THE

FLIGHT

OF THE

VEIL

BRUCE J. BERGER

Black Rose Writing | Texas

ISBN: 978-1-68433-559-6
PUBLISHED BY BLACK ROSE WRITING
www.blackrosewriting.com

Printed in the United States of America
Suggested Retail Price (SRP) $19.95

The Flight of the Veil is printed in Calluna

*As a planet-friendly publisher, Black Rose Writing does its best to eliminate
unnecessary waste to reduce paper usage and energy costs, while never compromising
the reading experience. As a result, the final word count vs. page count may not meet
common expectations.

For Laurie

THE

FLIGHT

OF THE

VEIL

"Because I remember, I despair. Because I remember, I have the duty to reject despair. I remember the killers, I remember the victims, even as I struggle to invent a thousand and one reasons to hope."

—Elie Wiesel, *Hope, Despair, and Memory*, Nobel Lecture, Dec. 11, 1986, © Nobel Media, By Permission

"For lo, the winter is past, the rain over and gone;
The time of singing is come, and the voice of the turtle is heard in our land;
The fig tree puts forth her green figs;
And the vines in blossom give forth their fragrance.
Arise, my love, my fair one, and come away."

—*Shir HaShirim,* The Song of Songs, 2:11-13

"When God so wills, the natural order is overcome, for He does whatsoever He pleases and what is beyond humankind comes to pass."

—Based upon The Canon during Great Vespers before the Annunciation

IN THE FACE OF CERTAIN DEATH

He moves when ordered, shoots when he must, eats when he can, but feels he no longer inhabits his own body. The fierce soldier that Nicky Covo has pretended to be, sardonically named Chrisma by his comrades in arms, has become a stranger, lost in a vapor of diesel fumes and rotting bodies, in the thunder of rapid gunfire and screams. Visions of children dying – deaths for which he feels responsible – stay fresh before his eyes when he's awake and plague his dreams, set in a maze of tiny bombed-out towns and fields shorn of their produce. His lust for killing the Germans and their collaborators has evaporated, yet he's unable to stop. The power of his Karabiner 98K and his pistol no longer thrill him, and he considers deserting, but deserters are summarily shot, and, irrationally, he still hopes that his band of partisans can press on into Ioannina and save the remaining Jews.

In early March 1944 they've reached the outskirts of the city, and there their forward movement stops. The *andartes* seem to be safe from a German counterattack for the moment, because the occupying forces care only about deporting the Jews trapped in the city and keeping open their own evacuation routes to the north. The German withdrawal from Greece is imminent, as the Wehrmacht is collapsing before the attacking Soviet Army. To the south, the Germans are fighting only a rear-guard action.

In Pedini, in Katsakis, and in Chionasa, Nicky's group collects every scrap of food and hunts down collaborators, breaking into houses, terrifying women and children, inspecting floors and walls for hiding places, stabbing bayonets through stacks of hay where traitors may be hiding. When discovered, traitors – any men of fighting age who haven't joined the *andartes* – are efficiently executed. Nicky kills to avoid being called a traitor himself and dispensed with just as abruptly.

One evening, while on guard duty, he sees a young man, perhaps fifteen or so – roughly his age – approach from Ioannina, waving a white handkerchief. He turns out to be a Greek Jew, like Nicky, named Matsa. They learn from him that the SS has confined Ioannina's Jews in their homes, under penalty of death. According to Matsa, the deportations will occur within days, if not hours. A convey of German military trucks has arrived in Ioannina for that purpose.

In minutes, Nicky's company of *andartes* prepares for an attack. This is the opportunity he's been hoping for. They approach cautiously just before dawn. As the blackness of night slowly grows lighter, the southern edge of the ancient city remains quiet. He and a comrade are ordered to check out a small, dark brown, brick church. It is the Church of Saints Constantine and Helen, but the sign has been blasted away by earlier fighting, and the two are unaware of its name. They enter, Mauser pistols drawn. A door leads off the sanctuary to what might be an office or closet. Nicky's comrade tries the door, but it's locked, a bad sign. The priest and his family cowering in fear? A Jewish family hiding with the help of the priest? A cache of German soldiers waiting to annihilate them? They are compelled to find out, one way or another.

They prepare to kick in the door, but a volley of gunfire from inside pierces holes through the wood and through his comrade's torso. Nicky jumps back, plastering himself to the near wall, and waits, expecting more bullets, but there's only eerie silence, save for the gasping of the dying fighter, whose blood pulses onto the floor. Nicky sees that the lock has been shot out, knows that the enemy is within, and understands that, if he's ever going to act, it must be now. If he had a grenade, this would have been the time to use it. He pushes his way into the room, discerning nothing in the dimness, and shoots wildly. Within seconds, just as his eyes begin to adjust to the darkness, he's emptied his clip. He hears a noise and comprehends that he's a helpless target.

Nicky has entered a small room; one window filters in the faint glimmer of dawn. He sees a young German springing from behind a desk. Nicky cannot fathom why the German is there alone and knows only that the enemy has killed his comrade and is about to kill him. That's why the German – only two meters away – brandishes a grenade, has pulled its pin, has let go of its safety lever. It seems that the German has a clownish smile, that he must be crazy, that the war has gotten to him. Like Nicky, tired of killing, yet not too tired to kill two more. Maybe he just wants to die a hero to his lost cause. The German must sense that the Third Reich is dying and that there'll be nothing left for him if he returned to his homeland. All three possibilities – trap, crazed man, suicidal martyr – cross Nicky's mind in an instant.

Then a flash of deep red, the color of sunset in the moments before dark, but the flash doesn't come from the grenade. It sweeps into the room from the wall with the window, from the window itself, and envelopes the German. The grenade goes off in his hand a tiny fraction of a second later, but the explosion doesn't deafen Nicky, as he would've expected. The explosion is muffled almost to inaudibility, like summer thunder heard from miles away. Shrapnel shreds the German's face, but nothing hits Nicky except a puff of warm air. The German has been caught in a whirlwind, but the grenade's metal shards leave Nicky unscathed, as if he'd been protected by an impervious blanket. The red flash, which has flooded the room in a ghastly, near-blinding light, swirls for a second and disappears as suddenly as it came. He imagines for an instant the scent of cinnamon.

Nicky stares with disbelief at the dead German soldier, a crumpled body without a head, a gaping hole where his neck had been, his ravished uniform barely holding his body together. He looks down to see that his own legs are still attached to his body; he studies his hands to assure himself that he still has arms. His rational mind tells him he must be mortally wounded, bleeding out, but the physical parts of his body are intact.

The German has destroyed himself alone. Nicky runs outside, yelling in the triumph of being alive.

BOOK ONE

CHAPTER ONE

Brooklyn, New York, February 8, 1990 (Thursday)

At the end of his long day, Dr. Nicky Covo sat at his desk and pondered his last patient, a woman he treated for depression. Of all the losses that one could suffer, the worst was the inexplicable death of a child, and so it had been for Alice, whose son had taken his last breath at five months. A year after the tragedy, her progress, if any, had been slow. As she'd recounted to Nicky, she'd dreamt the night before her appointment that her baby had suddenly appeared next to her as an adult, healthy, handsome, and successful, trying to console her, explaining that everything had turned out for the best. She'd reached out to hold him; she described the familiar feeling of his skin, his pure new-baby smell, and she remembered hearing from somewhere a lullaby she'd sung to him. And yet she'd not felt cheered by the dream. The dream had served only to remind her of the emptiness of her life without her son, how nothing could ever be good again.

Then Alice spoke for the first time about suicide. Her exact phrase, which Nicky had scribbled verbatim into her chart: "I'll join him, wherever he is, as soon as possible." When Nicky asked her to explain, she pretended not to hear him. When he demanded to know whether she'd formulated a plan to end her life, demanded in a way that she couldn't ignore, she denied the clear implication of what she'd just said.

"Look, Alice. You can't drop hints you're going to kill yourself and then pretend you haven't."

"I said no such thing."

"I hear the words you're saying and the meaning behind them ..."

"I didn't say ..."

"You said you'd join him soon and that can mean only one thing."

Her eyes had been red and puffed when she'd entered Nicky's office, and now she looked as if she wanted to cry again, covering her face with her hands. As Nicky let the silence grow, glancing once at his clock to see that their time was almost up, he regretted his aggressive tone. He made a note in her chart to consider changing her medication and wondered if that was enough of a response. If he couldn't demonstrate more empathy, if he couldn't at least find less confrontational means of questioning, he'd find his patients abandoning him. After a minute, as if to confirm his thought, Alice got up, straightened the skirt of her grey wool dress, and said she was leaving. He closed her chart with a sigh as she slammed shut the door to his office.

Long after she left, he could still feel Alice's despair. She'd looked straight at him as she spoke about joining her son, but he felt she was also looking at something well beyond him, a future without unrelenting pain. He understood her look because he'd often contemplated suicide himself.

Indeed, he'd twice tried to end his own life.

He feels his fourteen-year-old self once again unwrapping the leather straps from the yad, *the box of* t'fillin *meant to be wrapped tightly to his upper arm. His hands twitch as he twists the leather around his neck into a knot. He looks around to see an easy way to hang himself in this bedroom of a rectory of a Greek Orthodox church in Athens and realizes that he can stand on a chair, secure the leather to a pipe emerging from a wall, and jump. And he can still sense his shock as the door bursts open and the priest's daughter, Dora, marches in ...*

Nicky rubbed his eyes hard as if trying to press out the unpleasantness of his session with Alice. Then he opened Alice's chart and looked haphazardly at the notes he'd taken, seeing his handwriting but not thinking about her. Memories long buried had been floating into his consciousness often in the recent months, depressing him, shortening his temper, and making him a less effective healer. More than once, his patients had ended up trying to console him. He thought fleetingly of Adel, his wife, who'd died from a heart attack two years earlier and who would've been dismayed had she known how poor of a psychiatrist he'd become.

He took stock of his office. He'd set it up to convey a sense of comfort and wondered how he could expect his patients to feel at ease when he could not. He'd spent a lot of time selecting the books that patients would see on his shelves, mostly popular novels. Recently, he'd placed *A Prayer for Owen Meany* on his desk, hoping that it might lead to a conversation about God. Although Nicky was no longer a believer, had disavowed God when he realized that the rest of his family had been murdered in Auschwitz, many of his patients did believe. He'd long felt that getting his patients to talk about their beliefs in Divine intervention, in the existence of a Creator, could at least be a place to start a conversation. It was all about getting started, about searching for an opening, about gently probing to reveal what needed to be dissected and dealt with.

Occasionally, to get started, Nicky would encourage his patients to pace around his office and look, not only at the books, but at the curiosities he left within reach, things to pick up and examine, anything that might motivate his patents to talk. The Rubik's Cube acquired in 1976 sat on the table – red, green, yellow, blue, orange, and white squares seemingly distributed at random – between the chairs in which he and his patients sat. The device might lead to a discussion of particular colors, of puzzles, of complexity, of futility. On his desk, next to Irving's novel, sat the Newton's Cradle, which might lead to a discussion of motion, of momentum, of cause and effect. Somewhere in his office there were prompts for virtually every patient; it was only a matter of time to find the right key.

There were only two personal items. He often stared at them when alone, although he knew them well enough to describe them minutely with his eyes closed.

On his desk he kept a framed picture of Adel and him, and their closest friends, at their wedding. Nicky's smile, unexpectedly prominent in his thin face, was the only smile in the group that looked forced. On either side of Nicky and Adel were two old men. One, a tall well-built black man with a polished bald head, stood next to Adel. The second, a slightly shorter, broad-chested white man with sparse graying hair, stood next to Nicky. They'd served as surrogate parents: the black man, Norm Williams, had employed Adel at his diner, notwithstanding her schizophrenia, and the white man, Elie Saltiel, had sponsored Nicky into America, a Holocaust refugee from

Salonika, where the Saltiel family had lived for centuries. Nicky missed them all intensely and couldn't understand how he'd come to be the only one left.

On the wall behind his desk, between the two windows, hung a framed crayon drawing, one corner missing, its colors fading. The drawing, in blue, depicted a flying bird. Nicky had beyond all odds managed to save this last remnant of his family, given to him by his six-year-old sister Kalli, the night he fled Salonika to hide in Athens. He could still feel her pushing it into his hand seconds before he said goodbye.

"For you, Nicky." He grabs the drawing from his younger sister as their mother cries and their father urges him to hurry, Alex is waiting, the boat that will smuggle him down the coast to the capital must be at the dock. He must go now. It all happens in an instant and it's over. He's abandoned his home.

He sighed, turned away from the drawing and back toward his desk, put down the framed photograph, and rose to start his trip home. His secretary had left a pile of his mail, as usual, just inside the door on a small wooden table. Bills, he assumed, from his answering service, from Con Edison, from one of the psychiatric magazines, and perhaps also a few checks. The pile could wait. He was about to leave when he saw one letter out of the ordinary, a tissue-thin blue air-mail envelope with red edging. It clearly contained neither bill nor check, for its return address was written in confident Greek script: *ηγ. Φεβροϋια Οιϋoussα Ελλάδα*. Someone from the town of Inousa in Greece. He picked it up, returned to his desk, and turned on his lamp.

It was a letter from one Abbess Fevronia, unknown to Nicky, and his first impulse was to throw it away. It had to be a scam. The black-and-white Polaroid of a middle-aged nun could've been anyone. Then he read the letter again despite himself.

Dr. Nikolas Covo:

I have been in search for a long time, of exactly whom I was not sure, and you may not be the person I'm seeking, but I think you are.

The photograph is of Sister Theodora, a nun at the Holy Monastery of St. Vlassios in Inousa. She prays constantly to Christ, even more so than most nuns. She has a most pure soul and is well-loved here and listens to confessions of the villagers. She is a powerful force within our community.

However, her origins have been a mystery since 1944, when she was discovered here, then a little girl, perhaps six or seven years old. We don't know where she came from, because she chooses not to speak. She seems, quite honestly, afraid to speak. During a recent illness, however, she was delirious with fever. We thought she might die. Indeed, we gave her last rites. In her delirium, she mentioned the city of Kavala, which I'm sure you must know, and the surname Ganis.

Please forgive me for the long introduction, because you're certainly wondering what all this has to do with you. Through the grace of God, and after quite a lot of work, I must say, I managed to track down a woman named Tabitha Ganis, who lived in Kavala during the war. I heard from her the story of her brother, Alex, killed in 1943 while possibly trying to hide a young Jewish girl from Salonika. Miss Ganis has Alex's diary, and she told me he'd earlier helped one Nikolas Covo, then a teenager, escape from Salonika, to be smuggled to Athens. I am trying to find that Nikolas Covo. I've written to refugee authorities around the world and finally learned of you, that you apparently got to America in 1946 and became a psychiatrist. It took me a long time to track down an address. I hope you are the Nikolas Covo whom Alex Ganis helped escape.

If so, it's possible that Sister Theodora is one of your sisters – there are the vaguest of hints in Alex's diary – and I hope you will be able to come soon and verify my suspicions. Meanwhile, please call me at the monastery.

Yours in Christ,
Abbess Fevronia, Holy Monastery of St. Vlassios, Inousa

He picked up the photograph. The lighting was bad, but he could see a nun wearing a black habit, her hair completely hidden by its veil, her face looking at something other than the camera, as if she had turned away just as the shutter snapped. He could get no real sense of connection. One of his sisters? Could it really be Ada? Or perhaps Kalli? Could one of them have not gone to Auschwitz, survived, and never come looking for him? Never register with the agencies? Absurd. Much more likely that this letter was a fund-raising ploy, if not outright fraud. He'd heard about missing persons scams, promises to reunite the victim – a sucker – with a long-lost loved one in return for a small, or not so small, payment. He was too smart to fall for something like that. His impulse was to tear the letter and photograph into tiny pieces.

Yet, he stared at the photograph, as if intense study might bring the figure within it to life. He stared for minutes, hardly moving a muscle, straining to look through the image on the photographic paper into the room itself in which this nun had stood. Noise from the rush hour traffic outside his window began to grow and interfere with his concentration. He let out a lungful of air and put the photograph on his desk next to the letter.

If it was one of his sisters, it had to be Kal. Ada was nine in 1943 and couldn't have been mistaken for a much younger girl. And there was something about the set of this nun's jaw, something he couldn't define, that reminded him of his younger sister poring over a book or art project. It was a look of determination, of a willpower strong enough to focus on one activity, one thought, for an extraordinarily long time. And this nun's eyes did seem large, reminiscent of Kal's. Yes, it could have been Kal, but she was dead, murdered, gassed and torched, her ashes blown into the sky to settle on the town around the crematorium. Of that, he'd always been certain.

Nicky replaced the letter in the envelope. Still holding the photograph, he turned and stared at the faded crayon drawing over his credenza.

"For you, Nicky." Her bright smile and perky voice are completely at odds with the quiet sobbing of his mother and other sister. *"What is that, anyway?"* he barely manages to ask, fighting back his own tears, knowing that he will not be able to step out of his house if he succumbs to his emotions. *"It's a blue jay, silly! Can't you tell?"* To Kal, Nicky's leaving for Athens presages only a short separation; he's going on an adventure away from the family, that's all. *"Ah, of course, a blue jay. It's beautiful."* He folds the drawing carefully and places it into the pocket of his jacket.

Had he hugged her goodbye? Had he hugged anyone goodbye? He must have, but he couldn't remember. The last moments with his family were a blur, and Kal's gesture was the only image of his leave-taking that remained strong for the intervening forty-seven years.

CHAPTER TWO

Inousa, Greece, January 14, 1953 (Wednesday)

Sister Fevronia gripped the seat and prayed that the war-surplus black Morris, which bounced along the rutted road, would not overturn as it climbed toward the monastery. Prayer was serious business – she made sure to reflect on the work of God she'd do and on the peace and comfort she might bring to the people of Inousa if she survived. Yet Andros, who'd volunteered to drive her from the village, seemed not to hear her begging him to slow down through the racket of the engine. He pulled his black cap nearly to his eyes, and Fevronia thought the cap might as well have covered his ears for all the attention he gave her. Mercifully, the Lord brought them safely to their destination, allowing her to conclude that He wanted her to resurrect the monastery after all.

Andros cut the motor, and the sudden silence was eerily deafening. They disembarked and stood at the car for a half minute, staring at the ruined church. The church's stone walls were intact, but the arched door was gone. Walking closer, Fevronia reached out to feel the wall near the doorway. The stone felt grimy and cold, like a campfire doused with heavy rainfall. Weeds covered what should have been the floor inside. Moving along the perimeter of the church, Andros close behind her, Fevronia saw on the ground tiny glints of red, blue, and gold. She knelt to pick up a couple of pieces of stained glass.

"What's left of the windows," murmured Andros. He wore a faded gray wool jacket that might once have had a herringbone pattern over a light blue long-sleeved wool shirt and baggy brown trousers. He sported a three- or four-day growth of beard. Fevronia had learned that he was a widower in his mid-forties who earned his living in Inousa by repairing farm equipment, and his hands showed signed of lingering grease. He clearly possessed enough mechanical ability, thought Fevronia, to have repaired the windows and much more.

•   •   •   •   •

Behind the church they came to the one-story stone building that had held the monks' cells. An empty bird's nest sat in an opening on the east wall, where the early morning sun cast its pale orange glow. A blanket of ivy crept up the wall.

"No roof to speak of. Just a few rotting timbers left," Andros advised.

Despite the destruction, it was a holy place, solemn and ethereal, isolated from the bustle of the town by hills and forest. It had been all but forgotten by many, but it was a place that had been at the center of Fevronia's heart long before her first visit. She knew it as a place stricken by violence, grief, yearning, loneliness, and doubt. She knew it as a place of secrets as well, a place where her brother and other holy men had been murdered, their graves never found. She knew it as a place where mourners had cried out and recited the words of the Psalmist: "My soul is weary with sorrow; strengthen me according to Thy word." But she knew it also could be much more than a place noted in the history books. She could bring the monastery alive again, let it once more become a haven in which a select few of the most devoted could immerse themselves in the joy of the Lord, of the Savior Jesus Christ, and in the awesome power of the Theotokos, the God-Bearer.

First, though, she needed to meet the strange young girl the villagers had told her about. She crossed herself.

"Where's Theodora now?"

"Her cell, I imagine. She's usually there." Andros hesitated a second before continuing. "Not always, though."

Fevronia turned quickly to look at Andros. "No?"

"Sometimes she wanders out back." Andros gestured toward the north and the rolling hills behind the church.

"Wanders? Like she's lost?"

"Like she's looking for something in the old vineyards, and often I see her looking farther up the hill or across the valley. Sometimes we see her staring into space, like she's wanting to see beyond the clouds. Sometimes she's looking down, as if she'd dropped a holy icon. We got used to her wandering long ago, all nine years she's been here. It's just her way."

"She wouldn't be looking for the graves, would she?"

"No way to know."

Andros led Fevronia into the building. As with the church itself, the outer stone walls were largely intact, but the inside walls were destroyed. Only a few joists and planks remained, and those were scarred black; the smell reminded Fevronia of times in her family's house when the chimney had been blocked. The wooden ceiling too had burned through, and Fevronia could look up to see parts of the sky.

"So no one has ever bothered to try to clean this up?"

Andros shrugged.

Fevronia saw that, in one corner of the building, a makeshift cell had been fashioned with wide planks of wood, leaving a low doorway-like opening, about four feet high. They approached quietly, until Andros motioned for Fevronia to stop and look into the cell.

The girl whom Andros called Sister Theodora knelt in a corner, facing two icons of the Mother of God. Dim light flickered from a brass lampada near the girl but added little to the sunlight that leaked in from the sky. At first glance, the girl looked more like a child than a young woman, more like a five-year-old kneeling near her bed to say goodnight prayers than someone in her late teens. Fevronia couldn't see the girl's face, just a hunched figure, head near the wall, a mass of dark brown hair. She could hear the girl murmuring a prayer, but the words were not clear enough to be deciphered.

Fevronia recognized both icons. One was the golden-hued miracle-working Theotokos holding Jesus, and the other was the Theotokos wearing a dark red veil with a gold border, cheek to cheek with Jesus. Fevronia shuddered for an instant, imagining that she too could feel the uncanny softness of the Lord's skin against her. For a split second, not long enough to reach the realm of conscious thought, she imagined that she, too, was the Theotokos. Then her focus returned to the kneeling girl.

"Should I just go in?"

"No, much better I call her out. She knows my voice and won't be startled." Andros walked to the opening of the cell and spoke softly. "Sister Theodora. A visitor wants to meet you." Fevronia could see the girl cross herself three times and kiss both icons. When she emerged a few seconds later, it was clear that she was older than she had appeared earlier, but looked nothing like the teenager whom Fevronia had been expecting. She carried a small wooden bucket in her left hand and a sponge in her right hand. She was rail thin, her breasts forming the tiniest of mounds beneath her drab grey cotton dress. The dress could not have kept her warm even on a summer night, let alone the middle of winter. She had light olive skin, a gypsy look, but skin that was unblemished and smooth. She had large, dark brown eyes, but as soon as Fevronia tried to look more deeply into them, the girl dropped her gaze to the floor. Fevronia looked down too and realized that the girl was barefoot. Her feet, visible just under the hem of her dress, were black with dirt. Fevronia stifled the urge to comment on cleanliness.

"Theodora, I am Sister Fevronia." She opened her arms, as if expecting an embrace, but the girl retreated a step, continuing to look down. "Andros mentioned to you that I would be visiting."

"I pray to the Lord Jesus Christ to forgive me, a sinner."

Theodora's voice hardly exceeded a whisper, yet, as they were now only two meters apart, Fevronia could easily understand. The Jesus Prayer was part of her own daily ritual. Theodora's Greek was strangely accented, however, reminding Fevronia of a childhood friend whose mother had been Spanish.

"I have been looking forward very much to meeting you, Theodora." Fevronia tried to keep her voice gentle and non-judgmental.

Theodora looked up and smiled. Fevronia smiled back and suddenly, strangely, felt an urge to cry. She had no idea why, but it was the urge to weep with joy. Fevronia took a deep breath, blinked her eyes once, and suppressed the impulse.

"I pray to the Lord Jesus Christ to forgive me, a sinner," Theodora repeated.

The wish for forgiveness was as soft as velvet, but it struck Fevronia as grossly out of place, particularly in its repetition, coming from the mouth of such a young girl. Then again, she thought, this wasn't any young girl;

Theodora was a young girl who'd somehow secreted herself from the physical world in order to pray.

Andros gestured toward Theodora, his unlit pipe in his hand. "As I've told you, Sister Fevronia, she won't talk to people. When she speaks, it's always to God." Fevronia felt chagrined that, despite Andros's warnings, she should've expected Theodora to converse with her.

Theodora approached and knelt in front of Fevronia to begin the ritual that Fevronia had dreaded. The girl untied and pulled off Fevronia's shoes, removed her white cotton socks, and gently wiped her feet with the moistened sponge. The sponge seemed to be clean enough, although an old, faded red, and the water in the bucket from which the sponge had been taken was clear. It obviously had not been used on Theodora herself. Fevronia was grateful that she would not be washed with dirty water.

Despite her embarrassment, Fevronia lifted up the edge of her black cassock to allow Theodora better access to her feet, recalling how Jesus washed the Disciples' feet. St. Anthony had taught that only through extreme humility could one hope to inherit the Kingdom of God, and eternal residence in that kingdom seemed to be Theodora's intention. Theodora's face was only inches from Fevronia's skin, and Fevronia could feel a strange warmth, as if she'd walked too near an ember-laden brazier.

Theodora finished her ministrations, stood, and stepped back.

"May God's blessing be with you always, Theodora."

The girl turned suddenly and ducked into her cell like a mouse scampering to its hole, a splash of water lapping out of her swinging bucket. Back in her cell, Theodora knelt again and resumed her prayer.

After a few moments of listening, during which Fevronia heard the incantation at least ten times, she realized that she was shivering at the coldness of the floor and the air of the unheated building. The contrast between the ambient temperature and the heat she'd felt when Theodora was near her was striking. Fevronia put on her socks and shoes with difficulty. Because there was no chair, she was forced to sit on the floor to redress, and she reluctantly took Andros's offered hand when she was ready to get up. She could feel herself blushing. Once on her feet, she moved down a few meters farther from Theodora's cell.

"You call her Sister Theodora, Andros. She's not even old enough to be a novice. Obviously, she's not a nun."

Andros shrugged. "She's special," he said. "Appeared out of nowhere. Prays day and night. Pushes aside every nice thing we offer. And we feel she looks after us."

"How does she look after you?"

"We confess to her."

Fevronia thought for a few seconds. In her earlier conversations with Andros, he'd never mentioned confessions. It dawned on her slowly that she'd been purposely misled about the villagers' full connection with Theodora, but wasn't sure why. She knew, however, that if her mission at the monastery was to be successful, she'd need the strong support of Andros and his neighbors. "You have a priest in Inousa, a priest authorized to grant absolution in the name of Our Lord, Jesus Christ," she said evenly. Confessions to mature nuns were not new to the Church, yet they usually occurred only when no priest was available, and Fevronia had never heard of confessions to one as young and untrained in the ways of the Church as Theodora seemed to be.

"Yes, we see Father Economou, he does the Divine Liturgy of course, but on Sunday afternoons – after we receive absolution from him – eight or so of us come here to confess again to Sister Theodora. She's special."

"You've said so a number of times, but how? Because she just appeared one day? Because she's a mystery to you?" She tried to keep her voice unconcerned and pleasant, aiming to strike a pose of nothing more serious than curiosity.

Andros stared at her for a few moments, tugging down on his cap, frowning like a schoolteacher whose student was being intentionally obtuse. "You don't understand what it feels like when we tell her our sins."

"Tell me then, please."

"Maybe you should try confessing to her yourself, Sister."

"Maybe I will, but what is it in particular that confessing to Theodora does for you?"

"It's not at all like confessing to Father Economou. That's an important ritual, but still ... predictable, a formula. Approach and venerate the icons, stand next to the priest, say words of contrition, have the stole placed on one's head, hear that Christ has forgiven. With Sister Theodora, it's the real sense of deliverance, of utter acceptance, as if just her listening could bring us the forgiveness of the Lord. We're looking at her, and she's looking at us, as if she sees into our hearts, sees everything there that burdens us and understands. It's as if she has a light about her."

"How do you even know if Theodora understands what you tell her, if she doesn't speak?"

"She's smart. When she prays, she knows what she's saying. You can hear that in her voice, even though she keeps that voice very low. She has holy books in her cell, under her cot. When I talk to her, confess, that is, she looks me square in the eye. She nods. I can see she understands. And then there's the touch." Andros closed his eyes briefly, as if trying to experience that sensation again in his memory, then opened them and smiled.

"The touch?"

"The warmth. Didn't you feel it when she washed your feet? When I've said all I have to say, she grasps my hands for a second or two, and the sensation is incredible, as if she'd just been holding her hands above a roaring fire. She'll embrace the women, and they always say they feel it as well. And, however she touches us, the most important things is that we know that she feels what we feel, our sorrows and regrets, our moments of joy, and knowing that soothes our souls."

"Just like that?"

"I can't explain it any better."

Fevronia doubted that the Metropolitan who headed the Greek Orthodox Church had an inkling of what was going on at the Holy Monastery of St. Vlassios. She had many more questions for Andros, but they needed to wait. Andros had made it quite clear that Theodora's well-being and continued presence was a critical factor in obtaining his support, which Fevronia would need when she attempted to rebuild the monastery into a home for ascetic nuns. She'd need to learn more about this uncanny girl-woman who'd soon fall under her control and who had such a profound effect on the villagers. How exactly did Theodora soothe souls? How much did she comprehend when she looked the villagers in the eye? Why hadn't Theodora looked directly at Fevronia that way, but kept her gaze mostly at the floor? What did the grasping of hands and the embraces really mean? And Theodora might pretend to read, but, if she never spoke about what she read, then no one could be sure she understood anything. She could easily have picked up the Jesus Prayer by rote.

There would be plenty of time to learn more about Theodora. At present, there was only one more question, which Fevronia asked as they walked out of the building into the weak winter sunshine. "If she doesn't speak to you, then how do you know her name is Theodora?"

Andros relit his pipe before answering. "She told us when we first met her. For some reason, it seemed critical to her to tell us her name, Theodora, and then she fell silent, except for prayer. We've called her Theodora ever since, and you just saw her respond."

"Andros, let's go back in. Please call her again. There's more I need to say."

Andros turned and led her into the building for a second time. Fevronia had the sensation that he thought her odd, even objectionable. She couldn't blame him, as she was preparing to interfere with the way of life that had developed for him and others at the ruined monastery in the previous nine years. As she took control, she'd have to impose restrictions on the way that the local men, in particular, encountered Theodora.

Back at her cell, Andros stuck his head in and said, in a sharper voice than he'd used previously, "Sister Theodora, Sister Fevronia would like to see you once more." When Theodora emerged, this time without the bucket and sponge, this time fingering a crimson prayer rope in her left hand, she stepped right up to Fevronia and looked at her calmly. Perhaps the previous floor-gazing had been an act of faux modesty. Theodora's dark brown eyes were deep, intelligent, and focused. Theodora was a young woman who seemed to fear little.

Fevronia briefly explained her plan to move into the monastery, rebuild it, set it to winemaking again, and bring with her other nuns to share the holiness and beauty of the place. "There are eight others now who are committed to come here with me. We are devoted to the Theotokos, and with Her help, with guidance from the Mother of Jesus, this monastery will thrive."

Theodora's face brightened, as if Fevronia's news about the Theotokos was exactly what Theodora had prayed for. She whispered, "Unto you, O Theotokos, invincible champion" and glanced at Andros, who reached over to take her hand. Theodora looked up at him, smiling, apparently used to such familiarity.

Andros turned to Fevronia. "Will you promise to allow Sister Theodora to stay here with you and the others nuns, Sister Fevronia?" he asked. "Will you promise that she can be part of your holy group, that we can still see her, confess to her, as we've always done?"

"Yes. That's what I intended all along," responded Fevronia quickly, although she'd not actually made a decision until that instant. "That will make ten of us here, as ..."

"As there had been ten monks before the war."

"Quite so. But when the church is rebuilt, I ask that you – Sister Theodora – meet with the villagers and hear their confessions only in the nave. Your cell shall be yours only to enter."

Neither had Fevronia intended to say the words "Sister Theodora" until the instant she said them. She almost reversed herself, yet realized immediately that she couldn't. She'd seen Theodora's nod, tears of gratitude glistening in her eyes, and felt that what had been done should not be undone. She'd felt some Divine spirit guiding her through her meeting with Theodora.

"Andros, you will please spread the word among your friends."

"Very well, Sister Fevronia."

Fevronia turned to Theodora, who stared at the floor. She reached out and gently lifted Theodora's face to look directly into the warm, still glistening, eyes. Fevronia again had the urge to cry and was reminded of the warmth she'd felt as Theodora had washed her feet with cold water. There was something about Theodora that made Fevronia almost want to drop to her knees before her and confess her own doubts and half-truths. But that was something she couldn't do in Andros's presence, if ever. She was taking charge of the Holy Monastery of St. Vlassios, and it was of utmost importance for her to convey authority and control.

"Sister Theodora, we will meet again soon. As I've said, you may stay here at the monastery, for as long as you desire. We shall live in rejoicing of the Ever-Virgin, She who ineffably gave birth to the Light. Return now to your prayer."

CHAPTER THREE

Manhattan, New York, February 8, 1990 (Thursday)

Nicky drove home with only vague attention to the squalls of snow that made rush hour a nightmare. He toyed with the idea that there might be truth in the letter, but every time he imagined what it might be like to see his sister again, to talk to her after having long believed her to be dead, he felt his hopes smashing against a concrete wall. It was impossible. For Kal to have lived and remained hidden for decades, only to emerge out of nothingness, would have required a miracle, and miracles were the stuff of desperation, the stories that people told each other to ward off the void.

Miracles were the imaginary work of the non-existent God.

Coming off the Brooklyn Bridge, a large pothole that he'd not seen knocked Nicky's car into a skid. He corrected for the skid automatically and continued on his way, thinking of another jolt, one around which his life had revolved.

He's lying in the trunk of a Citroen, being smuggled out of Athens in late 1943, determined to join the partisans in northern Greece. The car bounces hard, and his head smashes against the trunk lid. Pain shoots down his neck to his lower spine and in that instant he knows there is no God. The idea of God had been an illusion maintained by his ancestors for millennia. As suddenly as he loses his faith, his fear vanishes. His racing heart and hyperventilation slow. He relaxes his death grip on his duffel bag as he realizes that he might yet live through the night. He falls asleep as the car starts to climb.

When he reached his street on the Upper West Side, Nicky was still thinking about how the Citroen had stopped, the trunk lid had opened, and the bright sunshine had momentarily blinded him; about how relieved and at ease he'd felt at that moment, without the burden of God; about the strange sense of strength that settled over him when he recognized that he himself, and not God, was in charge of his life, that he was in control. But for much of his life, the idea of control seemed as illusory as the idea of God. There had been so much that he couldn't control.

As Nicky entered his apartment, he shuddered at the sense that he was once again entering into a period where fate would push him wherever it cared to, regardless of what he wanted. As he brushed snow from his coat and hat, he shivered more from the memories he'd dredged up than from the cold. In the corner of the front hall closet, he spotted Adel's Dodger blue parka, still hanging where it had hung for the last two years. For what might have been the hundredth time, he told himself he ought to insist that Kayla take the coat and use it herself or give it to a thrift shop, but finished the thought as always, with recognition that the parka was much too big for Kayla and, in any event, that its disposal could wait.

Aliyah, the calico cat that Kayla had given him more than a year earlier, sidled up and whined for her dinner. He scratched her behind the ear, then walked to the kitchen and emptied a can of Fancy Feast into her dish. He watched her eat her fill before she wandered away to her favorite corner in his bedroom. Kayla's intentions after Adel died – to put another living being into the too large apartment – had been good, but Nicky and Aliyah had never truly bonded. A dog would have been a much better pet. He'd once suggested to Adel that they get a dog, but then reconsidered, fearing that Adel might hurt it. After Adel's death, his daughter's instinct had been right. A pet was needed, but Kayla hadn't consulted him before getting the cat. That was her way, to act on impulse with the best motives. She'd even named the cat Aliyah before giving it to Nicky.

Nicky should have been sleepy, but instead felt nervously alert, thinking about the letter from Greece that had floated into his office that day as if from a cloud. Lost in thought, he reached into a wooden kitchen cupboard to remove a mug and set about making tea in the microwave, bought only a year before Adel's death. Chamomile had been Adel's favorite, and he drank it automatically, longing for but never quite finding its supposed soothing effect. The tea, with its faint lilac odor, brought Adel to mind, as did everything else in the kitchen: the 50s era gas stove with four small burners and tiny oven, the Formica counter with the burn marks where someone – probably Adel – had set down a hot baking pan, her potted basil plants, which Nicky kept going even though he didn't cook, preferring instead to eat out or to heat up TV dinners. He also invariably used Adel's favorite mug, dark blue, adorned with the Dodgers logo, a baseball rocketing into the air behind the team's name.

Nicky took his mug into his office and sat before his Mac Portable, which he'd paid too much for. When Adel died, he felt freer to spend money on himself, but the Mac had clearly been an extravagance in light of its limited use. On most evenings, Nicky would ignore the Mac and instead relax with a psychiatric journal or very occasionally watch television, *The Cosby Show* his favorite. On this particular evening, however, he felt the need to write. He had to respond to the letter from this alleged – or maybe real – abbess. That much was clear. But what to say? He sat at the computer, wondering where to start.

His office had been Kayla's bedroom. Other than the absence of her bed and dresser and the presence of a larger desk, the Mac, and the Luxman CD player, the room had changed little from when Kayla slept there. Kayla had chosen the wallpaper when the family bought the apartment, a white background patterned with swirling yellow and green piano keyboards. Kayla's Beatles posters, darkened with age and curled at the corners, still hung where she and Adel had mounted them.

He picked up one of the CDs Kayla had recorded and popped it into the Luxman. It started with her rendition of Beethoven's Piano Sonata, No. 17, the Tempest. She was only sixteen when her CD won an Honorable Mention in the Gramophone Awards. Nicky pressed his fingers against his closed eyes to concentrate. The quiet, broken A Major chord of the first bars led to the pulsing rhythm underlying the D Minor theme. He let the music wash over him. He could see his daughter, with her unflagging energy, create and nourish the storm. His heartbeat quickened as Kayla took the first movement through the tumultuous development. Although he'd hoped that the music would help him relax, the first movement, if anything, put him further on edge.

As the sonata's slow second movement began, Nicky did relax. He sipped his tea, opened a new file, and began a letter to Abbess Fevronia. After the salutation, he continued:

Yes, I am the Nicky Covo whom Alex Ganis helped escape, and although I would so much like to believe the news that one of my sisters still lives, I know in my heart that she was murdered at Auschwitz. Somehow, you are sadly mistaken. Although I am sure you are good intentioned. If you actually knew my sister, you'd know that she couldn't now be the woman you describe, this Sister Theodora. She …

Why couldn't she be? He wanted to tell Fevronia of the deeply religious house he'd grown up in, how his ancestors had been persecuted by Christians and forced to leave Portugal centuries earlier, how he and his sister were the great-grandchildren of the famous Jacob Covo, the Chief Rabbi of Salonika, how it would be the last thing one could ever imagine, that it was entirely preposterous that one of his family would convert to Christianity. Better, far better, to die.

But to speak thusly would be horribly rude, and he prided himself on being a civilized man. If the letter wasn't the scam that he'd surmised upon first reading it, it could only have been an honest mistake. After all, Fevronia hadn't asked for money, hadn't even hinted of a need for financial support. So, if she was simply in error, he'd need to explain her error politely, clearly, yes, but in a way that would not be thought offensive. Perhaps all he had to do was describe his family and, in particular, his sisters, to talk about how his house revolved around Judaism, how his father, a doctor, used all his spare time in studying the Talmud and often studied with one of his children at his side, talking quietly about the lessons as he read. But could he describe this properly? His family life seemed to him further than dreams he'd long ago forgotten.

If you actually knew my sister, you'd know that she couldn't now be the woman you describe, this Sister Theodora. We all grew up in a very religious Jewish household in Salonika.

There, a start, touching immediately on his family's deep roots. As he reread the last sentence, though, it seemed flat. What could it possibly mean to the abbess of a woman's monastery in the Greek Orthodox Church, who knew nothing about Judaism? It said nothing of his family's very tight-knit Sephardic community. How could he convey that people so devout in their

Jewish beliefs would never accept any semblance of Christianity, let alone the extreme devotion of a nun? He'd never heard even the rumor of such a conversion. At least not in modern times.

Shaking his head in disgust at himself, he continued, starting a new paragraph.

I, myself, don't know the precise circumstances of the deportations from Salonika because, in March 1943, I fled to Athens to hide from the Nazis and lived there with a priest and his family. But after the German retreat, I returned to Salonika from the mountains to find my family gone, our house occupied by Bulgarian strangers. Not a single Jew had returned from the camps, as far as I could make out.

The last sentence was accurate, but misleading. He hadn't asked around. He'd concluded that not only his own family but all the other Jewish families he'd known hadn't returned and that all their houses were occupied by strangers, but he hadn't looked for Alex, the one person who might have told him what had happened. Why hadn't he? There had been no need to inquire further, so certain he was that his family had been exterminated. What if he had asked?

What would he have learned?

I fled Athens to hide from the Nazis ...

The sentence was dry and hard and heavy, like a boulder lying in a field. How could one capture the truth of what it felt like to be sent away from one's family, knowing that they were in grave danger? He could write a book and never get close to touching the shock and grief of learning, not long after he'd left home, that his family had been pushed into box cars and transported to Auschwitz to be gassed. Well, there was no need after all to explain to this abbess how he felt. He needed only to convince her to leave him alone, however innocent her letter was.

Lived there with a priest and his family.

And should he mention Father Liakos, who'd protected him at great risk to his own life and that of his family by taking him into their home as a purported relative? Would this suggest that there wasn't such a Jewish aversion to Christianity, or at least to obtaining help from Christians, as he wanted to convey? He remembered bitterly about how Father Liakos had initially wanted him to renounce his Judaism and convert. It was this wrongheaded desire on Father Liakos's part that had driven him to his first attempt at suicide. But nothing would be gained by telling the abbess that the nun of whom she spoke couldn't have been his sister because, when he was in peril of being converted, he'd tried to hang himself. Even to Adel he'd never confessed that he'd come damned close to ending it all that first night at the church. He had no intention of sharing his most private memories with anyone, let alone a Greek abbess.

Lived there.

He'd never opened up to anyone about how he'd fallen in love with the priest's twelve-year-old daughter over the months he stayed at the church. Oh, Dora, I remember your sweet shyness and intelligence so well.

With a priest and his family, indeed.

Nicky deleted everything he'd written and stared at the blinking cursor, then got up to make more tea. As he walked past the living room, listening to the pulsing third movement of the Tempest, he considered how large the apartment felt since Kayla moved her Steinway to New Jersey. Its absence seemed to make the floor tilt away from the wall where it had stood. He pressed his back against that empty wall, closed his eyes again, and listened. He did not move until the sonata faded into its final arpeggio.

With his second cup of tea, he sat again before his blank screen and tried to force himself to write the letter telling Abbess Fevronia what he wanted her to know, that Sister Theodora could not be his sister, that she'd have to look elsewhere to solve her mystery, but the solution to that mystery was of no concern to him. Nothing appeared on the page before him, however. Instead, he thought once more about the Citroen's trunk, this time, about getting into it just minutes before he stopped believing in God.

He squeezes into a fetal position. His face rubs along a greasy spot, almost making him vomit. The duffel thrown on top of him, the trunk lid pushed shut, the click of the lock reverberating in the total blackness. The engine starts. Movement. He hugs the duffel tightly, imagining it to be Dora, but the rough canvas feels grossly wrong – exactly the opposite of her softness. He wants to pray, but no suitable words come to mind. He's trapped, and everywhere outside his small hiding place people want to kill him.

CHAPTER FOUR

Inousa, Greece, January 14, 1953 (Wednesday)

Outside again, Fevronia sat next to Andros on a stone bench that bordered a path up the hill. Some hundred meters away at the top of a fairly steep but walkable climb sat the ruins of the monastery's ancient winemaking operation. Fevronia had learned that the nineteenth and early twentieth century monks, the last to have made wine here, had used mules to haul casks up and down, but she saw that motorized vehicles would be needed in the future and that a road would have to be constructed. Pine trees on one side of the path or the other would have to be removed. It would be a shame to destroy so much forestation, but, she imagined, the wood could be sold and the money put to good use.

"She's strange, Andros." Fevronia pulled her black wool coat tighter around her cassock, shivering. "That second time, when she looked at me, I felt she could speak perfectly well if she wanted. She doesn't want to. She's walled herself within a cocoon of silence and is happy to stay there, hiding."

"Is she hiding?" Andros nibbled on the dirty nail of his right thumb. He continued to smoke, holding his pipe in the other hand. A light breeze carried the smoke away from Fevronia, for which she was grateful.

"Isn't she?"

"Not when she washes your feet in the humility of Our Lord. Not when she hears our confessions, when she's as open and accepting as a human being could be. Not when she touches us. I wouldn't call any of that hiding."

"I wonder."

Among her other concerns, Fevronia thought about the complications that Theodora might cause her effort at the monastery and with her community of nuns. She wondered whether Father Economou even realized that Theodora was hearing confessions. In her cell, no less. He would certainly raise objections with the Metropolitan if he knew. And she wondered whether Theodora's presence – compounded now by Fevronia's promise to treat her as a full-fledged nun – would cause jealousy among the other nuns who'd soon arrive. Would they, for example, resent that Theodora had been at the monastery long before them and had developed a close, if unusual, relationship with the locals?

As if Andros could read her thoughts, he spoke to allay Fevronia's concerns. "Sister Theodora will be no problem, if that's what you're worried about. She has a soul as sweet as honey. You'll love her, too, when you get to know her better. As will the others."

Fevronia was savvy enough to realize that the problem of Theodora wouldn't be solved immediately. She still had much to learn about her. "Let's get up and move around, Andros. It's too cold just sitting here. Let's go back into the church, where at least we'll be out of the wind."

"As you wish."

Once inside, Fevronia saw that, not only was there no place to sit, there wasn't even a clean wall to lean against. So she and Andros just stood in the nave, looking around. She tried without success to imagine what her brother had felt as he'd prayed in this place. She herself felt nothing except absence. No cross, icons or icon screen, no Holy Doors, no candelabras, no sensors, no chalices. They had disappeared, first through Nazi theft and later through fire and more pilferage. They had been replaced, it appeared, by Theodora.

Fevronia had been curious about Theodora when she'd first heard about her, but it was an intellectual kind of curiosity. Now, however, having been touched by her, having felt her unnatural warmth, having had the chance to look deeply into her eyes, Fevronia felt a much greater emotional curiosity, a virtual hunger for more knowledge. She resolved to draw Andros out as much as possible.

"Here's another thing about her that's pressing on my mind," Fevronia said. "You and your friends give Theodora a special place in your hearts because of what you think is a miracle, that she appeared out of nowhere."

"She did. There's no other explanation."

"You're an intelligent man, though, Andros. You understand complex machinery. You know cause and effect. So bear with me. Theodora had to come from somewhere. She had to be someone's little girl. It doesn't make sense that you just found her here, abandoned."

"Alone, yes. Abandoned, I don't know."

"Aren't they effectively the same?"

"Theodora seemed to belong here. As I've said, when the Germans pulled out and we came to see that they'd burned down the church and that the monks were nowhere to be found – we knew they'd been shot the night before, we could hear the gunfire – she sat right there on that bench we just left, as if waiting. Waiting for us. You might say that she waited there preparing to welcome us."

"If she was really waiting for you, it doesn't make sense that then she refused to stay with you and your wife. Based on what you've told me, you offered her a haven, food, warmth, caring, none of which she wanted."

Andros shook his head. "She was happier here, even then, at the beginning. It's when we first realized how special she was."

"There's obviously something I'm not getting." Fevronia felt that Andros had to be holding back.

Andros sighed, still seemingly burdened by the task of teaching a recalcitrant student. "I'll tell you again. Euadne and I found the *koritsaki*. The timbers of the church were still smoldering." He paused, gesturing upward with the hand that held his pipe. "The beautiful dome had fallen in. It hurt to see this blessed place in shambles. And the monks were gone...."

"Yes, my brother among them."

"I pray to the Lord Jesus Christ for the peace of his soul."

"But back to the *koritsaki?*"

"This is all about her. She came in the monks' place. She was God's gift to us, to replace the ten holy men who'd lived, prayed, and were murdered here."

"Yes, certainly you could believe that, and you may well be right. Our Lord works in strange ways at times. Do you ever wonder why you and your wife were chosen to find her, as opposed to someone else from the village?"

"Does it matter?"

"No, I suppose not. I suppose the others from the village would have done exactly the same."

"Well, there was the *koritsaki* and we were shocked to see her. At first we thought she was a ghost, she sat so still, she looked so pale on that bench. But then we saw she was real. We asked her name, of course. Theodora, we heard her say. We'd never seen her in the village, so we asked where she was from, another village maybe, Serres? And she said nothing else." He tamped out tobacco ashes from his pipe and placed it into his pocket. "Nothing at all."

"Then what? I'd like to hear as much detail as you can recall."

Andros took a deep breath. "We asked whether the soldiers had hurt her, and she looked as if she has no idea what we were talking about. Said nothing." He stopped to reflect. "We asked about the monks, and she shook her head again, as if she had no clue. Said nothing. We asked if the Germans had brought her there, to the monastery, and once again she shook her head."

"She understood who the Germans were?"

"Your guess is as good as mine, but it seemed so."

"Then what? She's little more than a baby, she had to have had a home and family." Fevronia reflected that, if she herself had been lost, removed from her parents and brother, she would have told anyone who found her where she was from and who was likely to be looking for her.

"We asked about her parents, and she kept shaking her head. She shook her head no to everything we asked her. It didn't matter what we asked. Are you cold? A head shake. No. Are you hungry? Another head shake. On and on."

"Then?"

"We weren't going to leave her alone. We came closer and felt almost a glow from her, a warmth that had nothing to do with the sun. You've undoubtedly felt it yourself today."

"Maybe."

"And then Euadne noticed an orange glow around her, and I thought I could see it too." He closed his eyes, and when he opened them he looked straight at Fevronia and seemed to lean toward her.

"An orange glow, you say?"

Andros nodded and continued. "We coaxed her down to our house. Euadne washed her because, frankly, she stank of piss. I think her clothes were still damp with it, and God knows when she'd last had a bath. And, if I recall, her clothes also smelled a bit like wine. We gave her clean clothes that our daughter had outgrown. We showed her a place to sleep, next to our fireplace. We made a nice bed for her with blankets. The next morning, Theodora was gone. The clothes we gave her were in a pile on the floor. Her stinking shift was gone. So we climbed back up the hill to find her again. This time, however, she wasn't on the bench. She was in a corner of the cell building, the same corner where her cell is now, kneeling. Praying in a soft voice. The Jesus Prayer, of course."

"You still see her there in your mind?"

"I'll never forget a kneeling child, a waif, a *koritsaki*, saying the Prayer. The words flew out of her as fast as a person can speak. 'I pray to the Lord Jesus Christ to forgive me, a sinner.'" He repeated the sentence rapidly a few times. "Beautiful, in a way, but disturbing all the same."

Fevronia tried to picture Theodora as a child, wearing nothing but a stinking shift, yet emanating an orange light and a strange warmth, prostrating herself as a sinner and praying for forgiveness. "It's bizarre, the way you tell it. But let's go outside again and sit. It's too sad in here."

They continued their conversation as they made their way back to the stone bench on which they'd sat earlier.

"Beyond bizarre." Andros resumed their conversation as if it hadn't been interrupted by their walk. "We were stunned. Scared, in fact. We wanted to run, but we couldn't leave her there. That would have been un-Christian. We insisted that she return to the village with us. We took her by the hand, one on each side, and led her once again back to our house."

"Did she resist?"

"Not as I recall, but we weren't taking chances. It was clear she didn't want to go with us, but we were stronger, we were adults. Euadne and I were perhaps a bit more forceful than we needed to be. So we got her back, made her put on Rhaab's clothes again, but this time Euadne took away the dirty shift and destroyed it."

"Naturally."

"We should've ripped it up the night before. Well, Euadne fixed supper. Theodora took one or two bites, refused more. I thought she was hungry but maybe didn't trust our food. She was terribly skinny. Again, we asked her where she was from. She whispered something about a church. 'Εκκλησία,' she said, but so softly we might've imagined it, and whatever she said she wouldn't say again. She looked woefully scared at that point. We could tell she understood us, but she'd already mastered the art of silence. Don't ask me why she could talk about some things and not about other things."

"Did she say anything else?"

"We thought we heard her whisper the word έκρηξη."

"Explosion? What explosion?"

"She never repeated it, and we were never sure we'd heard her right. Well, of course, at her first opportunity she snuck out of our house and came back here. We gave up trying to keep her in the village. We brought her food, but she never ate much. We brought her clothes, but she wore the minimum for modesty. Blankets, an old mattress, we lugged up there, so she'd have a better place to sleep. We got others in Inousa to look after her, too. Ephraim, our son, and Rhaab would take food. Rhaab was the first to confess to Theodora, after maybe about a year, and told us about it. Then Euadne and I did the same, and experienced Theodora's touch, and it was remarkable. We chewed over whether we should tell anyone else and decided, after perhaps another year, to tell a few others, but only if they swore to Our Lord and Savior Jesus Christ not to spread the word further. We didn't want Theodora besieged. And Theodora grew up. Is growing up."

"How do I say this? Is someone looking after her feminine needs?"

Andros blushed visibly through the stubble of his days old beard. "That was Euadne's job, to teach her, to provide what she needed. Theodora's time started about two years ago. That was the last thing Euadne taught her about before she died. The other women now make sure she has what she needs."

"And you and Euadne decided she was a nun? A mere child?" Fevronia could not keep the disbelief out of her voice.

"I can't recall when, maybe about the time she started hearing confessions, but we started to call her Sister Theodora, yes. If that's a sin in the eyes of the Church, then I will seek absolution."

"I'm not saying it's a sin, Andros. Let's say it's unprecedented."

"We know she's holy. Could be a saint someday."

"Saints have to be associated with miracles, of course. Are you aware of any that Theo … Sister Theodora has brought about?"

"Showing up here like she did? Wouldn't that serve? Taking the place of the ten holy men who perished? And Euadne and I weren't the only ones to see that orange light back in '44."

Fevronia had severe doubts about almost every aspect of Andros's story, but the other villagers to whom she'd spoken briefly had repeated similar details, although nothing about smells of piss and wine, nothing about inexplicable words. Somehow this girl had appeared at the monastery from points unknown and lived there ever since. Somehow she'd glowed with an inner light that warmed those around her. Somehow she'd been holy and a person to whom believers might confess. Somehow her touch was magical and healing.

"All right. Well, you've heard me tell her she can stay. She can pray with us, help us with chores. You and your friends can always have contact with her, as I've said. And, perhaps someday she'll converse with other human beings and actually become a novice, beginning the road to truly becoming a real nun."

"As far as I'm concerned, she's there already. Whatever she's gone through so far has more than qualified her."

Andros tugged on his black cap and turned suddenly toward the top of the hill, as if he had heard a ghost at the defunct winemaking operation. Fevronia held her breath, waiting, for what she didn't know. A few seconds later, Andros turned back toward Fevronia, and she tried in vain to read the look on his face. Determination? Fear? Concern? A bit of all three?

"Yes. That's your position. Understood. Now, please show me around the old vineyards. We'll have to brave the cold and wind. I need to know the lay of the land."

Fevronia's hunger for more information about Theodora hadn't been satisfied in the least. Had there truly been a miracle surrounding her appearance at the monastery? Where had the orange glow come from? Where did that continuing, unnatural warmth come from? She realized, as she began to follow Andros into the vineyards, that her becoming an abbess would be infinitely more complicated than she'd ever imagined.

CHAPTER FIVE

Brooklyn, New York, February 9, 1990 (Friday)

The following morning, Nicky returned to his office, the sun not yet risen. Dark clouds blocked any light from the moon or stars. The weather hadn't improved. Although the previous day's snow squalls had stopped, the report predicted substantial additional snow in the early afternoon. He wondered whether he'd have to cancel his late appointments.

He reread Fevronia's letter, left on his desk. After a night's fitful sleep and numerous failed attempts to write a response to Abbess Fevronia, the letter seemed even stranger to him in the morning. The first strangeness was that he should have heard anything at all of a personal nature from the country he'd fled forty-four years earlier. The only Greeks he corresponded with worked at the University Mental Health Research Institute in Athens. The second and greater strangeness was that a letter purporting to be about his sister came from this small town. As far as he knew, his family had no connections with Inousa, a place deep in the mountains, far north and east of Salonika. The third and greatest strangeness came to him slowly. As he thought about the town, he recalled that something particularly gruesome had occurred there during the war. A Waffen S.S. massacre of civilians? There had been many such massacres in Greece, and it was impossible to keep them straight. The Germans' cruel idea of justice was that ten civilian deaths should be exacted for each death of a German soldier. But it seemed to him that Inousa was indeed a place where a massacre had occurred, a massacre of monks. From the same monastery? If his sister Kal had been there, then she obviously wouldn't have been left alive. Killing children was good sport for the Nazis.

Then he reread the letter yet another time and glanced at the framed crayon drawing on his wall.

"For you, Nicky," he hears again.

He saw six patients that day and found it impossible to concentrate on their stories. Could Kal actually be alive? With the last patient gone, Nicky reread the letter, now for the fifth time. "Prays constantly to Christ"? That still didn't make sense. Kal had invariably helped Mama on Friday afternoons, preparing *challah* with caraway seeds for the *Shabbat* dinner. Kal was even the one who said the *hamotzi* blessing every Friday since she'd been three. Something surely had mixed up this Abbess Fevronia.

And yet. Alex. Abbess Fevronia knew the name Alex, the young man who'd indeed helped him escape.

"You've got to leave now, Nicky. Alex is waiting."

His family's last words to him. Nicky couldn't imagine how Abbess Fevronia had discovered that Alex Ganis helped him avoid the deportations. Could there really be a diary? Had Alex, who'd risked his life helping Jews hide, have kept notes that could have led to his immediate execution? It made no sense.

And yet. Alex Ganis was a name he'd never forget, but he was sure he'd never mentioned it to anyone, not even to Father Liakos or Dora.

And yet. 1944? A year after the deportations. In 1943, his parents tried to find hiding places for all three children. He was the first who'd gotten away. Had they been able to send Ada and Kalli into hiding, too? Had it perhaps been the very next day when his sisters had been taken under the protection of righteous Christians? There'd been no way for him to find out.

Nicky placed the letter and photograph into his desk drawer, tidied his charts, and headed for his car. Should he try to call this abbess at the number she'd enclosed? Just the cost of a phone call to figure out where Abbess

Fevronia had gone wrong in her thinking. Go to Greece as she suggested? As if that was the only way to learn whether one of his sisters lived? No. He would call obviously, and that would put an end to it. Next week, when he was back in his office.

But the possibility of returning to Greece, a country he'd put behind him forever, gnawed at the edges of his consciousness. The wisp of an idea – revisit the Byzantine church in Athens where he'd hidden, Agios Nikolaos Ragavas, and see if anyone remembered Father Liakos or Dora – floated up where he could almost visualize it and then disappeared back quickly into the darkness.

CHAPTER SIX

Inousa, Greece, January 14, 1953 (Wednesday)

Following Andros around the church and up into the old vineyards, Fevronia pulled her wool coat as tightly around her black cassock as she could. The wind had picked up, somber leaden clouds were drifting in, and it smelled as though it would snow. The morning mist still lay like a shroud over the valley. The distant hills were dark purple; the air had a wavering, dreamlike quality, heavy with gray moisture.

As she walked, Fevronia thought about Silenos. Fevronia had loved him deeply, and his choice to become a monk led her to consider a similar path through life. She keenly felt her brother's presence in the fields upon which she now walked and rejoiced at the thought that Silenos had spent years here in God's presence. Through her devotion, in this sacred but scarred place that her brother had loved, she hoped to do honor to his memory and to someday understand the incomprehensible.

They picked their way through weeds and rubble, the remnants of vineyards planted, she'd read, in the thirties. The monastery had once been quite productive, but winemaking ended in the early part of the twentieth century after a severe blight, and the old winery had fallen into disrepair. The monks occupying St. Vlassios in the years before the war had planted new vines and had begun selling off their produce, intending to build a new winery, but the German invasion had ended their dreams.

Just as Fevronia and Andros reached the first rank of withered vines, Andros hesitatingly addressed her. "Sister Fevronia, you've told us that you're to bring other nuns and rebuild."

"Quite correct."

"Forgive me, but how could the Metropolitan have chosen someone so ...so ...?"

She waited a second to give him a chance to finish, but when he looked away, apparently embarrassed, she helped him. "Young? You know I'm twenty-eight already." She tried to turn his implied question – an accusation – into a joke.

"I wasn't thinking about your age."

"Inexperienced?" He turned to face her, and she smiled as warmly as she could to tell him she wasn't offended.

Nervously, Andros tugged at the bill of his cap. "Do you know anything about winemaking? Growing and caring for a vineyard? Or, do you know anything about construction, say? Anything about restoration of ancient buildings?" He cast his gaze at the ruins and waited for an answer.

She swallowed, trying to maintain her composure. Andros had asked the very questions that plagued her with self-doubt. She could do nothing but try on him the answers that had earned her the assignment in the first place. "I will see what has to be done. God will provide." When she saw Andros frown, she knew that she had not convinced him, but she hadn't really thought he'd be convinced with nothing greater than her faith in Divine assistance. He might be a devout believer, but he was also an extremely practical hardworking man, a man who expected others to work hard as well if they wanted to achieve anything.

"Yes, a safe thing to say, but wouldn't God provide by bringing here subjects of His who have the necessary knowledge and skill?"

She could not blame Andros for his skepticism, as skeptical as she was herself, as many were who'd heard her plans. "You're right. We might've expected God to find more knowledgeable people, if God worked and thought like human beings. But clearly God's will and efforts are beyond human comprehension. Here we are, years after this place was devastated, and no one else stepped forward, not even to replace broken windows or doors. No one else has offered to devote a lifetime to bring this place back to what it was. Perhaps even to make it more than it was. And I make this offer in the name of God. So what then is God's will?"

"Who can say?" As Andros spoke, small crystals of snow began to fall even though the spot where they stood remained washed with the pale sunlight.

"As you surmise, I've precious little understanding about winemaking or vineyards, other than what I've read in preparation for this task. The other areas, construction, restoration, none at all, and I'll require good advisors and enormous energy and commitment from many. People of faith, of course." She waited a few seconds, then continued. "People devoted to Christ. People like you, Andros, if you're willing to help me."

He said nothing, but turned and continued farther into the vineyard. She followed close behind, but his long stride required her almost to run in order to keep up with him.

"People devoted to Sister Theodora, Andros."

She heard what sounded like a grunt of assent, then thought she must have been mistaken, because Andros continued to walk in silence. Minutes elapsed before he stopped and turned toward Fevronia. "This has been her home for nine years. We've long ago come to love her, and she us. If nothing changes for her, then yes, of course, I will help you. And so would my friends in Inousa. And, I dare say, people I know in Serres, people with resources."

"Yes, we'll need resources."

Fevronia bent next to a vine that looked diseased, its leaves brown but marked with small splotches of orange and red. The challenges that the Lord, in His infinite wisdom, threw her way, she thought. She crumbled a leaf to dust with just the slightest pressure of her hand, then wiped off her hand on her coat, realizing suddenly the enormous amount of work necessary to weed out the sick vines and replant. Even as she tried to imagine how long they'd have to wait to see if the replanted vines thrived, she wondered at Andros's slightly veiled threat. She'd already given Theodora assurances that she could remain, already made it clear to Andros that she would be called *Sister* Theodora. Fevronia did not intend to send her away, but neither Fevronia nor anyone else could force her to stay against her will. As she matured, as other nuns arrived, as the nature of the monastery changed drastically from the home within the ruins that Theodora had known for years, she might well decide to leave.

Fevronia wanted to manufacture thousands of bottles of wine annually, the proceeds from which could be used to enlarge the monastery and make it a home for perhaps as many as twenty nuns. She wanted to set up a few guest houses where women pilgrims interested in experiencing the quiet life of the ascetic – for a weekend, a week, or a month – might find a welcome place. She wanted to be known as the abbess whose touch – love for Christ, skill at management, guidance of younger nuns – had brought about a miracle in the mountains. If she could succeed in all that, and she felt that she could, if God so willed, then Theodora might not want to stay at all. No one could be forced to stay.

Andros knelt near the base of a vine, brushed stones away, pinched soil between his fingers, and stood again. "Do you know they planted Xinomavro on about eighty percent of the land? Roditis on the rest? Do you even know these grapes?"

"I do." Fevronia looked away, afraid that Andros might see the uncertainty in her eyes. Her reading had been mostly about winemaking in general, not about specific grape varieties common to northern Greece. How could she not know these names? She had no idea what the monks had planted nor why.

Andros dropped the soil. "Would you be so kind, Sister Fevronia, to tell me just how it was that God is exercising His will through you? How you in particular you came to be chosen for this mission?"

"You ask a good question, Andros. I should've said so at once that I don't know Xinomavro from Roditis. Please forgive me. But I've been thinking about this monastery for many years, wanting to make this my home. I begged my abbess to take my idea to Metropolitan Spyridon himself and then, by the grace of God, he granted me an audience. I convinced him of my determination. The Lord was with me. The Metropolitan told me that he's wanted to rebuild but could find no one eager for the task. I imagine that the Metropolitan feels I make up in enthusiasm – in determination, in willingness to fail, if necessary – for what I lack in experience. So, we'll get funds for repair, for replanting, and for restarting wine operations. I will have a decade to make the monastery self-sufficient, His Excellency promises. That should be more than enough time. I will account to him directly. But additional resources, as you suggest, will be most helpful."

"With respect, Sister Fevronia, have you even drunk wine, besides the Blood of Christ?"

"No." She felt her face turn red. "I've always wanted to keep my head clear, the better to venerate Our Lord. Nama is all I've drunk."

"Hmph. You'll need a wine taster, of course, to advise about blending and fining before you start bottling. You'll likely want to call in a professional at some point if you're going to be serious about this. And I can tell you about the care of the vines, for sure, because I used to work here as a youngster long before the war."

"Ah, you knew the monks. I thought you might've." Fevronia tried to keep her voice level.

"So I knew your brother, if that's what you're asking."

"We have a lot to talk about. Come on, let's keep walking."

CHAPTER SEVEN

Manhattan, New York, February 11, 1990 (Sunday)

Over the weekend, through much mental struggling, Nicky decided that he didn't want to call the abbess after all. Although he believed he could probably end the mystery and correct Fevronia's misunderstanding in a few minutes with the convenience of the telephone, his desire not to do so left him stymied. Despite his doubts, Fevronia's letter had awakened the intense hope within him that his sister still lived. It was a feeling like nothing else he could recall, a mixture of intense happiness at the idea that something so preposterous could be true, that a beloved family member long known to be dead could actually be alive, combined with a feeling of utter sadness that he could've been separated for forty-seven years from his sister. He had to process these feelings, he felt, before acting in any way. He didn't want these feelings to disappear too quickly; he wanted to stretch them out, experience them more fully, play with them in his mind.

But Fevronia's letter had also awakened a fear. If he called, if he explained to the abbess how she'd been mistaken, he feared something beyond the likelihood that his hopes about Kal would be dashed. He knew that the horribly uneasy feeling had to do with not wanting to revisit his time with the partisans. He assumed that Fevronia would argue with him, talk about the utter chaos in Greece toward the end of the German occupation, and he imagined that their conversation would inevitably touch on things like the massacre. He would be reminded about his own experiences in the war, the blood, the dead bodies, the violence that he'd tried for so long to forget.

Three sullen men who meet him wear rifles strapped around their shoulders and ammunition belts, no uniforms. Like the Citroen, their clothes are encrusted with mud. The tallest, a bearded man with dark, gloomy eyes, has a red five-pointed star stitched onto his sleeve. The other two – one short and muscular, the other taller and wiry – lack beards as such, but look as if many days have passed since they'd shaved. Nicky stands as tall as he can, though his back and limbs ache from the hours he'd spent crumpled up in the trunk. "Nikolas Covo," he announces. The bearded man, obviously the leader, spits near his feet. "Covo? Forget that Jewish name. Best off you not let people know you're Jewish. And we use only nicknames here." He thinks for a second. "You're Chrisma, got it?" The bearded man laughs loudly, and the two other andartes join in. Great fun! The Communist guerilla has given Nicky the nom de guerre of the Christian god, a choice of exquisite irony for someone who only hours earlier had decided abruptly that there was no god at all. He doesn't want the name, but has no choice.

It was inevitable in his mind that, if he called the monastery, they would have to discuss the war. How could he talk to a nun about how Alex helped him flee to safety only for him to have later become – been forced to become – a killer? He decided to go back to writing a letter in response.

Through the weekend, though, every effort at his computer struck him as worse than the previous effort. He faltered every time he tried to explain. Who was he to judge what could or couldn't have taken place after having run away? If he could unwind the past, surely he would've stayed at home and refused to abandon his family. He might not have lived beyond Auschwitz, but at least would've known.

Dear Abbess Fevronia. As much as I would like to believe you, I cannot be the person you are looking for. While Alex Ganis did help me escape, I became overwhelmed, not long after last seeing him, by a desire for revenge for the murder of my family. When I fought with the partisans, I committed unspeakable atrocities in the name of revenge, and then multiple atrocities on top of those. If my sister had lived, as you claim, she would want to be reunited, not with a murderer, not with a war criminal, but with the brother she'd known as a child. I could never be that person again, so I don't see how

I could be of help to you or to your Sister Theodora. As I say, my sister Kal was annihilated in the gas chambers, just as the boy I once was no longer exists.

He wrote as if possessed, not thinking deeply about what he was writing until he'd finished the paragraphs and went back to read. As he reread drafts and erased them as fast as he reread them, he despaired of the futility of trying to deal with the past. The psychiatrist in him wanted to be rational and state bluntly that the past had to be dealt with, one way or the other, but Nicky couldn't approach his own trauma as would a psychiatrist. He was a patient, and a terrible one at that.

If it were possible to erase the past, of course, he would've taken back the bayonet he'd plunged into the belly of a German prisoner. He would've taken back the bullets pumped into the old man walking up the trail at dawn. He would've made sure his own Mauser was loaded when he'd placed his mouth around its muzzle and pulled its trigger. If it were possible to erase the past, he would've chosen to stay in Athens with Father Liakos, and he might've died there the next day at the hands of a German firing squad, killed in broad daylight on Kolokotroni Street, or he might still live in Athens at the age of sixty-two, never having become a doctor. Or perhaps he would've become a doctor anyway. He might've married Dora, who wouldn't have succumbed to typhus, if only he'd been at her side. He would never have had to visit her on her death bed, a few weeks after deserting the partisans.

"Do you still have the ... the ... t'fillin?" she asks, her voice weak and scratchy. "In my duffel right here. I could never throw them away, although I often thought about it." "I'm glad you didn't. Can you put them on me?" "On you?" "Yes, close to my heart, like you explained once. You told me, 'And thou shalt bind them as a sign upon your hand.' It's in Deuteronomy, isn't it? I want to wear them. Please?" Her voice barely registers above a whisper; she stays alive only by the sheer force of her will.

Nicky rose abruptly from his desk, grabbing another of Kayla's CD's, the one in which she'd recorded the Schubert Piano Sonata in C Minor. Shaking his head to clear the images and sounds and feel of a girl long dead from typhus, he put on the music in his bedroom. Its dark opening mirrored his mood. He'd hoped to be distracted by the music, but his memories of Dora intensified rather than faded. He could still just see her innocent face, could feel for an instant the love he'd suppressed, could remember the fiery heat of her young body on its death bed encased only in a thin cotton nightgown, could still detect the smell of ointments and feces in her bedroom. Against his will, he could see her opening her eyes in recognition of his subdued greeting, her failed attempt to take his hand, the dry and rough skin he felt when he took hers, her joy at his having survived the mountains and returned.

"Oh, that's good. So that's what it's like to be bound by the straps. It makes you feel close to God, just like you said, it really does. Thank you." He puts his head down on her chest, crying. "You won't forget me?" she asks. "Never." "Then do one more thing, before you go." "Anything." "Hold my breast, as if you were my lover." In a trance, he opens the top buttons of Dora's nightgown, then reaches in and gently cups her small breast, which feels as hot as anything he'd ever touched. Tears stream down his face. "That's so nice, Nicky, although your hand is cold." "Dora." "Just stay for a few more minutes, just like that, please, and, when you leave, don't come back. I want to remember you just like this."

Nicky found himself crying. As suddenly as the memories of Dora had come on, they disappeared, and in a minute he could hardly recall why he was crying. His mind pushed him back a month or so prior to his saying goodbye to Dora, to when he'd stuck the muzzle of his pistol into his mouth in the Church of the Trinity. Then his thoughts jumped forward decades to Alice, the patient who'd implied she was going to kill herself. From Alice, he thought once more about Fevronia's letter and his aborted attempt to respond, and from there his mind turned to his deceased wife. Next to where Adel would have lain, her weight pushing down the mattress so that he would inevitably roll toward her if he couldn't brace himself with a pillow, he gave up trying to sleep and began to imagine a conversation.

He would've tried to explain the whole thing to Adel, the one person who might have understood, the one person who'd ever suggested, so long before, that he might return to Greece to face his ghosts. Adel, a letter came to me from Greece. The abbess of a woman's monastery claims that my sister is still alive. It's incredible. Now I'm trying to write to her, and all I'm doing is remembering the terrible things I did, things I'm so ashamed of. - Nicky, war is shit. Tell me about it. You're the best. It's a quest. - Adel, hold me. - He could feel her grabbing him in one of those fierce hugs that crushed his breath out of him, he could hear her continued babbling as she became his therapist, reversing roles from their first meeting. – Adel, I was so afraid, alone with a rifle in the dark. The sounds from the forest. Knowing the Germans could sneak up on me from any direction. – Tell me your fears. So many gears. All these years. – It wasn't death so much I feared, but not knowing when or how it would come. A bullet through the neck? Rifle butts smashing my head, knocking an eye out of its socket? Maybe a searing knife in the gut, spilling my insides, the way I killed the prisoner? – Nicky, I remember fear like that. – Tell me. – Like when I was a kid, never knowing whether I'd feel the strap, never knowing when I'd be sent to bed without supper.

They would've talked for hours, sharing their hells. He had told her part, but hardly all.

Nothing about the grenade. Nothing about the girl in the yellow smock. Nothing about the old man. Why hadn't he revealed it all to her when she was alive? He longed for the comfort of Adel's ample body, a body in whose warmth he could lose himself and forget the world outside, a body whose needs took him completely away from himself and his memories, as if she'd been created solely to bring him oblivion. For two years he'd been so cold without her. He reached to her side of the bed, trying to imagine her weight against him, but could feel only her absence.

The warm Adagio of the Schubert sonata, played with great feeling by Kayla, did nothing to cheer him. In the winter of Greece's mountains, he at least could look for a blanket and huddle closer to his comrades. In his Manhattan bed, where he should've been warm and comfortable, he felt a cold that no blanket or music could thwart.

CHAPTER EIGHT

Inousa, Greece, August 14, 1953 (Friday)

Only months after Fevronia had taken charge of the monastery and earned the title of abbess, she and Theodora were next to each other during *Orthros*. The changes that had begun at the monastery – the carpenters and bricklayers, the other workmen, the other nuns – had not seemed to change Theodora at all. She still kept silent except for her prayer, still smiled at whomever was near her, still heard the confessions of a handful of villagers on Sunday afternoons. Fevronia was pleased that Theodora appeared comfortable, followed orders, and gave no indication of wanting to leave. With Theodora as firmly entrenched at the monastery as ever, most of the villagers were enthusiastic about Fevronia's efforts at rebuilding. Even Father Economou welcomed the possibility that there might be renewed wine production and an influx of tourists, as he felt such changes could only help Inousa's financial wellbeing. He seemed to have known that Theodora was hearing confessions – at least what the villagers deemed confessions – and didn't seem to mind.

Fevronia had even taken to spending an occasional half-hour with Theodora in her cell, reading out loud from one of the two holy books that she kept there. It was Father Economou who'd happily given them to Theodora a few years before. Theodora's favorite seemed to be an edition of the letters of St. Basil the Great, particularly St. Basil's letter to Eustathius, in which the saint bemoaned his inability, despite strenuous effort, to make personal contact with his friend over many years. And when Fevronia read

"Is not all this in the hand of Fate, as you yourself would say, and the work of Necessity?" Theodora would stop her there and motion to read it again. The letter having been reread, Fevronia would then counsel Theodora that the "hand of Fate" was in truth the hand of God – to which Theodora vigorously nodded – and that she should never doubt this truth. Accepting God's control over everything, Fevronia continued with one of St. Basil's key messages, was the only way to "keep the mind in tranquility." It was during these sessions in Theodora's cell that Fevronia felt herself and Theodora drawing closer to each other.

But Fevronia, as they prayed *Orthros* together, wasn't thinking about the time she'd spent in Theodora's cell. Indeed, Fevronia wasn't even conscious of Theodora kneeling next to where Fevronia stood; her mind instead had fastened as it often did on Silenos, lost in contemplation about why God, in control of everything, allowed massacres in His world. The murder of Silenos and his brethren had to be part of God's plan, but why? Her mind was far from tranquil as she listened to the readings, chanted by Sister Zoe, Fevronia's spiritual child and principal assistant in running the monastery. As Zoe's beautiful voice settled around Fevronia, she tried to pray.

Then, to her disbelief, Fevronia felt Theodora grab her about her lower legs and heard Theodora's shaky whisper addressing her. It was the first time Fevronia encountered Theodora's voice other than in prayer. Fevronia quickly knelt next to Theodora in order to better understand what she was trying to say.

"What, my child?"

"Mother, please forgive me."

Fevronia turned to see a tear creep down Theodora's cheek. What had she been praying about that would make her cry? Fevronia placed her hand gently on Theodora's arm. More tears followed, and Fevronia put her arm around Theodora and pulled her close. Another first. Theodora's tears grew into shaking sobs, and it wasn't long before Fevronia cried as well, not on account of Theodora, but still grieving for Silenos. Fevronia was dimly conscious that Sister Zoe's chanting paused and that the other nuns had stopped praying, as they glanced over to where Fevronia and Theodora now held each other. But then, with Zoe in the lead, their small choir of three nuns began to sing; slowly Theodora's sobs subsided, as did Fevronia's. It was minutes, though, before Fevronia spoke in a soft voice.

"Forgive you for what, my child?" Fevronia wiped her own eyes with a handkerchief, then offered it to Theodora, who accepted it and blew her nose. "Why on God's earth should I ever need to forgive you?"

"I'm unworthy of what you have done for me. I fear you'll send me away if I tell you where I came from, how I got here."

In the dim light, Fevronia could see Theodora shudder. She wondered about what could possibly have been the cause of such torment and why, at that particular moment, Theodora was willing to converse. Fevronia felt a frisson of excitement. She would learn about Theodora's origins and solve a great mystery.

"Of course we wouldn't send you away. This is your home. It will be your home forever, as long as you want it to be. You must tell me, child, what torments you so. What is it about how you got here, where you came from?"

Theodora crossed herself and seemed to struggle with what, if anything, she should say.

Finally, she turned to look at Fevronia and began, again in a whisper. "The Mother of God, the Theotokos ..."

"Yes? The Theotokos?"

"The Theotokos Herself brought me here. Had to bring me. Carried me with Her light and veil. Put me in a dark place."

"The Theotokos brought you here?" Fevronia caught her breath and couldn't keep the shock out of her voice. She barely suppressed a laugh, struck by the absurdity of Theodora's claim, and immediately felt ashamed for her disbelief.

Theodora continued, her whisper so faint that Fevronia was unsure she could hear Theodora's words correctly. "Because ... they died ... and the Theotokos lifted me from the closet."

"They died? Who died? And what closet? Where was it? Why were you in a closet? What was the dark place?" Fevronia allowed her voice to grow louder, and again the singing around them faded as the other nuns tried to listen.

Theodora shook her head, her eyes closed. "I cannot tell you more, or you will send me away."

"You must."

Theodora stood abruptly and eluded Fevronia's grasp, walking briskly out of the church and back toward her cell. Fevronia rose from her own kneeling position more slowly, her knees aching. She'd been so close and needed answers. The Theotokos? A closet? Carried by Her light and Her veil? Could the Theotokos have appeared to Theodora, yet never to Fevronia? Could it be that Theodora had a purer heart than everyone else at the monastery? And why the sobbing? Why the contrition? Why ever would Theodora worry about being sent away? Shouldn't Theodora's miracle have been the cause of incredible happiness? Or maybe the sobbing was because "they" died? Who were "they"? The monks who'd lived here before? The idea crossed Fevronia's find again that Theodora must have known what had happened to the monks and that, if so, she could lead her to their graves. If Fevronia could find the graves, then she could make sure that all received the proper Christian burials they were due.

By the time Fevronia reached Theodora's cell, she was kneeling in her usual corner, deep in the Jesus prayer.

Fevronia reached out to place her hand gently on Theodora's shoulder. "I'm sorry to have questioned you so … severely. I don't mean to scare you, Sister Theodora. To be saved by the Theotokos, to have been carried by the Mother of God, in Her light and veil, is one of the greatest blessings I can imagine. It is truly a miracle. Surely you know that there's no sin in that. Won't you please tell me more?"

Even as Fevronia begged, she knew her questions would go unanswered. It would be years before she heard Theodora's voice again in anything other than prayer.

CHAPTER NINE

Manhattan, New York, February 12, 1990 (Monday)

By late Sunday night, Nicky changed his mind again. He couldn't write an intelligent response, so he resolved to call the monastery early the next morning, calculating that it would be near midday in Greece. While Kayla's string quartet played very softly in the background, he dialed the monastery's number. To Nicky's ear, the music swayed and repeated itself mysteriously and endlessly. He didn't quite understand the music, but listening gave him a sense of pride.

After two rings, the connection he thought he'd made to Greece was lost, and he heard a dial tone. He shook his head in disgust and tried again, but his second effort resulted just in a series of clicks. His nervousness began to increase just as the tempo of the string quartet itself began to increase, and as the music turned darker, so did Nicky's mood.

Nicky was about to give up. Aliyah was whining, and he had to get to the office. One more try, though, through a long-distance operator. On this attempt, he heard rings again, higher pitched, and in a few seconds someone answered. He heard a deep-throated, rough woman's voice.

"*Ya sas?*"

Nicky slipped back into Greek as if he'd never left the country of his birth. "I'm trying to reach Abbess Fevronia. Do I have the right number?"

"I am she. Hold for a second, please." He heard the abbess giving orders to someone in the background but could not make out the words. The tone, however, was that of a person completely in charge and at ease. Then she spoke to him again. "Yes, I am Abbess Fevronia. To whom ..."

"This is Dr. Nicky Covo, Nikolas Covo, calling from America." He heard a gasp at the other end of the line. "You did write to me some months ago?"

"Dr. Covo. My letter reached you, Praise be to God. I thought, when you hadn't written back, that I'd been mistaken, that whoever had received the letter was the wrong person."

"You had an old address for my office."

To Fevronia, it sounded almost as if she were being chastised by the man whom she was trying to reunite with his sister. But maybe she'd gotten it wrong, had found the wrong person. "Are you ... the Nikolas Covo that Alex Ganis helped get out of Thessaloniki? The Nikolas Covo who had two younger sisters?"

"I *am* Nicky Covo, born in Salonika and, yes, I had two younger sisters who were murdered in Auschwitz. There's no record I could find of either of them surviving. Believe me, I tried." Again, it sounded to Fevronia as if she was being accused somehow of disappointing Dr. Covo, spoiling his view of what had happened to his family.

The first movement of the quartet, in sonata form, proceeded through its development. Nicky wondered whether Fevronia could hear it and whether she might now be annoyed that he was listening to music during such an important conversation. He could not reach his CD player, however, without having to put down his phone and decided to leave things be.

"But you were wrong, Dr. Covo," Fevronia said, trying to sound firm in her conviction. "One of your sisters is here. I'm virtually certain."

"I don't know how it's possible."

"For the Lord anything is possible," she continued.

"You'll please excuse me for saying so, but I don't believe in God."

"Then so much more the pity. Still. I need to know. Sister Theodora, the photograph. Does she look like one of your sisters? Or like your sister might be today?"

Her tone was breathless, imploring, yet strong. Nicky didn't know what an abbess was supposed to sound like, but had imagined that an abbess should sound meek, humble, and unused to dealing with the outside world. Abbess Fevronia sounded anything but meek and humble.

He looked once more at the photograph. The eyes, though in shadow, did seem large, like Kal's. The nose, possibly titled slightly to the right, like Kal's. Or was that just his imagination?

"I don't know. Maybe Kal, the younger one."

"Kal?"

"Kalmiri was her full name. We called her Kalli or Kal."

"Kalli." The name seemed to fit well with Sister Theodora, thought Fevronia. "Her soul is goodness indeed. I've tried so long to find out where Sister Theodora came from and who she was before."

"If she's my sister, she's most likely Kal. The other sister, Ada, would have been too old to be the girl you described in your letter. But how could this possibly be? My family didn't know anyone near Serres. They wouldn't have sent her to the north, up to where the German army was in control. If such a crazy thing had been in the works, I'd have known."

"Really? I wonder. If you'd been caught in Athens, if you'd been tortured by the Nazis, would you have wanted to be able to reveal where your sister was?"

"Well ..."

"Don't answer. That wasn't a fair question. Anyway, I don't believe she came here directly from Thessaloniki. She got here somehow from Kavala. As I said in my letter, I've talked to Alex Ganis's sister, Tabitha, and seen his diary. There are certainly suggestions that he helped your sisters, and Alex was killed on the road to Kavala, where Tabitha lived. He might have been trying to get Kal, as you call her, to his sister for safekeeping. But nothing is clear."

"I don't remember our folks talking about Kavala either, but haven't you asked her, this Sister Theodora?"

"That's the thing, Dr. Covo. She won't say anything, as I told you." Fevronia paused, reflecting that she wasn't about to disclose that Sister Theodora had told her that the Mother of God brought her to the monastery. This Jewish man, a non-believer, would certainly be rebuffed by the idea. "She clearly doesn't wish to discuss where she came from or anything else, for that matter. The only time we hear her voice now – and it's been like this for decades – is when she prays. Which she does constantly. She's most devout in her prayer."

"Well, she'll speak to me, if I'm really her brother. Tell her that her brother is on the phone, if that's what you think. Can you put her on please?" There was a long pause during which he heard the faint crackle of the long distance connection.

Reservations that she couldn't put her finger on nagged at Fevronia. What Dr. Covo suggested was reasonable, and she herself would have begged to speak to her sibling if the situation had been reversed, but it was the loss of control by handing the telephone over to Theodora that troubled Fevronia.

"I think not, Dr. Covo." She paused briefly, trying to come up with an excuse that might sound plausible. "As I said, she doesn't speak to anyone. It's more than that, too. I've no idea how she'd react if she recognized your voice over the telephone, and I'm concerned about the consequences. I think your disembodied voice might frighten her."

"You're kidding."

"I assure you, Dr. Covo, I'm not kidding. It's always been my hope that, if I could locate you, if you still lived, that you'd come to the monastery."

"You want a major donation to your church, right? St. Vlassios, I believe. This is all to get money, isn't it?"

"Glory be to Christ, Dr. Covo, that's not my purpose. I've not asked for money and I never will. We do quite well financially, with our pilgrims and our wine. Believe me, I just want to know who Sister Theodora is, where she came from." She hesitated, slowly coming to the conclusion that she had to concede at least one additional point if she was to make him see how important it was that he come. "Her arrival here has been a mystery for decades but could well be the result of a miracle. That's why I need to know. I need you to help me unravel the mystery. If she is your sister, I should think you'd want to know, too, and to see her, to make yourself known to her. Glory be to Christ, how could you not want to reunite with your own blood?"

"A miracle? Please. I want to *talk* my sister, right now, if that's who she is. Please tell her that a Dr. Nicky Covo must speak with her. No, in fact, just say Nicky Covo. She'd have no idea that I'm a doctor." Perplexed that Fevronia was being so difficult, he heard her sigh.

"Very well. I'll try to get her to come to my office. I have to tell you candidly that I doubt she'll come."

He waited for what seemed forever, unhappy that this abbess controlled the situation and that he could accept only whatever she doled out. As the minutes dragged by, he cursed inwardly, thinking of the mounting long-distance charges. Ultimately, after he'd waited five or six minutes, it was Fevronia, not Sister Theodora, who came back on the line.

"I'm sorry, Dr. Covo. I did try, I assure you. I told her you were on the phone. I specifically told her it was her brother. I used your name. I even called her Kal, Kalli, and Kalmiri. Then I used the names Kal Covo and Kalli Covo. She had absolutely no reaction. She just looked at me, turned back into her corner and continued her prayer, exactly as I expected." Fevronia stopped. "So, you'll come? I think it's the only way."

"Her corner?"

"The corner of her cell, where she usually prays, under her favorite icons, next to her *lampada*. She did not want to step away from her prayer."

He closed his eyes to think more clearly. Could he bring himself to go back to Greece after so many years, after the horrors he'd lived through there? With the possibility that his sister was alive and waiting, as it were, for him to show up at her monastery. He wondered if he could live with himself if he gave up the chance to see her again. But no reaction when she heard his name? He found that impossible to believe, if Sister Theodora had really been his sister Kal. The lack of a reaction could only mean that Sister Theodora wasn't Kal. What point, therefore, to seeing her in person?

"Dr. Covo, are you there?"

He wasn't sure how long he'd been silent, but Fevronia's voice showed impatience. He opened his eyes and saw how badly his hands shook. He noticed with surprise that the string quartet had ended, and that Kayla's "Six Incidental Solos for Cello" was now playing: somber, slowly changing double-stops alternating with frenetic and discordant arpeggios.

"Yes, I'm here. I'm not sure what else I can do for you if she doesn't want to listen to me on the phone."

"If you come, when might we expect you?"

The music distracted Nicky, but he didn't want to put down the receiver, even for a second. He was about to tell Fevronia he was sorry that she'd been mistaken and say goodbye, but remembered something he'd been curious about.

"You told me in your letter how you learned the name Ganis, but how did you track down his sister?"

"For that, I have to thank God. It's a long story, a lot of detective work and even more luck, and I was helped by one of the old-timers here, a fellow named Andros. Maybe you'll meet him when you visit. I can share the details of our investigation then, if you like. The important thing is that I did find Tabitha."

"All right, as you say."

"And with her story and Alex's diary," Fevronia continued, "and putting two and two together, there's no other explanation for who Sister Theodora is."

"She would've responded when you mentioned my name."

"Maybe the sister you knew decades ago, but not Sister Theodora. You'll see how she is. You're coming, right?"

"I don't know."

"You must."

"I'll be in touch after I think it over."

He expected her to hang up, but could still hear some indistinct sound, perhaps papers being shuffled, on her end. She was waiting for him to say something. He closed his eyes again, counted to five, and then knew what he had to say.

"Abbess Fevronia, thank you for taking the trouble to find me, whether or not your hunch is right. *Efcharisto para poli.*"

"I hope I've done as God wishes. She's your sister, Dr. Covo, I'm telling you with certainty, and you will see her again," she assured him in that strong voice, a voice in control, its owner very comfortable in telling people what to do and having her way. "I feel you'll confirm what I believe and, with your help, she'll tell us how she came to the monastery."

"And visiting your monastery is the only way that I'll ever know if Sister Theodora is Kal? That's your edict?"

"That is what God has decreed."

CHAPTER TEN

Inousa, Greece, July 23, 1986 (Wednesday)

Fevronia gave up questioning Theodora about the Theotokos within months after Theodora's brief description of how she'd arrived at the monastery. Every time Fevronia brought up the subject, Theodora would smile and remain silent or turn her face back into the corner of her cell and recite the Jesus prayer rapidly and with fervor. Fevronia resolved that she would no longer torment the young woman with her questions, which would only divert Theodora from attaining the state of grace that she hungered after. Fevronia simply had to accept that the power of the Virgin Mary – or Her essence, or Her spirit – had entered Theodora and rested there for reasons that Fevronia couldn't fathom. Fevronia acknowledged to herself grudgingly that Theodora had been touched by God in a way that she, Fevronia, had never been and likely never would be.

That Theodora had the power to share God's touch with others was also evident. Theodora's following among the villagers had grown quickly after Fevronia and the other nuns occupied the monastery. When the small group of villagers coming to confess to Theodora swelled beyond what was appropriate for the peace of Sunday afternoons, Fevronia had had to limit the visitors to fifteen and the time of each to ten minutes. In addition to the villagers' confessions, however, Theodora within weeks began to hear the confessions of other nuns, who visited her in her cell – with Fevronia's blessings of course – at least once a week. They'd been able to keep their visits a secret from Fevronia for a short time. Fevronia was concerned when she found out, yet she had no choice but to go along with what had developed under her nose and what she felt couldn't be stopped. She couldn't risk alienating those whose assistance was vital. She was astute enough to recognize that being in control of the monastery didn't mean she could act stupidly to satisfy her own emotional needs.

Although Fevronia maintained a fascination with Theodora's origins, perhaps a fascination tinged with fear, and despite what she recognized as an unhealthy envy, she did not allow Theodora to dominate her thoughts. Theodora seemed to need no spiritual guidance from Fevronia, although Fevronia continued to read to Theodora in her cell from time to time. Instead, Fevronia concentrated her energies on perfecting her own prayer and on the spiritual health of the other nuns. She prayed every day to be united in spirit with the Lord and with the Theotokos, for the spiritual peace of those whose poor souls were tormented by grief and loneliness, and, most frequently, to be guided by the Lord to her brother's gravesite. She often had to absent herself from prayer to attend to the business side of the monastery, the development of the vineyards and winery, and her efforts to attract pilgrims and tourists who'd buy wine and contribute financially.

By 1986, when the vineyards and winery had been productive for decades, Fevronia began once again to obsess about Theodora. All Fevronia's prayers seemed to lead back to wondering about Theodora. Why had Theodora feared being sent away, particularly if the Virgin Mother had carried Theodora to the monastery with Her Light and Her Veil? Fevronia well remembered her one conversation with Theodora, primarily because of the grandiosity of Theodora's claims: to have been lifted from a closet by the Theotokos and put into a dark place. Where and how had this happened? Why had this happened? In addition to her curiosity, Fevronia's long-suppressed envy emerged and, once again, deeply troubled her. Hardly a day passed when Fevronia did not ask herself why Theodora should have had this magical experience but not Fevronia herself.

Mid-year, Fevronia decided that her only option to find out more was to beg for help from a clairvoyant, Elder Porphyrios, long famous in the Orthodox Church for his holiness and uncanny abilities to discern the unknown. She had heard that Elder Porphyrios could meet you for the first time, hold your hand for a second, and know immediately where you were from, who your parents were, where you'd gone to school, and what you did for a hobby. She'd read accounts of people who, upon meeting Elder Porphyrios, would learn from him that they had diseases of which their doctors were unaware. She'd read how he'd been able to tell searchers where a lost child could be found in woods he'd never visited. If anyone could tell her about Theodora, it would be Elder Porphyrios. So she wrote to him, explaining that she wanted him to meet a nun at her monastery and why. She's found out from a visitor that Elder Porphyrios planned to leave Mt. Athos soon to visit mainland Greece. He would have to go out of his way to make it to Inousa, but she begged that he might do so. When she received his return letter, in which he agreed to her request and gave a date, Fevronia was elated.

On the day Elder Porphyrios arrived, Fevronia had already been praying for hours. She had not eaten and was faint with hunger. The day was excessively hot, and Fevronia had begun to feel dizzy.

Porphyrios had been driven up from Inousa by an aide and emerged from the car wearing his black cassock and black pectoral cross. He had a thick, unruly white beard and mustache, giving the impression of a true man of God who could not possibly hope to keep sartorial appearance in order. He was also thin, almost consumptively so; his cassock seemed held up merely by a skeleton.

Fevronia's first impression was of a man near death, but how close no one might say.

As Fevronia approached him, she introduced herself. He extended his hand, which she took, bending her head forward. "A blessing to you in the name of Christ, Abbess Fevronia." His breathing was labored, as if he had climbed from Inousa through a deep snowfall.

"Elder Porphyrios, welcome in the name of Christ. It is indeed an honor to receive you to the Holy Monastery of St. Vlassios." She spread her arms out and turned slightly toward a portion of the vineyard.

"You are far from your home in ... Igoumenitsa, are you not?"

Fevronia was stunned. Although she'd been born in Igoumenitsa, she'd grown up in Paramythia since the age of two. She doubted whether anyone knew of her birthplace except her parents, dead for years. It did not seem probable that the Elder Porphyrios, before visiting the monastery, had conducted an investigation of her birth certificate.

"I have not lived there in many years, Father," she said. "You surprise me by knowing my birthplace. May I share with you some simple lunch?"

"Ah, but it is not yet late enough in the day for my meal, you see. I have only but a few minutes to meet the Sister Theodora of whom you wrote. May we see her now, please?"

Fevronia led him around the church and asked him to wait. As anxious as she was to have Elder Porphyrios meet Theodora and to discover the truth about her, she'd assumed that she could sit for a while with the great clairvoyant and come to know him better. She was offended with his obvious intent to keep his visit short, as if she, the abbess of a monastery that had been brought back to self-sufficiency through her hard work, indeed, that had been brought back into its very existence, was not worth sitting down with for a ten-minute meal. And, as she turned into the hallway leading to Theodora's cell, she wondered whether Elder Porphyrios could discern the location of her brother's grave, but realized with regret that she'd not thought earlier to ask him about that issue. Or should she ask him now, anyway? He was already doing a favor for her in meeting Theodora. She decided that she'd limit her requests on this visit to that one subject. Perhaps, in another year, when once again he might visit the mainland, she could ask him.

Theodora was in her usual place, on her knees, face to the corner of her cell. Fevronia said Theodora's name softly, but had to repeat it a few times, each time a touch louder, until Theodora turned. Fevronia could see that Theodora wasn't annoyed with the interruption, but instead was curious. Fevronia explained that someone was at the monastery to meet her, a great elder from Mt. Athos, not telling her more. Theodora rose slowly, rubbed her knees, and stretched her back. Then she picked up her bucket and followed Fevronia, who led her out of the building, into the blinding sunlight. The heat of the day enveloped them, rising as much from the stones upon which they walked as sweltering down from the sky. The light breeze that touched them did nothing to alleviate the feeling of oppression. In the background, Fevronia could hear the faint voices of workers in the vineyard.

Once Fevronia brought Theodora up to Elder Porphyrios, she stepped aside. Theodora took the Elder's hand, kissed it for a blessing, led him to sit on the nearby stone bench, and washed his feet. Completing the rite, she backed away, staring at the ground. Elder Porphyrios rose and gently reached to lift her head so that they looked at each other eye to eye. They stood that way for what seemed to Fevronia a very long time, until Elder Porphyrios turned to Fevronia and asked about Theodora's prayer habits.

"She prays without ceasing." Fevronia could not keep a hint of pride out of her voice.

"Yes, I can sense that. She has a pure heart, maybe the purest I've ever encountered. Somebody who is Christ's must love Christ, and when she loves Christ she is delivered from the Devil, from hell and from death." He looked at Theodora again. "My dear one, please take my hands again to receive another blessing." Theodora reached out both hands to his. "Sister Theodora, I bless you in the name of the Father, the Son, and the Holy Spirit." They stood, hands lightly touching, but Theodora's gaze had fallen once again to the ground, as if the path to heaven lay through the center of the earth. When Porphyrios dropped his hands, he said "you may go back to your prayer." Theodora turned and walked quickly back around to the cell building.

Fevronia asked immediately what he'd learned. Porphyrios lifted his cross to his mouth, kissed it, and allowed it to linger in front of his face as he thought. The contrast between Porphyrios's black cross and his white beard was sharp and startling. He stood with his cross lifted for what seemed to Fevronia an inordinately long time, during which she felt a rapid increase in her heartbeat. Finally, Porphyrios lowered the cross and shook his head. Fevronia saw pain in his pale blue eyes.

"No, Abbess Fevronia. I am not able in this case to tell you anything." He turned to head back to the car, where the aide was waiting, when she put her hand on his arm gently.

"Wait, Father. Please. You can't tell me anything? You touched her."

Porphyrios turned toward Fevronia and took a deep breath before continuing. "I know that I can see many things that others cannot. How I see these things, I do not understand, but these visions are from God. What He chooses to reveal or to conceal is up to Him. If I see nothing, it is because God does not want me to see, for reasons that I cannot explain."

"But ... you see nothing at all?"

"What I see cannot help you, I'm afraid."

"But, Father ... still, you saw something? You felt something?"

Porphyrios paused, then knelt at the spot where Theodora had stood in her bare feet just moments earlier and placed his hands in the dirt. When he rose, he'd picked up dirt in each hand and let it fall slowly back to the ground. Fevronia had the sense that he was simply stalling for time, deliberating about what he should say, but she couldn't understand why. His reputation was to speak truth, without reservation.

After a minute, Porphyrios responded in a soft voice. "I see pain from the time she was a child. I see a young girl without hope. I see great danger. I see confusion. But these are all things you must have known yourself."

"Yes. But no, not really. These things you say don't help me figure out where she's from."

"She's from a place on the seacoast of Greece."

"Father, the seacoast is tens of thousands of kilometers long."

"Yes, it's long." Porphyrios paused, seeming to deliberate about sharing additional information.

"You see nothing else?"

"I see a house, well-furnished. I see a family, parents and their children. I see a bird."

"A bird? What kind of bird?"

He looked up to the sky as if the answer would be written in the clouds. "What kind of bird, I cannot tell you. It's a bird of hope. It's a bird of freedom, but it's not a bird at all. It's ... it's ..." He stopped, turned his back on Fevronia, and began to walk toward his car.

"Father, please!" Fevronia put her hand on his arm again and, once again, he turned to face her. The briefest hint of a scowl disfigured his face, but then his normal, cool gaze returned as if the scowl had never been there, and he considered Fevronia with renewed patience.

"Abbess Fevronia, sometimes the things I see are best not divulged, at least not immediately, without more thought. Souls are at stake. But I can see from your eyes, without any special gift, that you are quite desperate. Think carefully about the value of the knowledge you seek and why you want that knowledge. I see into your heart as well."

"I don't understand."

"I've tried to help you as best I can."

"Please, Father, something more?"

He sighed, and a troubled look crossed his face and lingered for more than a few seconds while he spoke. "All right. Something more. I saw a bird that was not a bird, but a child's idea of a bird. It's blue."

"Father Porphyrios, do you see a closet?"

He showed no particular reaction to the question, no surprise, no curiosity as to why it had been asked. Porphyrios thought for a second before responding. "There's blood."

"The monks who died here?"

"No, I think not. I know not."

Fevronia wanted to protest against what seemed to be his desire to pose riddles instead of providing clear answers. She counseled herself to remain as calm as she could and maintain the proper demeanor of respect. "Father Porphyrios, do you see a dark place?"

"Many dark places, intertwined."

"Their graves?"

"God will divulge in His own good time."

"Do you see the Holy Mother of God?"

"There's a lock, but there's a key to be found."

Fevronia had no idea what Porphyrios was talking about and wondered whether, in the frailty of his old age, he had lost something of his powers. Or, she thought, he'd lost the desire to communicate as clearly as he once had.

Porphyrios reached his car, and his aide opened the door for him. He turned for one last look around at the monastery. Moments later, Fevronia watched as the Elder Porphyrios was driven slowly away from the Holy Monastery of St. Vlassios.

CHAPTER ELEVEN

Brooklyn, New York, February 12, 1990 (Monday)

On his way to work, Nicky had been deep in thought about his highly unsatisfactory conversation with the abbess. It was hard to accept that, if Sister Theodora was truly his sister, she'd have had no reaction at mention of his name. It could mean only that the abbess had been mistaken. But how could she have made such a mistake and yet known about Alex Ganis? She claimed not to want money, but perhaps that had been a ploy. But if she was after a large donation, why insist that he visit the monastery? Was that where they'd put the arm on him? Fevronia had not sounded devious, however. He tried without success to picture her. Ascetics were supposed to be recluses, shut off from the world, mild-mannered to the point of obsequiousness, but Fevronia struck him quite otherwise.

Nicky parked near his office and caught sight of the large white stone church on Jensen Street. Its five-story bell tower was the highest structure on the block, and he'd walked past it every workday for a year. This wasn't an Orthodox church, but Nicky thought he might enter on his way home and talk to the priest, one Father Leonard, a man whom some of his patients had mentioned as an intelligent and caring person. Perhaps Father Leonard might advise him on how to interpret Abbess Fevronia's behavior.

After his last patient, Nicky crossed Jensen Street to enter the church. He picked up a pamphlet explaining that he'd entered Our Lady of Lebanon, the spiritual home of Maronite Catholics in the Northeast United States. It was an official cathedral. The sanctuary was poorly lit, and he smelled a faint, woody incense. Nicky sat in a back pew and pulled Fevronia's letter from his pocket. Reading in the dimness was difficult.

I heard from her the story of her brother, Alex, killed in 1943 while possibly trying to hide a young Jewish girl from Salonika.

Alex would have been in his seventies if he'd lived. He'd often imagined Alex as still alive, but had never tried to contact him. He was saddened now that he'd never thanked Alex. If Alex died trying to hide his sister, then what? A Jew lived and a Christian died. Would the world have been any worse a place if their fates had been reversed? It was a question that Nicky knew had no reasonable answer. It was pure luck that governed. People would fall where they fell, and that was that.

"And how may we help you, brother?"

The voice startled Nicky. Father Leonard had found him and sat in the pew a few feet away. He was a short, stocky man who wore the white collar, black shirt, and black pants donned by Catholic clergy. Father Leonard had a strong nose, close-cropped dark hair, and a warm, if uncertain, smile. He smelled of linseed oil, as if he'd just come from painting a wood cabinet. The priest wiped his hands with a white cloth.

"I'm Father Leonard. David Leonard." He stuck the white cloth into his pocket and put out his hand, which Nicky felt obliged to shake. "Haven't I seen you in the neighborhood?"

"No doubt, Father Leonard. I've heard of you from my patients. I'm Dr. Nicky Covo. My office is ..."

"Of course, Dr. Covo." The priest's smile broadened, as if Nicky had been the very person he'd hoped would drop in that day. "So some of my flock are your patients? I'm not surprised. We serve the same ends, spiritual cleansing, do we not?"

"I don't quite see it as spiritual. My job is talking through problems, assessing a patient's mood, deciding which medications are appropriate."

Father Leonard's smile fell for an instant, but then returned warmly. "How we approach problems of those who seek healing may not be the same, but our ends are the same."

"I guess."

"So, if you'll allow me, what troubles you, Dr. Covo? I take it you're here because you want to talk to me, yes?"

It had been many years since Nicky himself had been through therapy. As he'd entered the church, he'd sought nothing more than information. But of course he wanted to talk. Father Leonard was sincere, his concern seemed genuine, and he was anxious to hear Nicky's story. Nicky felt in that instant grateful that he had, perhaps, found a sympathetic sounding board. The idea of a potential friendship, something Nicky desperately needed, began to emerge.

"Yes, I think so, if you have a minute. Or more. I received this last week." He gave the letter to the priest, who looked at it and then up at Nicky in puzzlement.

"Greek? If it had been Arabic I might have given it a shot, but I don't know a word of Greek."

"Sorry. Quite foolish of me." Nicky took the letter and read aloud in English. He tried to keep his voice non-committal.

"And you're this Nikolas Covo? You escaped from Thessaloniki?"

Nicky nodded.

"Astounding, I must say. May I?" The priest pointed toward the photograph that Nicky had taken from the envelope and still held in his hand. Nicky shrugged and handed it over. "Is this your sister? Or could it be her?"

There was a catch in his voice as he answered. Indeed, he was on the verge of tears because, as he formulated an answer to Father Leonard's question, he pictured Kal, at age six, chanting *hamotzi*, the blessing before eating bread. "My sister – both sisters – were murdered in the Nazi gas chambers or in front of a Nazi firing squad, or at least so I've always thought. I've believed that since '43. We knew what the deportations were for."

The priest again looked closely at the photograph.

"You know, Dr. Covo ..."

"Nicky, please."

"Nicky, then. There *have* been cases of people long thought dead in the camps who turned up alive somewhere. Years later."

Nicky shook his head unhappily. "Of course. Few from Salonika survived, though, and certainly not children under ten when they got to the camp. Kal would've been six, Ada nine. Neither would've been selected for labor. I know that much about Auschwitz. That's where the Greek Jews ended up."

"Yes, I know they went to Auschwitz, but still ... you weren't there, right?"

"As the letter says, and as somehow this abbess knows, I escaped before the deportations. She knows that I hid for months in Athens. With a priest, as it turned out."

"Ah, yes. I've read that there were such priests who risked their lives. But does this nun look like one of your sisters? The woman she might've turned into forty-something years after you last saw her?"

"Forty-seven."

"Forty-seven, then."

Nicky looked at the photograph yet another time. What could he even remember about Kal's face? He recalled that Kal had abnormally large eyes. The eyes of the nun in the photograph could have been large but it was hard to tell. Were they brown? Impossible to tell. One part of his mind, he knew, was forcing him to see Kal in the photograph, and the other part was warning him not to see her.

"I don't know. It's too long ago. How could I imagine what they looked like now? But, if she was one of my sisters, she'd be Kalli."

"Kalli."

"Kal, the younger of the two. I was eight years older."

"She was the baby of the family?"

"Yes."

Father Leonard thought for a moment. "And you were like a father to her, maybe?"

"No, I don't think so, but I was proud of her. Kal was very smart. Read well for her age, had started before she was four. Loved to draw, too." He pictured the blue jay in flight. "She might've become an artist. If she'd been a boy, she might have become a Talmud scholar. She used to sit with our father when he studied."

"So she had a religious conviction?"

"Well, we all did."

Nicky leaned forward, his head resting on the pew in front. The church suddenly faded from consciousness for a second, during which Nicky fell into a black void and felt himself spinning in dizzyingly tight circles. He opened his eyes to stop the spinning, pushed himself upright with difficulty.

The priest placed his hand gently on Nicky's shoulder. "Are you all right?"

It took Nicky a few deep breaths to clear his head, remember where he was, and remember to whom he was speaking. "Quite."

"I see. Well, don't you feel that a child who immerses herself in religion, as your sister did, might continue to do so as an adult?"

"She was Jewish, through and through. She knew the difference between Jews and gentiles."

"We *goyim*," Father Leonard said with a smile.

"Yes. It's hard to understand how Kal could have become a Christian, but not only that, a nun, cloistered in a remote monastery. And, if she was alive, it's impossible for me to accept that she never tried to track me down."

"You don't know that she never tried, do you?"

"If the abbess could find me, then anyone else could've as well."

"You won't know until you talk to her. Haven't you called?"

"Tried just this morning and spoke to the abbess, who told me that her Sister Theodora won't talk to me. She didn't even react when she heard that I was on the phone. It's why I doubt that Theodora *could* be my sister. My real sister would've rushed to speak to me. And this abbess now says I need to visit the monastery. She wants me to prove to myself and to her that Theodora is my sister. She wants to know for sure where Theodora came from. It's bizarre."

Father Leonard was silent for a minute. He picked up a hymnal from the book rack and thumbed through for a second as if looking for something, then replaced it. "And so how can I help you, Nicky? Besides listening to you, which I'm happy to do. You're always welcome to stop in here."

"Tell me how a Jewish girl becomes a Christian nun, one whose only activity is to pray to someone the Jews do not believe is God."

"I can't tell you how in this particular case, but I can say with confidence that it's possible. Many Jews convert, for many reasons. Some young Jews hidden during the Holocaust with Christian families were undoubtedly raised as Christian and adopted the faith."

"But not Kalli, not a girl already devout in her Judaism. To turn herself into a nun? I think I'd better go. Thank you very much for your time, but there's lots of traffic back to the city." Nicky rose to leave, but Father Leonard put his hand on Nicky's arm and urged him gently back to sit.

"Wait, please. Perhaps I can explain better what it means for a Christian to live in a monastery and devote herself to prayer. To do what Sister Theodora does."

"My sister was not and would never be a Christian. Neither sister."

"Then let me speak in terms of a girl who *was* born Christian, baptized, grew up in an observant Christian home. Someone perhaps like this Abbess Fevronia."

"Go ahead."

"So, the believer wants to achieve as much union with God as we can have in this life. Every possession, every activity not absolutely necessary for life is seen as excessive, a diversion from fulfilling one's true destiny."

"Which is?"

"Immersion in God's love and wisdom. It's been said that the monastic is one who keeps up the life and flame of the world."

"I don't get it."

"It's not an easy concept to grasp, I'll admit. But isn't it a bit like what your father tried to do when he studied the Talmud? Isn't that the reason that many religious Jews will spend hours a day – so I gather – going through these difficult texts, to read about God's miracles and to learn what actions God wants Jews to undertake in their everyday lives? And by immersing themselves in these words, becoming closer to God?"

"Maybe. But I studied Talmud too, when I was young. It's really a game, solving a puzzle. Like solving the Rubik's Cube. The purpose is just to keep your mind sharp." Even as he spoke, though, Nicky's dim memories of studying Talmud with his father seemed more than just a game or intellectual project. He knew there'd been a time when such intense study had made him feel close to the *El Shaddai*, the Supreme Being.

"For Christian ascetics, those who succeed at it, it's the highest achievement possible. It's much more than solving a puzzle. It's surrendering oneself to the Divine, twenty-four hours a day, an unending quest to purify the soul, expressing continuously the utmost gratitude to Christ for His sacrifice."

Nicky suppressed a smirk with difficulty. "That's not how Abbess Fevronia came across when I spoke to her. That's not the impression I get of the woman who wrote this letter." He tapped the envelope. "And why, of all things, would a Jewish girl become devoted in this way to Christ?"

"I can't answer that."

"You're a priest and you yourself haven't taken that route."

"Sometimes I wish I had, instead of choosing the very mundane duties of a parish priest." Father Leonard looked about him, as parishioners started to file in and someone turned the lights up. He handed the photograph back. "I don't know anything about your sister other than what you told me, nor anything about Sister Theodora other than what you read to me, but you should know that, for the true ascetic there's pure joy in approaching God. I'd guess that Sister Theodora leads a most happy life, and Abbess Fevronia too. You should rejoice that your sister is alive and that she's found a way to live a full, meaningful life."

"I can't ... my sister? Kal was Jewish and would never be anything else." Nicky's voice, repeating what he'd said out loud many times and to himself even more, struck him as weaker, plaintive, almost expecting and wanting to be rebutted.

"We all find our own ways to serve God, Nicky. You'd have to understand what becoming a Christian meant to her, how that came about; you'd have to know how she saw that her prayer affected others. Perhaps she felt – feels – that in her devotion to Christ she can help bring miracles to the world. You'd have to feel what a believer feels in her presence."

"I don't believe in God, forgive me for saying so, and I don't believe in prayer, so I can't ... thank you again for your time, Father Leonard." Nicky got up once more to leave, but once more the priest put his hand on Nicky's arm.

"We have lots of doubters in our church."

"For me, it's not a question of doubt. For me, it's a certainty God does not exist."

"But you grew up believing? You did believe?"

Nicky turned his face away. "An illusion."

"I'd say you converted, too. Just in an opposite way. You chose atheism."

"I accepted reality."

"We have congregants in our community, here, who are equally certain. Yet, many who protest loudly that God doesn't exist keep coming back."

"They like you. They're fond of you."

Father Leonard shook his head, still smiling generously as if he relished the conversation.

"No. They come back time and again hoping for God to reenter their lives. They're waiting."

CHAPTER TWELVE

Inousa, Greece, February 12, 1990 (Monday)

Fevronia was sure that she'd found the right person and that Sister Theodora could be none other than Dr. Covo's sister, Kal. Instead of elation at the unexpected call, though, she felt a sense of foreboding. After hanging up with Dr. Covo, she returned to her cell to pray, but the feeling of closeness to God did not come. She thought instead about whether she'd been wise to press the search for Theodora's origins. Elder Porphyrios had seen something he'd not wanted her to know. He'd mentioned blood, as she recalled his purposely obtuse words. She worried about what would happen to Theodora if her brother did come to St. Vlassios.

Fevronia regretted lying to Dr. Covo, a sin she'd confess to Father Rukos as soon as she first had an opportunity. Although she'd intended originally to put Theodora on the phone with Dr. Covo, she changed her mind halfway to Theodora's cell. Instead, she entered the monastery's small library to think. She feared the shock that hearing her brother's voice might have on Theodora. Would Theodora, if she recognized her brother's voice, be suddenly reminded of her origins and forsake her devotion to Christ? Would she want to leave the monastery, even while maintaining her Christian faith, to reunite with her brother? Perhaps either scenario was unlikely, but suddenly Fevronia wasn't sure she was ready to take that chance. And why hadn't Fevronia thought of these possibilities sooner, before she went searching for Theodora's brother in the first place? Why hadn't she heeded Elder Porphyrios's implicit message to leave well enough alone?

It took Fevronia only a minute of reflection in the library to decide that it was not right to put the lost siblings together on the trans-Atlantic line. If they were to be reunited, it had to be in person, at a meeting that Fevronia could control. As she returned to her office, the lie – that she had tried and that Theodora hadn't responded – seemed the most sensible escape from the predicament into which Fevronia had placed herself.

Now, reflecting upon her conversation with Dr. Covo, Fevronia felt that she needed to dissect her ambivalence. She needed to confide in someone. She thought first of Sister Zoe, but decided that the person who would most likely understand would be Andros, who'd first introduced her to Theodora and, decades later, helped her track down Alex Ganis's sister. Yes. She would talk to Andros, her frequent advisor, main principal go-between with the villagers, and general sounding board on subjects she didn't want to share with the others at the monastery.

Fevronia trudged the two kilometers to Andros's house. The road was covered with crusted snow, but she steadied her descent with the beech walking stick that Andros himself had carved for her many years before. The stick always anchored Fevronia's hand when she ventured away from the monastery. She gripped its curved *glitsa*, which Andros had fashioned from olive wood. It had been a gift for Fevronia's fiftieth birthday, a possession she treasured, even while recognizing that a true ascetic should never treasure any worldly item.

As she arrived, she saw parked in front of Andros's house the beige DIM 652 of his son, Ephraim. Fevronia was happy to see Ephraim, who answered the door when she knocked. He was a large man with a gray, grizzled beard, a grandfather in his own right. Fevronia had attended the baptisms of his children and grandchildren. Ephraim had a gruff, common sense manner about him, and she wouldn't have any problem talking to Ephraim as well as to Andros.

Ephraim took Fevronia's coat and stick and pointed to Andros's small kitchen, where her friend sat, smoking his pipe. Andros invited her to sit and made a big show of putting out his pipe, which unfortunately did nothing to diminish the sickly sweet smoke already circulating through the air. The only available chair was covered with two old sweaters and a hat. She picked them up and placed them on the table in front of her, wiped her hands on her cassock, and sat on the chair's edge. As Andros prepared a pot of tea,

Fevronia blessed him, his son, and their respective households in the name of Christ and asked after Ephraim's grandchildren.

After they had chatted for a while, Fevronia explained that she'd heard from Dr. Covo and was sure she'd found Theodora's brother. She watched Andros carefully for his reaction, seeing what she thought was a slight grimace, but nothing more. He'd known Fevronia had been reaching out to agencies, Holocaust museums, and the like with the name Nikolas Covo, but was never a strong supporter of the enterprise.

"Wait a minute, Mother," Ephraim interjected. "Sister Theodora was Jewish?"

"I told you already, weeks ago, she might be Jewish," said Andros as he poured more tea for himself.

"I thought you were joking, Baba."

"You never listen. You think I'm just an old fool."

"Look, Mother." Ephraim tweaked his beard. "Everyone knows Sister Theodora is devoted to Christ and prays day and night to Our Savior. It doesn't make sense that she's Jewish. The Jews killed Christ."

Fevronia held back from reminding Ephraim that Christ, Himself, had been born a Jew and that the Blessed Theotokos was also a Jewess. That the Jews of Judea killed Christ was well ingrained in Christian doctrine as an undeniable historical point, but she saw it as irrelevant to Theodora. If born a Jew, she'd long since given up her connection to that tribe. What she needed was not an argument about what obviously *had* happened, at least in terms of Theodora being thoroughly Christian, but advice about how to deal with Theodora's brother.

She said, calmly, "It might not make sense, but there's a long history of Jewish converts to Christianity. Some of them are revered as saints. What I'm concerned about now is whether I've done the right thing."

"Now's a fine time to worry," grumbled Andros.

"I told Dr. Covo, who wanted to talk to Sister Theodora, that she had no reaction when I mentioned he was on the telephone. But that was untrue. I said nothing to her. I just told Dr. Covo he had to come here if he wanted to see his sister again. He told me, from the photograph, she's probably his sister named Kalmiri. Kal, he called her."

"That's no Jewish name, is it?" asked Ephraim.

"I don't think so, but then Nikolas isn't a Jewish name either," she responded.

"And so he'll come?" asked Andros.

"I want him to, yet I don't know if I've done the right thing."

"How important is it really, bringing the two of them together?" Ephraim continued, reaching for a *diples* on a tray Andros had put before them. "Why disturb Sister Theodora after all this time?"

With sorrow, Fevronia declined Ephraim's offer of the honey walnut pastries. She thought for a long minute about Ephraim's question. "Initially, when I begged your father to help me track down Theodora's connection to Ganis and Kavala, I wanted to know who she was and how she'd come to the monastery, something I've wanted to know for years."

"I told you when you first met her, Mother. Theodora's coming was a miracle," sniffed Andros, helping himself to a second *diples.*

"And when I found out she might have a brother, alive, it seemed only right to try to find him. And if I found her brother, I thought, he could come here and get her to talk."

"No guarantee she'd talk, even if he came," Andros observed as he chewed.

"No, but that's how I saw it happening. I wanted her to open up. Still want that, I guess. I wanted badly to understand what makes her so special." As she spoke, Fevronia knew that she'd never told anyone, even those closest to her, about Theodora's claimed encounter with the Theotokos and about how she longed to have a similar experience. She didn't feel she could share that, but she could, she thought, add additional reasons for her preoccupation with Theodora. "And I also thought there was a chance we could learn where the monks were buried."

Andros and Ephraim remained silent for a minute and glanced at each other. Fevronia was on the verge of saying more when Andros spoke.

"As I thought. It all comes back to Silenos. That's what's been driving you more than anything else, hasn't it, Mother? But what will you do if you do find the graves? Dig them up and rebury them? Can't they rest where they've been now for decades?" Andros set his teacup down a bit too firmly, the china rattling.

"They haven't had a proper Christian burial, as necessary to show proper respect for the dead. With myrrh and aloe, wrapped in linen, as with our

Lord. As necessary for resurrection of the body when He comes again." She made the sign of the cross; Andros and Ephraim quickly followed suit.

"But," said Andros softly, then stopped.

"But what?"

"Mustn't there come a time when we stop trying for a proper Christian burial, as you say, and just let the dead lie in peace? Can't we leave it to Christ Himself to attend to their resurrection?"

Fevronia knew he was right. The church did recognize there were times when proper burial was impossible; it even accepted that cremation might be necessary in some cases. Then she felt she could no longer hold back. "It's also about the Theotokos."

Andros and Ephraim both looked up sharply when she mentioned the Mother of God. She could almost hear her ears burning, almost see her heart beating wildly.

"Mother, what have you not told us?" asked Andros. "The Theotokos? For all the time I spent helping you get to Kavala, searching through old records, you had more information?"

She nodded ever so faintly, trying to find her voice when it seemed her throat was tightening. She took a sip of tea and prayed for the courage to speak. A few seconds elapsed before she could continue. "Sister Theodora told me once, soon after I got here, that the Theotokos had brought her to St. Vlassios. Had in fact lifted her out of a closet and brought her to the monastery with Her veil. To be more specific, brought her with Her light and Her veil. Something else about having been put in a dark place. And, yes, I didn't tell you because I didn't know what to make of the story. I beg your forgiveness for not telling you. But this story has bothered and intrigued me ever since."

"Amazing," said Andros, retrieving his pipe from the shelf on which he put it, filling it once more, and lighting it. "Amazing and unbelievable. Yet I believe it. I sensed her glow and her warmth at the beginning, and the warmth of her touch stays with her. I knew it was a miracle that brought her to us. And you've hidden it from us."

There was a long moment of embarrassment for all. Then Ephraim, as if to divert their attention from Fevronia's deceit, picked at her logic. "Mother, I don't see how Theodora could know anything about the massacre. She was found alive at the monastery, so must've had no knowledge of what happened to the monks. That's pure common sense."

"Perhaps it's your common sense, but there's more at work here. If it's true the Theotokos brought Theodora here, as she claims, then who knows what else is possible? If she was under the protection of the Holy Mother ..."

"If it's true?" whispered Andros, then allowed his voice to get stronger. "You doubt Theodora's story? You, a woman dedicated to a life of prayer? Is your doubt what kept you from telling me about this years ago? Where was your faith, Mother? Imagine what it would have meant to the villagers to hear of the intervention of the Mother of God in bringing Theodora here."

"I understand what you're saying. But Theodora never told me how, never repeated her story. How could I know it wasn't just a dream, just her imagination? I had nothing, still have nothing to prove, to show for sure, that she was touched by the Blessed Virgin. I wouldn't spread news of such a connection to the Theotokos without more; otherwise, I'd be thought injudicious, if not entirely crazy. And you'd be wise not to mention it either, without evidence. But we might get an answer if Dr. Covo comes and if his visit awakens Theodora's desire to speak again."

"But now you're unsure?" asked Andros.

"I'm afraid."

"You're afraid his visit will hurt her in some way?"

Fevronia couldn't answer Andros's question. She was afraid, but of exactly what she didn't know.

After a few moments, Andros added, "You're wondering why, if God wanted Sister Theodora to be with her brother, He separated them?"

She hadn't been thinking that at all, but Andros's question gave her something to grasp onto. "Yes. That must be at the heart of my doubt." She thought for a few seconds, unconsciously grasping the cross she wore over her cassock. "But I also ask myself whether, if God wanted them to remain apart, why He enabled us to find Dr. Covo? Why God even allowed Dr. Covo to live." There was a minute of uneasy silence. Fevronia looked from Andros to Ephraim and back again, trying to deduce what they were feeling.

"Rhaab and I are close," Ephraim reflected. "If something horrible happened to my sister when we were children, something to tear us apart ..."

"Then ...?"

"I'd want to find her again, Mother. I have two girls, two boys, six grandchildren. I'd want my own to look for each other, never to stop looking, if war separated them. I'd want others, if they had knowledge, to try to put them together. So I understand what you're trying to do for Sister Theodora as well as for this Dr. Covo. It could be good for both of them." Ephraim turned toward his father, who'd muttered something unintelligible. "You don't agree, Baba?"

Andros sat puffing. When he didn't answer, when he picked up his newspaper and turned to the football scores, Fevronia rose to leave, fighting the urge to cough. Ephraim offered to drive her back to the monastery, and she gratefully accepted.

CHAPTER THIRTEEN

Manhattan, New York, and New Brunswick, New Jersey, February 15-16, 1990 (Thursday-Friday)

After a stop at the Barnes and Noble on Broadway and 82nd, Nicky began reading extensively in the evenings about religious asceticism, trying to form a mental picture of what Father Leonard had told him, about surrounding oneself with the Divine. He knew the word *ascetic* itself had been derived from the Greek word for strenuous exercise and that the various forms of asceticism included lengthy fasting and self-flagellation, but beyond that he knew nothing. He learned quickly there had been Jewish ascetics, but that the practice as discussed in the Talmud had been viewed skeptically. The prevailing opinion of the rabbis had been that those Jews who professed to become holy by denying themselves even the slightly physical pleasures were, in fact, hypocrites, their true motivation not to seek oneness with God at all but to prove from outward appearances that their contemporaries were less holy than they were. In other words, asceticism was an unseemly contest of holier than thou. Yet, Jewish asceticism had never entirely disappeared.

The Greek Orthodox tradition did not view asceticism negatively. Rather, it was welcomed as the ultimate battle between the forces of good and evil, God versus the devil. The monks and nuns were championed as God's army on earth, obsessed with fighting all sins through their prayer and devotion. The first step along the way was feeling oneself a sinner, sinning as in having missed the mark, sinning as in having fallen short of regaining a lost likeness to God. The ascetics did not see themselves as sedentary at all, but rather fully engaged in the most important task they could imagine. The highest level of personal salvation – union with God, what some called "living Pentecost"– could be achieved only through repentance and self-denial, through a life of complete surrender and humility.

Nicky couldn't understand Kal feeling that she had to devote her life to repentance – what could she have had to repent about, a six-year-old girl? – nor could he picture Kal feeling that she had to fight the devil. She'd been brought up to obey God's laws as understood in the Sephardic tradition and had been eager to do so, never complaining about the restrictions of *Shabbat* or the holy festival days, but she was not one to deny herself the few pleasures available to her. She'd been learning to make *baklava* and certainly enjoyed eating them. She'd taken pride in her beautiful singing and in her artistic endeavors.

On Thursday evening, a week after Fevronia's letter had arrived, Nicky's ruminations about Kal were interrupted. So deep in thought had he been that the telephone's ringing startled him. He shivered as he reached for the receiver.

"We've got trouble, Dad. It's Kayla." His son's voice was frantic, scaring Nicky even before his mind registered that something had happened to his daughter. His daughter, two years younger than Max, had to be dead. This was the call Nicky had long dreaded.

"What is it Max?"

"She's at Robert Johnson psych ward. Can you get down here?"

Not dead, not dead. But the psych ward again?

"Tell me."

"Went off her meds, I guess. Dad ... she attacked Jackie, hurt him ..."

"Is he ..."

"But he'll be okay, I think. I happened to walk in just ... I found her throttling him, otherwise who knows what might've happened. I had to call the police, her doctor, her rabbi, I ..."

"Rabbi?"

"Kayla was screaming for him as the police took her to the second ambulance. So I called him. I thought he should know."

"All right." He looked at the clock. Nine-ten, rush hour long over. He'd been ready to fall asleep, but the desire to sleep had disappeared in response to adrenalin. "Be there as soon as I can."

·　　·　　·　　·　　·

The drive to New Brunswick and the hospital where Nicky had done his residency flew by in a blur of bad memories. Kayla, at Avery Fisher Hall, bowing to a standing ovation in her last concert, next to her the young Haitian violinist whom she'd accompanied, the man who seduced her and fathered Jackie. Kayla, screaming and running off-stage and out of the building before anyone had the sense to stop her. Kayla, missing for days. Alive or dead? Kayla, found hiding at a Chabad House. Kayla, fighting the recurring delusion of a fan stalking her, waiting for a chance to cut her throat. Kayla, becoming a mother. Kayla, learning to manage her paranoid schizophrenia with medication. Kayla, exercising, composing beautiful chamber music, gaining an excellent reputation in her second musical career. Kayla, too smart to stop taking her meds.

Or so Nicky had thought. But why now? What had the rabbi to do with this? Damn religion, damn the rabbi, damn everyone who rejected science. Damn Abbess Fevronia, for that matter, a meddler into his private life.

The psych ward was in a new building. It took Nicky a while to locate it, be identified and checked for contraband, and find Max, who was pacing in a cream-colored visitors' lounge.

"What's going on? Where are they?"

"Kayla's under sedation, Dad. Sound asleep, per the nurses. Not much you can do, although I knew you'd want to look in on her."

"And Jackie?"

"In the Peds unit, Building Two. They were still checking him out as of a half-hour ago. He could barely talk, still crying hysterically after all this time, didn't seem to recognize me. I had to pry her hands from his neck. A minute later and ..." Max turned away.

"Shit. Come with me. I want to look at her chart."

Through an intercom, he spoke to the on-duty nurse and both of them were buzzed through two heavy doors. Nicky marched to the nurse's station, identified himself again, and was given a thin sheaf of papers, which he scanned in a second. "Nothing particularly useful here. Let me go have a look, sleeping or not." The nurse led them to Kayla's room, where indeed they found Kayla sleeping deeply. Nicky took her pulse and felt her forehead, which was still damp with sweat.

"Why, Kayla?" he asked.

"Nicky?"

Nicky and Max both turned to see a woman at the door of the room, a woman whom Nicky knew and Max did not. Although Nicky hadn't seen Helen for more than two decades, he recognized her instantly. He'd lived with her family for his first months in America.

Helen leads him to a bedroom in her family's house that is to become his bedroom. It's a small corner room just up the first flight of stairs and facing the tree-lined street. She explains to him in Ladino that she and her sister Irene had shared the room when they were younger. On a dresser sits a basket of oranges, apples, and bananas, on the front of which leans a card reading, in English, "Welcome to America!" She's very pretty, Nicky thinks, smiling at her. She's wearing a white blouse and a light blue skirt with a pink and white floral pattern. He learns one of her brothers-in-law – Catherine's husband – was killed on the day the Americans landed at Normandy.

"Helen?"

"What are *you* doing here?" she asked, walking into the room and glancing at the young woman on the bed. "Oh my. Your daughter."

He nodded. "It's Kayla, yes. Let's step out, and I'll explain."

Back in the visitors' lounge, they hugged briefly, Nicky introduced Helen to Max and told her briefly what he knew about Kayla's situation and that of his grandson. There followed an awkward silence, until Nicky suggested they get coffee. He'd also wanted to check on his grandson, but felt that could wait. Max promised to look in on Jackie.

"Amazing running into you after all these years," Nicky said, smiling at Helen as they sat in the quiet cafeteria. At a nearby table, an older woman had put her head down and cried softly, making Nicky uncomfortable. "What are you doing here?"

Helen smiled. "I'm a retired social worker, still consulting. Usually I'm never here this late, but just this evening a patient on the psych ward died, a family I've known for years. I came to give the family support, see if I could help. But Nicky, how's Adel? You haven't said anything about her."

He shuddered for an instant, unprepared to hear his deceased wife's name. Helen couldn't have known about Adel's death, because he'd never called Helen or anyone else in the Saltiel family with the news. How could he have expected her to know without his making the effort to tell her? He said simply, "She's gone. Died two years ago. It was quick."

"Oh, I'm so sorry, Nicky. I ..."

"And David?" He couldn't talk about Adel without first asking Helen about her husband. From the look on her face, he knew, even before he asked, that Helen had a similar tale of loss.

"I'm a widow since '85, Nicky. *Zichrono l'vracha.* David had prostate cancer, which spread very quickly. It was over within a year."

"David gone," was all Nicky could muster. His memory flashed on how David in 1946 tried to explain to him, as they listened to the Saltiel's radio, the difference between a ball and a strike, on how David had taken him into nearby Donaldson Park to teach him how to play catch. It had taken months for David to pound baseball into Nicky's head, but finally the sport had captured Nicky's imagination. And now, to learn so belatedly that David had died. "I'm so sorry, Helen. That's tragic," he managed.

Their conversation turned back to Kayla. Daughter with mental problems, off meds, her son in danger. Nicky fought to control his sadness. Someone else might have given in to a teary display, but Nicky Covo would be calm, he told himself, even as his hands shook. He'd be the epitome of a rational approach to the problems in front of him.

"Oh, dear. Poor Kayla. And I hope Jackie will be all right. What a horror."

He nodded. "Jackie's old enough, unfortunately, that I fear he'll remember this for the rest of his life." He wondered how he might deal in therapy with a six-year-old who'd been choked by his mother. Children of that age could be damaged irrevocably by trauma, particularly at the hands of a close family member. Jackie would likely need long-term psychiatric care. Nicky was once again glad that he didn't treat young children. Too difficult. Too heart-crushing when, despite one's best efforts, the patient was beyond hope.

"Show me a picture?" asked Helen.

Nicky looked in his wallet and pulled out a photograph of Jackie holding a T-ball bat. "He's about three and a half in this one."

"He's delightful! What a sweetie."

They sat quietly for another minute, finishing their coffee. Helen played with her empty cup and seemed to be trying but failing to find something to say. But it was Nicky who broke the silence. As if Nicky had just noticed, he said "Helen, may I say that you look great? You're as beautiful as ever."

Helen blushed and started to tear her cup into small bits. Nicky took measure of her nervousness, unsurprising given the years that they'd been apart and the strange way they'd run into each other. With a patient this nervous, he might've suggested – if the weather was amenable – leaving his office and continuing the session during a brisk walk around downtown Brooklyn. Not an option now, though. It was almost midnight and freezing outside. Yet he didn't want her nervousness to end their conversation. He wanted to continue to enjoy her presence.

He reached out, took her hand lightly, and encouraged her to talk about her life. Although she looked up at him questioningly, she didn't withdraw her hand, and he could see with relief that Helen's nervousness began to ease. She stopped playing with her cup and began to summarize, in greater detail than Nicky would've imagined, the years they'd been out of touch. She was only six years older than he, yet he was shocked to discover she already had ten grandchildren, three grandsons already Bar Mitzvahed, two grandsons on their high school baseball teams. The oldest grandchild, a girl, was waiting to hear from colleges. Princeton or Penn? He was trained in listening carefully; yet Nicky soon became totally confused about which grandchildren went with which children, which sons worked where. He gathered mostly that, since David's death, Helen's two sons and one daughter looked after her, seeing her at least a few times a week.

When Helen paused, as if she'd exhausted the topic of her own life, Nicky talked about himself. How hard it had been to deal with Adel, her schizophrenia, her persistent hallucinations, her bouts of agitation, her tendency to rhyme whenever she became most agitated. He made sure to talk as well about the good Adel, her unwavering support for his career, her love for their children and grandchild, her devotion to making sure that the very young Kayla, a piano prodigy, could get to her lessons and find ample practice time. When he approached the subject of how Max and Kayla now lived together, Helen interrupted.

"I know a lot about Kayla, Nicky, I should tell you, should have said so earlier. I know about her career. Don't you remember calling Dad to tell him about one of her concerts? In Newark? Dad was sick and couldn't make it. He died not long after you called. I left a message at your office about his funeral."

Nicky had no recollection whatsoever. "I called Elie about one of Kayla's concerts? And you left a message? Gee, something must've come up, or I would've been at the funeral. Is it too late to say how sorry I am?" The man had been a second father. He had reached out to help a refugee, had virtually plucked him out of the displaced person's camp, and had paid for his education. Now it appeared that their last interaction had faded entirely from Nicky's memory as well as having received news of his death.

"It's never too late. Yes, you certainly did call him about Kayla, and he was grateful to hear from you. But I'd already learned about Kayla in the news and had been keeping track of her, right up to ..."

"Don't ..."

"That last concert. David and I were there. On the first tier. We weren't sure what we saw."

"That was awful, Helen."

"Maybe I shouldn't have reminded you. But that evening at Avery Fisher Hall, we spotted you on the main floor. When Kayla screamed, we saw you run toward the stage. What a mess. I called out, but you couldn't hear me in the chaos. After, I should've tried to get you on the phone, but so many years had passed since we'd talked, and I felt awkward. Or I should have sent a note. I can't say why I didn't. I did follow the story, though, and learned Kayla had gone missing for days. Months later I read about how she gave up concertizing and was expecting a baby."

Nicky nodded. "Sorel's."

"Sorel?"

"August Sorel is Jackie's father. The violinist you heard at that last concert. The jerk abandoned Kayla, left her pregnant at seventeen. Max pounded him into the ground just outside Juilliard later that year, and we haven't heard from him since. He's gone on to have quite a career, and yet not a penny of support."

"Poor Kayla."

"Her scream that night was just possibly the worst moment of my life, and there have been a lot of horrible moments."

She grimaced. "I remember you telling us about the war."

"I did?" Even as he questioned her recollection, a picture formed in his brain of his telling Helen's family about things he should never have confessed. But they'd pressured him to speak about his wartime experiences.

The partisans swear at the German prisoners. "Gamoto!" they yell. "Fuckers!" A few old women and a handful of children from the village demand that the invaders be killed immediately. General Stalin asks the crowd of younger andartes *in which he stands for a volunteer to execute a prisoner. Nicky cries out boldly, steps forward, is selected for the job and given a bayoneted rifle. In his mind, he's avenging the murder of his family. He studies the prisoners carefully before he chooses, taking his time, savoring the moment. He hates their pale skin, light blue eyes, and blond hair. Finally, he points to a clean-shaven corporal in the middle of the line, the largest of them, wanting to be sure he hits his target.*

"You did." Nicky saw Helen lips quiver. He reached out again to take her hand. "How did we stop being friends, Nicky? At one time ..."

"I got swept up in so many things." He wanted to elaborate about how he'd opened a practice, started a family, tried to raise a prodigy without the least idea of how, hindered by a wife whose psychiatric problems by themselves would've made his life overly complicated. All possible excuses seemed lame.

"I didn't mean to sound accusing." Helen's voice softened. "I could've reached out too, particularly after that concert. You needed a friend, but we were all busy, right? You know how much time it takes, how much energy, to raise kids and keep a career going." She withdrew her hand from Nicky's again. "And to care for David. He never overcame the trauma of war. Jumped at every loud, unexpected noise. Now we call it PTSD, pretty it up with a scientific name, but it's the same thing."

"The Battle of the Bulge," Nicky murmured, knowing Helen didn't need to be reminded.

"You live with someone long enough, sleep next to them every night, you know when they're fighting in their nightmares. You hold them when they shake. You had to deal with Adel like that, didn't you? Did she ever stop hearing Jackie Robinson's voice?"

"No."

Helen nodded solemnly, then looked around as if trying to locate the cafeteria's exit.

"Helen," Nicky drew in a breath. It had to be now, he thought, if it was to be at all. He reached out to hold her hand for a third time. "You were my first real friend here in America. Do you ... would you possibly want to see me again?"

Helen looked down at her left hand, the one Nicky held, apparently studying her wedding band and small diamond engagement ring, blushing again. "You know, even though I was married ... How shall I say this? You were good looking, exotic, mysterious, hardly knew a word of English, and so cute when you tried, always writing new words in your notebook, and ..."

"And?"

"You know. I could always talk to you when things were bad between David and me. You helped – just by being there, by listening, by being my friend. I've never forgotten. I've always felt I owed you so much."

"And you helped me feel welcome."

"So, if you're asking whether we can be friends again, then I can only say yes. Call me." She squeezed his hand. "Let's make one thing clear, though. Just friends, you understand. I'm sixty-seven. Too old to get involved with anyone seriously."

"Helen, I haven't looked at another woman since Adel."

Then he stood, pulled her up next to him, and kissed her on the cheek.

CHAPTER FOURTEEN

Inousa, Greece, February 13, 1990 (Monday)

Fevronia waited outside the church until Ephraim's beige DIM 652 disappeared around the curve and down the hill. His last words of advice to her still rung in her ears. Ephraim had said he would want someone with information to try to reconnect his own family if they had been separated by war. It was simple common sense. Resolved to do what she should've done earlier, during the call with Dr. Covo, Fevronia went to Theodora's cell.

"Sister Theodora, I'm sorry to interrupt your prayer. I'd like to speak to you."

Theodora looked up, rose from her corner, and nodded for Fevronia to enter. They sat on the edge of Theodora's cot. Fevronia rubbed her hand against the rough, dark grey wool of Theodora's blanket. It was an old blanket, one that had probably arrived in the 50s, but when Fevronia had offered years before to replace it with a newer one, Theodora had refused. Fevronia reached out to take Theodora's hand. It felt smooth, in contrast to the roughness of the blanket.

The two women, clad alike in black cassocks and veils, looked at each other closely, as if trying to gather each other's thoughts by telepathy. Theodora didn't seem particularly alarmed by Fevronia's visit and would've waited an hour without moving, waiting patiently for Fevronia's message, if she'd chosen to keep them in this preliminary pose for such a time. But, after a minute, Fevronia spoke softly.

"Do you recall when you were sick last fall? When we called in Father Rukos to give you last rites?"

Theodora nodded. She looked steadily at Fevronia.

"You were delirious, talking out of your head. Do you remember?"

Theodora looked down for a second, then back up at Fevronia. She shook her head in answer to Fevronia's question. Her face was a blank page. No recall.

"Well, you were. And during that worst night, when I sat with you, afraid you'd die, you muttered 'Kavala' and 'Ganis.' Does that help you remember?"

Theodora shook her head vigorously, then turned away toward her icons.

"You did. What happened in Kavala?"

"I can't say more," Theodora whispered.

That Theodora had spoken again in something other than prayer startled Fevronia but convinced her that she was on the right track. "Why can't you say more? I know you can speak in something other than prayer. You spoke to me once, a long time ago, about how you arrived at the monastery. I know you remember something. Can you tell me about Ganis? Do you remember Alex Ganis? And do you remember telling me about how the Theotokos brought you to the monastery? Lifted you from a closet?"

Theodora rose from her cot, knelt, and leaned her head on the wall of her cell, resuming her usual spot of devotion. "I pray to the Lord Jesus Christ to forgive me, a sinner."

"You knew Alex Ganis, didn't you?"

"I pray to the Lord Jesus Christ to forgive me, a sinner."

"Salonika? Can you tell me about Salonika?"

"I pray to the Lord Jesus Christ to forgive me, a sinner."

"All right, Sister Theodora, then listen please. I want to tell you a story. It's a story about you, before you ever came here. You're a little girl. You have a family.... Covo?"

Theodora seemed to slump against the wall, as if her knees had grown weak. She'd grown quiet.

"Your family name is Covo."

"No," Theodora whispered.

"Covo. You have an older sister. Her name is Ada. You have an older brother. His name is Nikolas. Nicky."

"No."

"Alex helped Nicky hide. Alex will help you hide, too."

"No."

What would leave Theodora no choice but to remember? Fevronia raised the pitch and volume of her voice, trying to match the urgency of the situation she was describing.

"You have to hide from the Nazis."

Theodora jerked her head up, her large eyes now even larger, wide in fear.

"If they find Jews, the Nazis will send you to the camps ..."

Theodora ran before Fevronia could react. Fevronia followed her outside as best she could, but was amazed to see how fast Theodora could move, faster than Fevronia would have imagined. She saw Theodora rush into the vineyard, heading west, getting almost immediately out of sight. She then spotted Sister Zoe coming down from the winery, yelled to her, and together they ran after Theodora, pleading for her to return. In minutes, though, not sure where Theodora had headed, they stopped. They were both exhausted, breathing heavily. The sun was already settling behind the purple mountains. During the night, the temperature would drop below freezing. Theodora would be in danger, but Fevronia and Zoe were equally unprepared and could not follow without putting themselves in extreme danger. Sorrowfully, they returned to Fevronia's office to call Andros. He promised that Ephraim and he would be there in five minutes. Within ten minutes, Fevronia had set up pairs of nuns with flashlights to venture into the vineyards in search. Within twenty minutes, two local constables summoned from Inousa had joined them.

It would've been a strange night even if Theodora hadn't run off. The clouds that had hung low during the day had been pushed away by the darkness, and the night sky was resplendent with stars. It would have been beautiful, and Fevronia would have welcomed the display as a sign of God, but for the fact that the temperature had fallen much lower than even she'd expected. Fevronia trembled with the cold and the fear that the night could lead only to death for Theodora, a death for which she, Fevronia, would be solely responsible. But just after midnight, when the world around the monastery should have been darkest, the temperature seemed to tick up again, and Fevronia sensed a dim, yellowish light toward the west, the direction in which Theodora had fled. The light hovered over the far edge of the monastery's vineyards, just under the descending arc of Orion's belt. Fevronia scanned the skies for long minutes, imagining she'd see a meteor shower or a hovering helicopter, but she could see nothing that suggested itself as the source of the glow, just the outlines of the purple mountains beyond. Then, the pale light gradually faded to nothing, the air grew colder again, and all was pitch black, save for the starlight.

It wasn't until two in the morning that Theodora could be seen returning, stumbling from the vineyard toward her would-be rescuers. Fevronia offered up a prayer of thanksgiving to Christ, without whose love Theodora would've died. Theodora was shivering violently, but otherwise appeared unhurt. She hugged Fevronia and Zoe and the other nuns, hugged Andros and Ephraim, nodded to the constables when they asked her if she was all right, but refused to answer questions. Fevronia and Zoe threw blankets around her, led her to the kitchen, and forced her to sip hot tea. When Ephraim suggested he take Theodora to the hospital in Serres, Theodora slammed her hands on the table and shook her head. Fevronia assured Theodora that they wouldn't force her to go to the city and counseled Andros, Ephraim, and the constables that the power of God had protected Theodora during the night and would protect her still.

A few minutes later, Fevronia led Theodora back to her cell. *Orthros* was just a few hours away.

CHAPTER FIFTEEN

Manhattan, New York, February 18, 1990 (Sunday)

Helen's brief reminder to Nicky that he'd told her family a bit about his travails in the war started a run of painful memories. Images plagued him throughout his waking hours and in his dreams. The fourteen-year-old he'd been, in his mud-encrusted clothes, and a Mauser Karabiner 98K strapped around his shoulders. The tricks he'd always used to repress memories – listening to Kayla's music, reading psychiatric journals, writing in and reviewing his patient charts – were no longer working. The harder he tried to avoid thinking about the war, the more he thought about it. He could feel it all as if it were happening right then. Fear. Cowardice. Filth. Adrenalin. Disgust. Hunger. Pride. He saw it play before his eyes. Spies. Traitors. Collaborators. Deserters. Executions.

He contemplated again the idea that he could stop these memories forever by killing himself, but he knew he couldn't remove himself from life that way. Not with Kayla in the hospital, fighting her own demons, not with Jackie already traumatized. Yet, his memories themselves seemed to be killing him. He recognized that he needed to talk to someone when he could no longer stand the constant nausea, the dryness of his throat no matter how much water he drank. He needed someone to steady him through a rough patch. He considered but rejected the idea of calling one of his psychiatric colleagues. He could not tolerate the likelihood that word of his instability would get around his small professional community.

If not a professional, who? Helen had been in the back of his mind the whole time. She'd started the series of memories, and he thought he might as well talk to her, not in her capacity as a retired social worker, but as a friend. She'd given him her telephone number at the hospital. Hands shaking, he dialed.

"Hello?"

"Helen, it's Nicky."

"Nicky! How nice. I hoped to hear from you again. *Baruch Hashem.*"

Blessed is the Name, she'd said. Blessed is God, a figure of speech she must've developed after their friendship had withered. He wouldn't argue with her about the existence of God. He wanted to talk and needed someone to listen.

Nicky felt duplicitous, though, sitting on the edge of his bed, looking at Adel's photograph. How happy she looked that day, a memorable day for the family; they'd just returned in joy and pride from their daughter's first solo recital at Carnegie, when she was only twelve. How much better it might've been for their marriage if he'd shared everything with Adel then, instead of hiding so much from her.

"Would you mind if I stopped by?" Nicky turned from the photograph and lay down, looking at the ceiling while he held the phone to his ear, the plastic clammy against his skin. He hadn't made his bed, and the lumped up sheets and blanket under him were uncomfortable. His hands still shook, and his pulse beat a fast march in his neck. "You know. To carry on our chat? We only just began to get to know each other again."

"That'd be lovely. Were you thinking of today?"

"If you're available, of course."

"I've no plans for the afternoon, if you want to drive down. Drop by for tea?"

"Tea's fine."

Within a half-hour, he'd showered, shaved, dressed, and headed out to purchase a bouquet, knowing he could not arrive empty-handed.

CHAPTER SIXTEEN

Inousa, Greece, February 14, 1990 (Tuesday)

Back in her own cell, Fevronia didn't try to sleep. She needed to pray, first to the Theotokos, the glorious Ever-Virgin Mary. To a woman called to God's duty, a much more glorious duty than Fevronia had been called. She begged for mercy and forgiveness for her lies to Dr. Covo and for her aggressive questioning of Theodora, which had nearly fatal consequences. She prayed in thanks as well for whatever divine intervention had returned Theodora to them unharmed. Then Fevronia turned her prayer to Christ Himself, asking for some sign of forgiveness from Him. She prayed for Christ to show her some sign that she'd made the right decision in tracking down Dr. Covo.

As she knelt, Fevronia shivered from a strange cold, despite the blanket she wore around her shoulders. Compounding her discomfort, her knees throbbed and her neck hurt. Suddenly, Fevronia felt as if a vice had caught her head in its grip and was pulling it off. Her penance, surely her punishment for lying, surely her punishment for almost killing Theodora. Just when she thought her head would be cleaved from her body, the uncanny hold relaxed. The pain in her knees and neck disappeared, and she felt weightless. Her breathing slowed, each new breath deeper and sweeter. An unimaginable warmth began to embrace her. She sensed, rather than saw, an orange glow.

Next to her knelt the Theotokos. Fevronia had longed for the presence of the Mother of God, who now presented Herself in the midst of Fevronia's deepest need. Fevronia wanted to speak but couldn't utter a sound. Instead, she studied the Theotokos, tried to memorize every detail of Her face, Her body, and Her dark red veil bordered by gold. The color of Her veil called to mind the tomatoes harvested in July from the monastery's garden. The fabric of the Theotokos's veil was worn, yet beautiful and powerful enough to illuminate the world with its light. At each side of the veil had been embroidered, with white thread, an eight-pointed star.

Fevronia was immersed by the love of the Theotokos's gaze upon her, a love she returned as fully as she could. She felt she could die in the happiness of that love and find herself immediately at the feet of Her Son, the Lord Jesus Christ, and that her life would thereby be given the meaning she'd prayed for. Before she could die, however, she had to hear the Theotokos's voice, and the Holy Mother of God did speak.

"Abbess Fevronia, you have called to Me and I am here for you, praise be to the Lord. What I can tell you? What do you need to know?" Her voice was an echo of itself, at once very near and yet coming from a great distance.

"Mother of God ..." Fevronia stopped, uncertain. What *did* she need to ask? Then questions flooded through her. Had the Theotokos actually lifted Theodora from a closet to put her in the monastery? Was Theodora a Jewess separated from her family in the war? Was it right or wrong for her to have tracked down Dr. Covo? Where had Silenos been murdered and buried? As much as she wanted to know, as much as she wanted to hear again the uncanny, beautiful voice, Fevronia hesitated.

The Theotokos seemed to sense Fevronia's confusion and questions. Fevronia heard the echo again. "*I apostolí sas edó eínai mia evlogía ston Yió mou. I Adelfí Theodóra eínai mia evlogía ston Yió mou. To thélima tou Theoú gínetai.* Your mission here is a blessing to my Son. Sister Theodora is a blessing to my Son. God's will is done."

Fevronia felt every word; the echo covered her like cool spring rain, a coolness contrasting pleasantly with the orange warmth of the Theotokos's glow. Every word tasted of cinnamon, sharp and sweet. *To thélima tou Theoú gínetai.* Fevronia breathed deeply of Her fragrance, of olive trees in bloom. She forced herself to speak. Her voice, in comparison to the Mother of God's, sounded to her like glass crushed under a boot. "Have I done right or wrong by inviting Dr. Covo to come to the monastery?"

"*To thélima tou Theoú gínetai.* God's will is done."

"And Silenos ... where may I find him?"

"*To thélima tou Theoú gínetai.* God's will is done."

The Theotokos vanished, but Fevronia continued for hours to feel Her warmth. In Fevronia's cell, the orange glow lingered until morning.

CHAPTER SEVENTEEN

Highland Park, New Jersey, February 18 (Sunday)

Within three hours, he'd parked his car in Helen's driveway and was trying to muster the nerve to go in. He studied the house in which Helen and David had ended up, only a few blocks from where Helen had grown up. Not bad. A two-story 1960s American contemporary, an attached one-car garage, a tall tree stripped by winter of its leaves in the center of the front lawn. He must've walked past this house scores of times in 1946 on his way to the park, but had never given it close attention. Now it had his full attention.

He breathed deeply, took up the bouquet of daffodils he'd purchased at the Cala Floral Studio, and walked to Helen's front door. There she waited. She wore dark green wool pants and a light green pullover sweater. He could see again what he'd noticed in the hospital, that she took care of herself and had pride in her appearance. He felt suddenly conscious of his expanding waistline. As he approached, he wanted to reach out and touch her short auburn hair, which glowed and showed just a touch of grey. He detected what he thought was a faint scent of citrus from her shampoo.

"Come in already. What are you waiting for? Sit down while I get these in a vase." After hugging him briefly, she took the flowers. He sat on her sofa and picked up a family portrait from the end table. "My favorite," she said, as she returned with the flowers in a vase. He stood and took her hands in his.

"Helen, you look great. Amazing, really. As beautiful as ever."

She blushed slightly and pulled her hands back, asking about Kayla. Nicky explained what he'd learned when Kayla had awoken, that her rabbi – one Rabbi Beck – had encouraged her to stop her medications.

"You're kidding. A rabbi said that? They're supposed to be educated."

"He told her medication is only for weak people, and she interpreted that as a command to stop. Outrageous."

"Quite."

Nicky explained he'd severely chastised his grown daughter and that she'd been counseled by her psychiatrist and by Max as well to never let that happen again, that she could not be cavalier about taking her anti-psychotics if she wanted to keep her son. Jackie had checked out all right, physically at least, with just a few bruises that would disappear in a couple of weeks, but the family expected that he would be in therapy for a long while.

"And the police didn't arrest her?"

"One good thing about her father being a shrink. Child Protective Services listened to me when I assured them this was entirely out of character and would never happen again. Well, they couldn't have believed that I could guarantee such a thing, but they signed off. My old friends at the hospital might have twisted some arms."

"*Baruch Hashem*. I'm glad things are getting back to normal."

"Maybe."

On the drive down, he had thought about what he'd wanted to say to Helen, why he'd called her in the first place, but now in her presence, he had no idea how to proceed. He worried about what Helen would think of him when he told her about the troubling memories he could no longer repress. He worried as well about why he should care what Helen thought, if she was just someone to talk to. After all, he'd been content to have her exist merely as a long-forgotten friend for years. But with the teasing scent of citrus about her, with her smile, with her being close enough to touch, he hesitated.

As if reading his thoughts, she asked "So, Nicky, there must've been a special reason you wanted to stop by today, yes? You did seem rather anxious on the phone."

He drew in a breath and took her hand again, warm and alive to his touch. "I just wanted to see you again, Helen. I've been thinking about my life, you see ..." He paused.

"And what ..."

"Please let me finish. It's just going to take some time, as I think this through. I don't have a speech prepared."

"I'll be patient. Go ahead."

She drew her hand away and settled back in the sofa, folding her legs under her. He imagined she looked at him as if he were a client. He imagined he saw the I'll-listen-to-anything look he'd cultivated in his own practice. Curious, non-judgmental, professional to the core. Except for her casual pose, he might well have been seeing her as a therapist despite his contrary intention.

Where to start? He thought back over the past days and realized it had all begun, not with Helen's question at the hospital, but with the letter from Abbess Fevronia. "Crazy things are happening."

"You're the psychiatrist." She smiled thinly. "Who better to deal with crazy things?"

"I got a letter from Greece. My sister, Kal, might be alive."

Helen sat up straight, placed her legs back on the floor, and reached out to touch his arm. He explained briefly about the claim that Kal had become a Greek Orthodox nun living in a monastery and refusing to talk and about how conflicted he felt about whether this woman might in fact be his sister. The warmth of Helen's hand, through his shirt, was comforting. When he finished the story with his failed attempt to reach this putative sister on the telephone, Helen finally commented, "You always said your entire family died at Auschwitz. Is it truly possible one of them still lives? *Baruch Hashem.*"

"I know what I said. I suppose it's possible. There's more, though. I've been thinking much more than is healthy, since we met at the hospital, about things that happened to me during the war."

"Things?"

"Things I did. You know about the prisoner, I told you back when, but you don't know about the other ... others."

"Then tell me."

Nicky is alone at night on the path down the mountain, running to catch up with his platoon, when a figure in the peasant uniform of mountain fighters emerges from the blackness, coming up at him from around a bend. He must be an enemy. Nicky kneels, aims his Karabiner, and orders the man to stop, but when the man keeps running, surely holding a gun, Nicky fires, keeps firing even as the man slows down, fires five shots, working the bolt as fast as he can, his rifle thundering. He can still see the man, falling forward, can still see the prostate form, as dawn inches its way over the hill behind him. In the man's outstretched right hand there's no gun, but a metal icon. The man, at closer inspection, seems old enough to have been Nicky's great-grandfather. The icon is in a rectangular case of silver, and Nicky can see, through a small circular window in the case, a gold image of the face of a woman. Nicky has seen images like this before, paintings on wood in the church in which he'd hidden. Dora had one on the wall of her room in the chancery. He throws the icon into the woods, toward a stand of trees, not noticing where it lands. He leaves the dead man lying without so much as a second glance and rushes again toward the rest of his platoon.

Helen listened, interrupting a few times to clarify a point. Yes, Nicky had known this man wasn't a German soldier. There weren't any in the vicinity, but Nicky's group of *andartes* had been fighting other Greek factions, angling for superiority when the inevitable time came that the German Army was forced to withdraw from Greece. Helen seemed most surprised at this revelation that Greeks fought other Greeks even when the Germans were their common enemy. She seemed little surprised or concerned that Nicky had killed the old man.

"Nicky, that's a horrible memory, but don't forget you were in the worst war in human history and just a teenager. You had no military training, and even if you had it wouldn't have mattered. Anyone else would've acted as you had to."

"Right," he said without conviction.

"Does this bother you even more because you threw away that icon, what you thought in the darkness had been a gun?"

"I don't know. I don't know anything anymore."

They sat quietly for a minute, a minute during which Nicky noticed his heartbeat had slowed and his hands weren't shaking as much. He sensed that it had been the right thing, after all, to share some of his burden with Helen. To speak about his deeds gave him the opportunity to analyze them, and he felt a measure of relief at Helen's comments that anyone else might have acted exactly the same way. And, as he began to feel grateful for her listening and sympathy, he began to think as well about her beauty, a beauty he remembered from decades earlier and had not diminished in the slightest, notwithstanding the wrinkles and the strands of grey.

Of Elie Saltiel's three daughters, Helen, the youngest, was by far the warmest and most animated. Now, long past their friendship of 1946, he felt the stirrings of sexual desire for her and realized he'd wanted her even as a teenager, even when he knew she was married. That desire couldn't have led anywhere. He shifted uncomfortably on the leather sofa.

"Are you okay?" she asked.

"There's a lot more I haven't told you. This is just … I just skimmed the surface."

"You're not seeing anyone, are you? In your field, I mean?"

"No. I don't want to. Word would get around."

"Have you thought about writing down some of this? Another way to get it out of your system?"

He wondered if her suggestion made sense. There were times when he'd urged his own patients to write about their traumas, and it could in fact be helpful, but he wasn't sure it was the right thing for him.

"I don't know. I might."

She tucked her legs under her again, her silk-stockinged feet in view. He wanted to take those feet in his hands, imagined them being warm to the touch.

She said, "When I've advised clients to write about guilt, it's for the purpose of helping them lessen the burden. I'm sure you know that. Or at least regaining control of their lives."

"Nothing's taken over my life."

She exhaled a bit too loudly, but then remained silent. Nicky waited. She looked up at him, as if she'd been patient with him but that her patience was wearing thin. He could no longer delay asking her the question he'd been tossing around in his mind for the hour they'd sat together.

"Helen, would you have dinner with me next Saturday night?"

"You're lonely, too, aren't you, Nicky?"

They leaned toward each other and kissed, their first real kiss, and it was the kiss he'd wanted for so long, the kiss he'd yearned for, ever since she'd showed him to her old bedroom so he could stow his duffel bag, within his first five minutes of entering the Saltiel house. They slid closer to each other for another kiss. When they broke, he repeated his question.

She laughed.

"You want to take me to dinner *next* week? Not this evening?"

"I'd been thinking about that too, but didn't want to seem ... to seem ..."

"Too eager?"

"Perhaps."

"Then let me ask you. Do you have plans for tonight? Only an hour or so before our wonderful Highland Park restaurants open for early dinner."

"Sure. I mean, no plans."

"Great, then in the meantime ..."

"But what about next Saturday night?"

"It has to be after *Shabbat*. Let me check the *luach* for the exact time."

"Of course."

"And I can open a bottle of wine for right now."

"That works."

CHAPTER EIGHTEEN

Inousa, Greece, February 14, 1990 (Tuesday)

The *Orthros* got started late, because Zoe had again been scheduled to chant and lead the singing of the hymns and had not awakened at her usual hour given the confusion of the night. She'd led Theodora into the church, then taken her position. As they chanted – "without speech or language, without a sound to be heard, their voice has gone out into all the earth" – Fevronia couldn't help but once again contemplate Theodora's great reluctance to utter words other than in private prayer. At communal prayer time, Theodora hummed the melodies in praise of God, hiding what Fevronia imagined would have been a beautiful voice if Theodora had wanted to sing. It comforted Fevronia on this particular morning to hear that Theodora's apparent enthusiasm for the service did not seem diminished from her recent ordeal. Indeed, Theodora's energy seemed greater than usual; the hours in the woods had done no particular damage.

Something nagged at Fevronia's mind, though. The Mother of God had told her she'd done the right thing in trying to reunite Theodora with her brother. It was God's will. Yet something wasn't right. It was more than her lie to Dr. Covo that worried her, more than the fear that he wouldn't come to the monastery as a result. It was something else that she was having difficulty putting her finger on.

Fevronia decided to remain in the church following *Orthros*, as the new daylight filtered in through the high-set windows. She sat on the cold floor alone, her arms wrapped around her knees, thinking of the words from the psalm about the sun emerging from his chamber like a bridegroom. Neither she nor her nuns could truly imagine what a bridegroom's emergence might be like, but it must be seen and felt, nonetheless, as the word of God, that which is pure, like honey, that which revives the soul. So, as the sunlight began to warm the nave, Fevronia struggled to understand her unease. It felt as if she had done wrong. "Who can discern his own errors?" she sang to herself, staring at the closest icon on the wall, letting her thoughts wander. "*Paratiomata tis synisel?*" It would come to her, soon enough. She told herself to relax, not to force it. She told herself to keep breathing. In, and out, and in.

Then somehow she knew that it was the icon that bothered her, the icon of John the Baptist anointing Jesus in the Jordan. No. It wasn't the icon per se, but something about its message. The icon was trying to point out to her what she had missed, what she had been trying to grasp.

The Baptist wore a red robe, Jesus a white loincloth. Fevronia had never liked this particular icon. Jesus looked surprised to find himself standing in the midst of a swirling waterfall and the Baptist, instead of concentrating with reverence on Jesus, gazed upward, presumably asking whether the Father was sure that Jesus was His Son. The Baptist's face held insufficient certainty of belief. Nonetheless, Fevronia rose and stood before the icon, crossed herself three times, each time bowing to touch the floor with her right hand, and kissed the Baptist's red robe.

As she stared, Fevronia slowly saw the outlines of the real problem. "The law of the Lord is perfect." How had she not seen it before? Baptism. A Jewish girl would never have been baptized in the Greek Orthodox Church. A dark flush of shame spread over Fevronia's face. She turned from the icon, fearing Jesus could see her. If Theodora had been Jewish, but never baptized, how could she have spent her adult life as a nun? How could she have been allowed to hear confessions? To be in the intimate presence of the other nuns – true Christians – to share the solemn prayers with them in the love of Christ? And how had she been allowed to receive last rites?

Fevronia half entertained the idea of confiding all of this to Zoe. As quickly as the thought arose, Fevronia rejected it. It wasn't Zoe who could help her now. For all of Fevronia's success at the monastery, for all her skill at management, for all her spiritual guidance of the nuns under her charge, she was now in over her head. An abbess could wield almost unchecked power within her chosen domain, but there were rituals she couldn't perform. Only a priest could conduct a baptism. The nearest was Father Rukos in Inousa, and it was to him that she now felt she needed to make pilgrimage. It took her a good hour to prepare herself and to walk into town. She steeled herself for the meeting by repeating in her mind what the Virgin Mother had said. "God's will is done."

Father Rukos was a short, slender man in his early thirties and wore a neatly trimmed black beard. He and Fevronia had maintained cordial, but distant, relations over the few years he'd been in Inousa. He welcomed Fevronia into the Ekklisia Panagia as he hung a gold censer on a wall. The sweet scent of cypress lingered in the air.

"So you want to talk about Sister Theodora? What have you learned?" They stood a few feet apart from each other, eschewing the rough wooden chairs placed against the wall of the nave, installed long prior to Rukos's arrival. He'd upset his parishioners when he'd suggested removing them and requiring congregants to stand at all times. Fearing that his church would be abandoned, he'd relented, but would not sit in them himself. Fevronia would have preferred to sit, but would not do so with Rukos standing.

"You won't believe this."

"I've heard many unbelievable things. Try me, Mother."

"I have information – I should say better I know – that Sister Theodora was Jewish at birth, rescued from a Thessaloniki family." She recounted, without going into much detail, the story of her recent investigations.

"Very strange indeed, Mother. She's such a good Christian." He paused briefly, then added, "By all accounts." Although Rukos had seemed startled at first to hear Fevronia's news, he now spoke in a calm, measured voice. "Could a Jew pretend to devote herself to the Lord for so long?"

"She's not pretending." Fevronia felt a surge of righteous anger mounting, anger she fought hard to suppress. To think that a man of God – a supposed man of God, this Rukos – would jump to the conclusion that Theodora was a fraud.

"You're sure about that?" he asked in a tone smacking of ridicule.

"She's devout. She's completely genuine in her belief and devotion. And, that she's Jewish by birth is the only possibility fitting the facts we know."

"Maybe."

"And if so, . . . Father ... I believe she's never been baptized. We'd need to get her baptized properly and promptly, wouldn't we?"

"Ah, I see the difficulty. Quite so, quite so." He picked up a copy of the prayer book from the closest reader's stand, thumbed through it for a second or two, then stood and read to Fevronia. "Queen of the heavenly hosts, defender of our souls, we thy servants offer to Thee a song of victory, for Thou hast delivered us from danger."

"Yes?"

"Your home for girls at St. Vlassios is a tribute to the Mother of God, is it not?"

"We venerate the Holy Virgin, but we are not girls," she said.

Rukos replaced the hymnal. "I can only pray for you now, Mother, pray that the Holy Virgin will protect your soul. If your theory about Theodora is right – perhaps that's not really her name – then it's quite too late for baptism, don't you think?"

"You know as well as I do it's never too late. Whenever a person's heart is in tune with Our Lord, whenever she wants ...."

"It's something that should've been addressed long ago. Many, many years ago. You've let her live at the monastery, made her a nun – you had me fooled – allowed the villagers to go to her when they should have been confessing to me. It's bothered me, yet I didn't say anything to you because it's accepted in the Church and it's been going on here for years. I didn't know she was a Jew, though. I don't see that you've exercised good judgment, Mother. Not good judgment at all."

Fevronia bristled, gritting her teeth, trying not to speak rashly. When she thought she could continue without snapping at Rukos, she responded. "Perhaps not, perhaps so. It was the group of villagers who first regarded her as holy, even before I'd ever stepped foot on the monastery. And when I first met her, I too could feel her special warmth. In my judgment, Sister Theodora has done a world of good for them and for everyone else, not the least of whom is me. She's been a rock of strength, from the time hope was most needed at the end of the war until today, and she must be allowed to keep playing that role. That is my decision as abbess."

"You have no right to consecrate an unbaptized woman as a nun."

Rukos turned from her and began to walk toward the door, signaling that in his opinion their interview, short though it was, had ended. Fevronia followed him but wasn't going to leave until she'd had her full say.

When Rukos turned toward her again, she spoke. "I'll be in touch to arrange a baptism when Theodora's identity is confirmed. That is, if I want you to officiate. There are other priests. Many in Serres who'd work with us."

She saw the color come into Rukos's face. He evidently didn't care to be challenged, she thought, particularly by a woman. She felt a distinct, guilty pleasure realizing she'd annoyed him immensely.

"As the psalmist says, 'Let the Lord destroy all deceitful lips.' What does that mean to you, Mother, to pass off a Jewess as a devout Christian nun? Don't you see that as the grossest kind of deceit?"

She felt her right hand form itself into a fist and had to consciously stop her arm from raising to strike the man before her, even knowing he wouldn't strike her back. But no one in her life had ever insinuated she was a liar. "The Virgin ... the Holy Mother ..." No. He would only mock her.

"Yes, you can pray all you want, but what's done is done. I'll be happy to hear your confession."

"I'll confess to whom I want, but not to someone of so little faith."

"You know, Mother, although I've no desire to embarrass you needlessly, this is something I will certainly have to take up with the Metropolitan. When Theodora's brother comes, of course, and confirms what you already believe."

"How kind of you, Father. I will now take my leave."

Rukos's mention of the Metropolitan, intended to bully Fevronia, actually worked in the opposite way. She felt a surge of inner strength, knowing that the Metropolitan, her spiritual father, was a strong supporter in light of the monastery's success. She'd managed not only to pay back all the funds that the Church had advanced but had substantially contributed above and beyond that amount. We'll let the Metropolitan settle this, she thought.

But Fevronia was nonetheless disheartened by Rukos's insufferably threatening tone. As she left, declining his offer of a ride and trying to steel herself for what would be a difficult walk back to the monastery, she could not disagree in his assessment of her judgment. She admitted to herself – far from the first time – that she might've been able to keep the villagers' trust even while taking a more measured approach to Theodora's status. She knew that she'd fallen immediately under Theodora's spell at their first meeting and that her equilibrium had never fully recovered.

Fevronia violently disagreed with Rukos's dictum that it was too late. As she'd told him, it was never too late to bring a soul into closer contact with God. If she had to have Theodora baptized, she'd make sure it was done properly, in a beautiful setting, and Theodora would be surrounded by those who loved her most. Perhaps the Metropolitan himself would officiate. She swore to herself that there would be no Father Rukos anywhere nearby.

CHAPTER NINETEEN

West Caldwell, New Jersey, February 20 and 23, 1990 (Tuesday and Friday)

When Nicky drove Kayla home from the hospital, he was pleased that she'd made an effort to dress nicely. She looked pale, with shadows under her eyes, and seemed to have lost a bit of weight. Her speech was hesitant. They spoke, carefully, not of her new medication, not of her feelings toward her psychiatrist or the hospital staff, not of Rabbi Beck's horrendous advice, but of her attack on Jackie. Kayla was unsurprisingly distressed about what she'd done to her son and offered no explanation other than that she'd been terribly afraid. As far as Nicky could glean from his daughter's confused remarks, she was under the delusion that Jackie was his father, August, and confused August with her delusional stalker, the one who pursued her throughout her meteoric piano career. In other words, in Kayla's mind, Jackie was an immediate danger to her life. She thought she'd been acting in self-defense, she admitted, crying.

Keep calm, Nicky told himself. Just listen, be supportive, understanding. He struggled to find something positive to say. "But you seem in control now, back in your usual steady state of mind. I hope."

"I do feel better. I feel I can face Jackie again. But will he be all right? And will he ever forgive me?"

"Kids are resilient. Therapy will help."

"Family therapy too. I've been told. I've made the appointments already."

"Obviously, staying on your meds will be critical."

"As I've promised a million times already. And of course I'll need to meet with Rabbi Beck and explain how I must, absolutely must, stay on my meds. I hope he'll understand."

Nicky wanted to scream that it was ridiculous to beg the understanding of the person who'd stupidly suggested she didn't need her medications in the first place. But he played along. Kayla chooses Chabad as the center of her life, so go along. She promises to stay on her meds regardless of what Beck says. Don't remind her of her nearly fatal idiocy. Don't tell her yet again that there's no God. She knows how you feel, has always known. Then it occurred to him that a major piece of evidence was missing from his assessment of the situation.

"By the way, I've never met your rabbi."

"Max has. We had Rabbi Beck over for *Shabbat* about a year ago."

"I think I should meet him. If you invite him again, perhaps you'll invite me too."

"Really?"

"Why not?"

"Let me talk to Max about his schedule."

•   •   •   •   •

On the next Friday afternoon, Nicky drove to the suburban house shared by his two adult children. They'd bought the house in the aftermath of Max's divorce and when Kayla desperately wanted to leave Manhattan. Nicky planned to stay overnight in their spare bedroom and continue to Highland Park the next day for his date with Helen.

He heard Jackie yell as he opened the door.

"Hi, Grandpa!"

Jackie was good looking, tall for six years, thin, and smiley. His skin was a warm ochre, his curly hair closely cut. He wore faded blue jeans and a light blue shirt with a brown collar. It looked to Nicky as if he'd lost another tooth. He showed no outward signs of the recent trauma, but as Nicky bent down to hug Jackie, the boy jumped back, suddenly cautious.

"No hug, Grandpa!"

"Okay. No hug." Nicky straightened up and tried to act as if nothing had happened. "So how's the clarinet going?"

"You want to hear? Let me get it."

As Jackie raced up the stairs, Nicky walked into the kitchen to see Kayla braiding the dough for *challah*. He put his arm around her briefly, the merest light squeeze around the shoulders. She was too busy getting ready for dinner and too covered with flour to reciprocate. At least she hadn't flinched. He sighed with relief.

"Glad you could join us, Dad. Max's been working like a dog; he's got a lot of work to make up, for time he lost taking care of Jackie, but he'll be here soon, as will Rabbi Beck and his wife, Miriam. Can you set the table, please? The dark blue tablecloth." Kayla picked up the hem of her "Glatt Kosher" apron and rubbed dough off her fingers.

As Nicky set their table, he told her he wanted to talk about something serious and that it had nothing to do with recent unhappy events in her life. It had to do with him.

"Just let me get this in the oven." In a minute, they sat together at in the dining room, facing each other across a corner of the table.

She wore a long black skirt and long-sleeved grey blouse. The dark circles under her eyes had faded a bit, and she wasn't quite as pale as she'd been a few nights earlier. Her short dark brown hair seemed to have regained its usual luster, no longer as dull as it had looked in the hospital. Her intelligent, hazel eyes reflected concern as she leaned toward Nicky. "So, what is it, this serious thing in your life?"

He told her briefly about Fevronia's letter, and before he could even get to his telephone conversation with Fevronia, Kayla interrupted.

"Your sister! I heard you right? Your sister may be alive?"

"So I'm told. One of my sisters."

"The letter from Greece, from this monastery, said this nun ..."

"Sister Theodora."

"Sister Theodora doesn't talk? Could she be amnesiac?"

"It's possible, but it's also the kind of thing one might say to create a mystery." He then told Kayla about the telephone conversation. "So this Abbess Fevronia wants me there, or whoever she works for wants me there, and once I'm there, I fear they'll put the tough arm on me for money." Even as Nicky spoke, he had the demoralizing sensation he'd once again gotten wrong a common American idiom.

"The strong arm, you mean."

"Whatever."

"You have to go. *Hashem* has meant for you to go and find your sister again. Oh, my. She would be my Aunt ... which aunt?"

"If she's my sister, if what Fevronia says is true about how old she was when this girl was found, then it would be Kal. The younger of my two sisters. The one you were named after."

"You have to go."

Just like Kayla, a believer, to take Fevronia's letter at face value. Despite the tragedy of her own life – her fall from stardom – she adhered to the goodness of a Supreme Being and now jumped at the chance to see first-hand evidence that this Supreme Being could bring the dead to life.

Nicky was hardly surprised at her reaction.

"One more thing, Kayla. I've run into an old friend, Helen Blanco, and ..." He realized as he spoke that he wasn't quite sure he was ready to confess to his children that he'd become interested in another woman. He'd assumed they would be fine with the news, but suddenly he became unsure. There was a spark of something in Kayla's eyes, and Nicky couldn't determine whether it was a glimmer of excitement or the beginnings of a tear.

"And ... come on, tell me."

"And, in fact we're having dinner tomorrow night. She lives in Highland Park, so I thought I might stay here tonight, if you don't mind, and drive down tomorrow afternoon. It would save me a lot of time."

"Of course you can stay, but ...?"

Kayla pulled herself up straight in her chair, her shoulders drawn back. The spark had disappeared. There was no tear, there was no excitement. There was just questioning.

"But what?"

"A letter from Greece announces your sister's alive, you're not sure if you believe it, but oh by the way you're dating an old friend? I thought I was the one with shocking surprises. Let me check on dinner. Stay right here."

He wanted to tell her that he was very happy to have met this old friend and to become interested in having female companionship again, but hesitated when he realized that, had it not been for Kayla's near tragic lapse in taking care of herself, he would never have run into Helen. Yet, he had to say something about Helen, something positive, as justification. Kayla walked back in from the kitchen and sat again.

"Yes, I've started dating an old friend, whose family came from Salonika a long time ago, by the way."

"Amazing. Almost like an episode from *Search for Tomorrow*. Too bad that show's gone. Well, now that you've confessed, I'll confess. You should know that I met Helen in the hospital. She came in to introduce herself the day I was discharged, and she explained how you'd run into each other and how you visited her. And had already taken her to dinner. I was wondering when you were going to say something."

"You knew all along?"

"If my being there was good for you, good in the sense that you and Helen met each other again, then I see it as part of *Hashem's* plan. Anyway, she came to check up on me. Offered to refer me to the therapist I ultimately called."

"I see."

"So I'm glad you bumped into each other. It's time you saw someone." Kayla reached out to lightly touch Nicky's hand, as if dispensing a piece of sweet candy to a child, almost as if she were the parent and he the offspring who needed guidance.

"She's religious, you know," Nicky continued. "Did you like her?"

"I won't like anyone just because she's *frum*, but I do like her. She explained about how her family had sponsored you, and I remember you talking about the three sisters in the Saltiel family. She told me a few good stories about things you did together."

"What did she tell you?" Nicky asked, with a touch of fear in his voice. He wondered whether Helen had somehow become aware of a certain indiscretion on his part in his time with her family.

"Nothing bad. Oh my god. Are you blushing?"

"No. It's just hot in here."

"It wasn't hot a minute ago." She paused and looked at him closely. "All she told me about was a picnic. And a Fourth of July celebration, where you got into a big fight with a couple of drunks."

"Oh."

"Did you really take on two soldiers who were picking on Helen's husband?"

How had he not thought about that for so many years? It was yet another unpleasant thing he'd suppressed, and now the memory came back full force. July Fourth 1946; the fireworks show in Donaldson Park nearing its climax. A bad place for returning veterans with PTSD. Nicky was never sure how the fight started, but David was clearly outmanned and in grave danger, and Nicky hadn't thought twice before he jumped in to defend his friend.

"Foolishly, perhaps. Couldn't let David be slaughtered, though."

"Helen made you sound like a hero. And she told it like it had just happened yesterday."

"Of course, she exaggerated."

Helen was not one to embellish, but Nicky did not feel up to assuming a hero's mantle. As he spoke to his daughter about Helen, though, he wasn't thinking about her propensity for accuracy in storytelling. Instead, he thought how very much he'd enjoy running his hands through Helen's auburn hair, how much he'd enjoyed their kisses the previous Sunday evening.

"And you're taking her to dinner again. It makes sense."

"She hasn't dated since her husband's death, I don't think."

"Are there kosher restaurants in Highland Park?"

"It always had a big Jewish community and hasn't seemed to change much in that regard."

"Maybe …" Kayla began, but was interrupted by Max's entrance. They'd not heard him come into the house.

"Hey, Dad. Let's have a drink. What's for dinner, Kayla?"

Max placed a heavy leather briefcase on the floor with a thud. He hugged Kayla, then walked to Nicky, who rose and kissed his son on the side of the head. Max was tall and dark, his black hair – taking after Adel's unruly mop – was curlier than Nicky's. Max seemed bleary-eyed to Nicky, who worried that his son worked too hard.

Then Nicky and his two children all jumped at a noise like that of a shrieking, wounded parrot: Jackie – standing behind them – blowing into the mouthpiece of his clarinet for all he was worth. Nicky laughed nervously, and a look of dismay crossed Jackie's face. Kayla assured Jackie that practicing was good, but that it would now have to stop for *Shabbat*.

Rabbi Beck and his wife arrived a few minutes later. The rabbi was a bearded man who looked to be in his seventies. He wore, as Nicky had expected, a dark suit and tie and black, wide-brimmed hat. He had a kind, intelligent look about him and spoke traditional *Shabbat* greetings in a soft voice with a Brooklyn accent. He didn't necessarily look like the kind of person who'd intentionally put one of his congregants into danger, but then Nicky wasn't sure what such a man might look like anyway. The rabbi's wife, Miriam, said little and seemed to walk quietly behind her husband, in his shadow.

The group assembled in the small dining room. After candle lighting, Jackie chanted the *kiddush*, although his cup contained only grape juice, not wine. Kayla pointed out to Nicky that Jackie – who'd just learned the *bracha* – followed the Chabad formula, picking up the cup with his right hand, transferring it to his left, then holding it again in his right. Rabbi Beck beamed and seemed to suppress a bout of delighted laughter. Following *kiddush*, the group returned to the kitchen and took turns pouring water over their hands from the ceramic *becher* given to Kayla by her friends at the West Side Chabad. All but Nicky and Max said the blessings. Lastly, back in the dining room, Kayla said *motzi* over the *challah*, and they sat to eat.

"This *challah* is delicious, Kayla."

"Thanks, Rabbi. Your compliment pleases me no end."

"It's a great *mitzvah* to bake *challah* every week in celebration of *Shabbat*. It's the one-hundred-and-thirty-third commandment, coming from the offerings to the priests in the time of the Holy Temple. And it helps keep our families together, to celebrate the great goodness of the Ineffable."

"I wish your mom had learned to bake *challah*," Nicky said.

"Well, she might've," added Max, "if we'd celebrated *Shabbat* regularly. Which we did not. And, let's be honest, baking was never her strong suit."

How true it was, Nicky reflected. Adel could cook well enough if the menu was what she might have served at Norm's Diner, where she'd been working when Nicky had first met her. She could sizzle her hamburgers, cook up rice and vegetables in short order, mix up a more than passable soup. But anything that required a lot of time and precision, such as baking, was usually beyond her level of attention to detail and patience. He wondered whether Helen might bake *challah*. He'd have to find out.

During the meal, at Kayla's urging, Nicky filled in Max and the guests about Fevronia's letter. Max agreed with his father that the letter might be a fraud, particularly in light of Fevronia not allowing him to talk to "this supposed Sister Theodora." He spoke about a case of elder fraud his law firm had recently handled.

"Don't encourage him to doubt," argued Kayla. "You and I might have an aunt living in Greece. Doesn't Dad need to find out?" She turned to her father. "Dad, you *are* going to this monastery, aren't you?"

Nicky ignored the question. He took a second helping of teriyaki tofu and cut a second thick slice of *challah*, which he slathered with butter.

"Well, aren't you?"

"Where's Greece, Grandpa?" Jackie pushed his tofu from one side of the plate to the other.

"Southern Europe, where I was born. On the Mediterranean Sea, a big, big sea. Almost as big as an ocean. I'll show you later on your globe, okay?"

"Are you going to Greece? Like *Ima* says?"

Everyone at the table looked at Nicky and waited.

"Jackie, it might take Grandpa a while to decide," Kayla said finally. "He had a hard time in Greece before he came to this country. He was in the *Shoah*."

"But you're alive, Grandpa. All the Jews in the *Shoah* were ... died."

Nicky could see that Jackie was befuddled. He bristled at the thought of Kayla having introduced the Holocaust to Jackie at such a tender age. Nicky knew some in the Chabad movement viewed the Holocaust as signaling the coming of redemption, but he'd never understood the argument. It seemed to Nicky that, although some Jews had strengthened their commitment as a way of fighting the ultimate despair and collapse of humanity signaled by the gas chambers, they had sorely deluded themselves. In any event, Jackie was way too young to comprehend any of it.

"He's what we call a survivor," Kayla continued. "He lived."

"That's right, Jackie, I'm a survivor. So we don't need to talk about it anymore, okay?" Jackie pouted and went back to pushing his food.

"I understand you're a psychiatrist, Dr. Covo." Rabbi Beck addressed him politely after a few moments of silence. It was as if he'd been waiting for the chance to ask the question. "How do you find the spirit of our times in your patients? There must be much longing for the peace and certainty that love of *Hashem* can bring, yes?"

The question triggered thoughts in Nicky that went immediately to Helen, not to God. He recalled the sweet taste of her mouth and his rush of desire to be more than just a friend.

"Dad?" urged Max.

"Sorry." It took Nicky a couple of seconds to remember what question had actually been asked of him. "Rabbi Beck, my patients have problems that no God can cure. I don't talk to them about religion unless they raise it. Which they often do. If they ask me about my faith – and I can't evade, because sometimes patients can be very persistent and annoying in that way – I tell them truthfully that I lost faith long ago, but I don't argue about it. I let them say what they want about their own faith or lack of faith. If they want to lecture me for a minute or two about why I should choose to believe again, I hear them out, it's their fifty minutes, it's their nickel, but then we move on to what I feel are likely to be more productive conversations."

Rabbi Beck meticulously refolded the napkin in his lap, as if arranging the books on his bookcase. "Kayla told me about your atheism. But you're still Jewish. Don't ever forget that. *Hashem* will have you back as soon as you decide to believe again."

"Never," Nicky said, his voice raising, although he'd not meant to sound so adamant. Neither had he meant to embarrass his daughter in front of her rabbi, although he suspected that she'd urged him to broach her father's rejection of God. Nicky continued, more softly, "I understand, Rabbi Beck, that you represent a tradition of faith, but no, I won't believe again. That was and continues to be a firm decision on my part. I gave all that up when I learned my family disappeared into the gas chambers."

"Yes, I see. But maybe not all of them, as it now appears."

After a few moments of uneasy silence, Kayla suggested that it was time for the closing blessings. "Let's b-*bench* and s-sing a few *z'mirot*." She passed around the *benchers*, then offered Rabbi Beck the honor of leading the prayers for thanks. He did so, in a great rush. The faster the better, thought Nicky. Jackie unsuccessfully tried to join. Max flipped pages, looking bored. Out of force of an old, long-ignored habit, Nicky joined the rabbi and Kayla in the chanting. He thought, not about thanks, but about Jews who undoubtedly praised God even as they were led to their deaths.

After the blessings, Kayla insisted upon their singing a Chabad song, informing Max and Nicky that it had been composed by the famous Cantor Yechiel Hacohen Halpern.

"I've no idea who you're talking about, Kayla," said Max. "Go ahead. I'll just sip tea, if you don't mind."

Jackie knew the song and joined in with Kayla, the rabbi, and Miriam. Nicky tried as well to join. The lyric, repeated endlessly, promised that the entire congregation of Israel would be forgiven. Nicky didn't understand. Forgiven by whom, for what? For dying by the millions? For loading themselves into boxcars? How had the entire congregation of Israel sinned? If there was a God, wasn't it God who had sinned in allowing the Holocaust? In perhaps purposely bringing it about?

The song continued, never wanting to end. Jackie closed his eyes and swayed in time with the music. Nicky could see that Jackie was enthralled with Kayla's sweet, pure voice, either not fearing her at all or able to hide his fear. Resilience of children, he mused. His grandson would end up being just as much a believer as Kayla.

CHAPTER TWENTY

Highland Park, New Jersey, February 24, 1990 (Saturday)

Before his date with Helen, Nicky took the opportunity to drive around Highland Park, remembering, weighing. First, to the house on Hill Street in which he'd lived with the Saltiel family for eight months, where he met Helen, Catherine, and Ilene. Where he lost his virginity. The house looked much the same as in 1946, save for an addition. On closer inspection, chunks were missing from the brick stairway and, where his bedroom window overlooked the gray house next door – Catherine and he had neglected to pull the shade in their haste – a gutter was ripped away. He tried to see himself walking into the house for the first time, on the edge of a life he could've never imagined only months earlier, but a clear image of his seventeen-year-old self wouldn't form.

He turned north on 1st, and then left again on Raritan, feeling himself a stranger to the neighborhood. No one living in Highland Park other than Helen would remember him. Driving toward Rutgers, he paused at the apartment building where Helen and David had lived. It too had seen better days; it was far dirtier than he recalled. Farther along, he saw familiar commercial buildings with new occupants. The Italian place to which he took Lorraine, his first date, was gone, replaced by a Mexican dive. The bank was still a bank, but the name of the institution hadn't existed in 1946. The 5 & 10 cent store had been knocked down, replaced by PK Kopper's All Day Café. He drove across the bridge and, at the edge of campus, saw that Rutgers wasn't as he remembered either.

As he pulled a U-turn, he heard Adel's voice break through the traffic sounds. – Highland Park's a lark; careful of the shark. Helen's a peach, so within reach. You cheated me, defeated me, deleted me. – He pulled over and closed his eyes until the unnerving voice in his head faded. Adel always sounded in death as she'd sounded in real life, as if she were about to laugh. The memory of her sound, what he assumed she might say if she knew everything in his heart, had been rudely pushing its way into his head since she'd died.

He waited in his car after arriving at the house on Valentine Street to let his heartbeat slow to a normal pace.

•   •   •   •   •

At 6:25 p.m., Helen declared it was time for *havdallah*. When she handed him the spice box as a reminder of the sweetness of the day of rest, the day now departing, he accepted it and sniffed the essence of cloves and cinnamon. He could not recall performing the rite since Salonika. Had the Saltiels engaged in the ritual? If they had, Nicky most likely would've been up in his room, studying. Helen extinguished the braided candle, turned to him, wished him *shavua tov*, and kissed him lightly.

"Where to, Helen?"

"Let's do Sushiana. Japanese kosher."

"Sounds like a plan."

"They won't be open for a while, though. Wine first?"

They opened a bottle of Yarden Cab, and shortly after their first sips, he told her that there was more he needed to say about the war, more than he'd told her on the previous Sunday. He'd been thinking about whether to write any of it down, but had decided against it, in favor of simply talking to her.

"I'm listening."

He stands in front of a ruined church, its dome collapsed. The front door has been blown off its hinges and lies like a corpse. With his heart thudding, he listens for a minute and hears nothing until a member of his platoon shattering the silence. "Chrisma! Get the fuck in there and check it out!" He enters with his Mauser semiautomatic pistol drawn. The smell of decomposing flesh washes over him as he darts in. A man and woman, covered with larvae, lie in blood on the floor. Next to them lie the bodies of two small children, a boy and a girl. Their eyes are open; larvae crowd over their faces. Nicky kneels in front of the dark red pool and presses his fingers down to feel the stickiness. Dead for days. He bends over, retching. The two older people are a middle-aged priest with a trim brown beard, and a woman – tiny, white-haired, shriveled – old enough to have been the priest's mother. Neither would've been a danger to the Germans.

Then a noise from the corner behind him, the sound of a chair pulled along a floor, and he wheels and fires without aiming, emptying the clip. Where he'd shot, another child, a girl of about eight, crumples over, blood pumping out of her. Nicky walks over cautiously, his pistol still pointed, scanning the back wall of the church. The girl is dressed in a plain yellow smock. She looks up at Nicky. Then her eyes cloud and she's still. Nicky sticks the barrel of the Mauser in his mouth and pulls the trigger, but he's not changed the clip. He hears shouts and a comrade rushes in. As Nicky kneels in front of the dead girl, his lips around his gun, the gun is pulled away from him. Nicky stares at the comrade, trying to identify this tall young man with blond hair as if he'd not been soldiering with him for months.

"Chrisma. Shit. It happens."

The comrade searches through Nicky's pockets to find another clip, reloads the Mauser, and hands it back to Nicky as he pulls Nicky up from the floor.

"Don't put that fucking thing in your mouth again. We need you."

The comrade pushes Nicky outside. Within minutes of trying to kill himself, Nicky is again fighting and trying to hide from the enemy's gunfire.

At the end of the story, when Helen was sure Nicky had finished, even as he began to cry, she said nothing. She moved toward him on the living room sofa and embraced him. Once her arms encircled him, the flow of tears seemed to increase, and Nicky couldn't do anything to stop them. Helen's warmth, what seemed like her forgiveness, were too much for him to bear. He didn't deserve warmth or forgiveness or anything but punishment. He was overwhelmed by her apparent determination not to punish him. He felt some minor relief at having told the story, but the relief was minuscule in comparison to his shame.

"Aren't you going to say anything?" he asked when his sobbing stopped, long minutes later.

She reached into her purse to pull out a wad of tissues and hand it to him. "I can't say I'm surprised by anything I hear about a war. You read one war novel – *The Naked and the Dead* for example – and you can't be surprised. It's very sad, your story."

"Understatement."

"I think you did the right thing, telling me."

"There's still so much more I haven't said yet."

"There's time."

They kissed, then Helen pushed herself back to arms' length. She looked to Nicky as if about to say something. He still expected her to chastise him for his rash conduct, to blame him for the girl's death.

"What else?" he asked.

"I've dealt with a lot of people who've gone through trauma, but I don't know any who had to go through what you went through. So that leaves me with a big question. In some ways, I'm not sure I believe what I see."

"What don't you believe? That I killed so many people?"

"No. That you lived through all the horror and you still ended up as well-balanced as you are. Well, as you have always seemed to be, even from the first evening in America, when you must have been totally overwhelmed on the inside. On the outside, you were in control."

"I don't know."

"I can't imagine what it's like to expect so often to die, when around every corner there might be an enemy machine gun nest." She looked down, preventing him from looking into her hazel eyes, where he'd hoped to see what she really felt.

"And?"

"And ... I'm getting hungry."

"Let's go then."

* * * * *

In better weather they might've walked, but it was February and bitterly cold. He opened the passenger door of his Eldorado and made sure Helen sat comfortably before closing it.

"You look very beautiful tonight, Helen."

"Ha. You keep saying. You know very well Irene got the best looks in our family, and Catherine was always much more elegant. You're sweet to flatter me, though."

"I should've asked before. How is Catherine?"

"Sick, I'm afraid. Breast cancer. She's a fighter, yet the beast is taking a toll."

"I'm very sorry. When you talk to her, please give her my wishes for recovery. I wonder if she remembers me."

"I'm pretty sure she does."

He could see the faintest glimmer of a smile, as if Helen had heard the punchline of a joke and thought it would have been rude to laugh out loud with Nicky unable to comprehend the humor. Then he thought he must have imagined the smile.

Shortly after nine, Sushiana was filling. Nicky and Helen found a table and ordered Alaska rolls and split pea soup. After they had tucked in for a few minutes, Helen turned the conversation to Nicky's family.

"How's Kayla? Did you know I stopped in to see her when I was on the unit recently?"

"She told me. I think things have returned to normal, as normal as they could be in the circumstances," he said.

"'Think?"

He sighed. "Her rabbi – Rabbi Beck, whom I met last night – still has too much influence in her life, if you ask me, and I'd rather she were more rational, let's say. Max is rational, whereas Kayla's got herself tied up into knots with Chabad. And she sure has Jackie going in that direction too. You know what they're like."

"No, actually, I don't know what you're talking about. They're a group of *chasidim*, they're faithful, observant, like I am. You're accusing her of not being rational because she's *frum*, that she feels obliged to obey every commandment?"

"Not quite. But Kayla goes too far. Stopping her meds because her rabbi directed her to stop was crazy. She might've killed Jackie."

"Everyone makes mistakes, and sometimes they're big mistakes. But you say Kayla has been chastened, that she won't do that again."

"She's staying in Chabad."

"Doesn't make her irrational, if Chabad helps her to be happy. Isn't it enough for you that she's happy?"

"I want her to be happy, yet ..."

"Do you know what Chabad stands for?"

Nicky stopped for a second to ponder her question, annoyed that she'd interrupted him. Chabad didn't stand for anything, as far as he was concerned, other than blind allegiance to the dictates of a *rebbe* and his disciples.

"As I was saying, think how much of her energy goes into religion and how limiting it is for Jackie, or will be." But he could see Helen's growing distaste for his argument; he could feel it in her glare, the way she slightly lowered the angle of her face as if she were getting ready to pounce. Her anger puzzled him. He knew she was Orthodox, but was pretty sure she wouldn't take foolhardy direction from a rabbi. She was a social worker, after all, a professional who often gave advice based on years of training and experience, based on finding practical solutions to life's problems.

"Chabad stands for wisdom, discernment, and understanding. Do you object?"

"No. Perhaps I ..."

"Tell me what you mean by rational, Nicky. The rational you're so proud of in your son. The rational you think you live your life by."

"Feet on the ground. Decisions based on evidence. Conclusions drawn from facts. What we learn in med school, what doctors do every day." To his relief, her look softened.

"What doctors do," she repeated thoughtfully. "Nicky Covo, psychiatrist. You know, I could've predicted within a month of meeting you that you'd end up a psychiatrist."

"How so?"

"You always found the right thing to say to make us feel comfortable and good about ourselves. You had a great sense of what people needed to hear, how to be of help. One of the reasons I was so fond of you."

She reached across the table to take his hand and smiled. He saw with gratitude that she'd had enough of arguing about faith and reason. They finished their meal chatting about how Highland Park had changed, and then, inevitably, their favorite teams, the Mets, the Scarlet Knights, the Devils, and the Knicks. On the way back to Nicky's car, Helen slipped on an icy patch and almost fell, but Nicky was there to catch her. They both laughed, disaster averted.

· · · · ·

Back in her living room, Nicky watched as Helen poured them each a small glass of Sabra.

He asked to see additional photographs of her grandchildren, and she explained again how old each one was, how they got good grades or played baseball or did gymnastics or loved to draw. When she put her photographs away, Nicky poured a second glass for himself, took a small sip, and moved closer to her on the sofa. As he took her hands, she leaned toward him, and they kissed, tentatively at first, then more urgently. Finally, gently, Helen pushed him away.

"You should go, Nicky. It was a lovely evening, but I need to get up early tomorrow." He reached for her again. She evaded his grasp and walked to the door. He had no choice but to follow. She handed him his coat, hat, and scarf.

"That was very sweet just now, Helen. Perhaps, next time, I might stay longer?"

She opened the door. "It's been less than two weeks since we saw each other for the first time in decades. Only *Hashem* knows exactly how long, but long. Good night, Nicky," she said, gently pushing him out. Heavy snow had begun to fall. She yelled after him to drive carefully.

It was past midnight when Nicky got back to his apartment. The long drive along icy highways, through poor visibility, left him shaking. In bed, he couldn't relax, excited by the time with Helen and the idea that he was falling in love again. Then he remembered his shame at having told her about the girl in the yellow smock. He thought again about the high tension of their brief spat at Sushiana. Could she truly care for him?

There was more he wanted to tell her, about the inexplicable. He'd almost ventured into the story at her house, but had held back. He thought now that, just maybe, this *was* the thing he should put down in writing. Could he recall correctly, if he sat down to write, those few seconds in the church in Ioannina, the tiniest fraction of his time on earth, and yet the most horrifying? Perhaps, contrary to how he now remembered those seconds, he had in fact been concussed by the blast and suffered from selective amnesia. The condition could be induced by hypnosis, so why not by trauma? Yet many details were clear. His brush with death had been neither hallucination nor dream.

He took a cup of chamomile tea to his computer and began to write. As he did so, he could almost feel himself again charging into that room.

.

Was I stupid to rush in like that? I just followed my instinct. I fired wildly at nothing, then saw the German crouched behind a desk. He stood, pulled the pin of a grenade, and released the safety lever to take us both out. I waited for the blast and then sensed a flash of deep red, the color of sunset moments before dark, but the flash didn't come from his grenade. It swept into the room from the wall with the window, from the window itself, and enveloped the German. The room flooded with red, the intermingled blood from our bodies. But the red was not blood at all, at least not mine. The German was caught in a whirlwind, the shrapnel hitting him only and leaving me unscathed, as if I'd been covered with an impervious, reflective blanket.

No. Couldn't have happened that way. Or could it have? I need to return to Greece, and I need to take Helen with me.

CHAPTER TWENTY-ONE

Highland Park, New Jersey, March 16, 1990 (Friday)

Nicky began to ask her, with every date, if she'd join him on a trip to Greece, and she invariably and politely declined. She was too old, too set in her ways. Her grandkids needed her. *Pesach* was coming. It would interfere with her consulting. She hated to fly. Yet Nicky didn't think she minded his persistence. He saw it as only a matter of time. When she was ready to go with him, she'd let him know. A trip to Greece could wait until then. A trip had to wait until she was ready to accompany him, because he didn't see how he could do it himself.

He thought she was near accepting his offer because she had invited him at long last to share *Shabbat* dinner with her. He'd meet her extended family. The invitation had to mean something.

Arriving at four, Nicky brought with him a large bouquet of white daisies. She hugged him quickly and hung up his coat. They kissed as if they might have been lovers who'd not seen each other for months, although it had been only a week. They'd already gotten to talking every day on the telephone. He'd thought often about telling her of the short vignette he'd written, or more accurately of the bizarre story it depicted, but hadn't been able to bring himself to do so. He didn't want to hear her say that his surviving the grenade blast was proof of God's existence. He didn't want to get into an argument in which he was forced to explain the inexplicable malfunctioning of the grenade.

"When does your family arrive?"

"Sunset is 7:03, so we have to light the candles by 6:41, so I told them get here by six-thirty. It'll be a zoo. Good luck if you remember any of my grandkids' names."

"I'll try."

He helped her prepare a salad without bringing up Greece, but when Helen offered him a glass of wine – "to help us relax before the onslaught" – he took a deep breath and decided to broach the topic once more. He made sure she started her own wine before he began.

"Helen, let's go back to my favorite topic. You know you want to go to Greece with me. Stop trying to pretend you don't. We could book tickets right after *Shabbat* and go right after *Pesach*."

She wiped her wet hands on her apron. "There's so much to consider, Nicky. The logistics alone . . ."

He laughed, in response to which she mock-pouted and turned away. He gently turned her back to face him again. "Logistics? Cab to airport, planes, cab to hotel, rental car, all of which I can easily handle. What else do we need? A guide book? I've already given you two. I can ask directions in Greek. I can discuss the finer points of the menus with the waiters who don't speak English. I can make sure only kosher food crosses your palate. What logistics?"

Helen sighed, leaned back against the kitchen counter, and put her hands on her slender hips. "Don't take this wrong, Nicky. How do I know I can trust you? What if we get to Inousa, say, and for whatever reason there's only one room at the only hotel? You know what I mean."

Nicky could see her color rising. He'd wanted a much more intimate relationship with her in the time they'd been dating but had schooled himself to be patient. He sensed now some deep fear of the physical on Helen's part – perhaps a reluctance to feel she was being unfaithful to David's memory – underlay her refusals to accompany him to Greece. "Well, it's not a problem."

"Not a problem? For you, maybe ..."

"No, I mean that I'll just sleep in a chair in the lobby. Every hotel has a lobby, right?" Helen smiled, apparently envisioning the humor of such a situation. "One condition, though."

"And that is?"

"In the morning, after you're properly dressed, after my embarrassing night in the lobby, you let me into your room so I can shower and shave and brush my teeth."

Helen burst out laughing, then caught herself. "We couldn't have you going around with bad breath, unshowered, and unshaved," she chuckled. "That'd be a tragedy of Biblical proportions. Maybe you'd consider growing a beard?"

She turned to her sink, grabbed a head of iceberg lettuce, and began to wash it, but Nicky once again, with great affection, turned her around to face him. As he pulled her close, she dropped the lettuce back on the counter and melted easily into him.

"Does that mean you'll come with me?"

"I suppose."

She kissed him on the mouth briefly, then pushed him back when he tried to slide his tongue into her mouth. "None of that now," she said. "Folks will arrive in a sec. We want to keep this G-rated all the way through dinner."

"Not even Parental Guidance?"

She ignored the remark and busied herself with final preparations.

In minutes, as promised, Helen's family materialized with blazing energy, as if from a thundercloud. Her elder son Jonah – she'd become pregnant with him when Nicky still lived with her family – his wife Naomi, their children; her daughter Sarah and son-in-law Morty and their children; and her younger son Kobi, his wife Shoshana, and their children. They'd all heard about Nicky. Helen's children claimed to remember being at Nicky's wedding, but Nicky couldn't recall that they'd been there. The magistrate who officiated hadn't taken more than that one picture hanging in his office, and it showed neither Helen nor her children. He wondered for a second why the participants themselves hadn't taken pictures. They'd probably been too stressed, perhaps by Adel starting to act up or by Norm needing to rush back to his diner.

Just after Helen served chocolate cake for dessert, she announced matter-of-factly that she and Nicky had decided to go to Greece together and the reason, that he might have a sister alive there whom he thought had died in the *Shoah*. There was a long moment of stunned silence, broken only by the squeals of Helen's youngest grandchildren playing in another room.

"*Ima*! Really! With Dr. Covo?" Sarah, swallowing, put her hand up to her mouth.

"With Nicky. Yes. After *Pesach*. You all can get along fine without me for a couple of weeks. I hope."

Again, for an uncomfortable couple of seconds, no one said anything. Then Jonah questioned Nicky about the itinerary. Nicky glanced at Helen. They'd not discussed the matter.

"Yes, Nicky, what *is* our plan exactly?" she asked.

"Well, of course, we fly to Athens. I'd like to spend some time there again. We'll need to see Salonika, where I came from, where your father's family came from. And, if you don't quite mind, I'd like to travel through the northern mountains and visit Ioannina. And, of course, the monastery outside of Inousa."

"The monastery?" asked Jonah. "What monastery?"

"My sister, the woman I think might be my sister, I mean, is a nun."

"No," said Shoshana and Sarah almost simultaneously, and Nicky proceeded to explain, to looks of amazement, what little he knew from Fevronia's letter and his telephone conversation with her.

"Well, your plan of travel is quite comprehensive, Dr. Covo, and it sounds like more than two weeks to me," observed Jonah.

"Please call me Nicky. Yes, it's comprehensive if we do all that, but it's something I need to work out with your mother. It's her trip as well as mine. And we'll want to visit Jewish sites, too, I assume. The old Monastir Synagogue in Salonika, where I had my Bar Mitzvah, is still in use."

"Well, *Ima*, you're one for surprises," Sarah said, pushing away the rest of her dessert. "Do you want help deciding what to bring? If you need new clothes, maybe I can shop with you?"

"Me, too," added Naomi.

"We can start at Macy's," suggested Shoshana.

"That's great, girls. That's what we'll do."

Helen's chocolate cake was the richest and sweetest Nicky had ever tasted.

· · · · · ·

After her family left, the dishes cleared and washed, the kitchen put in order, Helen and Nicky sat quietly in her living room, sipping Sabra. After a few minutes, she raised a new topic, one Nicky had been anticipating ever since he'd spoken at dinner of his ideas about the trip.

"I should've known, when you gave me those books, you intended more than just going to the monastery. I'm fine with seeing the rest of Greece, too, as long as I'm going, but do you think it's wise for you to go back to all those places?"

Her question was one he'd asked himself repeatedly. When he wanted to, he felt he could almost see those battle-scarred towns and roads in his mind, just as they'd been forty-plus years before, and he wondered what good could come of seeing them again. It could well be so much had changed that the places he wanted to see would be unrecognizable, and he wasn't even sure he could find those that tormented him most. Even the church in Ioannina, if it still existed, was one of scores that looked alike, and perhaps he'd only imagined that the grenade episode had taken place in a church. He hadn't been thinking clearly in the weeks after the girl in the yellow smock. He'd murdered her in a church, but his memories of the fighting after that small town, whose name he couldn't recall, were sketchier. And yet, despite his doubts, some inner force tugged at him to make expiation for his sins by guiding him back and forcing him to look again at the things he'd done. The weight of guilt had grown enormous and suffocating, as if he were struggling to breathe under an avalanche of snow and ice.

"I need to see those places again," he said uncertainly.

"To beat yourself up?"

"No. To help me process memories, to help me get them out of my system. And I want you to be there with me."

"You want me to make sure you don't blow your brains out?"

"I'd never blow my brains out."

Helen's blunt comment startled him. Bluntness, he was learning, was her way, and he'd told her about his two suicide attempts, one with his *t'fillin* and one with his Mauser, both attempts defeated by the purest luck. She knew as well, from the time she'd befriended him in 1946, that he could be impetuous, injudicious, and swept up by enormous waves of emotion. Even as he promised to Helen not to kill himself, at least with a gun, he felt unsure. The idea of taking his own life periodically surfaced during his bouts of depression. Could he keep such a promise?

"Forget I said that, it was rude." Tears glistened in her eyes as she leaned over to kiss him.

"It's all right."

"I need to learn better to think before I open my mouth. Look, let's get a calendar and pick the exact dates."

"You're still coming with me?"

"Didn't I say I would?"

"I mean, the whole trip, the side trips, the mountains, all that?"

"In for a dollar."

He frowned for a second until her remembered the idiom. "Right. Dime. Dollar. But you'll see. The mountains can be beautiful. You can feel close to ..." He caught himself from going on.

"Close to?"

"The sky. A beautiful sky in the mountains."

"And so I do need to buy new clothes, maybe good hiking clothes, for this great trek you're contemplating. Mountains. Hiking. I don't want to look frumpy."

"Frumpy nothing. Haven't I told you that you're beautiful?"

They reached for each other to start saying goodnight.

CHAPTER TWENTY-TWO

Manhattan, New York, April 16, 1990 (Monday)

Weeks later, Alice – the patient who'd lost a baby son – killed herself with a massive overdose of pain medications. She'd stopped seeing Nicky after their unpleasant February encounter. Alice's suicide, which he'd feared but hadn't been able to prevent, cast a decidedly gloomy shadow, even as his trip to Greece approached. He'd failed Alice, and it was not the first time a patient had taken that way out. Each time he lost a patient pushed him into a deep depression. Each time he'd managed to pull himself out by focusing on the other patients who still needed him. Now he'd have to bear the knowledge of Alice's death, not while treating others, but on his trip to Greece with Helen, a journey to revisit his own traumas, a journey to meet the strange woman who called herself Sister Theodora but who might well be Kal.

Not long after hearing about Alice's death, Nicky found himself packing for Greece and listening to the WQXR evening news, his suitcase open on his bed. An item on the radio caught his attention. He turned up the volume and stopped packing to listen more closely. Dr. Kevorkian, "the Doctor of Death," had participated in his first assisted suicide. The attorney general of Michigan was looking into prosecuting Kevorkian for murder.

Nicky admired Kevorkian's courage, although he wasn't sure that doctors should ever help patients kill themselves. He never wanted his own patients to end their lives, he knew it was his duty as a doctor to try to prevent such sad events, but he felt that suicide could be a rational decision for some, particularly when the pain of living became unbearable. As Nicky listened to the Kevorkian story, his thoughts turned to the pentobarbital in his own supply of drugs. It was his drug of preference for inducing a hypnotic state in some patients. He took a few vials from his medicine safe and added them to his toilet bag.

Just as he zipped his suitcase shut, he heard on the radio news about the Supreme Court reinstating the death penalty upon a retarded man convicted of murder. Dalton Prejean would perish in a Louisiana electric chair. As Nicky listened, he recalled a passage of *Torah*: "*Go-el hadam hu yamit et harotzach* – The avenger of blood shall kill the murderer."

There, at the heart of his ancestral religion, had been the law that murder must be punished by killing, that acts of violent revenge were an inevitable, if distasteful, part of life. The blood avenger would be a relative of the original victim. The revenge killing of a murderer would not end the cycle of violence but would provide some measure of justice. Only those who had killed others accidentally were to be spared, and only if they could make their way to a city of refuge.

There had to be multiple blood avengers waiting for him in Greece.

CHAPTER TWENTY-THREE

A Plane Over The Atlantic Ocean, April 17-18, 1990 (Tuesday-Wednesday)

Nicky insisted on paying for first-class tickets, even though Helen had protested that she would've been just as happy flying coach. On the Lufthansa flight to Frankfurt, Nicky enjoyed a roast beef dinner and was pleased to see that Helen was thankful he'd ordered her a kosher meal. They both had two glasses of wine and then reclined, hoping to sleep. In minutes, however, Helen complained that she was too nervous to sleep, first class notwithstanding. He took her hand lightly. She smiled at him. "This is so ... I don't know ... out of character for me? I'm still amazed I agreed to go with you. This trip is something I would've never imagined only a few months ago. I saw myself forever as a stay-at-home grandmother."

"A very intelligent and adventurous grandmother. I'm shocked you'd want to come to Greece with a strange man." He mock-growled, as if a wolf waiting in disguise for Little Red Riding Hood, then smiled at his own effort at humor.

"Down, boy." She thought for a minute. "How intelligent, I'm not sure. I'll buy adventurous though. Yet, I still have reservations. I hope I'm not a drag, getting in the way."

"I can't imagine you being in the way."

"Nicky, what if Sister Theodora isn't your sister? Have you thought of that? Well, of course, you have, we've talked about it, but I still wonder. Could you take the disappointment?"

He thought about the few additional times he'd called Abbess Fevronia and begged to talk to Sister Theodora and the equal number of times she'd refused. Each time, Fevronia had urged him to finalize plans to visit, and after each conversation Nicky was left with the distinct feeling – no reason for which he could give -- that Fevronia had been right and his sister was waiting to be discovered by him at the monastery.

"Sure. If she's not Kal, I'll be where I was before I read Fevronia's letter. But the more I think about this, the more I come to the conclusion she has to be Kal. Fevronia knows too much to be mistaken."

"And so here we are on our way to Greece."

"Here we are."

He turned from Helen and looked out the window into the night, where the reflection of the dim cabin lights played tricks in his mind and he imagined he could see Adel flying along with the plane. – You remember, Nicky, how I wanted to name our daughter Jackie? How you refused? A Dodgers fan like you, and you knew how much I loved Jackie Robinson and how he loved me? – That was just your illness, Adel, the voices you heard that no one else heard. – He told me he loved me and that my daughter should be named after him. But you insisted she had to be named after your sister. – It's true, Adel. But you ultimately got your Jackie and – And now it looks like there could be two of Kal. Two Kals, such pals, two locales. – No, we compromised on Kayla. Not the same.

"You're mumbling again, Nicky," said Helen, as she placed her hand gently on his arm. "Are you all right?"

Nicky turned from the window. "Just thinking that poor Adel didn't have a say about either of our kid's names. I tried to imagine my daughter as … a reincarnation of my sister? I'd listen to Kayla perform, hear the ovations – shoot, I yelled the loudest – and I could see my little sister on the stage. I'd think about what she might have done if she'd lived. All the possibilities snuffed out. And now, here I am, maybe on the way to meet her again, a nun. Hard to fathom."

In minutes, Helen was asleep. Nicky had not told her that he'd met with The Reverend Thomas Verdaris of the Annunciation Greek Orthodox Church on West 91st, told him the story and asked specifically about what it might be like for Sister Theodora to be transplanted to Manhattan. The most that the clergyman would say was that "it depended on her" and that she would be "welcomed in the name of Christ." Nicky had also learned a bit about the services of *Orthros* and *Paraklesis*. He wanted to assure Sister Theodora – if she was Kal – that he knew at least something about her chosen religion.

He pulled out from his backpack an envelope containing the short vignette about the grenade. Why had he lived when he should have died? Because he was somehow supposed to discover Kal again? It made no sense. He refolded the one page of typewriter paper, replaced it into the envelope, and returned the envelope to his backpack.

In a minute, he too closed his eyes.

He's driving a pickup truck in the north, the war having turned in favor of the Allies. The British have reoccupied Athens and Crete, and there are great celebrations, although the Germans haven't completely pulled out of Greece.

He travels from Kavala to Ioannina, on a mission to save the Jews there. He must warn them that they are about to be sent to the gas chambers. His pistol and 98K bounce on the seat next to him.

Clouds sweep in, the sky darkens, and a veil of deep blood red has been pulled over the sun. The day grows unbearably hot, like hell, like what it must feel like to be packed into an oven with the dead, the corpses of his family. The pickup runs out of diesel, so he must pedal to keep it going. Then the pedals fall off, so now he must push. He nears Ioannina, exhausted, yet cannot stop, every second precious. The road he must take leads into the mountains. There's a synagogue near the top where some Jews have hidden. It's not safe. The Germans are ready to storm it. He must get there first and load the Jews into his truck. He groans with the great effort of pushing the truck up the road; the truck turns into a bus, but he keeps pushing. He will load up the Jews, get them to safety.

Just around the next curve.

TEN OR ELEVEN

Hauptmann Wilhelm Rieger dragged on his black Nordiano and blew a cloud of smoke toward the bound man in front of him. The head monk, if that's what he was, sat and watched him, helpless to prevent the cigarette's nauseating miasma from washing over his heavy black beard and deeply lined face. The monk's arms were tied to the chair behind his back, his ankles tied to the chair's front legs. His gold cross had been ripped from around his neck and stowed in Rieger's pack. The monk had not resisted, had not even raised his hands to defend himself when Rieger slapped him twice on the face just for the fun of it. Now, Rieger sat opposite the monk. He held his pistol in his right hand and randomly tapped its barrel against his polished black boots.

"You're hiding Jews on this property, an underground bunker somewhere or a secret closet, and you will show me where they are, or you and your fellow bearded swine will be shot." Rieger was only a lower-ranked officer but spoke with the authority of a general; his combination of demand and threat varied little from what he'd been taught to say in such situations. His interpreter was a private whose mother had been Greek and who mimicked Rieger's volume and sneering tone as best he could.

"You needn't interpret for me, son," the monk said, turning to the private. "I know German."

"Then go," Rieger said to his subordinate, who complied, but not before spitting on the monk. The gob hit the prisoner's right ear, and Rieger watched it slowly change shape as it descended to the monk's neck. He thought for a second about wiping it off, then caught himself. The creeping saliva would accentuate the monk's feeling of helplessness and bring the meeting to a successful conclusion more quickly. When a minute had passed, Rieger continued. "So, where are they?"

"You have been misinformed, Herr Hauptmann. We have not hidden Jews here."

"We know some fled north from Salonika. We rounded up three in Serres. Shot them immediately, as they deserved, but that's not your concern, is it? We were told another three had come to ... what's the name of this stinking place?"

"The Holy Monastery of St. Vlassios."

"Holy my ass. Now, where are they?"

Rieger was tired after the day's exertions, and his voice began to lose some of its edge. His heart wasn't quite so much in his job as it had been when the forces of the Third Reich had first occupied northern Greece. He'd become suddenly important, the military governor of a string of villages, his only fighting an occasional skirmish with poorly organized partisans who, for the most part, wanted to stay hidden in the mountains. Finding and killing the Jews who avoided the deportations had been a defining part of his mission. He'd accepted all the teachings of National Socialism, the most important of which had been that the Jews were vermin and that the fate of humanity itself depended upon their being found and neutralized. It was war, and in war one had to do things that one would not do in times of peace. Since his time with the Hitler Youth, it had always made sense. And, he was happy to see, it made sense to most Greeks too. So many were willing to inform on their countrymen in hiding.

But doubts had begun to creep in as the tide of the war turned. The German brigades in Greece were in danger of being cut off by the Soviet army advancing across the Balkans. Rieger knew that, within days, he would be ordered to withdraw. In a week, he would be back in an active war zone, dealing with an unstoppable and vicious enemy. He would be lucky to survive such fighting, but if it was fate's decree that he die, then at least he could say – or others could say about him – that he had done his duty to the Fuhrer and the Fatherland. On the other hand, if he lived but the Allies ended up victors, hardly believable a year earlier but now very much believable, he might be judged very poorly indeed. The Allies might call him a murderer, as if he could be personally responsible for fulfilling his duties to the Fuhrer and following orders. Yet, fear of consequences could never be allowed to interfere with duty. Until the order of retreat, he knew what his duties were. Find and destroy the Jews and those who harbored them. He would continue to be an exterminator of the highest rank.

"If I knew – which I assure you I don't – I wouldn't tell you."

Father Augustin Kouris spoke with quiet assurance. He sensed that he and the other nine monks would be killed by the Germans regardless of what he said or did. He had no great aversion to death; rather, it would be the beginning of life eternal with Christ. He welcomed the idea that his life and those of his fellow monks would be martyred and hoped that someone, somewhere would discover their story and write about it. But, he thought with great regret, their martyrdom would be too late to save the lives of those who had come to them in fear and whom they had turned away. He had sinned greatly. He needed to make confession before dying, but how? Who could hear it and absolve him, when all were about to be killed?

The Germans had left St. Vlassios alone throughout the occupation, as long as the monastery provided no aid to the partisans and did not resist German rule, and he'd thought it his obligation to remain neutral. To have resisted would have been foolhardy, he had reasoned, and would lead only to the destruction of the monastery. And to what end? Throwing himself before a firing machine gun, as it were, would not have slowed down the Germans in the slightest. His body would be left where it fell unless the villagers took it upon themselves to bury it. At most, his death would cost the Germans a few bullets, and he was sure there were millions available and that those lost in his dead body would not be missed. If he managed to stay out of their way, he thought, the monastery could remain as a spiritual haven, and souls could be saved for the glory of Christ.

"You feel that life is so cheap that you can give up yours and those of your flock so easily? For the sake of a few shit-eating Jews?"

"What did you do before the war, Herr Hauptmann?"

Rieger flicked the safety off. Both he and Kouris stared at it for a second, then at each other.

Rieger was sorely tempted to end the discussion at once, in his typical way. Two months earlier, Rieger would have been quick to step behind Kouris's chair, place the muzzle of the gun up to the monk's lower neck, and fire. He would have done so without reservation, because as unpleasant as it was to kill a human being, particularly a priest, although of a religion that seemed bizarre to him, killing in the service of a greater good was an honor. No one would have reprimanded him. Now, though, that feeling of moral superiority on which he relied had all but evaporated, disappearing as the dawn's mist gives way to the sun's disinfecting rays. Rieger had a quick vision of his own father sitting there bound to a chair; he blinked, reminding himself that his father was hundreds of miles away, safe in Berlin. Kouris's voice and demeanor sounded to Rieger as if he was asked by his father what he had learned at school that day. But, no, it was only Kouris who sat before him, completely subject to his will.

"I studied accounting for two years, but enlisted in 1938."

"You knew war was coming."

"Everyone knew."

"There is still time to repent, Herr Hauptmann, still time to turn toward Christ the Savior and beg His forgiveness. He will forgive those who sincerely repent of their sins, no matter how big." Kouris spoke as he had spoken the same message to hundreds of believers and nonbelievers over the years. He had long ago found that a calm, steady voice was best suited to drawing to him those who were unsure. Belief had to come from within, where God's Grace could act only if the person was ready.

"Repent? It is not a sin to follow the wishes of one's father, and my father is the Fuhrer, and he is the father of all the German nation, and I will ..."

He was about to explain, although he felt no need to, why the Jews had started the war, why the Jews presented a mortal threat, not only to German people everywhere, but to all of Orthodox Christianity as well, and certainly to St. Vlassios or his monastery, and to the ten monks there with Kouris, when a private poked his head in and handed him a written order. Greek partisans had ambushed a German patrol, killing three. Reprisals were commanded. Rieger was to kill without delay all the monks and destroy the monastery. He looked up at Kouris and smiled. "Your death wish has arrived, Herr Monk."

•   •   •   •   •

No one could explain why there were ten in total and not eleven. When the Germans stormed into the monastery and tied up the monks, Rieger was certain that there were ten in addition to Kouris. No one could offer him even the wildest hypothesis about where the other monk had gone. Confronted by Rieger, Kouris looked at the other nine and said "They are all here. No one is missing," at which Rieger struck Kouris with his pistol, opening up a large gash over the left eye.

Kouris bled profusely. He fell to his knees for an instant as he tried to absorb the pain, as he watched in wonder at the spurting blood staining the floor of the church. He looked up at Rieger, ready for another blow, but Rieger had holstered his pistol. Kouris managed to regain his feet.

"There is still time, Herr Hauptmann."

"Time for what?" asked a sergeant, who kept his semi-automatic pistol aimed at the group of monks waiting to be taken to their deaths.

"Shut up," ordered Rieger, embarrassed that Kouris had spoken to him like that in front of the other soldiers.

Rieger's platoon marched the column of ten monks into the forest west of the monastery.

The terrain gradually descended, and the pine forest grew thicker around them. About two miles from the monastery, Rieger called a halt, had the monks' hands freed, and ordered them to begin digging their grave. The Germans stood, surrounding them, waiting. Although one might have thought that these condemned men would delay completion of their grave and thus extend their lives, even by a few minutes, the reverse seemed to be true. They dug with great energy, all the more surprising because some were quite old and did not appear to possess great physical strength. Rieger wanted the grave to be deep. He wanted to hide well the fruits of what he had commanded, of what they were about to do, although only a month earlier he would have been pleased to kill all the monks right there at the monastery and leave their bodies to be discovered by the villagers.

As he dug, Kouris murmured encouragement to the others, told them not to be afraid of death, and urged them to make the grave as deep as they could. He too did not want the bodies to be found. He knew that only ten monks, including himself, lived at St. Vlassios, but eleven monks had been tied up. The eleventh, the one that seemed to have disappeared, had been a visitor from a world that was not that of St. Vlassios or of the nearby town of Serres or even of the earth. For a second, upon first seeing him, Kouris thought that this visitor must be Christ Himself, that he was a witness to

Christ's Second Coming. The idea was outrageous though. The Second Coming could not coincide with the horrible war that was upon them. What then? An angel? The Devil himself? An agent of the Devil? Perhaps God had sent a messenger to guide Rieger, but the messenger had been unable to deliver the message and departed before he could be killed, departed the same way he had come. Or had the eleventh been a figment of everyone's imagination?

Meanwhile, even as the minute drew closer when Rieger would give his men the order to shoot, Kouris's invitation to repent weighed in his heart. He thought about a young Jewish girl he shot, the one whose face struck him as angelic just at the very instant of his pulling the trigger. He knew even as he shot that she was not the vermin that Hitler had imagined, that none of them were, but before the bullet had bored through her head the idea of their innocence had vanished. Now, as the ten monks dug their grave, her face came before him again, and he realized that repentance was out of the question. Not even a God of mercy could forgive Rieger for what Rieger had done and was about to do, if such a God existed. Rieger did not want Divine forgiveness, if by attaining forgiveness he was required to disobey his orders or abandon his true father.

As they dug, Father Souris began to chant the twenty-seventh psalm in Greek, and the others quickly joined. "The Lord is the stronghold of my life – of whom shall I be afraid? When evil men advance against me to devour my flesh, when my enemies and my foes attack me, they will stumble and fall." Then the grave was deep enough, even deeper than it needed to be.

"Lie down, face down," Rieger screamed. Kouris tossed his spade out of the ditch, which was now more than two meters deep, and lay prone in its center, his arms outstretched over his head as if he were preparing to dive into a pool. Rieger kept yelling, and one by one the other nine monks lay down, positioning themselves as Kouris had done. Only two monks could fit next to Kouris, the next three were forced to lie directly atop the first three, and then the four last monks were forced to lie atop the pile of six.

Rieger stood looking at them, his platoon ready to shoot on command. He listened closely to the sounds of praying, the chanting that he did not understand. He thought it only right that they should pray before death, because there was nothing after death, as we all knew, and he wanted to be able to say that he had been generous and thoughtful before carrying out his orders. We heard only the praying, which 1 understood, but no pleas for mercy, no last-minute confessions, no begging for absolution, nothing to indicate fear, nothing but quiet certainty.

We obeyed Rieger's orders and fired.

BOOK TWO

CHAPTER ONE

Athens, April 19, 1990 (Thursday)

They sat at a table on the open air rooftop restaurant of the Hotel Grande Bretagne, plates of fresh fruit, savory cheese, and mixed nuts before them. Nicky wolfed down a large helping of scrambled eggs, while Helen nibbled at cottage cheese, absorbed in her reading and ignoring Nicky's efforts to start a conversation. Finally, she showed him the Fodor's guidebook, opened to the page displaying the church of Agios Nikolaos Ragavas. "This is where you hid?"

He looked. "Yes."

"Fascinating." She resumed reading. "Eleventh century Byzantine. It was said to be the first church to ring its bells as the Germans withdrew."

"Yes, I know." He took the guidebook from her and turned to a map. "It's on Pritaniou. About nine blocks away. Can we go there first?"

"And then the Parthenon, like we agreed?" She looked past Nicky's right shoulder to the immense mountain hovering in the city, its walls bathed in brilliant, Mediterranean sunshine. "The view from here is amazing. It feels as if you can almost reach out and touch it. Not a picture book anymore. The Parthenon in real life. Close up. Wow."

Nicky followed her glance for a second, then pulled *drachma* out of his wallet and placed them on the table. "Once we get to the church, we'll already be on the slope of the Acropolis in Plaka. Just a short climb to the Parthenon."

"Short climb? You've got to be kidding."

"No, really. It's easier than it looks. At least it didn't seem so hard when I was young. Today, it might take as a bit longer than a half hour."

"I don't know."

"Trust me."

．　　．　　．　　．　　．

A long row of eateries, tourist shops, and travel agencies crowded along the sides of Navarchou Nikodemou. The street itself was jammed with motorcycles and cabs. Nothing like the mental images of Athens Nicky had carried. No signs of starvation. No crumpled bodies. No stench of death. Their walk to the church was the reverse of his journey to meet with the Citroen, in the trunk of which he'd been smuggled to the mountains. Left on Tripodon, right up a short stone stairway, right again, more stairs, a narrow passage between old apartment buildings so close to each other that residents on either side could almost touch hands from their windows, then left. When they at last emerged from the shadows into bright sunshine, they faced the front of the church, its stone walls bleached to pure white through the centuries, its glare blinding. They stood quietly for a minute.

"Never thought I'd see it again."

"It's tiny." Helen pulled out the Fodor's and located its discussion of the church. "In the book, it looks much bigger."

"Down the block," Nicky pointed, "across the street, the grey house was the rectory. May still be. Many memories there, good and bad." His voice turned softer. "It's where I first tried to kill myself."

"A first time?" She looked at him with raised eyebrows.

"I almost hanged myself the night I arrived." He briefly told her the story of his despondency when he realized he was being asked to forsake his Jewish identity. "When I saw how alone I was, how Father Liakos expected me to pray to Christ, not just to pretend, but to be sincere, I felt desperate. Suicide seemed the only way out, and I thought of the martyrs, Rabbi Akiva raked with iron combs and reciting the *Sh'ma*. I was devoted then, so committed, so serious, I felt I couldn't live in those conditions."

"*Baruch Hashem* that you changed your mind."

"That's not quite what happened. Someone walked in just in time to prevent me from following through. And then, she ..." But he couldn't finish the sentence immediately, wondering how to explain about Dora.

"She?"

He wanted to tell Helen, yet didn't want to tell her, how Dora's unexpected presence changed everything for him in an instant. The lingering memory of the girl he'd fallen in love with was still too private to share with the woman he now loved. They walked closer toward the door of the church; Nicky put his hands up to feel the warm stone, to touch the bottom of one of the arched windows.

"Maybe it was guilt as much as anything else," he continued. "My family was in danger, and I ran away like a scared rabbit. And I hated myself for being a coward. I literally couldn't bear to live with myself."

"And?"

"I was going to tell you," he said uncertainly, not sure at all. "Dora, the priest's daughter, a complete innocent, barged into my room, trying to be welcoming, wanting to know if I was hungry. That was all. The leather straps of my t'fillin were already around my neck, and she was naturally curious. I pretended this was part of a Jewish ritual, and what did she know from t'fillin? Two seconds later, had she not entered, I'd have tightened them into a noose. And then, for months, it seems I spent almost every waking hour with her."

"I see."

"She was twelve, I was fourteen."

"I get it."

They reached the front door of the church, set back in a shallow alcove, still in shade.

"C'mon, let's go in," Nicky said.

But the door was locked, and a sign told them that *Esperinos* would be at six. Nicky knocked. No one answered. He knocked again, louder. Still nothing. To the right of the door was an iron gate separating the street from a short stairway to a verdant garden. Nicky pushed on the gate to find out that it was locked too.

"*Dekara.* We have to go around back and look at ... well, I'll call it the cemetery." He pointed in the direction from which they'd come.

"We have to look at what?" Helen put her hands on her hips and glared at him.

"Climb fifty meters, that's all. Roughly a quarter of the way to the Parthenon. We didn't use markers, but I think I know where they are."

"Where what are?"

"Wait here if you want, Helen. I won't be long. Then I'll get you and we can climb to the top together."

"No. You're crazy. I have to stay with you. For one thing, I don't know a word of Greek. What is *dekara*?"

"Damn."

They walked back on Pritaniou toward the nearest corner, but instead of heading down the stone stairway on which they'd originally approached, they turned uphill to another much narrower stairway. The massive Acropolis loomed over them. As they climbed, they passed tall bushes that occasionally crowded out the sun. Beyond the bushes, as the slope steepened and their pace slowed, the stairs ended and a path beyond led to the top. They were both breathing hard and sweating when they came to a chain-link fence that bordered the path. Just beyond the stairway, where a small gulley had formed, Nicky pulled at the bottom of the fence.

"I'm climbing under. Are you joining me?"

Helen had worn grey pants and a grey sweater over a white, long-sleeved blouse. She crouched in front of the gulley and took off her sweater, placing it on a tuft of grass. She glared at him. "You're going to pay for this, Nicky."

"Look, Helen, you don't have to if ..."

"Oh, shut up." She pushed herself under the fence. When she stood again, she brushed dirt from her slacks and blouse. "If we're arrested, Nicky, I promise I'll kill you myself before we get to jail. There won't be anything left of you for a judge and jury."

"I don't think they use juries in Greece today."

"Greece is where juries were invented, you ignoramus. And you say you're Greek?" When Nicky joined her on the other side of the fence, she refused to let him take her hand. "Now, please just do what you have to do, and do it quickly. If you don't mind, that is."

He walked down the hill a few yards, behind a clump of bushes. Intermittently, he glanced toward the top of the Acropolis, trying to get bearings.

"What exactly are you looking for, anyway?" asked Helen. "The bones of the girl you loved? The girl you still love?"

"Please be quiet for a minute."

Nicky knelt in the shade of a bush, head bowed. It might have been here or meters away. What difference? Father Liakos had been too weak to help dig Dora's grave, too weak to help carry her body up the hill. Then, a month later, Father Liakos himself died, from grief as much from anything else. With help from a parishioner, Nicky buried his last friend in Athens near his wife and daughter. Their bodies long ago had melted into the earth, become part of it, like rain, like tears flowing into the harbor at Pireas. They'd seeped into and out of myriad fish, which in turn been caught in the fishermen's nets and served fresh in the finest Athenian restaurants.

Helen put her hand lightly on his hunched shoulder. "You say you were fourteen?"

"Fifteen when Dora died."

"You cared for her a great deal."

He stood, wiped his eyes with his hand, brushed dirt from his knees. "She was the first girl I loved. In a way, still love, yes, as one must, if love was true."

"I understand. I think I can see David here, in a way."

"It was impossible, obviously. Dora was Christian, and I couldn't stay with her anyway."

"Do you remember what she looked like?"

He paused for a second to consider the question. "Small for her age. Light brown hair. Green eyes. No, wait, they were gray. Or maybe a little bit of both?"

Helen hugged him as he cried. When he'd wept enough, he gently eased himself away from her embrace. "Let's get out of here."

●   ●   ●   ●   ●

At dinner, they chatted amiably about the day's activities, until Helen led their discussion to religion. "You know, the temples are much larger than I thought. One can't appreciate them from photographs. But one thing struck me today."

"Which is?"

"When the Greeks started the Parthenon, the Temple in Jerusalem was already hundreds of years old."

"The Temple." Nicky thought of his years studying the priestly rituals in place there before the Roman destruction. "I don't understand how Jews today still pray for its restoration, nineteen hundred years after the fact. It's obscene."

"Some Jews."

"Fine, just some Jews. They're nuts," huffed Nicky. "We need to kill more goats and sheep today? Weren't the millions already killed there enough? The only people who benefited were the priests who ate the meat."

Helen pulled her hand away from his. "Why did our ancestors bring their sheep and goats to be sacrificed? Wasn't it to show their devotion to *Hashem?* Better than human sacrifice. And, by the way, the prayer for restoration is still in the *siddur* we use at *Etz Ahaim*, although I don't actually think we should build a Third Temple."

"Sorry to offend. It's time for you to change the prayers. Why pray for something you don't believe in? And so what if Jews substituted animals for humans? Why is any sacrifice ever necessary? Why does a god require someone to kill a part of his flock? His livelihood? Why is any killing good?"

"So you're a vegetarian?"

"No."

She sighed. "You were devoted once yourself, Nicky. Even way back, when you first came into my folks' house, you studied Talmud with Rabbi Amar."

He shrugged. "Only for a few months, as I recall." He put down his fork, told the waiter who just then appeared that they'd not be having dessert, and asked for the check.

"It doesn't matter. You studied with him, even though you didn't believe in *Hashem?*"

"I studied Talmud to clear my head of college work. I needed a break every once in a while, and it was a hobby, an intellectual exercise, as engaging and complicated as the *Times* crossword. I haven't picked up a volume of Talmud since."

"I wonder if you're as much an atheist as you claim. I'm sure you know that most *Shoah* survivors didn't lose their faith in *Hashem*, regardless of their suffering."

"You'd rather that I return to believing, wouldn't you?"

"Honestly, yes. We're so different in that way. It's a wall between us."

"It doesn't have to be. It's a wall only if we make it such."

"It's there, the wall, whether we acknowledge that it's there or ignore it. And this is more than our relationship. It's you, Nicky Covo, with or without me. Who you are, who you became, who you forced yourself to be. Who you might still be someday."

"Our relationship. I do like the sound of that. That's what's important to me right now."

"Don't you see what disbelief has done to you, Nicky? What it's cost you? To turn your back on your heritage. Our heritage."

"Is my face such an open book?"

"We've spent a lot of time together. And I've ..."

"I've loved every minute."

"Nicky, please listen. Just stop for a second and try to listen to me for a change. I've had clients who were survivors. They suffered, as you did. They lost their families, as you did. Your choice – to reject *Hashem* – hasn't been good for you."

"So you want to cure me of atheism. You want to be my therapist."

Their check paid, they pushed back their chairs simultaneously. It had become chilly in the early evening, and Nicky helped Helen on with her light jacket.

"I'm not trying to cure you," she continued. "I don't want to be your therapist. That's the last thing I would want."

"Then what?"

"I'm trying to protect myself."

CHAPTER TWO

Athens, Greece, April 20, 1990 (Friday)

Their plan had been to spend a day in Athens, then fly directly to Thessaloniki and drive north to the monastery. When Nicky called from Athens to confirm, however, Fevronia surprisingly put him off. Easter had only just passed, and there were too many pilgrims and other visitors to the monastery who'd not yet left. She'd be busy dealing with them, as would Sister Theodora, who was being called upon to hear extra confessions. It would be much better to visit when they both had more time. Could Nicky and Helen possibly delay visiting until the end of their time in Greece?

Nicky reluctantly agreed. When he explained the change of plans to Helen, she seemed oddly relieved, observing that, once they'd met Sister Theodora, it might be hard to do anything else of a touristy nature. She'd hoped they might find a beautiful beach to lie on together under the delicious Mediterranean sun.

Two nights before they were to leave Athens for a trip by car into the mountains, Helen, after a brief kiss, pushed Nicky away outside her hotel room door. Nicky retreated to his room, angry with himself for wanting to prolong the kiss inside Helen's room and for allowing himself to be scuttled down the hall.

Although he'd known from the beginning that he wanted Helen along with him, he was wondering whether his intense desire for her could complicate things. The mission upon which he'd embarked would be complicated enough without being in love with Helen. Yet, he knew that he already loved her, had loved her for months, and had loved her decades before.

Even as he savored Helen's kiss, a tide of guilt washed over him. If Adel observed Nicky from another world, she would be enormously jealous. She'd know that Helen was beautiful, and she'd feel herself plain in comparison. She'd know that Helen was intelligent and clearheaded, and she'd know – as she'd always known – that her own mind was irreparably clouded by schizophrenia. She'd know that Helen was well spoken and know that she, herself, even at her best, frequently spoke in riddles, rhymes, and non-sequiturs. She'd know that Helen was healthy, hardly showing her age, whereas she suffered from side effects of psychiatric medications. In short, Nicky uneasily felt that Adel might watch him substitute for her a more desirable model of a woman. There was a small part of him that felt he needed to remain loyal to Adel by never involving himself with anyone else. He owed that loyalty to Adel because she'd been the only person to fully understand his pain. But the other part of him, the much larger and stronger part, loved Helen. She was his present and, he hoped, his future.

Unable to sleep, he dressed again, went down to the front desk, and asked for a road map of Greece and a highlighter. Entering the bar, he saw a few touristy-looking couples and an odd assortment of businessmen lounging with drinks. In the background, he heard a solo guitar playing Greek music, a tune he knew by heart but had not heard for ages. He sat at the last empty table, ordered a sweet local wine, Black Laurel, and spread out the map. With the highlighter, he traced his intended route from Athens to Ioannina to Salonika and ultimately to Inousa. He downed his wine quickly and ordered another, closed his eyes to listen to the music, and unconsciously began tapping his foot.

"Planning a trip?"

Someone had spoken to him in Greek. He looked up to see a good-looking man, likely in his mid-seventies, tall and thin, with blond hair turning whitish grey, a well-trimmed beard and mustache, another conservative businessman on holiday, dressed in a light grey sports jacket over a white turtleneck. Nicky was confused for a second until the man, smiling, pointed to the map.

"It looks like you're covering a lot of territory."

"Oh. I guess so," Nicky responded in Greek.

"I'm Georgios Raptis. You seem familiar somehow."

"Nicky Covo." Nicky extended his hand, and the stranger grabbed it firmly and held it longer than Nicky liked. Now the guitar chords that he'd appreciated only moments before began to annoy him. They were too loud, too aggressive, discordant. It was near midnight, and the music should have been softer, mellower, and perhaps sadder. He remembered finally that Raptis was still standing near him.

"Please, sit. I'm sorry, I don't recognize you. I'm American."

Raptis sat and ordered his own glass of port when the waitress immediately appeared. "American, you say, yet your Greek is flawless. Back to the homeland now, for business or pleasure?" Nicky did not respond, pretending not to have heard, pretending to be engrossed by the music, nodding his head ever so slightly in what he hoped was a semblance of the rhythm. He sipped his wine and looked away, wanting Raptis to move on after he was served. Raptis stayed, though, and asked permission to look more closely at Nicky's map. Permission reluctantly granted, Raptis studied it for a minute, then pushed it back and began talking about himself. Nicky's initial hunch had been correct; Raptis was a shipping company executive and had just concluded a client meeting. Then Raptis pointed to the map again.

"All the way to Ioannina, I see. I was born and grew up there, still have family there. Where in Greece are you from originally?"

"Salonika. A long time ago. In America since '46. First trip back."

"Indeed."

As Nicky refolded the map, Raptis studied Nicky's face. Nicky looked toward the bar as if trying to find his date, feeling more uncomfortable by the second. Suddenly, Raptis reached out and grabbed Nicky's arm. "Chrisma!"

Nicky jumped. "What?"

"We called you Chrisma. Comrade Chrisma. We fought together. Surely you remember?"

"You must be mistaken," said Nicky weakly, his heart banging but seeming not to pump blood to his brain. He felt faint. How could someone from that horrible time happen upon him in Athens of all places and, worse, recognize him? An intense wave of nausea broke over him. "Excuse me." He escaped to the men's room and made it to a toilet just in time. The wine pooling under his face had left a bitter, burning taste. Nicky felt the urge to hide in the lavatory until morning, but he heard the stranger's insistent voice from outside the stall; he'd been followed, and hiding was not an option.

"You okay, Nicky? Sorry I startled you. Please, let's talk about the old times. I won't bite."

Nicky vomited again, wiped his mouth with toilet paper, counted to twenty, slowly stood, and emerged from the stall. "Do you want me to get someone to look after you?" Raptis's voice was gentle.

"Not necessary, but thanks. I guess I'm not used to Black Laurel."

Nicky washed himself and wondered whether he was obliged by simple civility to sit with Raptis a few more minutes. He could certainly excuse himself in light of his having been sick, and the man would understand. But he felt in a way like a moth attracted to a flame. He was fascinated as well as appalled by having been discovered. He decided that they could exchange a few more pleasantries before he said good night. They returned to their table, where Nicky's map still lay, and ordered club sodas. The guitar music had been replaced by bouzouki and drums playing traditional Greek music with an insistent beat.

"I was Churchill then, remember?" Raptis asked sadly, frowning, as if he regretted having dropped so far in rank after the war.

Nicky remembered well that some fighters had chosen *nom de guerre* of prominent statesmen. He thought that there might've been a Roosevelt who'd shown him how to fire his 98K. And of course there was Stalin. Never forget Stalin, the leader of his band of *andartes* that had allowed him to eviscerate the German corporal. He shuddered at the memory, hoping that Raptis wouldn't notice. But was Raptis really Churchill? No reason there couldn't have been a Churchill in the group. In fact, it was likely that there *had* been a Churchill, yet he couldn't recall the face in front of him.

"I'm sorry, Georgios, you don't look familiar. Yes, I did fight and, yes, they did call me Chrisma. I didn't pick it. In fact, I hated the name. I'm amazed you recognize me after all these years, but when exactly were we together?"

"Give me your map again, please." He took it from Nicky, then traced a small arc over the yellow highlighting through Mt. Tsoumerka, Charakopi, and Ioannina. "All through here." He paused. "You're planning on going back, obviously."

"I wonder if there's still snow in the mountains."

"Chrisma ... I'm sorry, Nicky, I remember now that you had the most amazing luck."

"I'm not sure I want to talk about this. I need to sleep."

Raptis gripped Nicky's arm with the strength of a young man. "By God, do you remember that ruined church?" Raptis's voice turned sly, like a conspirator. He'd asked the question that Nicky feared most. Nicky tried to get up, but couldn't move. Raptis's smile was now ugly, sneering, cruel. Nicky could not move, frozen by Raptis's words. He tried to keep guilt from showing on his face. "A horrible scene," Raptis continued. "The work of *Phriké*, the Goddess of Horror, yes? We saw many such horrors in those months, *nai*? My poor father, killed by the Germans." Raptis's smile became grotesque.

Only then did it come to Nicky. Raptis – of course, he'd known him as Churchill – was the comrade who'd seen Nicky try to annihilate himself with his own Mauser, who'd lifted him to his feet, reloaded the pistol, and handed it back. Who'd seen the girl in the yellow smock Nicky had just killed. Had seen the blood still pouring from her body. You're needed for the fight, he'd said, so either kill yourself now or get a move on. We don't have time to waste because of your sorrow at the death of this girl. It's a war.

Nicky forced himself to stand and tossed a 10,000 *drachma* note onto the table.

"Perhaps we'll run into each other again," Raptis offered. "I'm visiting my sister in Ioannina in a few days."

Raptis extended his hand, but Nicky turned and quickly, although unsteadily, walked away.

CHAPTER THREE

Athens, Trikala, and Kalabaka, Greece, April 22, 1990 (Sunday)

They started to the mountains. He wanted to follow the route on which he'd been smuggled in 1943 but wasn't sure which roads had been used. He'd been asleep then, and decades later the roads were different and better. Traffic was light. They'd driven for an hour when Helen closed her guide book and said, "I've heard that the beaches of Chalkis are beautiful. Maybe we should stop there for the day? Or at least the afternoon?"

"Never been there." As they whizzed past the Chalkis exit on the E75, he glanced at her.

"Well, I did pack a bathing suit," Helen said, dejectedly. "Like you told me to? Or begged me to? I'd hoped ..."

"Don't worry, we'll have the chance, near Salonika. The beach at Peraia perhaps, although I imagine the water will be too cold for swimming. By the way, aren't you hungry?"

"Sometimes you amaze me."

"What?"

"Why did you invite me along? Why were you so persistent? Just to ignore me when I asked for something? I thought you wanted to see me in a bathing suit, modest though it is. Is losing one day to share a warm beach with me such a catastrophe that you can't even consider it?"

As if in response, Nicky sped up to overtake a slow-moving eighteen-wheel truck bearing the large white name "Accorsi" on its red-painted sides. "Of course it's not a catastrophe. We'll do it, I promise. And, yes, I'd love to see you in your modest bathing suit. But Helen, please. Can we put off beaches until after the monastery? There are so many other things I need to see and do now, and the mountains should be as beautiful as any beach. More beautiful in fact. The sky so close you can touch it."

"Whatever."

He stole a glance at Helen and was relieved to see that she was not frowning, although she couldn't have been described as smiling either. She was merely fussing with the settings on her Nikon. Grudgingly accepting, he thought. "Meanwhile, lunch. Shall we find a place in Trikala?"

"Do I have a choice?"

"It's only about another half-hour."

"Drive on," she ordered.

As he once again sped up, Nicky regretted his decision to ignore Helen's request for a side trip to Chalkis. A distant image of seeing Helen in a swimsuit formed, a faded memory of having been with her and David at a neighborhood pool in 1946 kept forcing its way into his mind.

Until now, their goodnight kisses in Greece had been sweet and short, their physical relationship not having developed since their first few dates. As they'd said goodnight on the previous evening, though, she'd let him touch her breasts briefly. The thought of Helen on a beach and his memory of the previous evening brought desire back into him, as if he'd been injected with aphrodisiac chemicals. Let's drop the pretense of being friends, he wanted to scream. We need to get past this barrier, make this a honeymoon, then it won't matter if we're on a beach. He decided to seize the moment.

"Helen, about tonight."

"What about tonight? We haven't even stopped for lunch." He thought he detected the sound of amusement in her voice, as if she'd been reading his mind, indeed, as if she were many steps ahead of him.

"Do you think, wherever we stay, we might do tonight with only one room?" With his right hand, he gently caressed the back of her head. She leaned into his caress, and he imagined that she was closing her eyes.

"Mmm. That's nice. One room, did you say?"

"Do we need more?"

"You're trying to save a few *drachma*, aren't you? You, a pretty well-off guy?"

"Not exactly. Although that might be a side benefit."

"Getting just one room might bring on a scandal, you know. Your kids. What would they say if they found out? What would Jackie say? What about *my* kids and grandkids?"

She didn't sound scandalized. He brought his hand to the base of her neck and continued as best he could to massage her, happy to hear her continued sighs.

"Well, I'm willing to take a risk. We don't have to tell anyone we don't want to know."

"Let me think about it."

For a couple of seconds, he wasn't sure what to make of her noncommittal answer. Was she truly thinking about the risk of scandal? Did it matter so much to her what her children might say? She was an adult, a woman in charge of her life and a woman who certainly deserved not to be lonely.

Then she started to laugh, and he feared that his appeal had been rejected, feared that he was being made fun of. He nervously laughed in return, and Helen's laughter increased. What was the joke? She had to be laughing at him, thinking him a fool. Helpless, unable to think, he punched her lightly on the arm, intending to divert her from her laughter, but his punch was not as light as he'd intended.

"Ow!"

"Time's run out. You've thought about it plenty. Say no if that's what you want to say."

"No? Why ever would I say no? One room. Sure." She reached out for his right hand and brought it to lips, offering a kiss of surrender. Then she bit down on his index finger, and he jerked back his hand. "That's for the punch."

"Fair enough."

They pulled into Trikala at two in the afternoon. Nicky – in giddy anticipation of their lovemaking – had half a mind to suggest that they find a hotel immediately, yet thought it better to get back on the road after lunch. There were still many miles before them on their trip to the mountains, and there'd be plenty of time later in the day to make real what Helen had promised.

As they sat at a sidewalk café, though, Nicky's exhilaration faded, replaced by the sickening feeling that Raptis had followed them. He knew the idea was crazy, but he felt the weight of Raptis's presence like a heavy wooden yoke. The air seemed thick with the smell of Raptis, a foul smell like sewage. Nicky looked around, trying to appear interested in the town, trying to pay attention to Helen's chatting, trying not to look worried. He felt himself sweating even though minutes before the air had been pleasantly cool. Then, to his horror, he spotted the tall, thin man with the neatly trimmed beard and mustache, white silver hair, ducking behind the closest corner. He almost got up to run after – it had to have been Raptis – and jump him, pummel his face into the sidewalk, order him to stay away, but he managed instead to turn back to Helen and force a smile.

"Nicky, what's got into you? Have you been listening to me?"

He'd not told Helen about Raptis, embarrassed to have been recognized by the one person in Greece who'd known that he shot and killed the young girl in a yellow smock. Inside a church, no less. Now, he wished that he'd told Helen about his strange encounter in the hotel bar as soon as it had happened.

"Oh, nothing. Just thought I saw someone I knew." He cast his gaze once more across the crowded square. Ordinary people went about their lives, nothing amiss. There were the usual restaurant smells of gyros roasting on rotating spits, of fish frying. Maybe he'd only imagined the sewage.

"This town isn't much, is it?" Helen observed, as a waiter handed them menus. The circular wooden table at which they sat was hardly big enough to hold two plates, although four chairs sat around it. "Order me a plain salad, please, and a diet Coke with lemon. When we Americans think of Greece, the pictures that come to mind are of ancient ruins and temples and ..."

"And beaches."

"And sun-bathed beaches, yes. Not plain vanilla towns, dirty at that." She brushed a few crumbs from their table onto the concrete floor.

"No, Trikala wouldn't be high on a list of tourist attractions. It's a place to travel through. Kalabaka, on the other hand, will be much better. That's the next town. We can tour the famous monasteries, then find a hotel." As he sipped water, he imagined Helen's body against his, neither encumbered by clothes. He worried that she might think him too fat around the middle and thought of pulling the shades closed to keep their room dark.

"Did you ever visit Kalabaka? I've seen the pictures in the guide book. Looks fascinating."

"If I did, my head was bouncing on the inside of the trunk of a car."

Helen winced.

"Let's change the subject, Helen. You look gorgeous." She was wearing a white blouse, a dark blue skirt, and a blue sweater. She rested her fingers lightly on his forearm.

"Well, thank you. I don't feel quite so gorgeous. The years have done a number on me, I'm afraid."

"Don't be ridiculous. You're as lovely as you were when we first met, and, as I think about it, you're wearing the same kind of outfit you did that evening." But the years had indeed had some effect on Helen, he thought, as they'd had on him.

"You're kidding. You remember what I wore on a certain night in February 1946? Come on."

Helen smiled, the smile told Nicky that she wanted to hear more, and he felt great relief and happiness that she enjoyed his company. Now that they were on the way toward real intimacy, engaged as it were, he relaxed. Stupid to worry that a man out of his past was following him. "One doesn't forget one's first day in America. I was obsessed with trying to observe everything, understand everything at once."

"You had your hands full dealing with English. That I well recall."

"True, I struggled with the language, but I also paid attention to details at the same time. I wanted very badly to learn about my new family. I wanted to fit in. I wanted not to make a fool of myself."

"Details, you say? For twenty dollars, the answer is: 'the clothing that Irene wore when first seen by Nicky Covo.'"

He thought for a second, then scrunched up his face, as if in deep thought. "What was ...? I haven't the faintest idea. I guess I didn't pay that much attention."

She made a buzzing sound. "I see. So, what was Catherine wearing?"

He shrugged. "You got me."

She looked at him as if wanting to say something, then simply reached for his hand. "This is going to be a big step for me, Nicky."

"For me too."

"In Kalabaka, don't you think we should find a place first, check in, and then tour the monasteries? I mean, after?"

There was an unmistakable quality of barely repressed desire in her voice, like a Siren call, which made his heart beat faster, yet, rather than give in to desire immediately, he wanted to demonstrate control. "Once we find a room, we're not going to want to leave it, so let's tour first." She looked down quickly, trying, he decided, to hide her disappointment. "Tour first, but not too much."

"All right." She pointed to a photograph in her guide book. "The Fodor's has impressive pictures of Varlaam Monastery."

"We'll make it our destination."

· · · · ·

An hour later, they drove into Kalabaka. High, craggy peaks crowded around them, atop of which sat the monasteries for which the town was famous. They found the narrow road that wound its way up to Varlaam, and the shadow of the mountain quickly enveloped them.

"God, there's no shoulder here. Slow down, Nicky. I'm afraid of heights." Helen gripped her seat with both hands.

"Sorry."

Nicky slowed the car to a crawl as he navigated a hair-pin turn, and the trees at the side of the road suddenly fell away, their world brightening again. From cramped darkness, they suddenly saw the countryside in a vista that spilled out for miles.

"*Baruch Hashem*! Stop so I can take pictures."

Nicky obliged, and she stepped out of the car with her Nikon, standing close to the sharp drop off, shooting at the town below and the facing peak. Then she fiddled off her regular lens and popped on a wide-angle lens, trying to gather the entire expanse before her in one good shot.

"So you're afraid of heights," he laughed, as she reentered the car.

"Drive," she commanded in a taxi passenger voice.

They found the turnoff for the monastery, parked in a small, crowded lot, located the narrow staircase, and climbed what seemed hundreds of steps, crisscrossing the face of a cliff, stopping often to catch their breaths. Nicky felt faint-headed with the exertion of the climb, compounded by the thin air. At the top, they were greeted by an even more breathtaking view than they'd seen from the road. After Helen shot more photos, Nicky dizzily leaned his head in toward her ear, and whispered, "Don't you think we've seen enough today? Want to find our room now?"

She reached a hand up behind his neck and held him close. "I'd ask you to kiss me, but we're in a holy place." She indicated the chapel and museum behind her. "Now be patient. I wanted to find the hotel first, remember? You said no. So we're here, we need to go in for a few minutes. We'll never be back to have a second chance, will we?"

"We'll make it quick."

They found themselves in a gallery displaying religious objects. Nicky was drawn immediately to a picture of Mary and Jesus painted on a wood panel. The legend explained that the icon was believed to date from the 14th century. He wanted to draw Helen's attention to it, tell her how much it reminded him of the icon he'd thrown into the woods, yet before he could say anything his lightheadedness returned, much stronger. It was as if a powerful fragrance of roses had infiltrated his head and blocked oxygen from reaching his brain. He was conscious of his knees growing wobbly and his inability to steady them. He began to shake like a dying leaf in a windstorm and instinctively reached for Helen. Luckily, she got her arms around him and guided him to a bench, where she forced him to sit with his head down.

"Take a deep breath and let it out slowly," she directed. "Again." He complied and felt the blood slowly return to his brain. "Do you have pain?" He shook his head and sat up slowly, concentrating on his breathing, Helen holding him. The floral scent had almost entirely disappeared, but Nicky wondered whether he'd ever forget it. When he felt he was breathing normally, he slowly lifted his head and looked at Helen, sorry to see the worried look on her face. Finally, she coaxed him to stand. "You had me scared, but you seem okay now, *Baruch Hashem.*"

"I'm so sorry. Not sure what happened. The thin air? The climb? I think I'm better now."

"Then let's get back to the car."

They walked even more cautiously down the steps than they'd walked up a quarter hour earlier. In the car, their kiss was short. Helen asked Nicky twice to slow as he drove toward town. Again, she gripped the seat. When the road leveled off, they saw a sign pointing to the Guesthouse Papastathis, and two quick turns brought them to it. Guesthouse Papastathis looked rundown to Nicky, hardly better than what they might've found in Trikala. Rundown, maybe, yet serviceable. He was mildly disappointed.

He signed the register as Mr. and Mrs. Nicky Covo. If Helen noticed, she said nothing. Their second-story room had twin beds and a balcony that faced the town and up to the mountain they'd just descended. Nicky pulled the curtains tight and locked the door. Daylight still seeped into the room; so much for hiding his paunch. He put his arms around her and they kissed. When he started to fondle her, she stepped back.

Helen said, with a nervous smile, "I've never made love with anyone other than David." He stepped toward her again and began to unbutton her blouse. "But I want you now, Nicky."

•　　•　　•　　•　　•

Nicky hadn't shared a bed with anyone since Adel. On the drive to Kalabaka, he'd been thinking about the difficulties he and Adel had experienced. Five years before her death, they'd given up sex entirely; the diminishing returns were not worth the effort. On the way down from Varlaam, he'd found himself worrying, not about almost passing out, but about not being able to perform for Helen. Now, all he thought of was the likelihood – no, the certainty – of failure. He went embarrassingly soft.

As it turned out, Helen was not a quitter. She held him quietly, telling him through her touch, as opposed to words, to relax. Her skin felt firm and smooth next to his. Her fragrance was musky and rich, and he imagined them lying on a field of freshly cut grass under a warm sun. He let his body grow heavy, like lead. She waited until his breathing slowed. When he inhaled deeply and sighed, she climbed on him, whispered to him to keep his eyes closed, and, after a minute, Nicky responded. They made love like two scared teenagers, he thought, or better like senior citizens long out of practice. Before either could climax, they ran out of energy. When a limp Nicky fell out of her, they both laughed. Their laughter soon turned to tears of hilarity, requiring them to use floral-scented tissues from the box on the night table. In a few minutes, they settled down to sleep.

•   •   •   •   •

Sunlight sneaking past the drawn curtains crept up the wall. Nicky awoke with a start. As he held Helen, still deep in slumber, thoughts tumbled through his mind: the coming encounter with Sister Theodora; his discovery by Raptis, otherwise known as Churchill; finding himself in the middle of Greece, lying next to a naked Helen; his inability to perform despite his desperation to please. Slowly, he turned, trying not to wake her. He thought again of the last night he'd spent with Adel, her sudden cry of pain, her gasping for breath, how he'd called 9-1-1 and started CPR. Adel died in the ambulance just the same. The ambulance was the last thing he envisioned before falling asleep again.

At about eight, Nicky – hungry, thirsty, badly needing to urinate – awoke, while Helen slept on. He wondered now about their relationship. Would it survive beyond Greece? Away from the strangeness of foreign soil, Helen might not want it to continue. If she did, either or both of their families might rebel against their romance. Her deeply religious family, because Nicky was a nonbeliever. His family, because they might feel – despite Kayla's assurances – that two years after Adel's death was too soon for his serious involvement with another woman. And how *would* he and Helen manage together? Would he keep his apartment in Manhattan and practice in Brooklyn and see her only occasionally? Give up the city to move to Highland Park? Either way, a host of sacrifices on his part.

Helen stirred and turned toward him.

"You've been up?"

"For a while. It was nice, just holding you, thinking about our making love."

"Mmm." Her eyes were closed; she'd not fully awakened. He traced his hand along her side and down to her knee.

"*Erotevménos.*"

"I love it when you talk dirty."

"It means we're in love."

"I knew that."

Her breath came faster. He felt himself stirring. His hand continued to feather small circles on her body. In a minute, she crawled on top again. Again, they were able to make love, just barely, and only for a minute until Nicky grew soft. As before, neither came close to orgasm.

"Don't worry, Nicky. We'll get there. It's the newness holding us both back, but it'll get better."

"Right," said Nicky, lacking conviction.

He headed into the bathroom, needing a shower, wanting to separate himself from her for just a while. Naked, testing the water with his hand, he thought of the drugs in his toilet bag, how it would be possible to be dead within minutes, long before Helen realized that the shower had run for way too long. Yet, he did not despair as he stepped gingerly into the shower, the bathroom filling with steam. He wanted to believe Helen's confident, loving promise that they would get there.

CHAPTER FOUR

Outside Kalabaka, Greece, April 23, 1990 (Monday)

The E92 climbed steadily out of Kalabaka. To the east, tall cliffs thrust themselves from the rolling land, like stegosaurus spikes. At their base, villages of stone houses capped by red tile roofs sped by. In late April, small patches of snow clung tenaciously to the roadsides. In Malakasi, they caught the four-lane A2 west. Now the mountains were to their right and the vast drop to the left splayed out for miles, the morning mist lightly screening hues of green, brown, and gray.

"Do you remember any of this, Nicky? It's amazing. Breathtaking."

"There weren't well-paved roads like this in '44. Driving here was rough."

Near Koutselio, they exited the A2, and in minutes Nicky admitted he was lost. For a while, he studied the map he'd marked up previously, only to toss it into the back seat next to Helen's Nikon. He felt stupid, embarrassed that he wasn't in as much control as he'd hoped.

"It's all Greek to you, right?" asked Helen, but Nicky ignored her attempt at a joke.

They stopped next to a small park to ask directions. Nicky approached a family – a mother, father, and two young girls – who sat at a picnic table eating their lunch. It was a scene more appropriate for July than April, but they seemed to be enjoying their Sunday outing together. After a short conversation, Nicky returned to Helen and saw her studying her own, larger map. Where had that come from? He took it from her and perused it briefly.

"This road goes up to the river and then farther into the mountains," he said as he pointed.

"You fought here?"

"Nearby," Nicky grunted. "We're actually not far at all."

They drove a mile outside the town and stopped the car on a bridge over rushing water. "Here," said Nicky. "This river. The Arachthos. This bridge." They got out to look more closely at the river, flowing fast with the spring thaw. Helen leaned against the rusted iron guard rail.

"It's beautiful, Nicky."

"As slender as you are, Helen, I wouldn't trust that to hold your weight." She stepped back quickly and clutched Nicky's arm.

"I need photos," she said.

He didn't see the beauty of the river or the surrounding woods, didn't appreciate the hills with their budding trees. Nothing was beautiful or breathtaking for him. He felt himself rather walking into a jigsaw of a battle, a puzzle piece with misshapen edges looking for its neighbors. Despite Helen's presence, he lost track of the fact that it was 1990. For Nicky, it was again the winter of 1943-1944.

"It's so peaceful," she said, letting her camera hang from its strap at her side.

"Here's where I saw the first dead NRGL soldiers." He pointed to one side. "Here's where I told them about the peasant I killed." He pointed to another. "Here's where I stepped in blood." He pointed to the middle of the bridge. "There was hardly a place to walk that wasn't covered in blood. Greek blood, sadly."

Helen shuddered. "It's just a road now, though, isn't it?"

"Let's get back in the car. We need to go farther." He pointed to the top of the mountain. "It won't take long."

Within minutes, they began their ascent, the turns as sharp as on the road to the Varlaam monastery. Helen said nothing, again clutching the seat.

"That winter, this was little more than a dirt path. Let's see. I think he came around this bend. I was up there." He pointed out vaguely toward the left. "Somewhere along here is .... Yes."

He stopped the car and studied the hillside above them.

Despite his claim that he'd found a familiar spot, everything along the roadway looked exactly the same to him as everything else. Each turn, each bunch of trees, duplicated every other. The puzzle pieces he looked at could have fit anywhere. Relief mixed with regret: if every place looked the same, stopping here was as good as stopping there. He'd spend a minute pretending to search, and they'd move on.

"Stay with the car, Helen, I need to look for something."

"Nicky, don't ..."

He slammed the door, crossed the road, and climbed, grabbing bushes and tree trunks to steady himself over the ground slippery with shards of ice and loose rubble. He knew dimly that he'd left Helen in a dangerous spot, their car vulnerable to collision with any other vehicle coming down the mountain at normal speed. Nonetheless, he pawed through deep grass among the pines until he saw Helen scrambling up toward him.

"You're kidding, Nicky. You're trying to find that icon?"

He frowned, annoyed that Helen had disobeyed his instructions. "Maybe."

"You are," she sighed. "Well, in for a dollar. No one who valued sanity would believe what I'm doing."

She herself began kicking through tufts of grass, gradually moving away from Nicky. After a few minutes, ready to call a halt, Nicky saw her bend at a clump of trees and reach down toward a cave of gnarled roots to pick up something. She brushed mud off the object as he approached. He took from her hands a dark silver, rectangular case with a small circular window showing the face of a woman.

"This must be it," she needlessly pointed out.

He turned the object around cautiously, as if it might explode, then opened the case to see the faint outline of a Madonna and Child. The shape he remembered, the general feel, weight, and image. He grabbed at Helen.

"How ...?"

"Easy, now."

He looked around him as if the object's owner might be lurking nearby, waiting for him, ready to ensnare him in an iron trap. But he saw no one other than Helen. The morning had grown still, the brisk April breeze that he'd been sure had ruffled treetops only moments earlier had suddenly taken a break. "It was lunacy to think this might still be here, even more so to think we would find it."

"*Hashem* just meant it to be."

"It can't be."

"This is the very icon you told me about. We wouldn't have found it here otherwise."

He wanted to deny, because he did not rationally comprehend how, after forty-six years, the object was where he'd thrown it and that he'd remembered. The chances were microscopically small. But he couldn't deny. As he looked at it, remembering its dead owner crumpled nearby, he knew it was the same. No doubt, it was the same.

"It is."

"Then consider it one of *Hashem's* miracles, Nicky."

He wanted to dispute with her that a supernatural force had aided their discovery of the icon, had even preserved much of the painting within the case. Even as he clung to Helen and fought the urge to cry, his brain told him that he must have remembered exactly where he'd killed the man, despite the astronomical odds. He wanted to tell her point blank that it was no miracle, that miracles were just a figment of the imagination, and that there were rational explanations for everything. Yet, as if a tiny circuit breaker in his brain had been deactivated, his desire to dispute disappeared. Helen's presence, Helen's having found the icon, made all the difference in what he would or wouldn't say. For the first time, he felt Helen's belief in God – whom she would refer to only as *Hashem*, "The Name" – to be a particularly lovable part of her. He'd say nothing to dissuade her, but neither would he credit her interpretation.

"Maybe," he said.

"I'm angry ...."

"Now that we've found it – that you've found it – we need to give this to a priest, someone who can take care of it properly."

"Angry. Did you hear? You shouldn't have left me there." Helen gestured toward the car.

"The man I killed probably thought this would protect him."

"Killed is what I might have been. Do you care? Are you even listening to me?"

"Sorry. Of course I care. Did you hear *me*, though? The man I gunned down was likely a grandfather. He loved his grandchildren, and they never saw him again. Just an old man out for an early morning walk."

She balled up her fists. "You told me that he was running toward you, not walking, but please, either way, stop tearing yourself apart. It does no good. Give me that."

Helen took the icon and rubbed more dirt off with the sleeve of her sweater. "You know, we're on our way to a monastery. We should give this to Abbess Fevronia. She must know the right people to restore it and say the right *bracha* or psalm. Maybe she'd even tell us something about this icon, what it means."

Nicky didn't answer, but shuddered as he felt the Karabiner still spitting out death.

CHAPTER FIVE

Dodoni and Ioannina, Greece, April 23, 1990 (Monday)

They drove down the A05 towards Ioannina, past broken fields bordered by scrubby pine and telephone poles, a VW dealership, the Epirus Palace Hotel, a few scattered houses, and a couple of commercial buildings that looked like they'd been abandoned before construction had been completed. The sky grew somber with rain clouds. Nicky slowed their car and pulled to the shoulder to allow a long stream of vehicles to pass.

"Where exactly are we?" asked Helen. "This road gives me the creeps."

"I think we've gone too far." He hated himself for having lost his way for the second time in the same morning.

"Now you tell me."

He again took the larger map from Helen, studied it for the fifth time that day, and looked around for signs, finding none. "Damn. It doesn't look like anything I remember along this road."

"Is it so important we find that church? We have the icon. Isn't that enough?" She tilted her head toward the back seat, where the piece of metal, wrapped in *H Αυγή*, a daily newspaper, rested next to her bag. "And how likely is it anyway that they rebuilt a ruined church in what you call a tiny village?"

Without warning, he pulled into the heavy traffic and made a sudden U-turn, barely noticing the horns of angry drivers. "Hold on, I think I know where we need to go."

"There have to be a lot more interesting things to look at," she pouted.

In a minute, he exited the highway and swung down a country lane. They climbed into low hills and passed a sign telling them, in English, to watch out for ice. The lane rounded the base of a hill and came to a wider road, which finally brought them into a village. He parked outside a small stone church topped by a red tile dome. Like hundreds of others in Greece, he thought. It faced a village square, two cafés, and a few shops.

"We're in Dodoni. That's it. I never knew the name before. Look there. Ekklisia Triada."

"Which means?"

"Church of the Trinity, of course."

"Of course. Well, now what? Go in and ask if they remember the people killed there during the war?"

"You're coming with me, aren't you?"

"No. I'm getting a Diet Coke in that café. Meet you back here in ten minutes."

Nicky wasn't sure what he intended to do in the church, but the idea suggested by Helen – talk about the war with anyone old enough to remember – didn't seem unreasonable. As he closed his car door, a familiar voice sickened him.

"Chrisma!"

Even as Nicky turned, he knew it was impossible, but, yes, there was Raptis approaching rapidly, dress in the same clothes he'd worn at the Hotel Grand Britagne. Raptis displayed a broad grin, like an evil clown ready to bite off his head. Nicky flashed on Pennywise, the murderous villain of Stephen King's novel *It*.

"Nicky! So good to see you again. Not surprised to find you here."

"How …" The grotesque smile disappeared, and Nicky wondered whether he'd really seen it. The face now looking at him was a mildly pleasant, cordial face, a face that might have been an old friend's.

"I'm doing the same as you. Visiting the scene of the crime, so to speak. Who's that sharp looking woman you're with?"

Nicky ignored Raptis's question and extended hand. Suddenly, the village had fallen quiet, like a morgue. The April breeze, which moments before had made the day quite pleasant, had also faded away with the noise. The uncanny change in atmosphere was exactly as it had been hours before on the mountain when they found the icon. Helen was nowhere to be seen, disappeared into a café. Had she still been in view, he'd have called and begged her to return.

"Let's go in."

Raptis pulled Nicky by the arm. Nicky cringed at the touch, helpless, a piece of flotsam swept along by a river.

The church was empty and tiny, smaller than Nicky recalled. Four rows of wood benches framed the small, rectangular nave, and a brass chandelier hung from the dome. Icons of various shapes and sizes hung on every wall, of Jesus, Mary and Jesus, and others whom Nicky assumed were saints. The smell of incense reminded him of his sanctuary at Agios Nikolaos Ragavas and of Father Liakos conducting the Divine Liturgy. He turned toward the western wall and looked at the floor, half expecting to see a chalk outline of the girl's body.

"Here," he whispered to himself.

Raptis looked down as well. "We can ask, if you really want to. I can introduce you to the villagers as the trigger-happy partisan, Chrisma, who shot the young girl during the war. I'm sure they'd be pleased to meet you. Maybe her brother still lives. He'd remember for sure how his innocent sister was gunned down. I think it was her brother who found her body. What was she wearing then, when you killed her? A yellow smock, wasn't it? You kept talking about it for days."

Nicky looked at Raptis with loathing. How dare this fake Churchill intrude on Nicky's private grief? "You think I'm here to find punishment?"

"Isn't that what you deserve?"

"*Ani go-el hadam*," Nicky whispered to the girl lying on the floor, who wore a yellow smock, her chest pierced by bullets, blood spilling out. "*Ani.*" She lifted her hands toward him with a question and took her last breath as her eyes clouded and her hands fell. He saw that she would've been a mother of three, a solemn and religious woman, if she'd lived.

"I'm sorry?"

"*I am* the blood avenger, fully capable of punishing myself. No one else need apply."

"I'll save you the trouble."

Raptis pulled a dagger from a hidden sheath and pressed its edge against Nicky's throat, like a chef ready to carve. Pinch of metal against skin. Nicky readied himself for death and without thought began to recite the *Sh'ma.*

Nicky knelt and bowed his head to touch it to the cold floor next to the girl. Hot blood bathed his forehead. He stayed like that until he heard Helen's voice asking him yet again if he was all right.

"Let me die."

"This is too much. We've got to go."

With difficulty, Helen helped him back to his feet. He looked around. No dead girl, no blood, no one else, an empty church save for Helen and him.

"Where is he?"

"Where's who?"

"Raptis, the guy who pulled me in here and tried to cut my throat. Tall, thin, good-looking. Whitish blond hair. Beard, mustache."

"I haven't seen anyone else in or out of here. Now, back to the car." She pulled him toward the bright light of the plaza.

• • • • •

An hour later, Nicky picked disinterestedly at his gyro, trying to explain. There were few patrons in the restaurant they'd found on the outskirts of Ioannina, in the town of Pedini. Helen munched slowly on her cucumber salad, watching Nicky closely, her face stern.

"For an instant, I could see her. Bleeding, dying, dead. Wearing that yellow smock. And then Raptis ..."

"Raptis again? The tall man I happened not to notice? Good looking?"

"Churchill was his fighting name," he said. "Like I was Chrisma. In my platoon."

"I get it," she said. "I see why you might have imagined his being there with you just now."

She's going along with my craziness, he thought, the way I used to go along with Adel's, the way I'd deal with Kayla's hallucinations. "Churchill's the only person who knows I killed that poor girl. He gave me the chance to kill myself. Loaded my Mauser and handed it back to me. And, Helen, he *was* there in the church. It wasn't my imagination."

"Just happened to arrive when you did?"

Her tone, unbelieving, almost derisive. Nicky didn't answer. It hadn't been a hallucination. His arm still ached from the strong grip that had pulled him into the church. His neck still tingled unpleasantly from the press of

Raptis's dagger. If he'd only told Helen of meeting Raptis at the hotel in Athens, she might now believe him.

"Nicky, are you sure you want to go on with this part of the trip, through the war zone? Haven't you had enough? Nothing's stopping us, we could leave right now for that beach near Salonika, take long walks, eat, sleep, and ... well. And then after a few days of rest, we'd go to the monastery when we're expected. There's too much in these memories for you to manage. It's why we, in bed I mean ..." She sighed, looking down for a second. "What I mean is, for me too, please stop this constant reliving of every horrible thing you think you've done."

Failure in bed! He tried to suppress his anger, tried to appear calm. A fight between them would do no good. He didn't want Helen to alter his plans.

"We're almost done, only one more place I need to see, the church in Ioannina. It's probably not more than a ten minute drive from here, if I can find it."

"How many times now have I had to literally pick you up or save you from falling on your face?"

"But that church, you see, is where the German ..."

"Yeah, I know. The grenade."

"You don't understand."

"You've told me about it. You showed me what you wrote about it. Nicky, what possible good will it be for you to go there too? You've got that picture clear in your mind, so let's leave it like that, leave it with the little vignette you wrote. What'll you achieve by putting yourself there physically? After so many years?"

"Despite the years, the dead girl was still in the church, wearing yellow. She saw me before she died. She reached out, yet she knew I was the one who'd shot her. She was still warm, her blood wet and warm on my head. Who knows what I might see ..."

"Cut it out, Nicky. I've had it."

He understood at last that he'd taxed her mightily and unfairly with his demands, pushed her too far by describing what seemed an all-too real, if horrible, experience. Now that they'd become lovers, he saw that Helen clearly wanted a honeymoon-like trip. Instead, he was leading her on an impossibly dark tour through a battlefield. To stay with him, she'd had to crawl through dirt at the base of the Acropolis, kick her way through weeds on a steep hill, and pick him up or steady him – how many times was it now? – as he grew faint, cried, saw dead people, and otherwise forced himself to suffer. It occurred to him, too late he feared, that she'd reached and been forced beyond the limits of her endurance.

"I'm sorry, truly."

"Right, but ..."

"No, wait. I don't have a good idea how it will help me to see the church, I admit. But I need to. I can't explain it. And I'd like to see the old synagogue, too. You've been incredibly patient through all this, and ..."

"All right. Let's get it over with."

With relief, he heard that her voice had lost a small bit of its edge. She sounded merely resigned, and he assumed he could deal with that.

• • • • •

A bit later, they drove around Ioannina, looking for the synagogue that had survived the war.

"It wasn't until April 1944 that we got here, Helen. Too late to prevent the deportations. Too late by a month." Nicky repeated what he'd already told her multiple times. "I naively thought we could save them."

"You wanted to be a hero, but the time wasn't right," she said. "It's what *Hashem* decreed."

Turning a corner, Nicky saw the sign. "Aha. *Kahal Kadosh Yashan.*" He pulled over.

"It's good that it's still here." She looked up at the building. "Does it still operate as a *shul*?"

"I think so. Why any survivors returned, I can't imagine. Crazy, coming back to where their neighbors helped push them into the Nazi trucks. Let's look inside."

The front door was open.

"No security," said Nicky sourly. "Any thug could barge in and finish the job the Nazis started."

He was surprised at the size of the sanctuary. The vaulted ceiling had to be at least thirty feet high. A narrow stairway of eight steps climbed to the *bimah* along one wall. Two men sat, conversing, on one of the long wooden pews and looked up at them questioningly.

"Do you think they're survivors?" Helen whispered.

"Let's ask."

As they approached, the men rose, and one greeted them with a hearty "*Shalom.*" Both wore *kipot* and were dressed in dark suits. The greeter, as it turned out, looked old enough to have been there in 1944. A short, stout man, he sported a trim grey beard and mustache, dark frame eyeglasses, and smiled warmly. Nicky engaged them both in animated conversation. Finally, switching to English, he introduced Helen to a Rabbi Frizi, the younger man, and a Mr. Teachis, the older. Nicky thanked them, then took Helen's arm to lead her back to their car.

"So what was all that about?"

"Mr. Teachis was at Auschwitz. As the Germans pulled out, they abandoned him to die, and he damn near did. The rest of his family were gassed the day they arrived at the camp. His wife would not abandon their children."

"Did he remember anyone there from Salonika?"

"He's sure there were some, although he doesn't remember anyone specifically, certainly not my family. He said that they took young girls from Salonika for their medical experiments."

"How sad."

"My sister Ada would have been one of them."

"*Baruch Hashem*, the true judge."

"You know, I never ripped my clothing for them, even when I'd figured out that they'd died. I remember Papa doing it when my grandfather died."

"You've ripped yourself, instead. You couldn't possibly have done more ripping than what you've already done to your soul."

"Maybe not. But if my parents hadn't sent me to Athens, I'd have been there with them when they died."

"And died too."

"This ripping of myself. Isn't it what I deserved for running away?"

"Your parents saved your life by hiding you in Athens. You should be grateful for what they gave you instead of wishing you'd died with them."

"But we wouldn't have been separated. You don't understand how painful that was, how I've always felt I was a coward." Nicky put the key in the car's ignition but didn't turn it.

"You need to forgive your parents, Nicky, before you'll ever be able to love yourself the way you should. And to love others the way they should be loved."

"Auschwitz. I should've died there. And here, Ioannina, another place I should've died. I thought for a second I *was* dead. Well, as you said, you read about it." He looked across the street at the moss-covered stone wall that faced the old synagogue.

"Nicky, please. Think about *k'ria*, the ripping of clothes, how it's done once and it's over with."

He turned back to face her, but in his mind he recalled his father ripping his shirt at news of death. Had it actually been his grandfather's death? He still heard the sound of ripping, still felt the shock of seeing his father's torn shirt. His father had worn the shirt throughout the week of *shiva*, then discarded it. To lose, but not to forget, to tear, but then to resume one's life. He'd been taught that there must come a time of turning away from despair.

"Helen ...," he said with hesitation, needing to be sure; there would never be another chance. "I did want to return to the place where the grenade should've taken off my head. But, just now ..."

"Just now?"

"I've changed my mind."

"*Baruch Hashem.*"

He smiled. "You would bless God again, one of the things I love about you. I hope you don't mind skipping that last visit. I don't think you'll mind."

She'd blushed and looked down at the sound of the word "love," then looked up at him immediately when she understood that he was relinquishing control, at least for this last intended visit.

"Are you kidding? No, I don't mind at all missing out on this church."

They fell quiet for a minute, then saw Rabbi Frizi and Mr. Teachis leave the synagogue. Nicky and Helen waved to them and they waved back.

"Let's find a hotel, Nicky." She picked up her Fodor's, flipped a few pages, and said. "What about the Lake Hotel? Right on the shore, obviously."

"I don't know why I should've been looking for that church, anyway," he said. "I think tomorrow it's time to move on to Salonika and to the monastery the day after. That's the reason we came here in the first place."

"Agreed. But today, right here, right now, after we check in, can't we goof around for a while? Make our own walking tour? Pretend we're regular tourists, not on a mission?"

"A walking tour sounds great."

She looked again at her Fodor's. "Or what about the Archaeological Museum?"

"Why not dig into history?" He waited a few seconds for a laugh, which wasn't forthcoming. Only a pained look on Helen's face. "And then the Lake Hotel and try again, only better?"

"You do have your ideas, Nicky."

"I'm persistent."

"By the way, what was the name of that church? You've never mentioned the name."

He thought carefully for a few seconds before answering. "I don't think I ever knew. But let me see your Fodor's for a moment." He thumbed through the pages relating to Ioannina. "Hmm. It might well have been The Church of Saints Constantine and Helen."

"It figures," she chuckled.

CHAPTER SIX

Ioannina and Salonika, Greece, April 23-24, 1990 (Monday-Tuesday)

That night, they tried again to make love, with no more success than their prior efforts, subpar at best. He feared growing accustomed to failure, to embarrassment, to disappointment. Even as he attempted clumsily to join their bodies, Nicky's thoughts kept returning to the exploding grenade and the church that he'd agreed not to visit. He now regretted the decision, imagining that, if he'd only reentered the room in which he'd confronted his own death, he would finally understand what had happened there. It was too late for him to change his mind.

Unable to sleep, Nicky dressed quietly at 2 a.m., grabbed a few sheets of hotel stationery and a ballpoint pen from the desk, picked up his backpack, and went down to the lobby. He sat there at a small table in dim light, removed the envelope with his vignette, reread it, then closed his eyes to try to see it again in his mind. Memory was playing tricks on him. It couldn't have happened as he'd written it, as he'd always remembered it, and yet, if not, what *had* happened? Now in Ioannina, now as close to that church as he'd ever be, he would try once more to reimagine the scene, how it must have happened, and get it down on paper. It would be his last, best chance to get the visions out of his system and allow him to sleep. He moved to a leather sofa under a better light and used a copy of *Athenaika* magazine as a base for the stationery. The writing went slowly, particularly as the pen kept skipping, like the first time a child tries to skate on ice. Nonetheless, in a half-hour he'd written it up as well as he could.

Why did I expose myself like that? I felt drawn in, didn't I? Compelled, as if my fate had always been leading me to confront what was in the room. I can recall now that the one window showed that dawn had broken. Why would I remember that, given that I was stepping into a death trap? But I do remember. I remember that the German soldier who'd been crouched behind a desk was coming toward me, and I knew that my life would end in a flash, because the enemy – a boy hardly older than me – held a grenade ready to explode. He smiled, crazy, happy to kill himself if he could kill me too. I was about to let him destroy me, as my legs wouldn't move, cement blocks anchoring my feet. I always had thought that I'd fired my pistol wildly as I entered, but now I'm not sure I did so or that I cared to live beyond that last instant.

Then that flash of deep red, which I thought was the color of sunset in the moments before dark, but now think it must have been the earliest rays of sunlight. The flash that didn't come from the grenade. The flash that still seems to have swept into the room from the small window, and – I can see it now, better than I ever have before – swarmed around the German. I know the grenade exploded because I saw the blinding light where the German had stood. How could I still be looking at the German, though, his face gone, his body crumpling? I must have been stunned by that light, but at the same time – or maybe it was minutes later – I saw him, and it was like I'd been covered, protected by some kind of impervious blanket, feeling perhaps only a small puff of air, almost like a kiss on the cheek. And, in a small space where a grenade exploded, I'd have expected the explosion to deafen me, but it didn't, it was muffled, like someone coughing into his hand. I sensed, rather than saw, that the red from the window, the red that had flooded the room and swarmed around the German, disappeared as suddenly as it came. What lingered in the air now around me wasn't the smell of explosives or burning, but the scent of cinnamon. And maybe a scent of roses too. Why am I now remembering that? But in front of me was the dead German boy, his ravaged body torn through with shrapnel, just a mangled mess of bone, blood, and charred flesh. I stared at the body in shock, for how long I can't be sure. Then all I thought about was running outside and yelling that I was still alive.

He sat for a few minutes reading and rereading, comparing the typewritten version to the handwritten version, ultimately deciding that there was nothing else to write. He folded the pages of hotel stationery and placed them in the envelope with his previous effort at capturing that moment in words. Now, he glanced at his watch, and somehow it was already 3:30 a.m. He'd been sitting there for much longer than he'd thought. His eyelids were heavy with the need for sleep.

Helen was awake when he got back to the room, sitting up in bed in a hotel bathrobe, reading her Fodor's with the light from the night table.

"Where were you? What happened?"

"Nothing happened. I went to the lobby to write. About the grenade."

"Again? Please let me see."

He held out the new pages toward her. After a minute, she said "It's pretty much what you've written before. More detailed here, though. Why did you write this now, when you should've been sleeping?"

"That's just it. I couldn't sleep, kept seeing this scene play out. Kept thinking that the first version needed more, that I might have missed things. I wanted to write it again as I went over it one more time in my mind. Now that I've read it, relived it as best I can, I still don't understand it. But I can sleep now. God, I need to."

"Come back to bed, Nicky. Hold me, please." She closed the Fodor's, tossed his pages on the night table, and switched off the light.

•　　•　　•　　•　　•

When they awoke, there was no further discussion of the event that Nicky had now put twice into written form. While Helen was in the bathroom, Nicky replaced both versions into the envelope and the envelope into his backpack.

At breakfast, Nicky couldn't get his mind off his encounter in the Ekklesia Triada with the dead girl in the yellow smock. Nicky was sure he'd dreamed about her before waking up and still saw her when he closed his eyes. For that matter, he still felt her blood on his head and Raptis's knife against his throat. He chose to say nothing to Helen about his continued immersion in that experience. She would insist that he was fantasizing, letting his imagination run rampant; she would tell him he needed to see a shrink; she wouldn't accept that a real girl had been lying there dead – very recently dead – in front of him.

Yet, she apparently saw his mind working. She asked, and he confessed that he was again in that room the girl he'd killed. She smiled sadly, shook her head, and said nothing. But Nicky knew he'd been foolish to admit the last thing Helen wanted to hear.

•   •   •   •   •

From a rest stop on the way to Salonika, Nicky called the monastery to clear with Fevronia their earlier arrival. They'd spend one night in a hotel, then head to Inousa in the morning. Nicky decided that they'd stay at the Electra Palace, in the heart of downtown, assuring Helen that a beach would still be part of their trip, but only after the monastery.

"Whatever," Helen assented.

As they continued their travel eastward, Helen was unusually quiet, and Nicky wondered what was on her mind. During the previous two days, she would've been praising the scenery and taking shots with her Nikon, but on the present drive she didn't even bother to look out the window. Whenever Nicky stole a glance, Helen seemed to have her eyes closed, as if fighting motion sickness.

He assumed that she was annoyed with his plans, perhaps feeling that he should have consulted more with her before making a decision about a hotel. Or before declaring that they would put off the beach. But why could it matter so much, delaying the beach for another day or two? Then he sensed that Helen was more than annoyed at something. It had to be her keen disappointment about his failures in bed. He ruminated on that silently, afraid to say anything, and it was not until they neared Veria that Helen spoke.

"Nicky, can we talk? About us?"

"We need to." Here it comes, he thought.

"When this trip started, I was unsure I wanted to become intimately involved, sex and all, although I thought there was a chance we would. I worried what that might mean, if we became lovers."

"We have. We are lovers now." He tried to sound confident, to banish any question about their status. He'd wanted Helen for so long and could not bear the thought that she might take herself out of reach.

"We've had sex together. We've slept together. I guess technically that makes us lovers. But I don't see how this can continue. The way we're going."

"What do you mean?"

"I care about you, Nicky. I love you. Yet ..."

"You're unhappy with me in bed. That's it, isn't it?"

"Of course not. I told you it'll come around, if we were to keep trying, that is."

"If? What do you mean?"

Minutes passed before she responded. "It's the larger question. Aren't we at bottom very different? Are we even compatible, long term? We're so different in our basic beliefs about the world we live in."

No, he thought. Don't let this happen to me. Where is the justice in her leading me on and then pulling away when I'm helplessly in love? "I can accommodate your beliefs. We're doing it right now on this trip, aren't we? Did I ask you to carry money on *Shabbat*? Did we drive on *Shabbat*?"

She began to cry. "There's more to being together than your accommodating me. That's so condescending."

"I'm sorry."

"Let me finish. You want to talk about accommodating my religion? I've accommodated your non-belief, if that's what you want to call it, yet shouldn't we actually share a belief system if we're a real couple? We're so far apart. How easy do you think it is for a person like me who believes so strongly in *Hashem's* goodness to be intimate with a man who considers me crazy for believing?"

"But I don't consider ..."

"Let me finish, I said. *And* – make sure you hear this good, Nicky, because this is even more important – it's not only religion. It's your obsession, which now I see clearly for the first time."

"I'm getting rid of the obsession. That's what this trip is about. That's why I gave up trying to find the last church."

"The trip is about giving up your obsession? I don't see you getting rid of anything. I see instead that you take joy in tormenting yourself, as if you wanted nothing more than pain, the same pain, over and over and over again until it kills you. If I weren't with you on this trip, I wouldn't have seen it."

He hated her accusations, knowing they were on target. "That's not it. I'm trying to ... get these fears ..."

"The guilt. Inexorable, crushing guilt. Oppressive guilt. Oppressive to me."

"Yes, guilt ... out on the table. I need your help, Helen. You can't desert me just because it's difficult. I'll get through this. We will, I mean."

"It was a mistake sleeping with you, knowing what I know. And, yes, religion does play a role. You reject *Hashem* with a vengeance. You feel I'm a misguided, unintelligent, superstitious woman. And you've got all this," she continued, gesturing toward the mountains and crying harder. "You've got all this weighing you down. I'm so tired of it. Some imaginary person you fought with is pursuing you. You fall down in churches, crawl into old graveyards, and see blood everywhere. You'll never escape this history, this overwhelming burden you're suffering from, and it's not a way for me to live. It rips me apart watching these memories destroy you. You're ripping me apart."

Still weeping, she fell silent, and he pondered how he might respond. He could pull off the road and put his arms around her, let her cry, try to comfort her, make the promises she wanted to hear. What if she pushed him away, though, and refused to be comforted? He could say nothing, let the motion of the car gently soothe her. Say nothing and thus admit she was right? He had to say something to get them over this rough spot.

"We're different, I grant you. But that doesn't mean this has to end. We can give each other what no one else can. And I'm working on the guilt."

"We can't give each other what we need, and if this is how you work on guilt, I can't stand it anymore. Count me out." She found tissues in her purse to wipe her eyes.

"There's no need to decide anything. Our trip isn't over. We have time."

She shook her head. "Look, Nicky. I'm going to put it to you as directly as I can." She gripped the armrest as if to keep herself from flying out. "I'm not going to fuck you, date you, or have anything else to do with you until you find a way to forgive yourself for whatever you did here in Greece. I can't say it any more clearly."

He was hardly able to breathe. They'd come so far, and now she was telling him it was over unless he fundamentally altered his outlook on the crimes he'd committed. Childish, just a schoolgirl threat, yet he knew Helen meant what she said, that she'd not have been vulgar, so far out of character, without good reason. He knew that she could be as stubborn as he.

"Helen, 1 ..."

"Do you understand?" She drew out the sentence well beyond normal cadence. "We're done, you never touch me again, unless there's a change."

"We can't be done. 1 love you."

She shrugged and lifted her hands in a gesture of helplessness. "You heard me, Nicky. Do 1 have to repeat myself? I'm not going to ..."

"Stop. Don't say it." If he hadn't been driving, he'd have covered her mouth to quiet her. He drove for miles, silent, pondering. There was only one thing to say, he decided, one thing that might get them past this unbearable place.

"Helen ..."

"What?"

"You're absolutely right."

"Of course I'm absolutely right."

"I'll do anything and everything in my power so we can stay together."

"So you say."

"Give me a chance. If 1 weren't driving, I'd get down on my knees to beg."

"That 1 can imagine," she said, with obvious sarcasm.

"1 do need to forgive myself. Shit. I'm sixty-one, I've spent most of a life wallowing in guilt, haven't 1?"

"Better late, they say. Better late."

"How? How do 1 learn to forgive myself?"

Helen was quiet for a few moments before responding. "Can you start by forgiving your parents for sending you away?"

"1 don't see what ..."

"You're still angry at them. 1 can sense it."

"That's ridic ..."

"Can you forgive Kayla for not living up to her promise as a classical pianist?"

"1 don't know what you mean."

"You certainly do know. Typical resistance of someone who doesn't want to heal, but you do know. You can't practice psychiatry for decades, make quite a good living at it, without understanding what I'm saying. If you learn how to forgive them, you might learn how to forgive yourself, the hardest one of all to forgive."

Nicky wondered whether he'd ever forgiven anyone for anything. Adel, for her schizophrenia? Max, for his divorce? Kayla, for allowing herself to get pregnant at seventeen, for allowing herself to be seduced by Sorel? Had he ever forgiven his parents, whose decision had precipitated the chain of events that led him to war? He began to comprehend how that sharp judgmental part of his personality had treated – yes, mistreated – everyone important in his life since he'd been sent away from his childhood home. He started to see that, among those he'd abused, not the least of them was himself.

After what seemed only a few minutes but might have been as long as an hour, while he was full of his thoughts and regrets, Nicky heard Helen's light snoring. She'd exhausted herself with her anger and her crying. Free from Helen's scrutiny, Nicky accelerated well past the speed limit. He slowed only when forced to by rush hour traffic around Salonika. The roads and buildings were unfamiliar, like the mountains on a different planet. Helen woke with the stop and go traffic, sighed loudly, and said nothing. At the hotel, they made their way to their room in continued, uncomfortable silence. Then Helen excused herself to shower. Nicky pulled the blinds across the glass patio door to block out the afternoon glare bouncing off the Aegean, then lay on the king-size bed, burrowing his head under two pillows to further block out light. Within seconds, he was dozing in the darkness. He awoke only when Helen emerged from the bathroom. Disoriented, smelling that she'd dabbed on perfume, he wondered for a second where he was.

"Nicky, what are you doing? You're not passing out on me, are you?"

Then he remembered the horrible conversation and his contemplation of the ways he'd held grudges against the most important people in his life. He remembered how hard Helen had been crying. But from her voice, though, he wouldn't have known that the tears had stopped only an hour earlier. He emerged from his pillow cave and turned to look at her. She wore only her bathrobe. Her having slept in the car, the shower's cleansing water, and a dab of fragrance had apparently put new life into her.

"Are we going to look at your old house tonight?" She leaned over him for a kiss, and the kiss stretched into a luxuriant minute of mutual fondling, of her climbing on his thigh, her robe parting.

In seconds, he'd lost his clothes and taken off her robe.

"Come here. Let's get under the sheet."

He nuzzled her breasts with his lips; their hands fluttered over each other like birds.

"Come inside me, Nicky. Stay longer this time."

"I love you, Helen."

Afterward, when they'd woken up, it was too late to do any sightseeing.

CHAPTER SEVEN

Inousa, Greece, April 24, 1990 (Tuesday)

Fevronia hung up from her call with Dr. Covo as nervous as she remembered being in a long time. Her equilibrium had shifted. The forces that she'd set in motion would now play themselves out in a way she could not anticipate or control. The success she'd achieved in bringing the monastery back to life was in jeopardy.

Could it have been only because of Theodora's presence that the vineyard regained – even surpassed – its former vitality? In the rational part of her brain, Fevronia recognized that her success had depended largely upon her own management, her skill in learning what had to be learned about growing grapes and processing them into wine, her maintaining good relationships with and getting help from the villagers, and her good judgment. Part of her recognized, however, that even before she'd arrived, Theodora had been there, at the center of everything, guarding the monastery by her mere presence. Fevronia believed that Theodora had been guarding Silenos's grave, as it were, even though unaware she was doing so. Or perhaps Theodora *had* been aware. With the mysteries that lived within her, she might well have been. Fevronia envied that, even after her own arrival, it had been Theodora who drew to the monastery Inousa's faithful and, later, the flocks of pilgrims. In her heart, Fevronia felt that the monastery's success had been due more to Theodora's presence than any other factor.

If Dr. Covo's visit upset the delicate balance of worship and productivity that kept the monastery going, what would happen to Fevronia and the other nuns? What would happen to Theodora in particular? Fevronia had struggled in vain to call back to her side the Theotokos, to hear from Her mouth once more "*To thélima tou Theoú gínetai.* God's will is done." The next day would bring home the truth or falsity of the words she'd heard so clearly.

CHAPTER EIGHT

Inousa, Greece, April 25, 1990 (Wednesday)

Late in the morning, Nicky and Helen pulled up to a small church built on the side of a hill. The driveway bordered an arched portico supported by four Doric columns. Standing on the portico was a short, heavy-set nun wearing a gold cross over her black cassock. Nicky pulled his backpack from the seat behind him as he and Helen got out of the car. As he approached the nun, the daylight seemed unusually strong, and he squinted, then tried to right the expression on his face into one of appropriate reverence.

"Abbess Fevronia?" Nicky spoke in Greek, as he had always done on the phone. "I'm Dr. Covo, and this is my friend, Helen Blanco. You do speak English?"

Fevronia approached with an outstretched hand, and her grip was firm. He towered over her by about a foot, yet she didn't appear to let their difference in size intimidate her. Her face was deeply lined and had the dark tone of a woman who often spent time in the sun. Her eyes were cautious, questioning. Nicky saw that she assessed him as intently as he assessed her. He wanted to understand who this woman was, the woman who'd searched him out, determined to track down Sister Theodora's origins.

Fevronia's English was fine and her voice pleasant with culture and hospitality as she shook Nicky's hand and then Helen's. "Yes, of course. We all study English in school, and we have lots of English-speaking faithful who visit here, so I've had many years to practice. So pleased to meet you both. Welcome to the Holy Monastery of St. Vlassios. Would you care for tea while we talk?"

"Is she nearby?" Nicky's voice, though firm, was soft. He looked around as if expecting that Sister Theodora might have been hiding behind one of the columns or in the shadows of the doorway.

"She's in her cell praying, as always, Dr. Covo. We will see her soon. Please do not to worry."

"Does she know we're coming?" he asked, his voice louder, but still at a shade less volume that his usual speech.

"Not that I am aware of," said Fevronia. She paused for a second before continuing. "But only God knows what He puts into the minds of His beloved children. Sister Theodora in particular. One can never be sure about her, what she can see and what she cannot."

"You've never said anything about the coming visit of someone who might be her brother?"

"You are her brother, I am sure, but no."

"Why for heaven's sake not?" he asked, finally letting his voice rise. He felt immediately he'd been too abrupt, but couldn't bring himself to apologize, nor did he see a way to retract the question.

"The time wasn't right," Fevronia answered, apparently not disturbed. "Please to follow me."

Nicky gritted his teeth, wondering how the time couldn't have been right, but said nothing in response. Helen looked back and forth to Nicky and Fevronia as they spoke, but likewise remained silent.

Fevronia was curious about Nicky, the man on whom she'd taken such a chance. She'd noted with relief that his facial features were similar to Theodora's, the dark brown eyes, the slight upward turn of the corners of the mouth, the straight ridge of the nose. More than assessing his facial features, though, she wanted to judge by his demeanor whether he'd create difficulties when he confirmed that Theodora was his sister. He looked to be strong and determined, yet anxious and impatient. His question about why she hadn't informed Theodora about his intended visit – particularly the way he'd phrased it – had bordered on rudeness, a rudeness that annoyed Fevronia, even though she'd lied in response. His impatience was ironic as well, given how for a long time he'd resisted the idea that his sister might be alive. Now that he was here, though, he wanted everything to happen at once.

Fevronia walked them around the back of the church and into a small, one-story brick building next to the dormitory. She brought them into her office, which Nicky thought was well organized. Its wood desk – most likely oak – was neat. A two-drawer file cabinet, made of a darker wood than the desk, sat along one wall and looked new. On the opposite wall, next to a window, stood a bookcase that might have been made of the same wood as the file cabinet. It looked to Nicky as if a fair amount of money had been spent to create a comfortable home for the abbess, and he wondered briefly about whether all ascetics were required to accept abject poverty or whether an exception might be made in the case of an abbess. The other article of note in the office was a crucifix that hung on the wall to the other side of the window. Nicky stared at the very lifelike Christ for a long moment.

Fevronia followed Nicky's glance and smiled. "I hope you do not mind meeting here, Dr. Covo."

"It doesn't bother me in the least, Abbess Fevronia, although I must say the sight is quite startling." He nodded toward the human form, wanting to say something conciliatory in light of his recent ill temper. "Your Lord suffers there, one can easily see."

"Yes. Very much. He suffers for us, you know. Well, please to sit." She poured hot water from an electric pot and offered them a choice of tea bags. As they took their first sips, she continued. "First, let me thank you, Dr. Covo, and you, Mrs. ....?"

"Blanco," said Helen.

"Mrs. Blanco, yes, for coming such distance, so far from home. Sister Theodora has long been a mystery, and for a long time I have wanted to understand where she came from, how she came here. If she is your sister, Dr. Covo, and I'm sure that she is, that may help answer questions that have plagued at me for a very long time. Now, first, please to tell me about Alex Ganis."

"Alex." Nicky breathed deeply, resisting the urge to ask Fevronia to bring them to Sister Theodora at that very instant and trying to conceal his irritation, given that he'd already provided to Fevronia the bare bones of Alex's role in his life. "I'll never forget him. He risked his life to get me out of Salonika just before the deportations in '43."

"He did more than risk his life. He gave his life helping your sister, trying to get her to a hiding place in Kavala."

"I have to say candidly that I don't remember my folks talking about Kavala as a place for my sisters to hide. I don't know of any connections we might've had there. True, though. They hoped to place Ada and Kal too with good Christians. They knew what was coming. I was lucky enough to be the first to get out. Or unlucky enough, because that's the last I saw them."

"They knew what was coming? How, may I ask?" asked Fevronia.

Nicky had to stifle a smirk. It was so easy for people like Fevronia to pretend, after the atrocities had been discovered, filmed, and thoroughly documented, that no one knew what was going on. "Yes, Abbess Fevronia, they did know. Word got out about the death camps well before March '43. Two prisoners who escaped from Auschwitz made it to Switzerland and told the world, and my father, may his name be for a blessing ..." Here, Nicky paused, a picture of his father looking up at him over a volume of Talmud having pushed its way into his consciousness. What would his father have said today if he'd seen that Kal, his precious flower, had lived and become a nun? Would he have felt that she'd died just as dead as if she'd been gassed?

"Yes, your father?"

"He was active in Jewish organizations, he heard the reports and, unlike most others, he understood that the deportations were for killing." Suddenly, he began to cry, hearing his father's voice explain patiently to him what was happening. His father had remained calm, trying to convey to Nicky the sad reality of the situation without causing panic. "Excuse me."

"Well." Fevronia paused while Nicky composed himself. Watching Nicky cry, she wanted to cry herself. Nicky's pain, she saw, was no different from the pain she herself felt when she thought of Silenos. They were equally victims of the Nazi brutality; they had both struggled in their own ways as survivors trying to comprehend what had no suitable explanation. The difference was, though, that Nicky's loss was not as complete as her own. At least one of his sisters had lived, and he was about to meet her again, whereas she would never see Silenos again in this world. She waited until she felt that Nicky was pulling himself together, then continued. "If we may please to get on to the business of your visit. I need to prepare you for one little oddity about Sister Theodora."

"And that is?" asked Helen, while Nicky wiped his eyes with a handkerchief.

"When she meets a stranger, she must wash his or her feet. It does not take long. It is a sign of humility. She is trying to be as close to Christ as she can be. I hope you will not mind." Nicky put his handkerchief away and looked at Helen, who shrugged her shoulders.

"But I'm not a stranger, if she is who you say she is."

"Nonetheless, I know her at least that well. I'm certain she will humble herself before you and Mrs. Blanco in this manner."

"We've come a long way," he said. "If that's how this has to start, then let's do it."

"In that case, please to wait here. We should be back in just a few minutes. I will tell her that there are visitors, and she will pick up her bucket and washcloth and return with me. Let her to take off your shoes and socks. You are obliged to put them back on yourselves."

Fevronia smiled wanly, as if Nicky and Helen replacing their own shoes and socks was the punchline of a weak joke.

•　　•　　•　　•　　•

It seemed like a long time before Fevronia and Theodora appeared, Theodora carrying a bucket as promised. Nicky, feeling weak throughout his body, and Helen stood simultaneously to face them, like subjects rising before a monarch. "Sister Theodora," Abbess Fevronia said in Greek, "these are your visitors."

Garbed in a black cassock like that worn by Fevronia, Theodora looked to Nicky just as she had in the photograph; a black veil covered most of her hair, with just a few strands of grey sticking out. Was she or wasn't she? Yes, Nicky thought, she could be. There was perhaps a faint resemblance to his mother, to their mother, or was that just a trick of his imagination? Briefly, their eyes locked on each other, but he saw no recognition in her look, nor in her pleasant but mild smile.

He wanted desperately to speak to her, but found neither the right words nor the voice. Something – a greeting, a salutation, a word praising God – had almost bubbled up from inside his being, but was caught by the stricture of his throat and a wave of nausea.

As Fevronia warned, Theodora lightly took Nicky's hand, pulled him back into his chair, and knelt in front of him. It was a relief that they were no longer looking at each other directly, because Theodora's gaze was now fixed to the servile task at hand. It was a relief for him to sit, because standing had caused him to feel a distinct shakiness, reminding him of his near collapse at the Varlaam Monastery.

Theodora took off his shoes and socks. The brief, light touch of her fingers on Nicky's ankles and heels was strangely soothing and warm. The warmth deepened steadily and unnaturally; it was a warmth well beyond what one would have expected, like a sun lamp brought too close for safety. Nicky attributed the feeling to his imagination and nerves. When Nicky's feet were bare, Theodora removed her wet washcloth from the bucket, and, with great care and attention to detail, bathed his feet. With a dry cloth, she wiped away the water, then held Nicky's socks up to him, indicating that he was to put himself together. Theodora then turned to Helen and repeated the process. When Theodora had finished, Fevronia pulled up another chair and placed it for Theodora between the chairs of her visitors.

Theodora sat, head down, apparently waiting, obviously expecting something. The only noise Nicky heard for a few long seconds was the excited chirping of birds outside. What next? His feet still felt abnormally, but pleasantly, warm. He looked past Theodora's bowed head to catch Helen's glance. She smiled at him and nodded. Did that mean he was supposed to start a conversation? He thought about doing so for a second, but then Fevronia's voice broke the silence.

"These people are your friends, Sister Theodora," she said in Greek. "They'd like to talk to you. Please lift your head and look at them."

It was a strange request, thought Nicky, because, from where she was sitting, Theodora couldn't have looked at them both. But Theodora turned immediately toward Nicky. She knows me, he thought, surprised and yet immensely relieved. He heard a click and saw Fevronia, who'd gone back to sit behind her desk, place a cassette tape recorder at its edge. Theodora then lowered her gaze again to the floor.

"Go ahead, Dr. Covo. I will record, with your permission." He nodded. "Mrs. Blanco," she said, turning to Helen, "I will interpret for you when it is over."

"Very well," said Helen uncertainly.

Then Fevronia and Helen turned to Nicky, and he had to start. "Sister Theodora," he said in Greek, "my name is Nicky Covo. Nicky. Do you know me?" He tried to keep his voice calm, as if he talked to a new patient, but the words rushed out breathlessly. "Do you remember Mordechai and Sara Covo? Your parents? Our parents?"

No visible reaction. Theodora remained in the same position, with her head down. Her breathing hadn't changed in the least, not even the slightest movement of a muscle. The stillness was grossly unnatural.

"Do you remember our sister, Ada?"

Still no reaction.

Seconds ticked by, as Nicky heard the continued but faint whirring of Fevronia's tape recorder, making its record of silence. Nicky remembered, or thought he remembered, a time when he was trying to teach Kal, then three, to read, how he would explain a letter or a word and Kal would just stare at the book quietly, not asking questions, not making a sound, but absorbing and learning. Was he seeing another manifestation of the same ability to concentrate? Fevronia's tape kept turning, and Nicky knew he'd have to press on if they were going to get anywhere.

"Let me show you something, Sister Theodora." He reached into his backpack and removed the framed crayon drawing of a blue jay. He stood and handed it to her. She took it from him and stared at it, in deep concentration. Then she looked up at him, a question of tears in her eyes, a mist, almost imaginary but there, her lips trembling. "Do you remember giving this to Nicky Covo, the last time you saw him? Do you remember giving it to me?" Tears how unmistakably welled, as Theodora looked back toward the drawing, then back toward Nicky. "Sister Theodora, were you once Kal Covo, my sister, my baby sister, from Salonika?" Nicky's voice broke, and he had to gulp back a sob, hardly able to pronounce the name of the city where they'd lived together as loving siblings.

Theodora shook her head, pushed the drawing into Nicky's hands, rose from her chair, and walked slowly but steadily toward the door, as if she were deep in thought. At the door, she turned to face the others. In a quivering voice, she said, "My real name is Kal *Ganis*, and I'm from Kavala." She left the room quickly, Fevronia a few steps behind, calling after her. Nicky got up to follow them, but Helen grabbed him. With her other hand, she turned off Fevronia's recorder. "Let them go, Nicky. Abbess Fevronia will handle it. Was that her? Did she say she was Kal *Ganis*? What was that about Kavala? I know where Kavala is, from the Fodor's, but I didn't understand."

"Oh, God." He sobbed openly now and saw tears streaking Helen's face too.

"What, Nicky?"

"I wasn't sure until I heard her voice. She's my sister, Helen. She's Kal."

•　　•　　•　　•　　•

Fevronia saw Theodora run up the hill toward the winery and, in Fevronia's mind, already rejecting prayer and her devotion to Christ. Had Theodora wanted to pray, she'd have been back in her cell or she'd have gone into the church. Fevronia's worst fears about Dr. Covo's visit had materialized. As Fevronia chased her, a woman she loved as if her own daughter, she realized that Theodora had never once, to her knowledge, climbed to the top of the hill. She'd been shocked by meeting her brother after forty-seven years, of being confronted by her lost brother without sufficient warning. The shock had obviously created a completely new Theodora, giving her a strange new energy and purpose. But why run all the way to the top? Why run away at all? And why Kal Ganis? Had she somehow been adopted by Alex? That made no sense. Tabitha surely would have mentioned that, had it been true.

Fevronia's short legs could not move her quickly, and the distance between them grew. She called repeatedly, yet her voice felt weak, she was ghastly out of breath, and she was fairly sure that Theodora couldn't hear her. Fevronia feared that Theodora would go right past the winery and down into the vineyards on the other side, to lose herself again, yet – thanks be to Christ – she saw Theodora kneeling at the last bench on the walk, some forty meters from the winery. Just wanting to find a new place to pray? Fevronia panted heavily; it took all of her willpower and energy and yet another five minutes before she came even with Theodora. She knelt beside her.

"Sister Theodora, are you … are you all right?" Theodora looked up at Fevronia and nodded. She wiped away tears with her sleeve.

"Let us pray to Christ the Savior for strength to get us through this," Fevronia urged. She held her cross in one hand and knelt. She prayed out loud. "Oh, Lord, we beg You to guide us, to guide Your humble servant Theodora, through the next minutes, hours, and days." Then she prayed silently. Theotokos, come back to tell me that God's will has been done. Tell me. Come back. Say to me again *To thélima tou Theoú gínetai*. Tell me. Come back. After a few long minutes, Theodora's soft voice awakened her from her reverie.

"Come, Mother, let's return. It was very rude of me to run, as they've obviously come so far. I must make it up." Theodora helped Fevronia get back to her feet.

Fevronia was amazed that Theodora was now speaking to her as if it were the most natural thing in the world, as if they'd talked to each other as close friends for decades. New energy and purpose indeed, she thought. She couldn't even try to imagine what was going to happen next. They walked slowly back down the hill, Theodora's arm around Fevronia. At one pause in their descent, Fevronia found the nerve to ask the main question that needed to be answered.

"Sister Theodora, do you recognize him? Is he really your brother?"

Theodora smiled at Fevronia, her cheeks still wet. She nodded. "Yes, of course, Mother."

"But Kal Ganis? Who is she?"

"I am Kal Ganis, too." Fevronia felt almost tipsy, anticipating that all would shortly be revealed.

"Do you have the strength and desire to speak with your brother and his friend? Her name is Mrs. Blanco."

"I think so. Yes. Of course, I must speak with them. That's why they're here, isn't it?"

"I believe Dr. Covo is as shocked as you are, Sister Theodora."

"Dr. Covo? Nicky is a doctor," she said thoughtfully. "Papa was a doctor too. But I shouldn't have been shocked. You asked me about Nicky months ago – now I recall that vividly – and I had no idea who or what you were talking about."

Theodora stopped suddenly and clutched Fevronia in a fierce embrace, with a renewed bout of crying. Theodora's frail body shook as she cried, and now it was all Fevronia could do, assuming the role of the strong one, to support her. Minutes passed before Theodora calmed down enough to continue walking.

"Are you sure you can do this?" asked Fevronia.

"Yes, Mother," said Theodora, crossing herself. "The Lord Jesus Christ will give me strength. Give me five minutes alone in my cell, please. I must pray."

•　　•　　•　　•　　•

The more time that elapsed, the worse Nicky felt. He swallowed the cold tea left in his cup in an effort to control his sweating and the shaking of his hands.

"Nicky, you're not going to have a heart attack on me, are you? Sit down." Helen guided him to his chair and pushed him down, felt his forehead, then leaned over and kissed the top of his head. He reached up and gently ran his hand through her hair.

A half-hour later, Fevronia returned to her office without Theodora.

Nicky could not hide his disappointment. "Where is she? Is she all right? Will she come back?"

"Yes, Dr. Covo, momentarily. She has had a good cry. A couple of good cries. Well, have we not all cried? She says that she will certainly want to talk to you. She knows that you're her brother."

"Why does she say she's Kal Ganis?"

"I hope she will to explain," said Fevronia. "Before she comes back, though, please to tell me about that drawing."

Nicky removed it again from his backpack and placed it on Fevronia's desk. "It's what Kal drew on the day I left home. She handed it me on my way out of our house, the last time I saw my family."

"And you managed to keep ..."

"Yes. Since '43. That drawing is the only thing I have from home."

"Amazing that you should have been able to hang onto that for so long. And that's a blue bird, isn't it?"

"A blue jay, she said."

"Somehow I'm not surprised. The Elder Porphyrios said something about a blue bird a few years ago, when he met her here. He was a clairvoyant." She thought for a second, looking again closely at the drawing. "There are things we somehow manage to hold onto long after they should have disappeared." She sighed, offering up a silent prayer in Silenos's memory.

Helen said "Nicky ... Dr. Covo ... showed it to me in 1946, Abbess Fevronia, when he arrived at our house in New Jersey. Our family sponsored him into America."

"So you have known each other for ..."

Fevronia didn't have time to finish, as Theodora appeared in the doorway. Nicky and Helen stood again, and everyone looked at each other, as if trying to deduce the protocols for such a meeting, before Theodora herself took charge. In Greek, she begged them all to sit, but Nicky would not. He held out his arms to his sister. After a second's delay, they embraced, both crying hard. He held her face in his hands for a long minute, kissed her on the forehead, hugged her again as hard as he'd ever hugged anyone. She felt frail within his arms, still not much more than a girl, he thought. Only with reluctance did he allow her to guide him back to his chair. She sat facing him. Fevronia clicked on her recorder.

"Sister Theodora ...," he started in Greek. He wanted to talk to her in Ladino, but Fevronia wouldn't have understood.

"Call me Kal, Nicky. For this morning, I'm just your little sister. Your baby sister."

"Kal ... I can't tell you what it means to me to see you here, alive." He reached for her slender hand, where it barely emerged from the sleeve of her cassock.

"When you left, Nicky, I ..." She stopped then, looked up toward the ceiling, then looked down again toward her lap, her hands brought over her eyes as if to hide them from the light of Fevronia's office. She sobbed as she sat there. Nicky understood that he had to let her cry as long as she needed. When she wiped her eyes and looked up again at him, he continued.

"When I left ..., then?"

"I ... thought I'd see you again the next day. Or maybe the day after. Soon, I thought."

"You had been told that I was going far, Kal. That's why you drew the blue jay for me."

"I didn't truly understand the danger, the meaning of deportations, the reason for hiding. I knew that Athens was the capital, that it was in the south, but didn't know exactly where or how far. When you didn't come back, when no one talked about your coming back, I thought you'd left me, that you didn't want to be my big brother."

"I did abandon you. And the rest of the family."

"Abandoned? No, you had to go. Back then, though, I still didn't see how all of our lives hung in the balance."

"I thought ... I believed ... you went to ... Auschwitz .... I believed that all of you had been murdered, as certain of that as of the sorry fact that I was still alive."

"Dr. Covo," interrupted Fevronia. "Perhaps now that Sister Theodora – Kal – is speaking with us, we might ask her about her coming to the monastery?"

Nicky wiped at his eyes again with his handkerchief. "Kal, can you tell us? I mean, the whole story? How you survived? How you got here?"

"This is very hard." Kal took a deep breath, her eyes resting on Fevronia for a long second. "I can tell some, but not everything, I don't think. A lot ... I've not thought of for so long. I don't know if I can remember all. I can try. Will that be all right?"

"Do your best, my child," urged Fevronia.

Kal turned to Nicky. "Nicky, I wouldn't be talking about this now, or ever, if you hadn't come back to me."

"I had to find you again, if you were really here."

"May the Lord Jesus Christ protect and defend me. May he take away our suffering and bring us into His Kingdom." There was a look of intense concentration on her face. She folded her hands together on her lap and rocked back and forth. Nicky thought she might still have been praying, but now Theodora's words were too faint to make out.

"Can someone please tell me what's going on?" Helen begged.

"Trust us," responded Nicky. "We'll fill you in after she finishes."

"Please go ahead, Sister Theodora," Fevronia urged. "God has willed this. The Mother of God has told me so. Praised be to Christ the Savior."

PHRIKÉ, THE GODDESS OF HORROR

I am Phriké, come to shed additional light on this story. I usually don't emerge from the underworld to help anyone. Yet, I'm not a perfect demon and so every once in a while I have these impulses to show a different side. Terror's my forte, but variety is the spice of life, as the Americans say. Ha ha.

So here's the first thing that I need to tell you. That vignette you read earlier, entitled "Ten or Eleven," was autobiographical and true. I know the truth of the story because I wrote it and because I was there, starting my appearance on stage, if you will, by playing the eleventh hostage that both Rieger and Father Augustin had seen. It's easy for a goddess to take on the appearance of a man if she needs to, particularly the appearance of a soldier. I can't vouch for the truth of everything else you've read in this novel and that which you are still about to read, other than to say that the few facts I know accord with the overall account – the German atrocities in Greece during World War II and the infighting among the various partisan factions are well documented, of course – and that the rest of this story is highly plausible, given what I know about the main characters.

Well, back to 1944. That's where everything happened that Fevronia is so intent on learning. My mission then was to make sure that the monks perished. God didn't tell me to do this; it was my decision, and God gives me pretty free rein to interfere in human tragedies as I see fit. He gives me a lot of power as well. In my view, the war hadn't yet gone on quite long enough as of 1944, the suffering hadn't yet reached its pre-ordained zenith, and adjustments had to be made, so to speak, before the Germans were forced to pull back. So. Call me a mass murderer, if you want, a serial killer. I own up to it. It's my job. After all, I am Phriké.

I entered the monastery, let myself be bound, studied the other monks, observed Rieger and his crew, and decided that, yes, the monks would die in a grave that would never be found. Fevronia will be very unhappy that she never learns where. When I decide that a grave won't be found, trust me, it won't.

So back to my story. As soon as I was sure about what I wanted to do, I prepared the order that required Rieger to kill the monks for "reprisals," an order I knew he'd obey, even as heavy as his heart had become, even as Father Augustin's plea for Rieger's repentance started to take effect. Afterward, it wasn't hard at all for me to assume the shape and trappings of a German soldier and march with them, through the vineyard and into the pines, to see that the execution was carried out properly. I was impressed by the monks' acceptance of their fate. Father Augustin was amazingly calm and brave. I admired that. To be perfectly honest, I was a bit moved by their final chanting of the psalm. Of course, resistance would've been futile.

You know that story in the Hebrew Bible about God hardening Pharaoh's heart so that he wouldn't let the Hebrews go? I helped in that. Took a rather big hand, in fact. That's one of my special skills, hardening of hearts, even my own, so Rieger had no real chance of countermanding the execution order. Had Rieger survived the Eastern front, he might well have repented later, might well have become a stalwart post-war German citizen, but that wasn't to be. I made sure that Russian bullets killed everyone who'd been in the German platoon at the monastery. There could be no witnesses to help locate the grave. I wanted there always to be the tiniest bit of doubt, and I wanted the searchers to be disappointed over and over again. I'm like Rubik, but I made my cube without a solution.

But here's the other thing. The Theotokos – I'll use the name that Kal prefers – goes about trying to perform miracle after miracle, and although often I've been able to parry her efforts through the eons, more often than not she beats me. She's a stalwart opponent. I should've won this one outright. The monks and Kal should all have been killed. The Theotokos having hidden Kal as carelessly as she did, where Kal so easily could have been found, made it easy. The Theotokos is full of miracles, dashing about the world as she does to save one person or another, but often she's not practical. She'd chosen an obvious hiding place, the first place that Germans always looked when hunting Jewish children. Well, let me not get too far ahead of myself. You're about to hear the story from Kal's mouth directly, but this is the small part that Kal doesn't know.

Before I explain what happened, you need to learn a bit more about the relationship that the Theotokos and I developed over the centuries.

It wasn't pure coincidence that we should have arrived at the monastery at almost the same time. My main field of operation – my specialty, if you will – is war, but the same is true for the Theotokos. So we do run into each other from time to time, working with the same raw materials, so to speak, but with opposite ends, artists who paint in clashing colors. There we both were, recognizing each other at once and understanding each other's deepest thoughts, having tried to out-maneuver each other thousands of times and, in the process, having becoming friends, with healthy respect for each other. I knew instantly that she would try to save the monks, and she knew instantly that I wanted Kal to die, too. We came to an instantaneous agreement. A *quid pro quo* as the Latins would say, and there was no need for it to be written out. The Theotokos would not intervene in the killing of the monks, and I would protect Kal. I made sure, damn sure, that the Germans never found the cask into which the Theotokos had placed Kal. Along with heart-hardening, blindness is one of my special skills when I need it.

I figured this was a good deal for me and most strange that the Theotokos would have gone along with the bargain: ten lives to be lost, one to be saved. Ten who worshiped God, Christ, and the Theotokos herself would surely perish; one frail, scared little girl, who might not survive the first cold winter in the mountains, would be allowed to live a little longer. Clearly, the Theotokos saw something special in Kal, and despite the fact that I've come back to the monastery from time to time and listened to Kal pray in her cell, I still don't know what makes her so special. So what if she hears confessions? She's far from the only nun to do so. So what if she was Jewish at birth? Aren't most of us, though we don't want to admit it?

How was I to know that Kal would be found by the villagers after I'd left for the Eastern front, the German execution squad in tow? How was I to know that they'd protect her? How was I to know that Fevronia, the sister of one of the monks I killed, would come to the monastery and continue to protect Kal? In the end, I cannot escape the gnawing suspicion that the Theotokos may have gotten the best deal. And it bothers me that I don't know why. Maybe with Kal's brother showing up, I'll find out. I'll need to get into his head, I think.

Well, I'm glad that I've gotten all this out of my system. I had to add in my two cents before you finished reading this story. Thanks for not skipping this small chapter. Now, I go back to my main business of terror, and you go back to the novel. But be warned: I am always close by!

BOOK THREE

CHAPTER ONE

Salonika, Kavala, Ioannina, and Inousa, Greece, March 1943-March 1944

Sister Theodora, the nun who as a child had been Kal Covo, repeated the words of Abbess Fevronia and crossed herself slowly, looking at the figure of the crucified Christ about which her brother had commented only an hour before. "Praised be to Christ the Savior." Then she looked into her lap and was still, as if she'd said all she was going to say.

"Please tell us, Kal, what happened to you," encouraged Nicky softly after a few seconds. Ever since he'd discovered that Kal might be alive, he had hoped that – if they met again – she might give him an account of what happened to his family after his departure. Now, about to be told, he could barely restrain his nervous excitement. And he realized that Kal understood his great need. She turned toward him, and it was to him directly that she told most of her story.

"I said that I didn't realize the danger, Nicky, yet in a way I did." She paused for a good ten seconds, her eyes closed in intense concentration, before continuing. "I think Mama and Papa talked about Eleftheria Square? How the Germans beat the Jewish men there, humiliated them, taunted them. Do I remember that right?"

"They told me about it. Luckily, Papa was too old for the Germans to call that day, and I was too young. I didn't know you and Ada heard, though."

"Mama and Papa always whispered after that. We – Ada and I – tried to pull together whatever scraps of meaning we could. But it was all about fear. They were so afraid, for us children in particular. I remember a name ..."

"A name?" asked Fevronia, startling Nicky, because for a second he'd imagined that he and Kal were alone.

"Eichmann this and Eichmann that, and I didn't understand. And I tried to ..."

"Yes?" urged Nicky.

"I tried to find out what was wrong. I begged them to explain, but they didn't. Or wouldn't. I prayed to God for ..."

"For what?" Nicky asked.

"For the nightmare to end."

Nicky tried to remember whether he, too, had been praying then, still a believer, but came up blank. He most likely would have been going through the daily ritual of *t'fillin* and prayer, he would have been addressing a Supreme Being as one who heard and answered prayer, but he suspected that his observances were rote, that he'd been too preoccupied by the danger that they all were in to devote himself wholeheartedly to prayer. "Mama and Papa knew that they needed to hide us or we'd die, Kal. Papa had learned about Auschwitz. They tried for so long to find ways to hide us, protect us. I knew they were looking, struggling."

"You knew, but I didn't. But the changes in our family life were stark. I could feel it even as a young child. Papa stopped studying the Talmud – you remember how I used to sit on his lap? – and I saw him bury Mama's jewels and still didn't understand. I asked you what was happening, and even you wouldn't tell me. 'Go ask Mama and Papa,' you said. Mama and Papa would only say 'God will make sure His will is done.' And then, it happened so suddenly, you were to leave that very evening and I drew the picture and before I hugged you goodbye, you *were* gone. Gone with Alex. When you didn't come back the next day or two ..."

"You thought I'd deserted you."

"I felt deserted, but I started to understand that Mama and Papa would send Ada and me away too. I didn't want to believe it, though, I thought maybe ... until ..."

"Until?" asked Nicky.

"Maybe three or four days after you left, I was finishing my lunch, and Mama rushed in, she pushed a small cloth bag into my hands – I think food was in it, I never learned – and she dragged me to the door, shouting that I had to go somewhere with Alex." Here Kal stopped, closing her eyes again, her body tensing as if she were reliving those moments. Then she continued, her voice slightly altered, slightly louder and deeper, first in Ladino and then back in Greek. '*Vaya con Alejandro ahora!* Go with Alex now! He'll take care of you.'"

"I cannot imagine," said Fevronia. She folded her hands in front of her face, elbows placed on the desk, and bent her head in silent prayer.

"Bless the Risen Lord," Kal said in her own voice, a bit shakily. "I can still hear Mama's shouts."

"What did you do?" asked Nicky softly, needing to know but not wanting to upset Kal further by his questions. He envisioned his family's house, he saw his mother dragging Kal toward the front door, but he could not see their faces, distorted with anguish as they must have been.

"I tried to run back into the house. She grabbed me again, yanked me. She almost yanked my arm out of my body. I can still feel it. She dragged me to Alex's truck. I screamed, crazy with fear. I punched her, Christ forgive me, the poor wretched sinner that I am, I punched Mama in the face. I scratched at her face, my fingers drew blood, I did everything I could to free myself. I kicked her. I twisted, contorted my body, bit at her. I couldn't let her send me away. Then Alex was there, and I was no match for both. He helped her push me into his truck, they slammed the door, I tried to get out the other side, but Alex was too fast. He hopped in and got the truck moving."

"Horrible, Kal," said Nicky. "Utterly, utterly horrible. I knew I had to leave home and why, but you were too young to understand. It must have been crushing."

"And I saw Mama crying, bent over, as we drove off, as if I'd hurt her, bent over like she'd be sick, no, like she was ready to die at that instant, and I knew I'd hurt her and I screamed again, this time because I thought I'd killed her too. We turned a corner, and that's the l last I saw her."

She stopped, letting her own tears flow. The only sounds were the soft purr of Fevronia's cassette recorder and Kal's sobbing. Helen came over to Kal's chair to hug her and whispered something to Kal in Ladino that Nicky didn't quite hear. It took Kal a full two minutes to regain her composure sufficiently to continue her story. Wiping her eyes, she again looked directly at Nicky, trying to smile, as if in contrition for her crying.

"Alex drove fast. Before I knew it, we were climbing out of the city on a dark country road. Then came the lessons."

Fevronia leaned toward her. "Lessons?"

"I knew him, the young man who'd captured me in his truck, only as Alex. He told me his last name was Ganis. If anyone asked, I had to say I was Kal Ganis. I argued with him. No one could tell me my name wasn't Kal Covo. He almost yelled at me, ordered me to be Kal Ganis, told me over and over that our lives depended on it, that I should not, never, never let anyone know I was Jewish. It was an order: Be Kal Ganis or be shot. It finally dawned on me what he was trying to say. He made me repeat my new name, over and over, for hours. Then he told me that I had to call him 'Uncle Alex' and that he was bringing me home, to a city called Kavala, where I lived with my mother, and I had to repeat over and over that I was Kal Ganis of Kavala. When he said we were almost there ...." She hesitated and closed her eyes once again.

"You're doing fine, Sister Theodora," said Fevronia.

"Soldiers stopped us. They had blocked the road. Alex jammed the brakes, I hit my head on the dashboard. Alex yelled for me to run. A soldier pulled me out of the truck, but Alex ..."

"Yes, go on, Sister Theodora," urged Fevronia.

"Alex fought them and I ran away. I ran and there was this very loud ... I knew it was a gunshot ... seconds later. Somehow I knew, although I'm not sure I'd ever heard a gun before. Then voices, soldiers chasing me, I knew, but I was deep in the woods and kept running. Something made me keep running, running like I'd never run in my life. Lost the bag Mama gave me. When I couldn't run any farther, I lay at the base of a tree. I waited, ready to die, expecting to die. But they never found me."

"You must've been so scared," said Nicky solemnly, then realized how trivial and obvious his comment sounded. He vowed to himself to try to keep him mouth shut until Kal had finished her story.

"I was too tired to be scared, Nicky. I was at the point where I didn't care. I just waited. I don't know how much time passed, but I fell asleep, as cold as it was, and then Demetrios was waking me up, and it was close to morning."

"Demetrios?"

"He was about Alex's age. A man who studied and lived with a priest. Demetrios was going to be a priest himself someday. He was nice. He took care of me, talked to me." She smiled briefly, her tears momentarily dried.

"He asked my name, so I told him I was Kal Ganis of Kavala. What else could I say? I was sure he didn't believe me, but I had to stick to my story."

"Then what?"

"He took me to their church, and I met Father Theodoros, who was very old, old and sweet, a calm, caring man with a big white beard. They didn't want to send me away. They wouldn't give me up to ... Was it the Bulgarians? Bulgarians, they said, yes. So, I lived with them for a few months. I didn't talk. I was afraid they'd find out I was Jewish."

"Surely they knew that anyway," observed Fevronia.

"I didn't realize that. I could not be Jewish, because, if I was Jewish then I'd be shot. Alex told me so."

"May the Lord Jesus Christ protect us all," Fevronia continued.

"I stayed in their small house, kept quiet, always, but they talked freely around me all the time, about the Risen Lord and the Theotokos. And I'd look at their books, and they'd read to me too, but I still I wouldn't talk. Then, they locked me in a closet."

Fevronia drew in her breath sharply. "The closet. You told me about that once."

"They said ... soldiers were coming, searching. I had to hide. In the closet. Cover myself with a blanket. In the corner. Father Theodoros and Demetrios would say they lost the key. They locked me in, but I heard. They prayed so I *would* hear, and ... they knew they'd die. They got ready for their deaths. Soldiers came, shouting, gunfire, the house shook from the bullets. They shot my closet full of holes, too, but I was in the corner and they didn't get me."

"That by itself is a miracle," said Fevronia.

"I tried to get out once I thought the soldiers had gone far away, but I was locked in. And so, once again, I expected to die, but I prayed to be saved. I prayed the way Father Theodoros and Demetrios had prayed. And I had to pee on the floor. I might have been in there for days."

She paused, and while she did so, Nicky almost felt himself trapped in the same closet with her, despairing. He almost found himself praying with her, just for a second, until he caught himself, because he knew that he wouldn't have prayed. He would have already decided that prayer was useless. Had it been him locked in a closet, he might have yelled for help, yelled himself voiceless, and perhaps a passerby might have come to investigate the racket, discovered him locked away, and found the key. But he wouldn't have prayed.

"I stayed," Kal continued, "until the Theotokos came to rescue me."

"The Theotokos?" asked Nicky, unable to hide his surprise.

"Yes," responded Fevronia. "Mary, the Holy Virgin, the Bearer of God, the Mother of Our Lord, Jesus Christ."

"Yes, Mother. It's true, Nicky. I knew who She was, yet I didn't expect Her to be so beautiful, that's the only word, isn't it? So radiant, so warm. She glowed with an orange light that filled me inside in a way I'd never been filled before. I didn't know that She would come to me, but I'd prayed for Her."

"What did the Theotokos look like? Besides the orange glow, I mean," asked Fevronia.

"She looked like she does in the icons, Mother. She wore a dark red veil. She was beautiful. She was holy."

"And then what?" asked Fevronia. Nicky felt himself in too much shock to ask anything.

"She asked me who I was. I told her. 'I am Kal Ganis of Kavala.' And she said 'Kal Ganis. Kal Ganis of Kavala. You've prayed that I come to you?' Yes, I told Her, and I want to be saved. Don't let me die in this closet."

"And she responded?"

"Oh, yes. I'll never forget what she said. 'Prayer that rises up in someone's heart serves to open for all of us the door of heaven, my child.' The Holy Mother asked if I wanted to serve God all my life. She asked if I wanted to draw as close to God, to the Divine Essence, as a person might draw. Her words exactly. She asked if I wanted to help open the door of heaven. I had no idea what She was asking me, what it truly meant. Still, I agreed. I wanted to be close to God and to be saved. And then ..." Kal looked at Nicky, as if he'd know what happened next.

"Then what?" he asked, finally, barely able to get the words out.

"She said 'Take hold of my veil,' and I did."

Kal paused in telling her story, as if preparing herself for an even greater revelation. Nicky wondered why she'd looked at him in that peculiar way, a way that reminded him of when they were children and she'd found something amazing but conceivably dangerous too – a wounded bird, had it been? – and wanted to tell him, needing his help and support.

"Listen, Nicky, and tell me if you remember."

"What?"

"The veil of the Theotokos. She told me to take hold of it, and I did. I held it gingerly at first, but then at Her urging gripped it more firmly, and suddenly we were outside, we were flying above the church, and I saw the entire city of Kavala and the Roman aqueduct and the sea and the island of Thasos, and we flew through the clouds above the countryside, the Theotokos and I, and we flew over the mountains toward the setting sun, and we flew faster than light. I asked Her where we were going, and She said 'My veil will take us where we need to be right now, Kal Ganis of Kavala.' And after the mountains we came down to a city on the side of a small lake and we flew into a church, into a room where two people faced each other, and you were there, Nicky, and a German soldier pulled the pin of a grenade and it exploded and I rushed toward you and pulled the veil of the Theotokos between you and the grenade."

"No," he said, frightened, not wanting to hear more. Kal could not have known what had happened to him in that room. He had the nauseating sensation that she'd managed to jump into his brain, that she wasn't Kal anymore, a human being just like him, but a ghastly spirit that was spying on him, a camera into his mind that had been implanted there without his knowing it and was now conjuring up his innermost secrets.

"Yes, Nicky. And you lived. That's why you're here today. And then the Theotokos and I were back in the closet in Kavala and I let go of Her veil. And a piece of ... no, there were many pieces, fragments of metal, hard, misshapen, torn, hard ... fell from her veil onto the floor."

Nicky stared at his baby sister, not a muscle moving in his face.

Fevronia said, "A grenade, you say. Then those were pieces of shrapnel, no doubt." She urged Kal to go on.

"And the Theotokos asked me again if I wanted to serve the Lord God for the rest of my life. I still wasn't sure what She meant. But I knew that She'd saved you, Nicky, spared you from death. So I repeated as strongly as I could, yes, yes, that's what I wanted. I asked Her how I could serve the Lord God for the rest of my life. I wanted that so badly then, because of what She had done for you, Nicky, and knew that it was the Lord God who gave Her that power. The Theotokos said, 'Before there's a how there must be a will. Is it something that you desire to do, to love the Lord God with all your heart and with all your soul and with all your might such that you'll be the person to open the door of heaven?' And I remembered that sound, that saying, from when we prayed at home and I felt such burning desire, Her warmth filled me even more, and so I said, I told Her a third time, 'I do. I promise. Forever.' And the Theotokos said, 'Then come with me, Kal Ganis of Kavala. Blessed is the young girl who has consented to become the close friend of faith and of prayer,' that's what She said, those were Her exact words, and so that's how I got here."

Kal looked at her brother, bit her lip, and nodded, punctuating the end of her story. Seconds passed. Nicky closed his eyes, trying to digest everything he'd heard. The mental picture of what had occurred in his family after he'd left was far from clear, but he realized that Kal had only described what had happened directly to her. He suddenly found himself with a myriad of additional questions he wanted to ask. Had they ever received word that Nicky had made it safely to Athens and the care of Father Liakos? What had Mama and Papa's demeanor been like after Nicky left? Were they able to express some happiness that he'd escaped from Salonika? Had Alex come back to their house and talked with Mama and Papa between Nicky's departure and Kal's harrowing trip? And what was Ada doing all this time? It wasn't even clear to Nicky whether Ada had been sent away to hide before Kal got her chance. Nicky steeled himself to be patient. Now that Kal had been found, now that she was talking, remembering, there would be plenty of time for all the necessary questions and answers.

Fevronia leaned closer to Kal and asked, "How did you get here specifically? To the monastery? I mean, did you hold Her veil again to fly from Kavala?"

"I cannot remember, Mother. She brought me so close to the light that I thought I would be blinded and burned, and She held me so tight, as if to press everything out of me, but Her embrace brought me peace for a long time, hours, days, weeks, months, I don't know how long. I don't know where I was or with whom, if anyone. There was light, and there was the essence of cinnamon and roses. Somehow, sometime, I found myself at the monastery, up in a back shed of the old winery, in an old, large wine keg, tarps thrown over the top, a canteen of water, a small loaf of bread with me, and somehow I knew I had to hide for days until I thought it was safe to come out. And then I came out. And that's when Andros and Euadne found me."

"Sitting on the stone bench."

"Yes."

"There's more to your story though, isn't there?" asked Fevronia.

"A bit more. Here is my last memory of the Theotokos, whom I never saw again and don't expect ever to see again. She said, just before She disappeared, 'You are now Sister Theodora.'"

"So that's how you got your name," observed Fevronia.

"That's when I was given the name Sister Theodora, Mother, but I knew my real name was Kal Ganis of Kavala."

CHAPTER TWO

Inousa, Greece, April 25, 1990 (Wednesday)

As he listened with rapt attention, Nicky easily pictured his baby sister, the young Kal, ignorant of what was happening, as their family disintegrated, as Mama forced her from home, outwardly impervious to her screams. He sensed Kal's panic as she fought with their mother, the woman who, instead of protecting her from harm, was violently and unlovingly pushing her away. He could feel Kal's fear as she and Alex were stopped by murderous soldiers and as she ran into the woods at Alex's command, escaping with her life beyond all odds. He felt understanding and sympathy with her refusal to speak when she believed that doing so would reveal that she was a Jew. He could see how she gravitated toward the Orthodox Christian mindset, immersed as she was for months in the lives of the religious men who sheltered her and ultimately gave their lives to protect her. He felt the deepest gloom when he pictured Kal in the locked closet, praying to be saved, but hidden where she felt that no one would ever find her.

When she spoke of her rescue by the Theotokos, however, Nicky could not believe, even though Kal sat before him. Prayer didn't work that way. Certainly, Kal must have been screaming, yelling to be rescued, certainly her screams brought a parishioner into the church, someone who discovered the bodies of Father Theodoros and Demetrios and found the closet key. Perhaps not a parishioner. Perhaps a visiting nun whom Kal mistook as the Mother of God. Any deliverance would smack of divine intervention to a susceptible young mind, a girl in delirium from lack of food and water, a girl suffering from post-traumatic shock.

Seconds later, Nicky's world turned on its end again, as Kal described her flight across Greece to the town near the lake. Ioannina, the small church, the German soldier exploding a grenade. He knew he had to be dreaming such nonsense and tried to wake himself, only to discover, in horror, that he was awake. She had said what she had said.

For a full minute after Kal explained how she'd gotten the name Sister Theodora, Nicky and the others sat in silence. Nicky looked at Helen, who appeared to want to say something but held her tongue. He regretted that the conversation had been in Greek and wanted Helen to understand, but felt that it was too soon. Kal had to be interrogated. No, challenged. She had to be challenged as to the fantasy inherent in her account. Nicky felt no option other than to pick at the parts of Kal's story he couldn't believe.

"Kal, you realize that your story is impossible, don't you?"

"For God, nothing is impossible, Nicky."

"Right, right, although ... tell us again about when you first grabbed hold of the veil. You were in the closet and this woman ..."

"The Mother of God. The Theotokos. Not just a woman."

"The Mother of God. Fine. And about your ...

"Flying with Her."

"Yes, and about that church in the city near the lake. What you saw."

"You were there, Nicky," she said emphatically as a prelude to repeating the whole story, starting from her being locked in the closet, her certainty that she'd die, her prayers, her glowing visitor, her flight with the Theotokos, and their intervention against the grenade to save Nicky's life. It had happened decades earlier, it had all unfolded in a second, yet Kal described the scene vividly, as if it had happened in slow motion the day before. Nicky and Kal stared at each other, Nicky struggling to comprehend and Kal remaining firm in the details.

He listened quietly to the repetition, all the while thinking, all right, trauma victims often hold onto exact details as they recount their stories, they remember some things in excruciating detail and other things they cannot remember at all or misremember. Kal was a trauma victim, multiple times, the trauma with Mama leaving home, the trauma of the soldiers' barricade and her dash into the woods as they killed Alex, the trauma when soldiers murdered the priest and his acolyte, and the trauma of the locked closet. Her story had all the elements of post-traumatic stress, particularly the vagueness in her recollection about how she got to the monastery. Maybe, if he explained to her that her imagination had overcome her rational ability to recall, perhaps she would see that, as a suggestible young girl, she'd created a myth for her life, a myth to help her live with things that were too terrible to remember as they were.

"Praised be to Christ our Savior," Fevronia said, in English, crossing herself as Kal finished her story once again. "That is certainly a miracle, Dr. Covo, a miracle that will bring everlasting glory to Sister Theodora and to the Holy Monastery of St. Vlassios. That is, if you will confirm what your sister has said."

"Confirm? I can't believe what I've heard. How can I confirm? You're asking me to do ...."

He stopped short when he saw Kal's face. Even though he'd spoken in English, she'd clearly understood the gist of his denial, and he saw a look of horror, horror that he disbelieved her.

Before Nicky continued, Helen spoke up at last. "Would someone please, in the name of *Hashem*, tell me what's going on?"

It had been cruel to keep Helen in the dark for so long about Kal's story. Nicky filled her in as succinctly as he could. Fevronia listened carefully to make sure that Nicky was telling the story correctly, and Kal sat quietly, eyes down. At the first mention of the Mother of God, Helen gasped as if she'd been slapped. As Nicky continued with Kal's story about the flight to Ioannina and the grenade, trying to keep derision out of his voice, Helen jumped in her chair.

"Nicky. It's what you wrote. It's all there."

And then he knew Helen was right. It was that knowledge he'd been fighting all through Kal's story. He had written down the events exactly as Kal had described. The force that protected him had flown in from the window and flown out again just as quickly. He reached into his backpack and withdrew the envelope with the one typewritten page and the additional folded sheets of hotel stationery. He read both versions over twice, quickly, then handed them to Helen, who likewise read them. The entire time Kal sat silently, head down, looking into her lap.

"Abbess Fevronia," Helen said, handing the pages to Fevronia. "What Kal has just told us did happen, as she says. Just exactly what Nicky has written there." Fevronia read silently for a minute, until she looked up at Nicky with a smile on her face. She read out loud from the typewritten version, in English first, then translated into Greek.

"I waited for the blast and then I sensed a flash of deep red, the color of sunset in the moments before dark, but the flash didn't come from his grenade. It swept into the room from the wall with the window and enveloped the German. The room flooded with red, the intermingled blood from our bodies. But the red was not blood at all, at least not mine. The German was caught in a whirlwind, the shrapnel hitting him only and leaving me unscathed, as if I'd been covered with an impervious, reflective blanket."

Hearing the translation, Kal nodded. She was utterly unsurprised, it appeared, that Nicky confirmed her account.

"I told you," said Helen.

"Amazing," Fevronia marveled, "yet not amazing when one considers the power of our Lord, the power of prayer, the power of our Holy Virgin Mother of Christ." Even as she spoke, she thought about her own visitation from the Theotokos, a smaller miracle, perhaps, yet a miracle still and her very own. She pushed the button to stop the recording.

Nicky was speechless. There must've been a rational explanation for everything, including a malfunctioning grenade, yet he couldn't formulate such an explanation for what he now knew to be true. His baby sister, Kal, and the Theotokos, together, had saved his undeserving life.

He had always loved Kal as strongly as a brother might love a sister. He had always thought of her as an intelligent, exceptional child. Now he stared her with awe and more than a touch of fear.

CHAPTER THREE

Inousa, Greece, April 25, 1990 (Wednesday)

"May I return to my cell, Mother? I've been away from my prayer too long, I fear."

"Yes, of course, Sister Theodora. I'll talk with Dr. Covo – your brother – and his friend for a while. Perhaps you'll see them again before they leave?"

"I'll do as you bid me." Kal rose and turned to Nicky, who reached for her, and they embraced again, a long embrace. He felt again the strange warmth of her body. The fear that Nicky had felt only seconds before had disappeared. As he clung to his sister, he understood that she was but a human being, no more supernatural than he. He could not fear her, yet there was a feeling of something inside her that exceeded humanness, something he would never understand. He murmured her name repeatedly through his tears. Then she smiled and said, "Praise be to God, the Father of our Lord Jesus Christ." Nicky felt pity in her look, a look in which she sorrowfully noted that Nicky would never glimpse the reality that had sustained her life; indeed, that had sustained both of their lives. She gently pushed herself out of Nicky's embrace, hugged Helen, and left Fevronia's office quickly, without turning back or a word of departure.

Nicky turned to Fevronia. "Does she expect me to believe what she believes? Did you see how she looked at me when she said that? When she said 'the Father of our Lord Jesus Christ? *Our* Lord?"

"You are not to be offended, Dr. Covo. Sister Theodora was simply trying to express thanks that you and she have met again. It is our way to praise

Christ whenever we are truly happy, whenever the world takes a positive turn, for which we bless Our Lord. You see, she is still as devoted as ever to her faith and her prayer."

"I thought I'd have more chance to talk to her," said Nicky.

"But she's been through an awful lot already today," observed Helen. "Surely she needs a rest from all this. Surely she needs time for prayer in her cell."

"Quite true, Mrs. Blanco," Fevronia responded. "And for us, prayer becomes addictive. When we are away from it for long, we feel the irritations, the unpleasantness of withdrawal." As if to illustrate her point, she withdrew a currant-colored silk prayer rope from her black habit and held it in her left hand. "Surely you have dealt with withdrawal in your patients, yes?" she asked.

"Yes, but not ...." Nicky started.

"Then that's how it is with us, too."

"I've never encountered someone who is addicted to prayer, if there is such a thing," he protested, resuming his seat, replacing the envelope and its contents into this backpack.

Fevronia considered the argument, ultimately deciding not to delve into the subject with this unbeliever. She cleared her throat, then spoke in a more formal voice, as if she were a corporate executive conducting a directors' meeting. "Do either of you know who St. Vlassios was? The St. Vlassios venerated by this monastery?"

"No," said Helen, as Nicky shook his head.

"A shame. You might have looked it up. He was a physician and often referred to as a healer of souls. You might say, Dr. Covo, that St. Vlassios was the first psychiatrist. Your profession reaches back to the early ages of our Church."

"If you say so, Abbess."

Fevronia waited a few seconds to see if he'd ask more about St. Vlassios, then decided the move on. "Let us please to proceed to the next order of business, if you will. In light of what we have all just witnessed, I will ask you, Dr. Covo, or, should I say I would very much like you please to fill out an ... an affidavit verifying Sister Theodora's story."

"Why should I do that? What good is it to anyone if I say that such a thing happened? How does it help Kal, for instance?"

Fevronia saw that Dr. Covo was being difficult because he'd not had time to absorb the reality of Sister Theodora's flight with the veil of the Theotokos, even though he'd recognized the truth upon reading his own description of how his life had been saved. She saw that he needed more time to contemplate what the story meant to him – might mean to him, if he gave it half a chance – and to talk the situation over with his friend. Mrs. Blanco at least appeared ready to accept the truth, even if that truth didn't align with her religious tradition.

"You ask good questions, Dr. Covo. It might not make any difference to you, because you don't want it to make a difference. That's your choice. Whether or not you sign an affidavit surely doesn't matter to Sister Theodora – Kal, let's call her that – because Kal knows what happened to her and what she and the Theotokos did to save your life. What Kal wants is just that you believe her, not whether you sign anything. And to me it makes no difference personally, because I heard Kal's story and read your notes and I know what happened and believe fully. It might make a difference to others, though, the people here who love Kal and have loved and taken care of her for many years. It might well matter to the people here she confesses every week, the people whom she touches to make their hearts lighten. The people here for whom she has helped open the door to heaven. And it might matter to others in later generations who want to believe and who need miracles to help them believe. We will always need our miracles and our saints. There are too few documented miracles these days of any type, and none of this great magnitude. Perhaps there would be more if there were more believers."

He was ready to tell her no, absolutely no, a thousand times no, but Helen intervened before he could say anything.

"Nicky, let's give ourselves a little space to think it through. We need to consider everything carefully. Surely, we'll want to come back and spend more time with Kal before we leave Greece. We can give Abbess Fevronia an answer when we return."

Nicky realized that Helen had a good point. His short visit with Kal couldn't be the end of their reunion. He had plans. And, yes, thinking things through before giving Fevronia a definitive answer would be for the best. Kal still lived, because ... well, who knew why? But she was alive, and he desperately wanted her to stay in his life. He had no choice but to cooperate with Fevronia, the woman who'd looked after Kal for so many years and brought them together.

"All right, Abbess Fevronia. I do need to take some time to absorb all this. Both of us – Kal and I – should've died, and yet here we are, forty-plus years later, holding each other, crying over each other."

"God has done that, Dr. Covo."

"Some force that you call 'God.' I don't recognize God, but yet ..."

"Nicky, please let's not argue about that right now," implored Helen.

"I suppose you're right. I apologize, Abbess Fevronia. May we come back tomorrow morning?"

"Our Divine Liturgy will be over by nine-thirty. You may come at ten."

"And so we will."

·　　·　　·　　·　　·

In part, Fevronia was excited by the realization that, with Dr. Covo's help, if he should choose to give it, she could attribute a miracle to Theodora's account. And she perceived that Theodora, documented as a Jewish survivor of the Holocaust who'd made a lifelong commitment to the Church that had saved her, would bring honor to the monastery where she lived out her life of prayer to Christ. Yes, Fevronia would have to arrange a formal baptism, which would be done in Kerkini Lake, not far from Inousa, with a small group, Andros certainly, Ephraim, a few of the sisters. She'd strong-arm Rukos into doing her bidding if the Metropolitan was unavailable. Do the baptism quickly, be done with it, and get back to life as the mother abbess of a miracle-working nun. Imagining the baptism, the widespread dissemination of news about the miracles, the name Holy Monastery of St. Vlassios on the lips of every Orthodox Christian, made her almost giddy.

Another part of Fevronia was more subdued, though. If the Theotokos had been able to save the life of this Jewish girl and her older brother, why had She not also saved Silenos and the other monks? The Theotokos must have been nearby when they were murdered. Had She not seen what was going to happen? Why did God Himself and his Holy Son and the Mother of God let them be killed, and why did They allow the grave to be kept hidden? Sister Theodora's life had been a blessing to the world, but God could've chosen to spare others in addition, those whose lives would likewise have been a blessing. Even as Fevronia wondered, though, she knew that mere human beings would never decipher God's will.

Perhaps everything unfolded as it did precisely to bring Dr. Covo and Mrs. Blanco to St. Vlassios at this very instant, for reasons no one would ever know.

CHAPTER FOUR

Thessaloniki, Greece, April 25-26, 1990 (Wednesday and Thursday)

They drove in silence toward Thessaloniki. The stop-and-go traffic, choked with heavy trucks, gave them a lot of time to reflect. Nicky felt uneasy with the way Kal had left them, looking at him and praising Christ as "our lord." As Fevronia said, it might well have been Kal's way of saying thank you to God for their reunion. But had she truly needed need to run off to pray just then? She couldn't endure visiting with him and Helen a bit longer? Withdrawal as from an addiction? A bunch of nonsense. Perhaps Kal hadn't liked Helen? Or had Nicky said something wrong? Then it hit him that he had, in fact, acted poorly. He'd doubted Kal's story. He'd said as much directly to her face, accusing her ... well, of being crazy. That was wrong. That's why she needed to go back to her cell. He'd offended her, and she could no longer stand to be in his presence.

He had to fight the instinct to turn around to revisit the monastery that afternoon. If it had been easier to get off the highway and reverse direction, he might well have done so. He attempted to imagine without success how he could explain to Fevronia and Kal why they'd returned so soon after they'd left.

As he continued to drive and think about the situation, his anger grew. He imagined Father Theodoros and Demetrios drilling Christ into the head of a scared six-year-old Jewish girl, telling her that the Jews had denied God, murdered God, and were a sinful people because of it. Then, however she got to the monastery, maybe drugged and brought against her will, all Kal had was a handful of Christian villagers who didn't have the sense to try help her find her real family. And Fevronia, meddlesome, worried about documenting miracles for the glory of her faith, with that stupid tape recorder. He should've told her to turn it off. She met Kal in the early 50s? If she'd tracked him down then, Kal could've been with him in America for most of her life. She'd have known her nephew and niece, her grandnephew. She'd have known Adel, been at his side when he and Adel were married, helped to comfort him when Adel died. He might've had a life with his sister if the people around her hadn't been so concerned about making her into something she wasn't.

And yet, he thought, I wouldn't have been anywhere at all, except thousands of torn pieces of flesh plastered on the wall of a small room inside a church, had it not been for Kal's faith. I know that now, as surely as I know I'm sitting here in a car, next to Helen Blanco, driving south. I can tell myself a million times over that what happened was impossible, I know it was impossible, yet it happened, and I'm here now only because of the impossible. I owe my life to something I can never believe. I was taught from an early age that God created the universe from nothing, and I believed that for so long, even though that was impossible. Then I saw truth. My life has since been devoted to truth, to facts, to science, to medicine, to the grim realization that there's nothing beyond death, no world of dead souls gathered waiting for us, no Messiah. I've formed my life from these truths.

And yet, why was I here for all that time, trying to devote myself to truth and facts, adamant in my disbelief? I had the freedom to disbelieve only because my supposedly dead baby sister, Kal, and the Mother of God, her God, flew across Greece in the blink of an eye and protected me in the very instant I should've died.

I don't understand. I'll never understand.

●　　●　　●　　●　　●

They bumped their way through the thick downtown traffic of Thessaloniki for the second time in two days. "Have you talked to Kayla or Max lately?" asked Helen, as they neared the Electra Palace. "I wonder how she's doing. And Jackie, of course."

Nicky made the call from their room.

"Hello, Jackie. This is Grandpa. How are you? .... I'm in Greece, remember? Is *Ima* home? ... Yes, yes, the clarinet is hard. Stick with it, okay? And how's Aliyah? Good. Put *Ima* on the phone, please."

Helen took a pair of grey wool slacks from a hanger and sat on the bed next to him, openly eavesdropping.

"Kayla, everything okay with you? ... How are you feeling? ... Good. ...Yes, she *is* my sister. She *is* Kal. She told the most amazing story, but I'll save that, to tell you both when we get home. ... Yes, she recognized me, after a while. ... Her whole life is a prayer to Jesus. Look, we'll relate all when Helen and I get back. I wanted you to know we're okay. We'll see you in a few days. Both of us." He replaced the phone into its holder.

"Both of us?" asked Helen.

"Well, only if you want to. I thought we should tell Max and Kayla about us. Maybe we should tell your family first."

"What about us? We haven't worked anything out, have we?"

"Helen, will you marry me?" He reached for her, but she jumped from the bed as if from a live electric wire, stumbling back a few steps until her way was barred by the dresser.

"No."

"No? That was too quick. Don't you want to think about it?"

"Not really." She returned to sit next to him and took his hands in hers. "How can you go from seeing your sister for the first time in forty-seven years to proposing marriage in the space of five hours? Where's your sense of timing? You make this so casual, as if it's preordained just because we're sleeping together."

"I'm sorry, Helen. I love you. I've told you that, and I thought you felt the same way. I guess I've just been ..." He shook his head, not sure at all what he'd been.

"Who says I don't love you? I need time. I have to think everything through. This is too big a step to take lightly."

"I'm not taking it lightly."

They kissed. "Let's talk about this tomorrow," she said, as she pressed her hand lightly to his chest.

"I'll put up the privacy sign."

He did not expect results better than what they'd previously achieved, yet this time he surprised himself. As drained as he felt by the emotions of the day, by the torrent of thoughts, by anger, by confusion, by thankfulness, inexplicably his lovemaking was more relaxed. It had become too hard to think, and with the loss of thought came a renewal of his body's natural instincts. He didn't rush. He sensed her needs and reacted. He held and caressed her as if time had gone on vacation, and to his joy it all came together as nature intended. He was ecstatic to hear her whimper his name as she climaxed, an urgent murmuring of his name that quickly brought him along.

And then, as they rested, when every fiber of his body pushed him toward sleep, he heard her singing ever so softly. It was too beautiful to stop, but he could hardly make out words. He squeezed her to urge her on, and she picked up the volume slightly. "*He-nach yafah rah-yah-ti, he-nach yafah.*" He knew the Hebrew; it was from the Song of Songs. "Behold, thou art fair, my love, behold thou art fair."

· · · · ·

The next morning, as Helen snored lightly, Nicky got out of bed, dressed in the bathroom, removed the pentobarbital vials from his suitcase, and went to the lobby. No one else besides the desk attendant was around. Nicky asked if he could borrow a Thessaloniki phone directory and a city map, then carried them outside. It was just beginning to get light, and the Aegean was still a misty, dark cobalt. When the sunlight hit it in an hour, it would turn dazzling blue-green. He walked to a bench overlooking the harbor, about a quarter-mile from the hotel. There, he sat and looked through the directory. After he dog-eared a page, he turned his attention to the map. In another ten minutes, he walked to the side of a pier, opened his vials, and poured their contents into the water, tossing the vials in afterward. He returned to the Electra Palace and, in a few minutes, had his party on the line and made the necessary arrangements.

When he got back to the room, Helen was dressed and greeted him with a kiss. "Good morning. What were you up to? You always seem to be gone when I wake. I looked for you in the lobby. How could you have left me?"

"How about an early morning stop here in the city before we go back to the monastery?"

"What? You're not anxious to be back? We told Fevronia ten."

"We'll call her and set it later. There's someone in Salonika we should meet. We need to meet." After breakfast, where Nicky explained what he intended, they were back in their car, threading their way through traffic.

"Hey, I've got an idea," ventured Helen brightly. "Since we're driving in the city, do you want to show me where you lived?"

"Might as well." He turned at the next corner, and in fifteen minutes they were on Delfon Street, where Nicky's house had been. They saw, though, not houses, but block after block of three- and four-story apartment buildings, stores, and restaurants.

"This doesn't look like the street you described. Are you sure you know where you are?"

"Yes, I know. It looks nothing like what I remember, though. Every house along here was torn down in the sixties and seventies, I've read. Urban renewal. I knew it. Still, I hoped that I'd see the old place again. Well, let's get on with our mission. I can't imagine ..." But at that instant, he swerved to the curb at the corner of Miaouli. An angry pedestrian, narrowly missed by their car, gave Nicky the finger.

"What is it?"

"Here, to the right, was our house." He pointed.

"You lived across from a church?" Helen turned from the drab apartment building indicated by Nicky to the impressive looking house of worship across the street; its façade shined brightly pink in the sunlight.

"No church there in '43. The Yahons, also Jews, lived there in a house almost as big as ours. Dr. Yahon took care of our teeth. His son Albertos, three years older than me, disappeared weeks before I left. Papa thought he'd gone off to the partisans. If he did, I never ran into him. There were scores of different groups. For all I know, I fought against him. And right there, Helen, Alex snuck me into his truck. We drove down Miaouli and in ten minutes made it to the pier at Navarinou."

"Hard to imagine, your rushing out of here, away from everything you knew."

"Let's scramble."

"Scram, I think you mean."

"Whatever."

He pulled back abruptly into the traffic. It took them another twenty minutes to find Eptanison Street, in a quiet rundown neighborhood rife with boarded-up buildings. As in Athens, graffiti were painted along many of the walls. The apartment they were seeking was on the second story of a nondescript building. A door opened for them as they approached, and a stooped woman with straggly grey hair, wearing a simple grey wool dress, welcomed them.

"Dr. Covo?"

"Yes, and you, I presume, are Miss Tabitha Ganis?" He spoke in English.

"Please to come in."

Nicky considered offering her his hand, then thought that the gesture might be too informal and simply walked past their hostess, nodding. But Helen, he could see as she came in behind him, took Tabitha gently by the shoulders and air kissed her on both sides of the face, as if she'd lived in Europe her entire life. Tabitha's reaction to Helen's gesture showed only pleasure, no offense.

Tabitha showed them to her living room, where she offered seats on a threadbare sofa. She asked if they'd like coffee, which they accepted. They spent a few minutes of conversing about the weather and about crime perpetrated "by the young hoodlums," until Tabitha turned to the business at hand.

"Dr. Covo, you remind me of your father."

Nicky raised his eyebrows. "You knew him?"

"When I was a little girl and started having seizures, he was my doctor. I saw him at the hospital. Then, when Alex began working there, I met Dr. Covo again on occasion. He treated Alex well, took interest in him. No doubt, that is one of the reasons Alex helped you get to Athens."

"I owe my life to that effort, Miss Ganis, and I want to thank you."

"I did nothing. Your debt is to Alex, but on his behalf, I accept your thanks."

"Do you have a picture of him?"

"Wait here. I will show you, and the diary too."

Tabitha returned with a framed photograph of her younger brother and a small leather diary. She placed the diary on a side table and handed the photograph to Nicky. The young, pensive looking man in the photograph sat on a park bench and held a cigarette. The dark sweater he wore matched his neatly combed dark hair.

"I remember him," Nicky offered. He showed Helen.

"And a father of two boys, my nephews. They were so young when Alex died. I wish they'd known you were coming this morning. They would have wanted to meet you."

"Perhaps someday. So, I would like to also offer thanks to your brother, and his family, for what he did for my sister, Kal."

"When Abbess Fevronia explained to me that Sister Theodora might have been a Jewish girl that Alex saved, I could not believe it. A nun! No one here knew exactly what Alex was doing when he died. We suspected it had to do with some little girl, though. There were cryptic notes in his diary."

"Helen and I," he said nodding to his companion, "heard Sister Theodora – Kal – tell the story yesterday, and there's no doubt. Your brother, may his memory be for a blessing, fought against the Bulgarian soldiers who stopped them and gave Kal a chance to escape. She ran for her life, she heard the shot. Alex was a hero, Miss Ganis."

"Please to call me Tabitha."

"Then please call me Nicky. Alex was a hero, Tabitha. And I think that needs to be recognized."

"What do you mean?"

"Have you heard of The Righteous Among the Nations?" When she shook her head, Nicky continued. "There's a commission in Israel that documents and honors gentiles, like Alex, who risked or gave their lives to help Jews during the Holocaust. They are honored in a museum in Jerusalem, a place of remembrance, known as Yad Vashem. If you consent, I'd like to nominate Alex."

She sat up straighter in her chair. "With all respect, Nicky, Alex did not do this for honor. His Christian faith required it of him. His love for Christ compelled him to do as he did. He felt he had no choice."

"Still, so many others who might have helped stayed silent, did nothing. So many others helped the Nazis. It's right to honor those who were true to their faiths."

"*Ochi.* No."

Nicky was about to argue, but Helen stayed him with a question. "May I try?"

"Go ahead."

"Miss Ganis, I'm Jewish, too, and my family came from Salonika long ago. We – my family and I -- were lucky. We weren't here when the Germans invaded. Nicky's family wasn't lucky. One person in the world saved both Nicky and his sister, the little girl who became Sister Theodora. That was your brother, Alex."

"My Alex was a very good man."

"Yes. He was. Well, Nicky's gone on to become a successful psychiatrist and has helped hundreds of patients."

"His father was a very good doctor, too."

"I'm sure that's true. Sister Theodora, whom Alex saved, devotes her life to serving Christ. She prays all the time."

"Yes, yes," responded Tabitha eagerly. "Abbess Fevronia made sure I knew that, yet I had long ago heard of her. Sister Theodora's devotion and life are well known in the Church. I have been there once myself, to confess to her."

"Abbess Fevronia says that Sister Theodora's prayers help open the doors of heaven. We can't know for sure what effect her prayers have, although Christians and Jews share the belief that God hears our prayers," Helen continued, as Tabitha nodded. "Those prayers wouldn't have reached God's ears had it not been for Alex. The people in Inousa who confess to Sister Theodora and other pilgrims like you who do the same wouldn't have had her blessings without Alex's heroism. Nicky's patients wouldn't have had his devotion and care had it not been for Alex." Helen looked at Nicky, who felt she was about to ask him to take over the argument, but she went on after drawing in a healthy breath. "So, Tabitha, even if Alex wouldn't have wanted to be honored, by honoring him we also honor the good that his courage brought to the rest of the world. We honor the faith that led him to do what he did. We honor your true faith."

Tabitha nodded again, then looked down for a second, and finally looked up with a warm smile, tears in her eyes. "Very well, I understand better now. In honor of my brother and his faith, in honor of God Almighty,

I will consent and will do what I can to help. May Christ's Name be blessed."
She crossed herself.

"Thank you, Tabitha." Helen walked to Tabitha and they hugged. Then
Tabitha picked up the leather book at her side and held it out to Nicky.

"Now, do you want to see the diary?"

CHAPTER FIVE

Inousa, Greece, April 26, 1990 (Thursday)

They were gathered again in the office, Fevronia, Nicky, and Helen. They'd exchanged pleasantries, started on tea, and then fallen silent for a few moments until Fevronia, needing to know how things stood, began the discussion for which they'd been readying themselves.

"Now, Dr. Covo, I have to ask you. Please to put aside for a moment the question of documenting the miracle. Please to tell me honestly. What are your intentions with regard to Sister Theodora? Do you plan to ask her to go home with you, to leave the monastery where she has lived since she was a little girl, where she has been venerated? Where she is greatly loved?"

Nicky answered almost before Fevronia finished her question. "Yes. That's exactly what I want to do. I've thought thoroughly about that possibility and see that it's entirely practical. I've plenty of room in my apartment, and there are many Orthodox churches in the neighborhood. Manhattan is full of them."

"I see. I was hoping you would not feel that way."

"Why shouldn't I? She's my sister, my flesh and blood. She's the only living connection I have with my family."

"Dr. Covo, do you realize how stressful that would be for her? Can you imagine how moving away from here will irrevocably interfere with her prayer? Do you want to be responsible for that?"

"Abbess Fevronia, I want her to come home with me. No. I need her to come with me. She knows who she is now. She's hidden too long from her identity." He paused, expecting a response, but Fevronia merely looked at him quietly. "It only makes sense that she'd want to stay with me, now that we've found each other again. Doesn't it?"

Fevronia sighed. "Her leaving here would devastate us and the town."

"I'm sorry, Abbess Fevronia. Inousa has had the benefit of her presence for, what, forty-six years? For that long time, Kal hasn't had anyone from her own family. Don't you think she deserves that connection for the rest of her life?"

"You think she has changed so much because you've come here? Yes, she has been able to talk, to remember, that is a blessing and an upheaval in her world. Underneath all that, at her core, at the very meaning of her life, she is still Sister Theodora. You saw her leave yesterday to return to her prayer. You heard her praise Christ the Lord to your face. You've been told how much she means to the people of this village. She cannot shuffle off her calling as easily as you would like."

Fevronia picked up a flyswatter and waved it at an annoying insect whose buzzing Nicky heard, suddenly, as if the creature had waited for the end of the conversation before making noise. She missed, sighed, and flipped the flyswatter back onto her desk.

Nicky waited to see if Fevronia would argue further, but she just stared at him. Was she angry because he wanted to take Kal from her or fearful of what Kal might decide if offered the opportunity to leave? He said, "Of course we'll let Kal decide what she wants to do."

"All right, we will let her to decide."

$$\bullet \quad \bullet \quad \bullet \quad \bullet \quad \bullet$$

Fevronia knew that she couldn't force Theodora to remain. The more Fevronia argued with Dr. Covo, however, the more confident she became that Theodora would remain of her own free will. Theodora would see that the Mother of God had saved her for the Church, to devote her life to Christ, and had found her the best possible home for that purpose. Theodora would understand that in every fiber of her body. She would insist on staying, and Fevronia would not have to urge her to do so.

When Sister Theodora returned to the office, the four resumed the seats in which they'd sat the previous day. "Sister Theodora," Fevronia said in

Greek, "your brother wants to ask you an important question. Please give him your full attention." She once again clicked on her tape recorder.

Nicky was annoyed that the conversation would be recorded. He'd not given his consent, but it wasn't the right time to argue. Instead, he turned to Kal and took her hand. She looked at him with what he felt was sisterly love in her large, clear, intelligent, dark brown eyes.

"Kal, Abbess Fevronia and I have been talking. Well, let's get to the point. I'm asking you to come back to America with me."

He paused, expecting Kal to say something, hoping that she'd immediately agree, yet she remained silent. The warm pressure of her hand in his did not change. She continued to look directly at him, calmly, not upset by his appeal. Good sign, he hoped.

"You'd have your own room in my apartment in Manhattan. You have a niece and a nephew, my children. My daughter, whom I named Kayla, whom I named after you, in your memory, composes music. My son, Max, is a lawyer. He's named after Papa, of course. You have a grandnephew, Jackie. They live together, close to New York City and would love to get to know you."

Kal continued to look at him patiently, silently.

"There are your churches, Kal. There's the Annunciation Greek Orthodox Church on West 91st. Only a short walk from where I live."

More silence. Kal continued to smile as if listening to the sweetest music. Nicky reached into his backpack, pulled out a pamphlet with a photograph of the church, and showed it to her. She glanced at it, still saying nothing. Nicky waited a few seconds before continuing.

"If you don't like that one, there are others a short subway ride away." Her gaze fell suddenly, and she seemed for all the world to be examining her dirty feet. Oh God, let her say yes, he thought. "What do you say, Kal? Can we be together again, brother and sister, as we once were? Before I ran off to Athens?" He pulled out the framed drawing of the blue jay and handed it to her as he'd done the day before. She glanced at it, then put it down gently on the floor.

As they waited for Theodora's answer, Fevronia's fears disappeared altogether. She breathed deeply in relief, now certain what Theodora would say, if anything. Theodora's head was down, her lips moved, and Fevronia knew she was praying. Finally, Theodora looked up at her brother.

"Nicky, Nicky." She handed the drawing and pamphlet back to her brother. "Thank you. Thank you for living to this point and remembering me, caring about me. Thank you for coming all the way back, to this little mountain, to find me. Thank you for wanting me in your life again. Thank you for allowing me to meet your special friend, Mrs. Blanco. As much as I love you, Nicky, I want to stay here. What's kept me alive all these years is my greater love for Christ, to Whom I pray as much as I can. I promised the Theotokos to serve God my entire life. I could never abandon that promise. I wouldn't be here today had I not made that promise. And my cell here, my prayer corner, is my true home. I could never leave it. And the villagers need me. They confess to me, and I help them feel better. When they tell me what they need to tell me, they feel closer to heaven, and so do I." A tear slipped down her cheek. As she spoke, her voice grew faint, ethereal. She closed her eyes.

"Kal, please." Nicky rose from his chair and knelt in front of his sister, putting his arms around her as she sat, his head against her bosom. She placed a thin hand lightly on the back of his head, then let her hand drop.

Fevronia felt deep sorrow for Dr. Covo. He'd come so far in the hope of finding his sister, yet she wasn't the same person he'd known before. They shared memories, a family history, and grief at the loss of their parents and sister; they shared trauma; they shared the drawing passed between them, her child's gift that had nourished his spirit for decades, yet they would never share the same time and place in the world.

Theodora remained silent, but Fevronia heard her words through her heart. "I pray to the Lord Jesus Christ to forgive me, a sinner."

They sat quietly for minutes while Kal prayed, until Fevronia spoke in a low voice. "I think, Dr. Covo, that you have your answer." He sat back in his chair, closed his eyes, and motioned that Fevronia should take Kal away.

Fevronia reached for Theodora's hand and urged her from her chair. "I will walk you to your cell, my sweet child, my life."

•　　•　　•　　•　　•

While Fevronia was away, Nicky related to Helen, as exactly as he was able, what Kal had said. He saw that Helen understood, even before he began to speak. He imagined that the great heaviness in his heart was more than apparent on his face. When he finished his account, Helen hugged him.

"I'm so sorry, Nicky."

"How did I think she might leave? How stupid of me. Selfish."

"You had to try. You couldn't just leave her here without trying, without doing your best. *Hashem* knows I would've done the same."

"My best didn't add up to very much, did it? Now what?"

"Now the rest of our trip. Now you and I."

"*He-nach yafah rah-yah-ti, he-nach yafah*," he sang, as sweetly as possible.

"Exactly."

They discussed briefly whether they should stay in in Salonika for a few days and visit the monastery one more time, try to talk to Kal again, but it didn't take them long to recognize the futility of hoping that she'd change her mind. They were discussing which beaches they might visit, and whether perhaps they should tour the tomb of King Philip II of Macedon, when Fevronia returned.

The three remained together for another hour in Fevronia's office. Fevronia apologized to Nicky for needing to turn their attention to a matter that was important only to her and her church, but she begged him to sign a statement confirming Theodora's story, how his life had been miraculously saved by her and the Theotokos. Nicky was willing, and Fevronia typed out a declaration to that effect in Greek. A problem arose when Fevronia asked him if he'd swear to God that his statement was true and Nicky was reluctant to acknowledge any deity. Yet he wanted to accommodate Fevronia, without whose determination he wouldn't have found Kal.

"Helen, help me here, please. How do I do this?"

Helen hesitated for only a moment before answering. "When you left Kal back in '43, when she handed you her drawing, that very instant, you believed in *Hashem*, yes?"

"Yes."

"It is to *Hashem* of your childhood and of Kal's childhood that you can swear an oath."

"All right." He turned to Fevronia. "I'll swear. Just say 'God' please, Abbess Fevronia, nothing Christian if that can be avoided." She complied, finished typing, and gave him the document to read and sign. It included not only his story about being shielded from the grenade's blast but Theodora's account of her flight with the Theotokos. He signed it, and Fevronia reread it and placed it in a file, thanking both Nicky and Helen profusely.

"And I guess you'll be on your way now?"

"Back to Salonika and then to the beach," Nicky answered. "We still have four days left before our return flights. I need time to think about what's just happened. I can't believe any of this, yet ... well, I've sworn it's true. Will I be able to write to her, do you think? Will you give her my letters?"

"Of course I will give them to her. I cannot promise you she will write back, though. She may, but in all the years I have been here I have never to see her write anything. I cannot even promise that she will read your letters. You can see what has happened just now. She has returned to her old self, her real self, completely Sister Theodora, focused only on prayer. Nothing else matters to her, nothing else ever will matter to her. I am not sure even if *I* will ever hear her to speak again." Fevronia thought for a second that she should've asked Theodora if she knew anything about Silenos's grave, that she'd missed a great opportunity, that she'd probably never have another chance.

Nicky wondered what, if anything, he might write to Kal now that she was fully and forever Sister Theodora. Memories of their childhoods together in Salonika? Updates about the lives of Kayla, Max, and Jackie, family members whom she'd never meet? An announcement of his and Helen's wedding, should such a thing ever take place? It might be pointless to write. But how could he not continue for the rest of his life to reach out to her?

"I understand. I'll write anyway. No one can know what she will or won't do, whether she'll even remember I was here and that we spoke as brother and sister. That we embraced twice more. That she remembered for a time that she'd been born and lived six years as Kal Covo. Thank you for everything, Abbess Fevronia."

"You are most welcome. Praise be to Our Lord."

"There's one more thing, though." Nicky reached yet again into his backpack and took out an object wrapped in newspaper. He unwrapped it and handed it to Fevronia. "I'm sorry that this is as dirty as it is. I think you should have it."

She looked at it carefully, brushing away some additional dirt, and opened the case. "The icon of Iveron," she gasped. "Where did this come from, Dr. Covo?" Her voice now sounded difficult to keep under control, laden with emotion, not the annoyance that Nicky had expected and feared.

"We found it off the side of a road on the other side of Greece. In a clump of trees. In a little cave formed by tree roots. Near a small village called Charakopi. Outside Ioannina."

"Just like that?"

"In truth, we were looking for it. It was something I'd thrown away many years ago, after I took it from a dead man." He looked directly into her eyes and heard her unspoken question. "I removed it from the hand of an elderly peasant I killed."

Fevronia looked to Helen and back to Nicky.

"Whom I killed during the war," Nicky added. "When I thought he was about to kill me."

"The *riza* still works," she observed, opening and closing the case. "This blessed icon was there in the woods for decades? It's hardly damaged; the scar on Our Lady's right cheek is still visible. We will of course to keep it here." She crossed herself and kissed the icon, praying out loud "oh pure Theotokos, deliver us from dangers," placed it carefully on a bookshelf behind her, and turned to Nicky. "It is rather a miracle that you should have found something like that so long after the fact. We will note if it gushes myrrh. I would expect that, based on your story."

"You see, I thought it was a gun." He had the crazy urge to beg her forgiveness.

"It might well have been a gun, for all you knew. You have put it in its right place now, though, with the faithful. Thank you both for bringing it here, to me. If Sister Theodora agrees, I will hang it in her cell, as a remembrance of your visit."

On their way out, at Nicky's request, Fevronia led them past Theodora's cell so that he could see how his sister looked when she prayed there. Fevronia pushed the door open a few inches, and they observed her quietly. Then Nicky began softly singing a lullaby Kal had loved as a child. He felt it would mean a great deal to him if Kal heard him sing it again, but immediately remembered that it wasn't Kal to whom he was singing, but Sister Theodora. Caught up in her prayer, she might not acknowledge him or his song. Fevronia sighed deeply as he sang, as if barely able to tolerate this intrusion on Sister Theodora's devotion.

"*Nani, nani, nani kere el ija de la Madre. De chica se aga grande. Ay el durmite el alma que tu padre viene. Ay, ay, durmite mi alma, durmite, mi vida.*"

There was no reaction from Sister Theodora. Nicky stopped and turned, walking away from the cell.

"Do you know the song, what he was singing?" Fevronia asked Helen in a whisper.

"A Ladino lullaby. Let's see. The daughter of his mother has grown. Sleep, my sweet one, sleep, my life."

Fevronia felt that Sister Theodora must have heard her brother's singing and had willed herself not to react, but had found it very difficult to pretend she hadn't heard. Fevronia sensed that Sister Theodora too wanted to say one more goodbye.

. . . . .

Nicky and Helen were almost back at their car, Fevronia alongside to wish them a safe journey, when Nicky had yet another idea about how he might try to connect once more with Kal. Fevronia reluctantly agreed – what Dr. Covo was asking was highly irregular – to take him back to Kal's cell. Helen said she'd wait in the car.

"You'll be back soon, I imagine," said Helen.

. . . . .

Left by Fevronia at Kal's cell, Nicky looked in to see her still kneeling in her corner, praying, exactly as she'd been when he'd seen her five minutes earlier. He knocked on the wall and cleared his throat loudly enough to cause Kal to turn around. A slight nod of her head and perhaps the glimmer of a smile. He entered.

"Sister Theodora, may I talk with you?"

"Call me Kal, Nicky. You're my brother, whom I love. You are as dear to me as any other living person. You came back to find me. For you, I'll always be Kal." She gestured for Nicky to sit on her cot and sat herself on the other end of it.

"I've heard you have the power to forgive."

"No, Nicky. Only God has that power."

"Abbess Fevronia said you hear confessions. I thought ..."

"I do. I listen to many poor souls who tell me their sins. It's always a first step. Do you need to confess?"

"How does this work?"

"You just tell me what you want to tell me."

"Fine." He took a deep breath, felt ridiculous, yet needed to talk. "I killed many people during the war," he said evenly, "people who didn't deserve to die." He felt her steady gaze through him, as if she saw everything hidden in his heart, and he knew she could never truly love him unless he confessed the very things she saw. "A prisoner. I gutted him with a bayonet." Her gaze did not falter, no look of shock, not even of sorrow, crossed her face. Just waiting. "And I shot to death an elderly peasant."

"Yes? There's more?"

"And I killed a young girl in a church, who wore a yellow smock. Others."

"Is that all?"

"No. I fled my home, leaving you and Mama and Papa and Ada to be caught and murdered."

"What else, Nicky? Now has to be the time for you to say it all. To speak the words that struggle within you, the words you fight against."

"I tried to kill myself."

"And?"

He thought.

"I made love to Helen's sister, my friend Mrs. Blanco's sister, years ago, on Helen's bed, which had become my bed, when their mother was in the hospital dying. I was unfaithful to Adel, my wife. She's dead now. I never knew how to take care of my daughter, Kayla. She was a piano prodigy and went mad because I couldn't protect her as a father should. I haven't been a good doctor at all. Some of my patients killed themselves, I should have done more. I spent too much time at work, not enough with my family."

"Nicky, please tell me everything."

"I rejected God."

Still, she waited quietly, not moving a muscle save for moistening her lips. What else? Then he knew.

"And, when I heard you were still alive, I didn't believe. When I heard how you survived and how you saved me, just yesterday, I didn't believe."

"But now?"

No answer emerged through his tears, and he saw that she cried as well. She slid closer to him on the cot and took his hand, squeezing gently. The touch. He sensed her absorbing his pain, and as the pain departed he knew a profound relief, near lightheadedness. After a while, he stopped crying, they hugged, and he left.

At the car, Nicky and Helen embraced, and he knew she felt his still wet face. She asked him what had happened.

"I confessed to Sister Theodora."

CHAPTER SIX

Over the Atlantic, in Manhattan, and in West Caldwell, New Jersey, April 29-30, 1990 (Sunday-Monday)

On the plane to New York from Frankfurt, Helen asked whether Nicky wanted to talk about their trip. She added, "You know, the whole thing. Now you've seen whatever there was to be seen in those places you fought? Now you've been with Kal?"

They had managed for three days to say nothing about the executed prisoner, the dead peasant on the mountain path, the dead girl in the church, the appearance of Churchill, otherwise known as Raptis – who fortunately seemed to have disappeared as unexpectedly as he appeared – or the events in Ioannina. Nor had Nicky talked further about his confession to his sister. The only part of their visit to the monastery they'd commented about was how peaceful Kal had looked when she returned to her prayer, how even her old, favorite lullaby hadn't been enough to distract Kal from her devotion. Nicky had accepted that he and Kal might never be together again.

Nicky took a small sip of bourbon and shrugged. "Sure. We can talk about it all, now that it's over. Time to digest, I guess. Now that I've dragged you through most of Greece, I expect you do have more to say."

"I sure do. Everything that happened to you, Nicky, everything you did or thought you did, tells me one thing, that you're only human. Welcome to the club."

"What do you mean? I'm only human?"

"The worst thing you did," she said as she took his hand, "was what you had to do to live. All the good things you've done in your life, the things I spoke to Tabitha Ganis about, none of that happens unless you survive. Adel has no one to marry, your children don't appear in this world. Kayla's music, your grandchildren, Jackie, his clarinet. Us. None of those things come to be unless you get through this war alive."

"Us?"

"Us." She squeezed his hand.

"I get that, but perhaps, if I'd not ... if I'd died, others would've lived. The unborn children of the young people I killed never had a chance to be what they could be, they ..."

"You were only fourteen, fifteen, Nicky."

"An adult under Jewish law."

"You did what you needed to do to survive. And so what if you were an adult under Jewish law? Jews believe that life is the most precious thing. You can eat *treyf* if you must to stay alive. But let's say you made mistakes. We all make mistakes, Nicky, that's part of being human, and *Hashem* forgives us if we're sorry for our mistakes. He'll forgive you, too, if you ask for forgiveness. Yes, I know, you're a confirmed atheist. For a minute, though, just be ... can you just be the Nicky you were when you turned fourteen? He's still inside you. Let that Nicky see the light for a minute, let him breathe again. Don't hide from him. Don't hide him from yourself."

"I don't know what you're saying."

"Of course you do. That fourteen-year-old boy *davened* every day, didn't he?"

"He did." He pictured himself in that instant as the young man who daily wrapped himself in his *t'fillin*, devoutly, intent on reaching communion with God, beseeching God. He suddenly remembered, with a force that pushed him back against his seat, that he'd left his *t'fillin* with Dora, and now here was Helen trying to grab them back for him, when perhaps he might still need them.

"Did that Nicky pray daily '*S'lach lanu, Avinu, ki chatanu,* ... Forgive us, Our Father, because we have sinned?'"

He choked out an answer. "He did."

"Did he mean that?"

Seeking comfort, he reached toward Helen, hugging her as best he could, strapped as they were in their seats.

·　　·　　·　　·　　·

It was late afternoon when they arrived in Manhattan and they were jet-lagged. They decided to spend the night in Nicky's apartment, relax the following day, and, in the end, Helen agreed that they would visit his family first, the next evening.

In the late morning of their first full day back, Nicky proposed they take a long walk in the park. They needed the exercise, he claimed, to help unwind. Nicky was honest about wanting to stretch his muscles, although he wanted even more to breathe in the aromas of his home city and hear its cries with the realization that his sister would never join him there. As they hiked around the Central Park reservoir, he smelled the blooms of spring and heard the voices of children playing, singing. The children reminded him of Jackie, and he intensely missed his grandson at that moment. The clarinet. Perhaps he'd bring his Artie Shaw CD down to West Caldwell and leave it with Jackie. And the Jimmy Hamilton CD too.

As they continued their stroll, he caught sight of a large church on the other side of Fifth Avenue and convinced Helen that they should go in just a minute to look around. He couldn't have articulated why he wanted at that minute to go into the church. It felt like the thing to do. The church turned out to be Episcopal, and walking into its sanctuary created no special feelings in Nicky. They walked a few yards down the center aisle, but Nicky stopped abruptly, grabbing Helen's arm, as he saw at the front of the sanctuary a tall, thin man who looked vaguely familiar. The man, dressed in a business suit, might have been watching them.

"Let's leave." He turned, and Helen followed suit.

"What's all this about, anyway?" she asked.

He struggled for an answer. Walking back out into the sunshine, still holding Helen's hand, he said "I thought maybe to better imagine my sister in a church here in Manhattan and get a sense of what that might feel like. Another stupid idea."

"What did it feel like?"

"Nothing much. That was not a place Kal would've liked. In fact, she wouldn't have liked anyplace in this city. I should've known that. New York is the last place in the world she'd want to live."

They kept walking for another half-hour, until they were both tired and ready for lunch. Nicky recommended crossing Central Park once more and dining at the Atlantic Grill. There, they enjoyed salmon and a bottle of wine. Throughout the meal, Helen was unusually quiet. Nicky wondered whether she was worrying about their abrupt departure from the Episcopal church. As she put down her fork with her salmon only half-eaten, he felt that she was about to berate him about something.

"Nicky?"

"Is something wrong, Helen?"

"I should have probably told you sooner."

"Go ahead. Whatever it is, I can take it." He knew now that, for reasons he wouldn't understand, she would tell him their relationship was over. Not only would she not marry him, she wouldn't date him. What had he done wrong this time? He knew the dismay he felt at that moment was written all over his face.

"Oh, no. It's nothing bad, Nicky. It's about Catherine."

Loud warning bells sounded in his brain. She couldn't know about Catherine, could she? But of course she did.

"Catherine?" he croaked.

"I know about the two of you."

He felt himself blushing. Even as dark-skinned as he was, she had to have seen. This can't be.

"You know ... what?"

"Don't act so innocent. She told me how she seduced you. Her words were, as I recall, 'I jumped his bones.'"

"Oh, God. I'm so sorry, Helen."

She laughed, her eyes sparkling. "Why sorry? That was forty-four years ago, by my count, and you were a kid, and you didn't stand a chance against her when she wanted you. Catherine always got what she wanted. Why, when we were young kids, she'd appropriate the dolls our folks gave to Irene and me. If we wanted to play with our own dolls, we had to play her way."

"When did you find out? I mean, about Catherine and me?"

"Right after our first date, Nicky, when I called her to tell her we'd seen each other again. She told me there was something I needed to know before I got involved with you, that she had a confession to make, and, well, her conscience had always bothered her."

"I don't know what happened."

"Sure you do. Anyway, I don't want you to think you're still keeping a secret from me. Would you have told me yourself, about Catherine, ever?"

"I don't think so."

"Well, now you don't have to worry anymore. It's out in the open."

"And this doesn't make a difference to you, about us I mean?"

She paused for more than a few beats. He felt she was trying to increase the suspense, making him suffer for his indiscretion in her old bedroom. "I can accept how you and Catherine got it on one night when you weren't married and she was a widow and you found yourselves unexpectedly alone in the house."

"She was your sister. Your mom was dying. It was wrong."

"I think I understand why Catherine did what she did that night. I might've beaten her to it if I hadn't been married. I'd always thought you were cute, from the minute you walked into our house." She looked at the dessert menu, and he saw that she was now the one to blush. "Can we order something sweet?"

"Why don't we split the warm apple pie?"

She looked up at him, her eyes still bright and warm. They held a question. "One thing I don't understand, though. Maybe you can tell me?"

"Which is?"

"Why Catherine stopped after only one time."

•   •   •   •   •

They took Nicky's car and headed to Max and Kayla's home in West Caldwell. Although it was past eight when they arrived, a school night, Jackie had waited up, excited to see them. He greeted Nicky and Helen, whom he'd never met, with hugs. Before anything else could happen, he insisted on playing a short piece on his clarinet. Nicky thought it sounded like "The Farmer in the Dell," which Jackie proudly confirmed.

"Good work, little guy! I see you've been practicing." He then gave Jackie the Artie Shaw and Jimmy Hamilton CDs with a strong build-up of how great they were on the clarinet and how Jackie too might be great one day if he kept practicing.

"I'm glad you're alive, Grandpa!" The adults laughed, although Jackie looked disconcerted, not clear at all what the joke was.

"Well, so am I, right now." He hugged his grandson again, tightly. "Guess what, Jackie?"

"What?"

"We found an aunt for you in Greece. Or a great aunt, I guess. I have a sister who lives there, and Helen and I found her."

"You did?"

"Her name is Sister Theodora. She lives at a church. Maybe you and I, and *Ima* and Uncle Max and Helen can go back and visit her someday. Would you like that?"

"Sure."

At that instant, Aliyah walked over to Jackie, who began to scratch her. When Nicky reached his hand out as well, she darted away.

"Have you been taking good care of Aliyah while I was gone?"

"She sleeps with me."

"Well, good. If you promise to keep taking good care of her, maybe *Ima* will let you keep her. What do you say?"

"Can I?" He looked hopefully at his mother.

Kayla frowned when she glanced at her father, then smiled again at Jackie. "Sure. I think Grandpa wishes I'd given Aliyah to you, instead of him, to start with. But, yes, you can keep her. Maybe Grandpa wants a dog instead."

"Thanks, *Ima.* Thanks, Grandpa."

"A dog for you sounds like fun," Helen said to Nicky.

"We'll talk about it."

Kayla got Jackie going into his bedtime routine, and when she returned to the others, Nicky again related the story about their meeting with his sister. This time he included the details from Kal's narrative that he'd not mentioned on the telephone, Kayla and Max listening with stunned attention. How Mary, the mother of Jesus – whom the Greeks called the Theotokos – had appeared to his trapped sister and rescued her from certain death in a locked closet. How according to Kal they had flown together across Greece in an instant. How both of them had saved his life from the exploding grenade, something Nicky had written about, something Kal couldn't have known about unless she'd been there. He ended with Kal back in her cell, having again become Sister Theodora, oblivious to Nicky's singing of the lullaby she once loved. He didn't mention his confession. When Nicky finished, Max shook his head.

"Dad, that's … an amazing story, but you're not buying into it, are you? The Mother of God? Grabbing onto the Virgin Mary's veil and flying into a church with her to save your from an exploding grenade? It's delusional, obviously."

"Max!" said Kayla. "I don't think you c-c-can talk to Dad like that. Of course he buys into it. Can't you see that?" She reached into her purse, took out a small plastic container, snapped it open, and removed a smooth stone, which she then rubbed between the thumb and fingers of her right hand. Nicky knew the stone had come from near Adel's grave. The ritual – one Rabbi Beck ordered her to perform – seemed to calm her.

"I'm no more a believer in miracles than you, Max." Nicky sighed. "Still, I know that's how my life was saved. I knew I was going to die in that instant I saw the German with the grenade. I had nowhere to go. So now I do believe Kal swept into that room. I swear she did. I have sworn, in fact. I've left an affidavit in care of the abbess. Someday, I imagine, it'll be used to make Sister Theodora a saint. There you have it."

"Incredible. I can hardly make sense of what I'm hearing, but all right. It's whatever you say." He turned to Helen. "You heard this, too?"

"Your Aunt Kal spoke in Greek, of course. Your dad filled me in. He's not making up any of this. He knows what happened to him, and Kal told her story without being prepped about what he'd already written."

Nicky yawned, look at his watch, then at Helen. She turned toward Kayla, who finally spoke. "Helen, my dad doesn't seem to need Aliyah anymore. I didn't want him to be lonely when I moved out of the apartment. You guys are … you're like … together now? Really a couple?"

Helen answered for both of them. "I'll say yes to that. For now. I know you've an extra bedroom, so …?"

"Let me show you, Helen." The women hugged before walking out.

. . . . .

It wasn't more than five minutes after they closed the door of the spare bedroom and made sure Kayla had retreated downstairs that Nicky and Helen were in bed, naked, holding each other gently, nuzzling. Nicky was aroused, but, after a few minutes, Helen asked if they could wait until morning, it having been a long and, in many ways, emotionally draining day. Nicky wasn't sure what, in particular, Helen had been drained by. The walk in the park? The discussion about his long-ago tryst with her sister? The full explanation to Kayla and Max about what they'd discovered at the monastery? It could've been all or none of those things. Nicky kissed her again and turned away from her, ready to begin the slow descent into what he hoped would be a peaceful sleep.

It was not to be. As he lay in the dark room, as he heard Helen's breathing fall into the regular, slow pattern of slumber, his mind wouldn't let go. He again saw Max's look of doubt at his story, a look tinged with contempt. But what bothered him more – what he uncovered in his thinking only after an hour of lying in bed – was having seen Raptis at the Fifth Avenue church. The more he replayed that scene in his mind, the more sure he was the man and could've been no one else. It was impossible, but true. Nicky turned and tossed, trying to make sense.

Then he found himself back in northwestern Greece, a fifteen-year-old, running through a village, looking for food. Somehow he knew that cheese, milk, and olives had been hidden in a church. He, Chrisma, would teach the villagers a lesson for hiding food from the soldiers fighting for Greece's freedom. He barged into the church, firing, but the church was empty. There was no one to shoot. The priest and his wife and their grandchildren must have hidden. Nicky placed his Mauser on a table and began to search, finding only a small cheese in a cupboard.

He'd just left the church in the hunt for more food and realized he'd forgotten his Mauser. About to retrace his steps and rearm himself, Nicky awoke. The early spring morning had lifted the darkness from their bedroom.

CHAPTER SEVEN

Inousa, Greece, June 3-4, 1990 (Sunday, Monday)

The services celebrating Pentecost had concluded, the nuns had eaten a simple late afternoon meal in the monastery's *trapeza*, and it happened that Fevronia and Theodora were together, alone, clearing away plates and wiping away crumbs. Fevronia spoke to Theodora about how the vineyard was doing, noting the healthy look of the grapes, all except for the one area that never supported strong vines, that lowest, thin plot near the edge of their property that seemed to point into the woods. Fevronia didn't expect a response from Theodora. She was talking to Theodora just to hear her own thoughts out loud, yet, on this occasion, Theodora chose to respond.

"Wine is for the bitter in spirit, isn't it?" Theodora's words were just loud enough to hear.

"What did you say, my precious one?"

"I ... I think ... it must have been something Papa said to me. He quoted ... *mishli* ... What is that?" Theodora, turning pale, dropped her broom and sat quickly. Her lips trembled.

"Quoting? ... Are you all right? Stay here while I look for something."

Theodora nodded and Fevronia ran to the tiny library, pulled down a Bible concordance from the shelf, and spent a few minutes looking up the reference. Proverbs, as it turned out. She grabbed a Bible and rushed back with both Bible and concordance.

"How did you ... I mean, that is a saying in Proverbs. You could certainly have read it there, but is it something you remember from home?"

"Papa would say things, important things, things I had to memorize. I was so little, yet he tried to teach me. We sat ... the Talmud ..."

Theodora hadn't talked about anything in the six weeks since Dr. Covo and his friend had visited. Fevronia had been sure that the memories then stirred up in Theodora had been buried deeply once again, unlikely ever to emerge. It now seemed though, apropos of nothing, that these memories of home did return.

"Yes, the Talmud, you told us once how you studied with him."

"He told me a story."

Theodora looked questioningly at Fevronia, seeking permission to continue, and Fevronia nodded. She saw Theodora held within herself much more than Fevronia could ever appreciate and she yearned to know Theodora more fully, to know and understand and feel everything about her prior life. Theodora thought for a minute before continuing.

"He told me Rav Huna had 400 barrels of wine, which turned to vinegar."

"That's it?"

"No. There was a miracle. The vinegar turned back to wine and Rav Huna was saved. He would have been destitute had it not been for the miracle."

"That's a story in the Talmud? You're sure?"

"If I can trust Papa's teaching, I'm sure."

"So, was there a lesson with that?"

"Yes. Rav Huna lost his wine because he mistreated a worker. The wine reappeared when he admitted his wrong and sought to make amends."

"How is it, Sister Theodora, that you recall this today, of all days?"

"Do you know *Shavuot*?"

"Something Jewish, I presume?"

"The Hebrew name for Pentecost. When I woke this morning, I knew it was Pentecost, but in the back of my mind I couldn't help thinking '*Shavuot*,' a word, a holiday, I haven't thought about since I was a girl."

"Tell me."

"Our family celebrated by eating dairy. Imagine. Cheese-filled torts. Milk. Sour cream. And Papa taught me ... we sang blessings after our meal? Do I remember right?" She thought for a second. "Of course. Psalms, but we sang in Hebrew or Ladino, not in Greek."

"Extraordinary that this comes back to you today."

"No, I don't think so. Nothing is extraordinary for our Lord Jesus Christ, even the resurrection of memory. He was resurrected and He gives us the power to do the same, for whatever has died in us or around us."

"Your memories died and were laid in a tomb and ..."

"The rock guarding the tomb was pushed away ..."

"And ..."

"Some of them live again."

Fevronia contemplated Theodora's words. Was Theodora trying to tell her that her Judaic soul – in addition to memories of her early life – was reborn, just weeks after her baptism in Christ? Did this mean that, ultimately, she'd follow her brother back to America? Or did it mean simply Theodora would choose to remain a devout Christian nun, one at peace with her Jewish heritage, who allowed that heritage to enhance her already profound religious faith? And would she, Fevronia, ever know for sure? She looked at Theodora again, waiting, feeling that Theodora hadn't finished bringing memories to the surface. Five minutes passed, after which Theodora began to sing softly, uncertainly, in what Fevronia knew was Hebrew. A song repeated the phrase "*u'vishem adonay ekra.*" When Theodora stopped, she smiled at Fevronia, apparently waiting for a compliment.

"That was beautiful. Can you tell me what that was, please?"

"A song of praise. A psalm."

"The words? What do they mean?"

"I hardly knew the Hebrew, but, since we sang it in Ladino, I recall that as well. 'Death encompassed me, and the grave opened for me ... and sorrow.' Yes, something about finding trouble and sorrow and calling upon the Lord and being saved."

It was only too clear to Fevronia that, for Theodora, the words were literally true. Based on what Theodora had told them, no words truer to Theodora's life could be found in the Bible.

Fevronia paged again through the concordance, then looked at the Bible.

"Here. The One Hundred and Sixteenth Psalm." She read it out loud.

"Yes. We sang such a song on *Shavuot.*"

"Sister Theodora, do you know what this holiday means for your ... for Jews?"

"No."

Fevronia stared at Theodora for a few seconds, wondering whether she truly didn't know or whether she simply didn't want to discuss her heritage further. Fevronia would have to research the meaning of this holiday.

"It's getting late."

"Let's go back into the chapel and pray again that our Lord's Holy Spirit will ever descend upon us."

• • • • •

The next morning, Fevronia trudged up the path from the church to the winery. Although it was only a bit after eight, the day already promised to be warm. She perspired heavily. It would be a good day for the grapes.

At her side, keeping her steps small to match Fevronia's pace, walked Theodora. The last time the two were this near the winery together was the day her brother arrived. Since then, two letters from Dr. Covo had come. Fevronia knew they sat unopened in a corner of Theodora's cell. Based on the previous day's conversation, Fevronia felt sure it would not be long before Theodora read them. On her way up the hill, Fevronia thought about what might happen afterward, but she couldn't formulate a clear vision. All she could think of was the assurance she'd received from the Mother of God that she'd done the right thing. *To thélima tou Theoú gínetai.*

As they neared the winery, as they passed the bench at which they'd prayed the day that Dr. Covo had arrived, Fevronia resisted the urge to ask Theodora if she knew anything about the monks' final resting place. There would be time for that. She couldn't resist, though, asking Theodora why she'd chosen this particular morning, the morning after Pentecost, to accompany her to the top of the hill. Fevronia wasn't sure she'd receive a response; Theodora had been silent, even at prayer, since their conversation about Pentecost and Rav Huna. Yet, Fevronia understood that a new Theodora – one who might sing Hebrew psalms – had begun to blossom. Fevronia's hopes for an answer were not disappointed.

With her usual peaceful smile, Theodora stopped and turned to Fevronia. She whispered, a secret only the two of them could share.

"To see God."

ACKNOWLEDGEMENTS

I thank my professors at American University's M.F.A. Program in Creative Writing, particularly Stephanie Grant and Roberta Rubenstein, for their teaching, for their confidence in me, and for their patient, sound advice in helping me craft an earlier version of this novel as my Master's Thesis.

I thank my cousin Steven Berger, his wife Barbara, and their daughter Elizabeth, for patiently explaining to me their practice of Christian Orthodoxy, and for taking me to services at the Holy Monastery of St. Paisius in Safford, Arizona. I also thank all those who live, work, and worship at the monastery for their hospitality and for allowing me to observe their practices and break bread with them over the course of a weekend. I thank Steven as well for his many suggestions on multiple drafts of this novel, most of which I incorporated, particularly regarding the Elder Porphyrios. And I thank Steven additionally for reading the latest draft and pointing out my errors and deviations from strict Orthodox practice. I have incorporated many of his proposed corrections, and any lingering mistakes are purely of my own making.

I thank my many other friends who have read and commented upon early drafts of this novel, including but not limited to Tom Leitch, to Joan Davan, to Aimee Lehmann and Gary Glass (who read the first draft at the Colgate Writer's Conference in 2015), and to Pierre and Deena Dugan, Elliot Rosen, Sharon Cohen, and their book group, which read a much later draft. Some of their suggestions were incredibly on point and useful. Pierre has by now read three drafts, always giving generously of his time and encouragement.

I thank Salvador Levy and Hella Matalon, who took me and my wife, Laurie, on Jewish walking tours of Athens and Thessaloniki, respectively, in the summer of 2017 and who were (and continue to be) fountains of pertinent information.

I thank Wilderness House Literary Review, which published *Ten or Eleven* (January 2017) and *Kal Ganis of Kavala* (January 2018), early versions of two portions of this novel.

Finally, I thank my wife, Laurie, my son Marty, and my daughter Jean, for their love, support, and patience. I thank Jean as well for her careful line editing and for her larger comments on the story. And I thank my grandchildren, Cole Ronin Haim and Neely River Haim, because I now realize how much I want this story to live for them.

ABOUT THE AUTHOR

Following a legal career of 40 years, Bruce J. Berger received his MFA in Creative Writing from American University in Washington, DC. His short stories – including two based upon this novel – have been published in a variety of literary magazines, including *Prole, Wilderness House Literary Review, Jersey Devil, Buck Off Magazine, A-Minor Magazine, The Raven's Perch,* and *Scarlet Leaf.* He now teaches at American University.

NOTE FROM THE AUTHOR

Word-of-mouth is crucial for any author to succeed. If you enjoyed *The Flight of the Veil*, please leave a review online—anywhere you are able. Even if it's just a sentence or two. It would make all the difference and would be very much appreciated.

Thanks!
Bruce

Thank you so much for reading one of our **Literary Fiction** novels.
If you enjoyed our book, please check out our recommendation
for your next great read!

The Five Wishes of Mr. Murray McBride by Joe Siple

2018 Maxy Award "Book Of The Year"
"A sweet...tale of human connection...
will feel familiar to fans of Hallmark movies."
-Kirkus Reviews

"An emotional story that will leave readers meditating on the
life-saving magic of kindness."
-Indie Reader

BLACK ROSE
writing™

CPSIA information can be obtained
at www.ICGtesting.com
Printed in the USA
LVHW041456161020
669012LV00001B/149

9 781684 335596